VOLUME ONE

Indelible Lovin'
Max & Jane's Story

d. w. cee

Indelible Lovin' - Max & Jane's Story

D. W. Cee

This story is a work of fiction. Any similarity to real persons, living or dead, is entirely coincidental.

E Book Edition
Chickygirl Publishing

ISBN: 0615913148
ISBN 13: 9780615913148

This volume is dedicated to all my blog Reiders.

You have brought new joys to my Mondays and Thursdays and have possibly helped me discover a new writing genre.

Shall I try for a Romantic Thriller, next?

Author's Note

elcome to the blog world of Jane Reid and Max Davis. This blog/book is a compilation of blogs that were posted every Monday and Thursday on my website from December 2012 to Aug 2013.

This story stars Jane Reid, a fiery twenty-seven-year-old lawyer, whose tough girl persona is tested on a daily basis because of her relationship with Max Davis. You'll all remember Max from the *Indelible Love* series. He never found his happily ever after, and he's working overtime to earn it now with a girl who is so different from Emily.

Each blog is a story in and of itself. It's more casual than a novel and doesn't go into much of the daily minutiae, but trust me when I say, it does not lack in plot line. In fact, you will soon discover as my readers did, (and cursed me on a weekly basis) that each story is filled with twists, turns, and of course, cliffhangers.

The prologue and epilogue were not a part of the original blogs released on my website. And this book in e-form was split into two volumes because the blog ran for many months, and so many readers requested a book to read in one sitting. There are from several different points of views in the prologue and epilogue. **But once you get into Max & Jane's Blog, it will be only from Jane's point of view**. In keeping with the original e-book version, I kept the different book covers and still "separated" the books. Now, as a print version, you will have it all in one sitting, one book.

With all the housekeeping matters done, sit back and enjoy the rollercoaster ride. It's sure to be a thriller!

Table of Contents

(Max) April 19, 2012 The End…Again!

Prologue

" Jane! Seriously? We're breaking up, again?" I was sick of the cat and mouse game we'd been playing the last few months.

"I can't take not being number one in your life. I'm tired of being second choice." She yelled in the maternity ward.

"What the hell are you talking about? You've never been second choice to anything or anybody. What would make you think that? I just don't understand you."

"That's just it! You don't understand me, I don't understand you, we don't belong together. It kills me whenever I see you looking at my sister-in-law. There's so much love in your eyes. It's like she's never left your life."

"Are you nuts?" This time, I was the one who yelled. All the nurses stared at this idiotic conversation taking place in the middle of the corridor. "She's married to your brother. She just had twins today! What could I possibly have done to make you think I was still in love with Em, and what can I possibly do now to change your mind?"

Women! What the hell was wrong with them? I had enough trouble with one woman—trying to understand her and keep her happy. Did she really think I had the energy to love another one at the same time? Maybe this was for the best. When we first started dating, Jane lived in New York and I was here in Los Angeles, so whenever we saw each other, it was like a first date all over again. We were excited, eager, and willing to give in to each other's demands. Once she moved here and we saw each other on a regular basis, everything changed.

The fact that Jane lived at home, and I lived with three room-mates, did not help our cause. We saw her family—who are all wonderful people—much too often. We had no privacy. This is where our troubles escalated. Since Jane lived on the same block as Em, I saw Em almost as often as I saw Jane, and Jane never warmed up to the idea of me and Em. It did not matter that Em and I had broken up ages ago, and that Em and Jake were beyond happily married. Jane didn't like how emotionally involved I was with Em and there was no way I could make Jane understand that I would always love Em like family. That was something I couldn't change...I didn't want to change.

"There's nothing you can do. Let's just end this now. I've decided to move back to New York," she announced.

"You decided to move away without discussing this with me?" Shit! I'd had enough. It was time to finish this conversation. "Go ahead, Jane. Move away. Hope you have a nice life!" I walked away from her, and went to visit Em in her room, instead.

Em was lying in her bed, looking radiant with both babies in her arms. I couldn't believe this was the same girl I met in Dykstra Hall on a hot September day. That timid girl—whom I loved, and who loved me with all our hearts—just became a mother to a baby boy and girl. There were few words to express my overwhelming joy for her. With so much goodness in her heart, and with so much love to give, she found her family to dote upon and to love the rest of her life. I couldn't have conjured up a better man than Jake Reid and today, seeing her with the babies, I was convinced I did the right thing on graduation night. She was finally where she belonged.

"Hey," she smiled. "Did you meet Elizabeth and James?"

"Em…" I was speechless. "…they're beautiful! They look just like you."

"Thanks Max. I think they're beautiful, too. Can you believe how both our lives have changed so much in a span of two years?"

"They've definitely changed, and you're exactly where you should be—here with Jake and your beauties. I see you named them after your mom and dad."

"Yeah…" My sweet ex-girlfriend and my dear friend started tearing. It always broke my heart when I saw her crying for the parents she lost too early in life. "I wish they could've met my babies. They would've loved them so much." Now she started crying.

"It looks like these babies are the reincarnation of your parents. From the pictures I remember, Elizabeth looks just like your mom, and James is the spitting image of your dad. You did right by naming them after your parents."

"I know this is going to sound ungrateful, but no matter how wonderful the Reid family is to me—and they have been beyond a dream where family is concerned—I can't help missing my parents. Especially on such a special occasion, I wish Mom, Dad, Grandma and Grandpa were here with me. The Reid family can't quite fill that void completely. Isn't that terrible of me to say such a thing?"

"It's not. I know how much you miss your family. That was something I could never complete for you either. But, I'm happy you found Jake. If I could have built a man out of dust for you, it would have been someone like him. He will fill in all your voids."

"He does..." She smiled her beautiful smile. I was a lucky man at one point, and Jake definitely will be a fortunate man to live with such inner and outer beauty the rest of his life. "Did Jane give you her big news?"

"Yeah. She also broke up with me."

"*WHAT*? Why???"

"She and I are like oil and water. We just don't work, Em. I don't know what it is that'll make her happy."

"But you love her, Max. Hold onto her. I know she'll stay if you ask her to stay. Don't let her go, again."

"I don't know how I feel about her. She makes me feel like the luckiest man one moment, and then she drives me up the wall the next moment. Regardless of how I feel, I don't think she wants to make this work." I didn't feel the need to tell Em about Jane's unnecessary pettiness where Em was concerned.

"Max Arthur Davis. I see the love in your eyes whenever you're with her. Give in to her demands." Em softly laughed, while giving each of her sleeping babies a kiss. "Jane grew up sandwiched between two overachieving brothers. She's always felt the need to prove her worth and demand her rightful attention. In my mind, she outdid both brothers, but I don't think she feels the same. I wish you'd stop her from moving away."

"I think it's out of my hands. She's made her decision, and she only told me after she broke up with me. I don't have the energy to stop her."

"Do you want to break up with her?"

"No...I don't." That was the last thing I wanted to do...I sincerely hoped this time we'd stick together—through thick and thin, for richer for poorer, till death do us part—type of together. I guess it wasn't meant to be.

Em was right. I was already in love with Jane, and could envision a lifetime of battling the wills and learning to compromise. But, Jane needed to decide where I belonged in her life and she needed to battle her own insecurities, first. I'd miss Jane, but perhaps this was for the best and we'd try again a few months down the road.

"Did you make my wife cry, Davis?" Jake walked in with more flowers for his family. "No one is allowed to make her cry," he said ominously.

"Congratulations, Jake." I shook his hand. "The babies are beautiful, just like their mother."

"I know," he smiled at his wife while answering me, and I knew it was time for me to leave so the Reid family could have some privacy.

"Bye, Em," I kissed her cheek one last time knowing I wouldn't see her or the Reid family for a while. Em gave me a funny look and tried to hold onto my hand, but I gently shook it loose and waved good-bye to Jake as well.

Walking down the corridor, I saw Jane talking to her family. I walked over to her one last time, and she had the good sense to meet me halfway.

"I hope you find what you're looking for in New York, and I'm sorry I couldn't be what you wanted in a boyfriend. I'll miss you..."

I thought I heard her whisper my name, but I didn't turn around to find out if my ears were playing tricks on me.

And that's how we ended...again.

(Jake) July 4, 2012

Happy Anniversary

"Hey, you got a moment?" I hadn't seen my buddy, Donovan, in months. Between my life with the wife and kids and his busy schedule, we couldn't meet unless he stopped by the house.

"What brings you here?" We shook hands and gave each other a hug.

Donovan was one of the groomsmen at my wedding and he was my best friend since our toddler days. Our fathers went to med school together and I had dated his sister, Kelley, years ago.

"I just finished at the hospital and I have a favor to ask of you, so I thought I'd drop by. Plus, I haven't seen you in a while."

"What's going on, proud father of two? You have time for dinner or drinks tonight?"

"No time for dinner or drinks, and even if I did have time, I'd rather be home with my wife and kids. I am in absolute heaven as a married man and a father of two children. I highly recommend it. You should try it too."

"No way, that's not for me."

"Isn't that why you came back to LA? Didn't you want to slow down, find a wife, get married and have a kid or two?"

"Speaking of women, how's your sister doing? I saw her about a month ago when I was out in New York, but I didn't get a chance to talk to her much. We were both busy at the firm and we tried to connect for dinner, but it didn't happen."

"Yeah...keep it that way. Stay away from my sister. She's not the girl for you. Don't you think it's a bit incestuous to be interested in someone you've known since her diaper days?"

"No more incestuous than her dating your wife's ex-boyfriend."

Donovan always had to rub that one in my face whenever I nixed the idea of him and Jane.

"Hey my wife came to me as a virgin bride. It doesn't matter to me that she had an insignificant relationship back in undergrad."

"Insignificant, my ass! Wasn't she thinking of marrying this guy?"

"*Anyhow*, the reason I stopped by was to ask you for a favor." Donovan laughed at me because I cut off whatever he was about to say concerning Emily and Max. "Can you ask Kate and see if that house up in Napa is available for rent, from the fourth of July till Sunday? I want to take Emi and the kids there for our anniversary."

"Kate, as in Kate Beauvais?"

"You know any other Kates? You remember that house we stayed in several years back? It belonged to a client of hers, and he used it as a rental?"

"Yeah, I know which house you're talking about. I'll ask." As soon as he said those words, my foot was almost out the door. I was itching to get home to my family. "You seriously bailing on me already? You won't let me date your sister, you go incommunicado for months, and you only stop by when you need something from me. You're a shitty friend, you know that?"

"Oh well. If you don't like it, find yourself a wife and kid and we can do family stuff together." I laughed and dodged his prized A-Rod baseball I knew he wouldn't throw at me. "See ya. Come by the house. Ellie and James say they'd like to see their godfather." I threw in one last jab before leaving.

Life these days had taken on an enjoyable routine. I'd get up early with my wife to help with morning rituals, go to work, and then come home for the nightly rituals. The number of diapers we went through on a daily basis could overflow a landfill. These kids had a good life! All they did was eat, sleep, pee and poop—interspersed with play dates, baby gyms, baby music classes, and outings with their mama. When I asked Emily about all these activities, she explained that if she didn't have a sched-uled activity once a day, she'd never see sunshine. I guess I understood.

The Chief eased up on my schedule at the hospital, at least for the time being, and I enjoyed teaching at the med school, immensely. But of course, my favorite time was when the little critters fell asleep and gifted Emi and myself the evening. The happiest day for the both of us since the babies were born was not when they first smiled, nor when they learned to bat at their toys while lying on the floor, but it was when they both slept through the night. I was not one who needed much sleep *UNTIL* I had kids. Sleep deprivation caused by two beings who weighed less than a combined twenty-five pounds was nothing to laugh at!

"Hello, Love." I snuck up on my wife who was doing…laundry! This was one machine in the house that never got a break.

"Hi," she smiled her beautiful smile. "You're home earlier than expected."

We made out in front of the washing machine until I realized something was not right.

"Why are we stopping?" Emi whispered.

"Why is it so quiet in the house at this hour? Where are our babies?"

Emi laughed. "They've been hijacked by your cousins. Laney came and picked up James, while Sam got Ellie. Everyone is back on the block for the fourth of July, so I don't know which house the babies are in right now. They may not even be in the same house for all I know."

"Fantastic. Can we go upstairs?"

"What, for all of ten minutes? Who knows when the kids will be back!"

"We can accomplish a lot in ten minutes." I answered with a sly grin. "Think of the other day when I popped in for lunch. The kids had no idea we were in the other room *playing*."

"Let's save whatever it is you have in mind for tonight. I'm not thrilled about your cousins finding us during our *playtime*. Dinner is at Mom and Dad's tonight. You want to help me fold laundry till then?"

"Not really."

Emi gave me a funny look, and I chuckled at how domesticated our lives had become. My travel-bugged wife hadn't been on any trips since our honeymoon, the foodie in her hasn't eaten out since the babies arrived, and the thrifty woman that I married refuses to get any hired help around the house. She insists on doing every job on her own, and she's accomplished it with aplomb. Our big house has become a cozy home, our once preemie babies are healthy and considered big on the growth chart, and her lack of dining-out has only refined her cooking skills. Yes, I won the lotto with this woman.

"Emi, Donovan is getting us a house up in Napa from Wednesday to Sunday. How quickly can you get the kids ready to travel?" Emily didn't look thrilled at all. "We talked about this the other night—about going back up to San Francisco and Napa, as well as having another baby?"

"Are you crazy? I am *NOT* having another child right now—maybe in a couple of years, but not now! And Jake, I really don't want to pack up everything but the kitchen sink and go away for four days. Let's just stay here and hang out with the family."

"Then let's go away without the kids for a few days!"

"And what about nursing? You think this milk will just hold off till the babies latch on again? You are seriously insane today."

"I'm going to put my foot down on this one. I want to take you away—with or without the kids—this weekend. You've been cooped up in this neighborhood for months. You need a change of scenery. Come on, Beautiful! It'll be fun." I pulled her into my body, and tried to coax her into my fabulous idea. "We'll leave the kids for a few hours and I'll take you back to French Laundry."

The idea of delicious food was working its magic—kind of.

She let out a big sigh and said, "All right...I'll get things ready. When do we leave?"

I answered, "In two days," and left the utility room before my wife yelled at me again.

Damn! My wife was right, was all I could think, while lugging two car seats, two large suitcases, a double stroller, and crying twins sitting in the double stroller. *What the hell was I thinking traveling with two three and a half-month-olds?* Emily just smiled an *I told you so* grin and leisurely strolled the babies through the airport. After checking in the two suitcases, I was about pushed over the cliff when we got to the TSA check-in. After practically disrobing in public and quickly placing my shoes, belt, cell phone, keys, laptop, and Emi's Kindle on the ever moving conveyor belt, I folded down the double stroller while Emi held on to both kids, then placed the two car seats on the belt for inspection. Then, before all of our items went through and caused a backlog on the other end, I took James and ran through the metal detector. Of course, the damn detector went off and one of the frickin' inspectors insisted on checking over James while another frickin' inspector performed my pat-down.

Was it really necessary to check over a three and a half-month-old? At this point, I wasn't going to argue. After taking out the loose coins in my pocket, they let me through one more time with James and we passed this time. Emily laughed her way through with Ellie, and she quickly took a crying James in her arms and calmed him down while I unfolded the stroller, put my clothes back on and placed all the electronics in my messenger bag. *Shit!* I was not doing this again until the babies could walk, talk, and handle their own pat-downs.

"Go ahead and say it," I told my wife. "I know you're dying to tell me!"

She quietly laughed and gave me a brief kiss on the lips. "I love you," was all she said. She was truly the mega millions of the lotto world.

Being so preoccupied with settling down our unhappy children, Emily not once realized that we were not headed to San Francisco anymore. And, as soon as the plane took off, she and the kids all fell asleep, and I didn't bother her until we touched down.

"Love," I whispered and kissed her on the head, "we're here. Let's take this one-man circus act back on the road."

We took our show all throughout the airport and stepped out onto the curb, waiting for our car.

"Jake..." Emi said while finally taking in her surroundings. "This isn't San Francisco. Is this where I think it is?" Her voice broke the moment she realized where she was.

"It is, Love. We're here to see your parents."

She immediately molded herself into my body and cried. "How did you know I've been wanting to see them...to show them our babies?"

"How could I not know, my sweet wife? With the pregnancy and the birth of the twins, you haven't seen your parents since right before the wedding. Of course I know you miss your parents."

"Thank you, Jake," she whispered and pulled herself together so the kids wouldn't get upset.

We got to the cemetery, and she walked as fast as she could with James in her arms to go see her parents. I came prepared this time and brought several packs of tissues.

"Mom and Dad's graves are so clean." Emily looked surprised. "And there are yellow Gerber daisies on Mom's grave and hyacinth on Dad's. Did you do this?"

I nodded yes.

"When?"

"Every week since we first came here."

She just stared at me.

"You can hire people to keep the grave area and bring fresh flowers, Love. I've been doing this since I met your parents. I promised you I'd love your parents as though they were my own."

"How come I never knew this?" Emily wiped away the tears and tried hard not to upset the kids.

"This was something between me and your parents. You didn't need to know," I winked.

She forced a smile, and started talking to the kids and to our parents, in every jumbled fashion.

"Mom. Dad. I've wanted so badly for you to meet James and Elizabeth. These are your grandchildren. Jake and I had twins back in April, and they are the most darling babies. I delivered them naturally and when James came out, I thought I was seeing Dad again. The sight of James made me so happy and so sad, all at the same time. Then I lost it when Elizabeth came out howling. She is a spitting image of you, Mom. She's so beautiful, just like you!"

I took out the tissue and held my wife through her sniffles. Her eyes watered, but she spoke with a smile on her face. Sitting comfortably in their stroller, the kids watched her intently, not knowing whether to smile or cry with her.

"I've settled into married life and family life without any problems. The Reid family has loved me, and taken care of me since I came into their fold. Sandy, Bobby, and the rest of the Reids love these kids unconditionally. They actually fight over who gets to hold them, and I don't think these kids will ever crawl because they are never let down. I love our family and they love us more than I deserve. But..."

This is where my wife couldn't hold back.

"I wish you were here to have watched their birth, and their first birthday and every birthday after that. I wish you'd be here to tell me what to do when their teeth are about to fall out, and how to handle the first day of kindergarten, and what I do about sibling rivalry. Ellie and James will need both sets of grandparents on grandparents' day at school, and they will wonder and ask about you, but they'll never have a clear picture of what wonderful grandparents you would've been, and what you look like...why did you have to leave so early?"

I took both kids who started crying like their mother, and walked away for a while to calm them down and to give Emily some time to cry. I believed that the kids and I had finally filled her emptiness, but I guess I was wrong. I'd have to try harder and hopefully one day, she could come here and only smile.

"I'm okay, Jake. Can you please bring the kids here? I'd like to tell them about their grandparents."

Emily sat with each kid on her lap and oddly, the two quietly listened to their mother the entire time. They watched her forced smile as she animatedly told them about their namesake. The kids would have a lot to live up to in the years to come as James Logan Reid and Elizabeth Logan Reid. Each name represented a myriad of personalities, accomplishments, and adventures—but the common denominator of them all was love. That's what we all shared, deep abiding love.

"Thank you, Jake, for the best anniversary present, ever," were my wife's last words as she fell asleep on me before consummating our first anniversary. I laughed, as this was the story of our lives these days. To many more happy anniversaries.

(Emily) August 7, 2012

Happy Days

"Come back to bed, Love. It's too early. The kids aren't even up yet," my husband complained.

"I can't. I have so much to do before the babies get up. I need to get the lamb chops frenched and seasoned, chop up all the veggies for the quinoa salad and put the red velvet cake in the oven so it'll be cooled for me to frost later in the day. It's a busy day." I pulled away from Jake's warmth and willed myself to get ready for a long, but joyous day.

"Emi, you need to get some help. This can't go on. What will you do when we have another child?"

I stopped dead and stared at my husband, who was deliciously naked under the sheet. "What other child? Why do you keep mentioning another child already?" I asked in semi-mock horror. "The twins are barely four months old. How can I possibly carry another baby? I don't know that that is physically possible."

"Oh it's possible. Especially since you're not on anything and I can't keep my hands off of you." He gave me that wicked smile that almost brought me back to bed.

"My cycle is still not back. I'm going to assume my body is not ready to reproduce yet. And I don't want to be on the mini-pill. Between nursing the twins and remnants of the first pregnancy, I don't need any extra hormones in my body." I pulled a dress over my body, brushed my teeth, washed my face, and pulled my hair into a ponytail, ready to attack the day.

It was only five am, but I needed the extra two hours to prep for the dinner party we were hosting in honor of Jake's cousin, Laney. It was her 22nd birthday today and sadly, both her parents were out of town at a doctor's convention in London. Aunt Babs tried to stay home with her to celebrate this day, but Uncle Henry wouldn't hear of it. He wanted her with him on this trip, plus this was a chance for one of the Reids to check in with Gram.

Gram left for London unexpectedly about a month ago, and she's been somewhat m.i.a. Every time I call her, she asks a plethora of questions about the babies, but is not as forthcoming with what she's been doing with her time. We all believe she's struck up a friendship with Sir Roland Ascot again, but no one can be sure. Aunt Babs was charged with finding out what was going on with our dear grandmother.

So, it was left to me—and of course, I happily accepted the challenge—to give Laney a wonderful birthday surprise. She has no idea that we are all getting together at our home and throwing her a party. She believes that her brother, Doug, is taking her out for a meal tonight, while the rest of us pretend to be busy.

"Waaa..." I heard through the monitor. Peace and quiet were done for now...

"What's the matter, my baby?" I whispered to James, who was crying in his crib. "You're going to wake up your sister." I thought I got to him in good time, but Elizabeth woke up right as I picked him up.

Not liking the sound of her brother, her lips turned into a frown and her pout was just a step away from turning into a cry.

"Are my prince and princess up, already?" Jake put a smile on our girl's face as he nuzzled her cheeks with a flurry of butterfly kisses. He tried to do the same for James, but James was in an unusually bad mood this morning. He wouldn't let his father get near him for fear that I may let go of him.

"Did you have a bad dream, my little one?" I did my best to smile while changing his diaper but he wouldn't be appeased. "Let's see what's wrong, handsome boy." I proceeded to check his temperature. "You're not hot, you're not wet anymore, maybe you're hungry?"

The rocking chair was calling my name and since the twins were too big to be nursed at the same time, and since James was in a mood, he went first while Jake occupied Ellie in the playroom. I know it sounds crazy, but a couple of weeks into what seemed like non-stop nursing after the birth of the twins, I decided to nurse them simultaneously. It was awkward for a few days, but once I got the hang of it, I was done in no time at all.

"What has you in such an unhappy mood, my baby?" My baby boy had beautiful blue eyes that were turning somewhat green now, and his straight black hair was showing signs of getting lighter and slightly wavy. "What can Momma do to make you feel better?" I did what James loved when he was nursing. I lightly combed my nails through his scalp and hair. He immediately placed his chubby little hand on my chest and dozed off.

I loved being a wife, and I loved being a mother. There was no explaining the happiness I felt when carrying James and or Ellie in my arms, or the pride I felt when either child accomplished a milestone. And there was no explaining the love that multiplied exponentially in my heart, every time I looked into my child's eyes and felt the smile, the trust, the unconditional love from my babies. Motherhood, times two, was God's greatest gift to me along with my husband Jake.

"You ready for your daughter? She's getting restless." I'd kept James a bit longer than usual just to calm his irritable temper and it was taking a toll on my daughter's hungry belly.

"I think he's sleeping, again." I tried to unlatch James and next thing I knew, "Ouch!" I said a bit louder than necessary. It startled James and he did one of those open-mouthed hollers. That's when I noticed what was wrong.

"You okay, Love? Did he bite your finger?"

"Nope, he bit down on a more sensitive body part," I grimaced while saying this, "and I've figured out what's got our son so upset. He's teething. Look here." I pointed to the two bottom areas of the gum where the teeth had cut through already. "He's getting the two bottoms one at the same time. It looks painful. No wonder he's unhappy."

"Son, your daddy will be unhappy if you keep chomping down on my favorite body part," he warned while attempting to pry away James from me. The loud holler voiced James' opinion. He didn't want to leave my side. "Your sister has to have her breakfast, too. Daddy's going to feel offended if you keep giving preferential treatment to your mother. I know she's your food source, but where will you be come baseball season if Momma is all you want? You think she can teach you how to catch a ball?" Jake lightly threw him up in the air—something James loved—to get him smiling. It did the trick.

"Can you take him downstairs and get a plastic teething ring from the freezer? Good thing I bought some the other day and put in the freezer. That should keep him happy for a while."

"Will do, Love." My loving husband kissed me one last time before he took James out of the room.

"Oh and Jake?"

"Yes?"

"I talked to Jane yesterday, and she's not happy. She needs to come home, she needs to rest, and she needs Max."

"Nothing I can do, Hon. That was her choice to go back into the rat race of partnership, and it was her choice to leave Max."

"You have to help them. They're both unhappy, but they're both too stubborn to admit it and do something about it."

"What can I do?"

"I'll work on Jane. Can you meet with Max? He won't return any of my calls. I'm feeling a bit hurt, to be honest with you, that Max won't talk to me."

Jake rolled his eyes at me. "I'll only promise to talk to him if you promise me that you'll erase Max from your thoughts—immediately!"

This time, I rolled my eyes at him. "Just talk to him. Knock some sense into him." Jake started walking away. He was done talking about Max. "Oh, and invite him to dinner tonight, if you can get a hold of him," I yelled before Jake got away from me. He did some waving of the hand that probably signaled, *"I don't think so,"* or something to that effect.

At a few blinks of the eye, the day flitted by. James' mood paralleled a bell curve, and his sister followed suit, in a milder form. I checked Ellie's gums too and though she wasn't teething, these twins had a strong bond with one another, and were privy to each other's moods before even me, their mother.

Dinner was done, the cake was frosted, and the present was wrapped. The twins decided to reward my extra efforts tonight by going to bed even earlier than their 6:30p.m. bedtime. It was blissfully quiet as soon as their eyes shut. I loved them dearly, but I enjoyed my quiet time.

"Sleeping already?" Jake tiptoed into the room, and kissed me quietly on the cheek. "I tried to get home earlier to help you today, but my students wouldn't let me leave the campus. How'd you manage our cranky son, all day by yourself?"

"He wasn't all that bad. I held him as much as he wanted to be held and gave him the extra attention he needed, and he was as content as a teething four-month old was going to be."

"And dinner? Did you use the same methods and dinner suddenly appeared?" Jake pulled me out of the kids' nursery and onto our bed. Next thing I knew, he had me laying right on top of him. It felt wonderful to lay my head on his chest and to be cradled and cherished, as always, by my husband.

"While Ellie napped in her crib, James napped in the baby carrier. It wasn't easy cooking with him glued to my chest, but it all worked out and everything got done in time."

"You think some more about getting some help? It would do you a world of good to have someone come in while I'm at work. I worry about you when I'm not here." Not once did my husband stop kissing or caressing me while he spoke. I hoped all the other women in the world felt as loved as I did, daily.

"I like the craziness of each day. I don't want anyone else to experience anything with the children that I can't experience. I want to be there for both kids, all day and every day." I spoke into his chest. "I know I sound like a control freak, but along with you, I want to be their only love for a long time."

"All right, my sweet wife. We'll table this for now."

Jake pulled me up and had me under him in no time with the intent of starting something I knew we didn't have time to finish. As soon as the clothes started coming off, assuredly the doorbell rang, and this day continued on.

An Unexpected Confidant

I got an unexpected text from Jake while I was in class today.

You have time to stop by the house after rounds today?

Yes. What's up?

I want to talk to you about a summer internship you might want to apply for, and I also want to talk about Jane.

If your sister is involved, let's meet outside. Drinks? Can you come alone?

I can meet you after I help Emily put the babies down. Text me the location and time of where you want to meet and I will be there.

Okay see you soon.

I was paired up with a group of smart, responsible, and fun third-year med students. I considered myself very lucky this time. There was nothing worse than being with a bunch of lazy med students.

"Max, do you want to grab some dinner with us?"

"Thanks for the invitation Joyce, but I'm meeting somebody right now."

"Who are you meeting?"

"Dr. Jake Reid."

"Okay. Don't forget we are all catching a movie this weekend."

"I haven't forgotten. See you tomorrow, Joyce."

I rushed out to meet Jake. I looked forward to talking to him about his sister since I hadn't been in touch with her the past four months. As much as I missed her, I wasn't going to contact somebody who told me not to ever call her again.

"Hey, over here," Jake called out to me. "How were rounds?"

"I'm with the fantastic group of people this time so it was great. We are also trailing Dr. Henry Reid so it's even more fun. I can't believe he has time to take around third-year med students. As Chief of Staff, I'm sure this is not part of his job description."

"Uncle Henry loves working with the students. And when I'm lucky enough to fill-in for him, I understand why he does it. It gives us a fresh perspective."

"So what's up?" It was a genuine surprise to read the text from Jake. Last I talked to him, Em had just given birth. Even though I was at the same hospital as Jake, we never ran into each other and I didn't make an effort to catch up with him.

"I got this in my inbox today, and I wanted to see if you were interested. I'll send in my recommendation if you want to go."

"What is it?"

"Our hospital supports a small village hospital in Mexico, and we always send some doctors in the summertime for a month or two to help out their clinic. It's dirty, the weather is crappy, and conditions are rougher than you're used to...but it'll be one of the best experiences of your life."

I looked over the printouts after we ordered dinner and listened to Jake explain more about this program. It was exactly what I was looking for in my quest to be a pediatrician. I could help under-privileged children for a short time, and see if this is honestly what I wanted to do the rest of my life.

"Have you done this?"

"Yeah, I did this the summer before I graduated from med school. I've wanted to go back since, but my schedule has not allowed me to, and now with the twins, I don't think I'll ever get back there. Maybe after the kids are all grown and out of the house, Emi and I can go out there. However, I thought this would be perfect for you. Take some time and read it through."

"Thanks for the information Jake. I will consider it. Though it does concern me if Jane and I were to get back together, how she will react to me going away for the summer."

"You can do the short one where you are only gone for a month. Don't tell me that you can't be away from her for thirty days. Haven't you guys been apart for more than four months now?"

"Yeah." I said feeling like crap again. "How is she doing?"

"She's busy. All I can say is that she doesn't have time to come up for air because the firm keeps her so busy. Don't you miss her?"

"I miss her like crazy."

"Then why haven't you called her? Emi tells me the two of you haven't communicated since the twins were born."

"Jane made it clear she didn't want me to call her ever again."

"And you believe her? You're stupider than you look."

"I don't know what the hell to believe. She's so infuriating and yet..."

"And yet...?"

"Your sister has this crazy notion that she ranks below Em in order of importance in my life. She's under this stupid ass assumption that I am still in love with your wife."

"Are you still in love with my wife?"

"Are you fucking insane? I have a difficult enough time dealing with one woman. Do you think I can handle another one, plus her husband, her kids and the rest of her family breathing down my neck, if I were to be in love with her? You're as idiotic as Jane if you believe that. I don't give a rat's ass if you don't like it, but I will always love your wife like family...maybe even more so than my own."

"Calm down." Jake chuckled. "I know you don't have any inappropriate feelings for my wife, but I needed to check one last time. And by the way, you should give my wife a call. She says you've been avoiding her, and you haven't seen her nor the babies since April. Don't upset my wife, Davis. Call her and say hello. God only knows why, but Emi misses you. And as for Jane, you know she's being an irrational woman about the whole Emily situation. It's next to impossible to change Jane's mind once she has an idea in her head."

"Great, then how am I supposed to convince her that I don't have any feelings for Em?"

"That's for you to figure out. I've done my crazy courtship and paid my dues. It's your turn!" Now Jake was laughing at me. "This is your just punishment for making my life miserable a few years back." His moronic laugh got even louder.

"Thanks for the advice, but I don't know if there will be a next time for me and Jane. She was pretty adamant about me not ever calling her again."

"You give up too easily. You gave up too easily with Emily when you left her on graduation night as well."

"Didn't that work to your benefit?"

"It did, and I thank you for selflessly letting Emi go so she could find me, but now I'd like for you to fight for my sister. I think you two are good for each other, and Emily believes with all her heart that you two are meant to be. It hurts my sweet wife to see you both miserable."

Now I got it. This tête-à-tête was Em's doing. I'm sure Jake was concerned for my welfare as well as the welfare of his sister, but it all came down to making his wife happy. Those two were a match made in heaven.

"What's with the smile?" Jake asked quizzically.

"I'm just glad Em found you. If there is any person on earth who deserves to live a blessed life, it's Em. Make sure you keep her content the rest of her life."

"Yeah, I plan to do that!"

We finished dinner and went our separate ways.

She's Home!

"What's got you grinning from ear to ear?" Pete, my best friend since undergrad asked.

"Jane is back. I'm going to call her right now and see if she wants to go out with me."

"How'd you know she was back?"

"I saw Jake at the hospital today, and he told me she came home unexpectedly late last night. Apparently, no one knew of her plans till she arrived with her bags."

"You sure you want to go there again with her? She was nothing but heartache for you the year you guys dated on and off."

"I gotta try again, Pete. I wanna try again..."

"It's your heart, Bud, not mine!"

"Let me make this phone call and we'll go shoot some hoops."

"Sure. I'm gonna heat up some pizza. You want some?"

"Yeah," I answered, and walked into the bedroom to talk to Jane privately.

"Hello?" Jane had no idea it was me on the line since I called her parents' land line.

"Hey," I called tentatively. "How are you?"

She was silent.

"It's me, Max." Damn! Had she forgotten my voice already? It'd only been eight months. "Did you really forget who I am or are you pretending not to remember me?"

She was still silent. Shit! This wasn't going to be easy.

"I don't know how you could forget such a good looking face, but if you give me a few hours on Friday, I'll show you what you've been missing." She didn't laugh. I guess humor wasn't going to do it. "You might have been so busy that you've forgotten to miss me, but I know I've missed you something fierce the last eight months. How about it, Jane? Can you spare a few hours for a guy who hasn't gone a day without thinking about you? Can we try again...? Slowly...? Cautiously...?"

"Hi Max." She finally answered, sweetly, carefully.

"Hi. You wanna hang out on Friday? Are you free? I have the whole day off."

"Yeah. I'm free."

"I'll pick you up in the morning? We can go for a ride and spend a day together?"

"Sure. I'd like that. See you Friday morning."

"Bye!"

"Bye."

I was fist-pumping like a moron. I didn't know why I was so excited to start up again with a girl whose mind and heart were so unreadable and unpredictable. Hell, she was more unpredictable than LA weather in the wintertime. But, I wanted to make it work this time. When things were good between us, it was heaven. This girl had spunk to her personality and fire to her soul. She wasn't half-bad to look at either. In fact, she was sexier than all the girls out there and she knew it.

"Hey Pete, I'm off to go look at bikes. Join me?"

"Bikes as in a bicycle or a motorcycle?"

"Bikes as in a Harley Davidson. There's one I've been eyeing. Let's go check it out, man."

"Dude, seriously? You have money to invest in a bike?"

"Yeah. I've been saving up a bit, plus I want to go riding up the coast with Jane on Friday. Come test drive one with me."

"All right! Let's go."

Two hours later, we came home with a Harley Davidson Switchback. It had that classic Harley Davidson throwback look with a powerful engine. I added a large saddlebag for our luggage if we wanted to go away for a few days, and a backrest pad so Jane would be comfortable whenever she rode with me. The bike was perfect for the both of us. It gave us a chance to be close together and yet the freedom to enjoy the ride, any which way we wanted. I was positive Jane would love it as much as I did.

"Max," Pete called from the living room. "Your phone's ringing."

I bolted from the bed, hoping it was Jane calling. "Hello?" I answered expectantly.

"Hi Max. It's me, Joyce."

"Uh, hey Joyce. What's up?"

"Well, a few of us wanted to see if you wanted to go to the movies on Wednesday, after rounds?"

"Um..." I hesitated because I didn't want to go and because of Jane. Knowing she was back home and knowing I'd have a chance to see her again in a few days, I had no desire to spend my time with anyone else.

"Everyone's going and it'd be a bummer if you didn't come," Joyce left her statement open-ended and hanging. I felt bad saying no since the rest of the group was going.

"Yeah, sure. I'll be there." I agreed reluctantly.

"Great!" I'll see you tomorrow?

"For sure, bye."

Pete shook his head at me. "She asked you out, again?"

"She wasn't asking me out. Everyone's going to the movies after rounds. I can't just slip away," I answered unconvincingly.

"Dude, she's majorly into you. You need to be extra careful, especially if Jane's back in the picture."

"There's nothing going on me and Joyce. We're only friends."

"It doesn't matter what *you* think you are, it only matters what Jane and Joyce think. This ain't gonna end well," he warned. "Don't go out with her."

"I'm not going out with Joyce," I insisted. "*We* are all going to the movies. It isn't a date!"

"Whatever...don't say I never looked out for you," Pete chuckled.

"Shut up, and let's go shoot some hoops."

(Max) December 5, 2012

Uncomfortable!

I took my time getting to the theater after we all parted from the hospital. I didn't really feel up to all of Joyce's questions and attention. Though I denied it the other night to Pete, I knew that Joyce's interest in me went beyond the friendship boundary, but I figured it was no big deal. So she crushed on me. I enjoyed her company as a friend and she understood that I had a girlfriend, or at least I did...and soon I would again? Shit. Life was more complicated than I ever imagined it would be.

"Max!" Joyce was already there waiting for us. Unfortunately, no one else had arrived.

"Hey, Joyce." She motioned for a hug so I had no choice but to oblige. Damn! Pete was right. I needed to be extra careful and this definitely would not sit well with Jane. "Where's everyone?"

"Crazy thing..." She laughed nervously. "They all got called back to the hospital. It's just you and me."

Shit! How was I going to explain this one to Jane?

"Okay, well let's go in and watch the movie," I let out that same nervous laughter.

The movie was of no interest to me. There was no way I could concentrate on the film when Joyce sat right next to me, insisted we share a tub of popcorn—though I drew the line at sharing a drink—and kept smiling at me during the movie. I decided to look only at the movie screen and forget that I was sitting next to a girl who wasn't Jane.

"So...are you seeing anyone?" Joyce asked during dinner. Rather than pretend-concentrating on the movie, I should have come up with an excuse as to why I couldn't have dinner with her. She caught me off guard right after the movie and here we were, eating dinner at 10p.m..

Here was my chance to nip this in the bud. "Jane is back from New York and we're going to give our relationship a try, again. In fact, I'm going to take her up the coast this Friday. Maybe we'll spend the weekend up in Santa Barbara." That should do it.

"Oh...okay. Jane was the girl you've been seeing on and off?"

"Yeah. I think we will only be on from here on out. I don't plan to lose her again."

"She's a lucky girl." Joyce sighed.

"No, I think I'm the lucky one," I answered with a hopeful smile. Hopeful that Jane would stick with me this time and hopeful that Joyce would let go of me immediately.

"I wish you and Jane well..." Joyce called out eerily as we parted from dinner.

Damn. I was never going to doubt Peter's words ever again!

VOLUME ONE

Indelible Lovin'
Max & Jane's Story
d. w. cee

Dec. 7, 2012

A Harley Man?

I looked out my window as a loud roar of pipes rolled up the driveway. Max pulled up in a sleek new motorcycle. At least I thought it was new. I hadn't seen Max in about eight months so I couldn't be sure when he got the bike.

Max was so not the Harley type of guy. He was the straight-laced, straight-A, straight-shooting type. 'The boy next door,' my sister-in-law, Emily, described him. Those monikers, as well as Max's ex-girlfriend, and my new sister, Emily, were the reasons why we took a break for a while.

I stared at the good-looking, brown-haired, brown-eyed guy. With more ease than I preferred, he gave Emily a hug and a kiss.

"Max! What a wonderful surprise. What are you doing here...and so early in the morning?" Emily greeted.

"Hi Em. I see motherhood agrees with you. You look beautiful even at this early hour." *Really???* Did he always need to find her so enchanting?

"Hey!" Of course, where Emily was, my brother wasn't far behind. "Get your hands and lips off my wife!" he demanded.

"Lighten up, Dr. Reid. I was just saying hello to my beautiful ex-girlfriend."

"Must you always bring up the fact that you and my wife once dated?"

"We didn't just once date; we were together twice the length of time you and she have been together."

The irritation in Jake's eyes was cracking me up. He was so easily riled. Though, the conversation outside was making me feel a little snarky, myself. *Relax*...my new mantra, as we were going to try again. I needed to get over my "hang-ups" as Max called them.

"Cut it out, both of you," Emily warned while giving her husband a loving embrace. "Good morning." Now she was only addressing Jake. "I brought the kids out so they wouldn't wake you. You got in so late last night from the hospital."

"It was lonely in bed without you," Jake announced loudly, so the whole neighborhood could hear. "I wanted to be out here with my family." My brother's voice got louder with each word, but not as loud as his twin son and daughter—Elizabeth and James.

"Da! Da! Da!" The twins screeched. The four of them made a gorgeous family and the smile on Max's face warmed my heart. For a change, he didn't look like he was still in love with Emily, but instead, he looked like he was in love with the idea of a happy family.

Time to make my grand entrance!

"Hey," I greeted.

"Hey..." His voice was soft as he locked eyes with me. Had he really thought about me in the past eight months? Had he missed me? Had he been dating around? Would we be able to make it work this time?

"Is this what you meant when you said you wanted to go for a ride?"

"I thought we'd ride up the coast for a while?"

"Okay, I guess..." What would happen today? Things had ended so abruptly between us. One day we were, then the next day we weren't.

"I can't wait to spend the day with you. I've been looking forward to it all week."

Really?

He somehow heard the Doubting Thomas question in my head.

"Hey." He gently tugged my chin up with this thumb and forefinger. "I guess you haven't missed me as much as I've missed you? Can we try this again and see where it takes us?"

Twenty+ words was all it took to melt away the bitterness of the past year and make me want to start again. I smiled. *Pushover!* Yeah... pushed-over and falling again. I was such a LOSER.

"Don't let go of another good one!" My brother sarcastically yelled as Max tried to muffle his words with the roar of the bike.

"Hold on tight!"

Ominous and yet very promising words...

Dec. 10, 2012

Well... That Didn't Go So Well!

"You're back!" My sister-in-law smiled with more enthusiasm than totally necessary. "You spent the night?"

"No," I cut her off, "I mean yes, but no."

"Explain, Sister." The thing about Emily—as sweet as she is, she's ruthless when she wants something from you. Whether it's the dazzling smile she throws your way, or her sweet innocent pleading look, you can't say no. Does this woman have any negatives in that beautiful frame of hers? I love her, but *ugh!*

"We rode up to Santa Barbara and were having brunch at the Four Seasons, when everything went downhill."

Emily didn't need to know that the ride sucked. There was too much wind, the seat was uncomfortable, it was cold, and we didn't say one word to each other for an hour and a half, but did I complain??? No! I was accommodating—as accommodating as Jane Sydney Reid was ever going to be.

"And..?"

"Max's cell phone kept ringing. After about the fifth ring, I kinda yelled at him to pick up the phone, and guess who was calling him?"

"Who?" Emily's big brown eyes were bugging out. It was cute, in a freakishly bugging sort of way.

"*Some GIRL!* He was so uncomfortable talking to her and he couldn't—no, he wouldn't tell her that he was out with me. I was so pissed, I felt like walking out on him, but I sat through his awkward conversation to get some answers."

While I was pining away for him the last half of the year, apparently, this jerk was dating around.

"He explained that he had 'group-dated' this girl, another doctor at his hospital, briefly." Emily's mouth opened, but I didn't give her a chance to start. I had too many things to say. "And though it bothered me, all would have been okay except...his last date with her was just 'a few days ago.'"

Those were the jerk's words, verbatim! What kind of man tells one woman that he misses her and would like to try for a relationship with her one day, then goes out with a totally different woman the next day? Am I wrong to want someone to love me and me only? Forget love—way too soon for that concept. I just want someone to want me and me only. Maybe it's an LA thing? Perhaps I should move back to New York and work a hundred hours a week and be on track to become the youngest partner at our law firm.

"No!" Emily was horrified, then mad. She pulled out her cell phone and before she could call Max, I took it away from her. "Let me call him and yell at him. He can't treat you like that! Oh Jane..." Then, she hugged me. I think she was more hurt than I was. No matter what I thought or said about my sister, I loved her and she genuinely loved me. The rivalry was only on my part and solely in my head. "So where were you all yesterday?"

"I left Max, got myself a room, then a rental car. After calling around, I got a hold of my girlfriend, Hilary, and we hung out the whole day. The thought of sitting in the hotel room and gorging on ice cream was tempting, but I spent a boatload of money on clothes and shoes, instead."

"Oh, sweet Jane! Your knight in shining armor will come around. Max just needs to sort out his life and grow up some more."

At this point, Max ≠ a knight in shining armor. Well...back to the drawing board!

Dec. 12, 2012 Another Date...

And His Initials Aren't MD

*T*his text greeted my morning.

Can we meet for a quick lunch? You need to give me a chance to explain.

I *need* to give you a chance?

Okay, sorry. Not the right thing to say. A lunch for a chance to grovel?

That made me laugh. Since I left without hearing the full explanation, I suppose I needed to give him a chance. Ha! It was more like I was dying to know who this Joyce girl was that he had been dating. From what my brother Jake told me, she was this brilliant doctor from Stanford who had been after Max for a while. When I asked what she looked like, he shrugged saying that he hadn't paid attention to another woman's looks since he met Emily. *Whatever...Dork!*

OK but you've gotta come my way cuz I only have 30 min.

Perfect. See you soon.

The morning flew by between meetings and prep work for a case I was assisting.

"Jane, you have a moment?"

"Um, sure."

Donovan, the head lawyer in mergers and acquisitions, waited for me to get up from my seat and practically held my hand into his office.

"What's up?"

He handed me an envelope and gestured for me to open it.

"I just got these tickets to a Laker game and I was wondering if you wanted to go with me."

"Like...as in a date?" I sounded so sophomoric, or better yet, so moronic asking this in a high pitched voice.

"Yes, as in a date. Dinner at The Palm, floor seats to watch Kobe, Pau and Howard in action? Unfortunately your favorite player is still injured."

Damn!

Double Damn!

Floor seats, Laker game, hot successful lawyer...why couldn't he have asked me out just a few days ago? Do I go? Do I need to explain about Max? What would I say? *Um...I'm kinda re-seeing this guy who had been dating around while I thought about him constantly?*

"Hello. Earth to Jane?"

"Wait, how'd you know Steve Nash was my favorite player?"

"I heard you mention it the other day and bought these tickets with you in mind."

A man who listens to what I have to say even when I wasn't talking to him? Was he for real? Was I an idiot for letting this one go?

"Sure. I'd like that."

"Great! We'll take the company shuttle. I'll pick you up at six?"

A goofy smile crossed my lips. "See you at six."

That high didn't last long as the speakerphone buzzed. "A Max Davis waiting for you in the lobby..."

Triple Damn!

10 hours, 2 hot dates, Part 1

"Do you go anywhere without your Harley, now?"

"This is my transportation of choice these days. I like the open air, the freedom..."

...the bugs, the dirt, the helmet head, was how I wanted to finish his sentence.

"Thanks for giving me a chance to explain." Max pulled me in for an impromptu scorching kiss, tongue and all, before placing the helmet on my head. I had to admit, rather than enjoying the make-out session, I was more worried about Donovan walking out of the revolving door to our building. Did this officially put me in the slutty girl category? Making out with one guy, then going on a dinner date with another guy?

"So...Joyce?" I casually asked, right before I bit into my egg salad sandwich.

"About a month ago, a group of us from the hospital went out for drinks. Joyce and I sat next to each other and spent a few hours talking. Then she invited a smaller group of us to her parents' beach house in Laguna and we hung out the whole weekend. This same group of friends decided to go out to dinner and a movie last Wednesday, but three out of the five of us got called back into the hospital. So, Joyce and I had a solo dinner and movie date."

"Did you kiss her? Have you slept with her?" Crap. Obviously, the brain-to-mouth filter was off.

Max smiled that gorgeous smile.

"No and no, Miss Green-eyed Monster. The only girl I've kissed in the past year is you—and not nearly enough, if you ask me."

His confession made me happy and mad at the same time. "Why didn't you tell me this up in Santa Barbara? I stewed the whole weekend, thanks to you."

"I was pissed that you were willing to walk away without listening to my explanation. So, I wanted you to stew."

With that lingering thought, he brought me back to work and immediately frenched me in front everyone walking by. We stayed lip locked for a while. It felt so good, so right, to be with Max again.

"I'm at the hospital tonight but have tomorrow off. Dinner?"

Dinner.... Tonight I was having dinner with a man who wasn't Max. Confession time.

"Pick you up at your parents' around 7:30p.m.?"

Pause, pause, pause...

"Yeah, okay."

The freakin' coward that I was, I confessed nothing. I then ran into the building letting Max believe all was right in this world.

"Jane! Wait up. Hold the elevator." Donovan slipped in. "Was that you on that sweet Harley?"

Quadruple Damn. Karma was a vengeful Biatch!

Dec. 20, 2012

10 Hours, 2 hot dates, Part 2

"Harley...me...yeah...ummm, that was me." I was so busted. What had I done in my lifetime to receive this kind of punishment? Two hot guys, two dates, on the same day—why me? "So, let me explain?"

Donovan contained his smile as deftly as humanly possible. "Okay, Jane Sydney Reid, let me hear your explanation. I've known you since you were born, and know what a clever girl you are. I'd like to know how you're getting out of this one."

Lucky for me, Donovan wasn't mad. In fact, he was finding my predicament funny. If this situation weren't entirely my fault, I'd almost call him out for being so ungentlemanly.

"That was Max, we had lunch and we are kinda back together again, I think."

"What does it mean to be 'kinda back together again, I think'? From the way you two were going at it on the sidewalk, it was more than being kinda together."

"We were together for a while last year."

"I remember Jake mentioning something like that—some incestuous relationship involving him, Emily, you and this guy, Max. Wasn't he in love with your sister-in-law?"

Damn. He was still smiling through all this.

"Was."

"Now he's in love with you?"

"Not really. I don't think so..." I pulled Donovan into his big office, closed the door and sat him down. "Here's the deal, as I know it. Max and I met right before my brother and Emily got married. We dated for a while, but I was still in New York, and between the distance, my work, and his med school schedule, it didn't work." I didn't mention my total insecurities about, and Max's obvious feelings for, Emily. "When you asked me out this morning, I was not expecting what happened at lunch to happen. And I..."

Donovan cut me off. "Are you married?"

"No..."

"Are you and Max together?"

"I don't know. I think so? I don't have an answer to that, yet."

"Do you still want to go out tonight with me?"

"Yes?" Did that make me a bad person to want to hang out with Donovan tonight?

"See you at six. Now, you've got to go 'cuz I need to jump into this conference call."

I got out of that one with relative ease. I did feel super guilty for going out with a guy other than Max. Maybe if it weren't Donovan I'd have canceled the date. Like he said, he's known me my whole life and I had a massive crush on him when I was little. It was cool that my childhood obsession asked me out.

Fast-forward seven hours. We were sitting courtside, watching the Lakers lose to the Bobcats. Dinner went better than any dinner date I'd ever been on, and now we were sipping beer chatting about old times.

"How do you like working in the LA office?" With his body slouched on the chair, his legs out and crossed, his arms across his chest and his tie loosened, he looked so sexy asking me this humdrum question. "Very different from the New York one, huh?"

"Yeah. I feel like I can have a life here. Is that why you finally made the move?"

"Yep. All my friends were getting married and having kids while I was billing hours around the clock."

"Have you dated much since you got here? I thought I heard Jake say you were seeing someone."

"Naw. I was waiting for you to grow up and notice me." He smiled a devastating smile. I died a thousand deaths from his romantic profession. Damn, Damn, Damn.

"You know I had the biggest crush on you when I was like, seven years old."

"But not now as a twenty-seven-year-old?"

I was so screwed.

Max? Max, who???

Noticing my obvious discomfort, he put his hand on my neck, pulled me to him and kissed the top of my head. It was the hottest brotherly kiss, *ever!*

Conversation jumped from embarrassing moments from our childhood to what he'd been doing while living in New York for the past fifteen years. I don't think we watched much of the game. In fact, if you asked me now who won, I couldn't answer that question.

We got back to the office and went up to collect our briefcases, when I saw my three main bosses in their office, working. Last thing I wanted to do was ask if I could help in any way, but since these people were heavyweights in the firm, and could probably nix my chance of ever making partner, I walked into their office and offered to help. There went my sleep for the night.

5:00am—I was jittery from being over-caffeinated, and under zzz'ed. Dragging myself to the elevator, I ran into my dinner date.

"What are you still doing here?" he asked. "I thought you left a long time ago."

"The big-three asked me to help. Why are you still here?"

"Our deal almost fell through. I sat in a conference call for a couple of hours, then had to rewrite the contract and get it sealed. That's why I couldn't come out and say good-bye. I was going to send you a text just now. Did they give you the day off?"

I laughed. "Yeah, right. A lowly peon in this massive firm given a day off? Nope. I was told to go home, do what I needed to do, then be back here by nine."

"Can I give you a lift home? I have the company car and driver."

"That sounds fantastic. I wasn't sure how I was getting home with my eyes closed."

"Come on, sleepy-head. Let's get you home."

A roar of Harley pipes jerked me awake. Disoriented, my eyes opened to the backseat of a car. My head felt the cushion of someone's thigh, and a dark suit jacket covered my sleeveless arms. It smelled faintly of Donovan's cologne. I popped up looking disheveled and knew something wasn't right in my world.

"You okay?" Donovan asked, chuckling. "You were dead to the world the moment we got in the car." He tried to tame my unruly hair. "We're at your house."

"Home, right."

I heard the roar again and knew something was seriously wrong.

As I stepped out, I saw my brother, in the midst of saying good-bye to his wife, looking our way with a gleam of mischief in his eyes. However, Emily looked down right terrified for me. I knew what was behind me. Better yet, I knew who was behind me. I turned to face the music and saw Max putting his helmet back on, covering the hurt and angry look in his eyes.

No!!!

"Max! Max!" The more I yelled, the harder he stepped on the gas pedal to drown out my voice.

To hell in a handbasket, on the express train...

Dec. 24, 2012

Movie Title—Unintentional Walk of Shame

*W*hat happened this morning was straight out of a movie script.

EXTERIOR. MY STREET—MISSION BLVD.—5:30A.M.
The scene opens with the main character Girl (me) yelling frantically and making a mad dash to the Harley Davidson sitting in front of her house. Main character Boy (Max) totally ignores the Girl's pleas, takes the bike off the kickstand, and begins to ride off into the sunrise. 2nd, and very minor in importance, Girl (Emily) pulls away from her husband and starts chasing down the Boy. When 2nd and minor part Girl (Emily) trips on a bump in the sidewalk and does a quasi face plant, her husband runs to save her. With Hollywood special effects in play, the Boy is the first one there, picking up his ex-girlfriend and minor character Girl (Emily) and tenderly checks the wounds on her hand. Minor character Girl usurps the starring role, and has both men wanting to take care of her. The husband is not a happy camper. Not only is his wife hurt, but the ex-boyfriend is also the first one on the scene to take care of his wife. He growls at both the Boy and the Girl and takes his wife into their house. The Girl, too, isn't happy with the way the minor character Girl stops

the Boy's life with her every hiccup and usurps the starring role. BUT, she is grateful for the chance to make everything right with the Boy.

THE GIRL
(pissed off)
Let's talk!

Boy follows.

DONOVAN
Jane, you need a ride back to work? You want me to pick you up in a few hours?
Girl forgot that her "overnight" date was still there watching this circus act.

THE BOY
(angry, territorial, resolute)
No!

Donovan chuckles and cruises right up to the Girl. Girl is a bit freaked out—no, she's more than a bit freaked out.

DONOVAN
(whispers the words, then pulls the GIRL in for a chaste kiss on the forehead)
If you need me, don't hesitate to call, okay?

The Boy gives a f*** off look and pulls the Girl away.

INTERIOR. GIRL'S BEDROOM—A FEW MINUTES AFTER 5:30AM

THE GIRL
What the hell was that with Emily?

THE BOY
(ANGRY! and hollering)
You spend the night with another man, he kisses you in front of me, and you're the one mad?

THE GIRL
(also angry and yelling)
I beg you to stop so I can explain, but noooo that's not enough. Then Emily has a tiny little fall and your life stops till all is right in her world. You got to her even before my brother, her husband, did.

THE BOY
(still yelling)
You drive me freakin' insane!

The Boy grabs the Girl and pulls her into his body and kisses her—no, devours her—as if their life depends upon this kiss. His kiss is possessive...demanding...seductive...and the Girl matches him, lust for lust.

INTERIOR. THE BED—ANOTHER FEW MINUTES LATER
Just about all clothes are off and the Boy and the Girl struggle for dominance on the bed. The Boy allows the Girl to take the lead for a while until he roughly shows her who's boss. Moans, Groans, Oohs, Aahs, happen until the phone rings...and rings... and rings...

The Boy
(annoyed, but answers the phone via speakerphone)
What is it?

THE MINOR GIRL'S HUSBAND
(amused)
Everything okay over there?

THE BOY
(not as annoyed)
Your sister is in bed with me close to naked, and you're interrupting.
Draw your own conclusion, Dr. Reid.

THE MINOR GIRL'S HUSBAND
(not as amused, grossed out)
Not funny, Davis! Get off her bed and get some clothes on. You, too,
little sister or I'm calling Mom to do a bed check.

THE GIRL
Why are you bothering us?

THE MINOR GIRL'S HUSBAND
Santa has come early for my Emi. Pack your stuff. We're going to
New York, Christmas morning.

THE GIRL
You found an apartment?

THE MINOR GIRL'S HUSBAND
I did. I just reached a verbal agreement and will sign all the papers
today.

THE BOY
How's Em doing?

THE MINOR GIRL'S HUSBAND
That's none of your concern, but thanks for asking.

THE GIRL
I don't know if I can go because of work.

THE MINOR GIRL'S HUSBAND
Donovan is taking care of that for you. You'll have Christmas to New Years off. Davis, you want to join us in New York for the holidays?

THE BOY / THE GIRL
(happily surprised)
Seriously?

THE MINOR GIRL'S HUSBAND
(amused)
Yeah, if you get off her bed and promise never to give me any more details about your relationship, there's a seat next to Jane with your name on it.

THE BOY
I can't leave till a few days after Christmas, but I'd like to join you and your family. Thanks, Jake.

THE MINOR GIRL'S HUSBAND
Don't ever say I never did anything for you two. Sis, I'll call you later with more details and your to-do list.

THE GIRL
(so grateful that the to-do list doesn't bother her)
Bye and thank you...

INTERIOR. STILL IN BED—LAYING IN EACH OTHER'S ARMS—MAYBE HALF HOUR LATER

THE BOY
You still owe me an explanation as to why you spent the night with another man.

THE GIRL
I didn't spend the night with Donovan. I worked the whole night, and Donovan gave me a ride home because he had the company car and driver.

THE BOY
(sounding insecure)
You mean to tell me that kiss meant nothing to him...or to you?

THE GIRL
(reassuring and repositioning herself to sprawl on top of the Boy)
Donovan is Jake's best friend since childhood and he's known me since I was born. He asked me out to a Laker game yesterday and I accepted because...

THE BOY
I'm listening.

THE GIRL
Because...
1. He's a good friend and I enjoy his company.
2. I used to have the biggest crush on him when I was little.
3. I didn't know where we stood, after the whole Santa Barbara fiasco, and it felt good to be wanted by somebody.
Was that honest enough for you?

Boy looks tenderly at the Girl and kisses her lovingly.

THE BOY
(looking into her eyes with conviction)
You don't need anyone else to want you because I want you. You and I are going to make this work. You understand me, Jane Reid?
(next, sounding very alpha-male)
Bring on all the Donovans in the world. I am not going to lose you again. You are mine from today on. It drove me nuts to give you that

year away from us. From now on, we are going to figure life out together. You got it?

The Girl looks upon the Boy somewhat uncertain but dazzled, nonetheless.

THE BOY
My Jane, you are the kindle to my fire, the spark to my flame, the burning sun that starts my day. My life was miserable when you went back to New York. Let's start fresh. Forget Joyce, forget Donovan—it's just you and me, baby. All right?

THE GIRL
(about to cry)
All right.

After making out a bit longer, the Girl realizes she has to get back to work. The Boy gives her a ride on the Harley and they plan to meet for dinner—their first date as a newfound couple.

FADE OUT!

Dec. 25, 2012

Merry Christmas

My Precious Jane,
You light me up with your smile
Your fiery spirit brings new meaning to life
Just being with you gives me hope
(Truly) I would not wish any companion in the world but you
(the first three lines plus Truly—me; the fourth line—Shakespeare)

*T*his crazy heartfelt (and slightly funny) card, sitting atop a Christmas present, waited for me on my seat on the airplane.

This morning, the Reid family had an out-of-control, over-the-top, Christmas at my brother's house. The twins got presents from *EVERY* member of the Reid clan. Not only did my aunts and uncles indulge these almost nine-month-olds, each one of my cousins came bearing gifts. The most hysterical part about all these gifts—the twins had no interest in any of them except for the nesting boxes that their favorite aunt, yours truly, bought for them. Nick and I stacked them up, James and Elizabeth knocked them down, and then the cackles ensued. The entire family was mesmerized with their laugh. I had to admit, there was something magical about watching little bodies practically fall back in glee. It made me feel warm and fuzzy as well.

After the fastest clean-up known to man and a chauffeur-driven ride to the airport, Mom, Dad, Uncle Henry, Jake, Emily and the twins were ensconced in first class, Nick and I sat in business class, Doug and Laney sat in coach. Nick and I would have sat right next to Doug and Laney if it hadn't been for all the miles I'd accrued flying back and forth from the New York office to the LA one. Lucky Nick—this upgrade was my Christmas present to him.

"How'd you get a Christmas present waiting for you on board the plane? After 9/11, I'm surprised anyone allowed an unsupervised package to just sit there."

"Shut up, Nick." I (literally) cried. In this beautifully packaged box was a framed pencil sketch of me laughing away—not much differently than my baby niece and nephew. Shockingly, it was signed Max Davis with *Whenever I think of you, this is the beauty I see* written above his signature. I looked so carefree and beautiful. I didn't know Max could be this romantic, and I had no idea he could draw.

"Emily," I worked my way up to first class before they made us all buckle up. "Did you know about this?" I held out the drawing.

"Wow! Did Max draw this? I didn't know he could draw."

FINALLY! Something about Max my sister didn't know. Though, I had no idea, till now, as well.

"This is gorgeous, Jane. But then again, you are gorgeous, so it wasn't a difficult draw." My sister was always so sweet.

"Did Max tell you about this gift?"

"Kind of. He stopped by the house early in the morning to drop off a gift for the babies and he asked me to put this on your seat on the plane. Pretty romantic, huh? I didn't know Max had it in him. He never ever did anything this sweet for me."

I was feeling mighty good right now!

"I'm sure you can see how much he adores you, Jane. I hope you'll go a little easier on him." That felt like a compliment and a slap on the wrist at the same time. "Has he told you about his family, yet?"

I shook my head no.

"He'll tell you, soon, I'm sure." Emily patted my hand. Once again, she knew something about Max that I didn't know. *Aargh!*

"Sit down Jane, and stop bothering us. Emi's had a long morning already. Let her sleep while the twins are sleeping." My brother could be so annoyingly protective of his wife. Maybe it was only annoying because I didn't have that same kind of protector in my life.

"We'll talk more, later?" she smiled.

"Sure." I returned her smile. "Thank you for the theater tickets, Emily. Max and I will enjoy them."

"What did you get them theater tickets for? I already spent a fortune on their plane tickets," said my cheapo brother who put us in coach. Bratty...I know. But that was the kind of relationship my older brother and I had.

"That was *your* present to them. I wanted to do something for my one sister and one ex-boyfriend." Her impish smile surfaced.

"Emi...! I hate it when you mention Max as your ex. It bugs me enough to not give you part two of your Christmas gift."

"There's more than this trip to New York? Jake...this is extravagant enough. I don't want anything else."

"There's a lot more, Love. Wait till we get to New York."

This was my cue to leave. They were getting those lovey-dovey eyes that made me want to throw up my breakfast. I would wager my first-born, if anyone thought there was another couple on earth who loved each other more than my brother and his wife.

Floored!
Astounded!
Close to faint!

That was how my sister-in-law looked when she saw her new apartment on the upper west side. Sparsely furnished by Aunt Babs, who had been in town for her sister's birthday, this spacious four bedroom apartment overlooked Central Park and was a short walking distance to the Time Warner Center at Columbus Circle. Jake looked impossibly smug with himself when he saw how delighted the love of his life was with their new living arrangement.

After helping the happy family settle into their new dig, Nick and I went to our rinky-dink apartment in Soho and unpacked.

"Hello?" I answered a call from an unknown number.

"Merry Christmas, Jane."

"Max..." I let his name linger on my tongue for a bit because right now, I was seriously (almost) in love with him.

"Flight was all you expected it to be?"

"It was more than I expected it to be. Thank you for the phenomenal gift. I can't believe you drew that picture of me. When did you learn to draw?"

"I've always liked art, but didn't really try to sketch till I got into that accident after Em and I broke up. I did it out of sheer boredom and discovered a new talent."

"When did you draw that picture of me?"

"When you left me for New York. I missed you a lot and none of the pictures I had of you captured the beauty that was in my head. So, I decided to draw a picture of my own and that was the result. I used to look at it whenever I wanted to talk to you."

"You missed me?" I seriously wanted to cry, again—and I'm *not* the crying-type.

"Of course I missed you, Jane. Why would you think I didn't? How could I not?"

"Why didn't you ever call me when I was in New York?" *I would've transferred back to LA, immediately.*

"You said you wanted space and that you needed time to think. So, I honored your wish till a few weeks ago when your brother told me you'd moved back into town." There was a bit of a pause to our conversation. "Jane..."

"Yeah?"

"I want you to know that I'll frustrate you many times over. I'm neither eloquent nor romantic. You, having lived with a brother who seems to have cornered that market, will be disappointed with my feeble attempts. But, I want us to work. I love your spitfire personality, I love your tender heart, and I love all that is you. I can't promise you anything just yet, but my hope is that you, too, would not wish any companion in the world...but me."

A poem, a sketch, a heartfelt confession...this was the best Christmas of my life!

Dec. 27, 2012

Getting to Know You, Getting to Know All About You...

jumped my new boyfriend the moment he came out of JFK Terminal 5.

"Whoa!" Max hadn't quite braced himself before I lunged at him. We almost fell to the ground. "You are quite the welcoming wagon."

"Uh-huh...wait till you see what's waiting for you back at the apartment," I answered between sucking on his lips.

"What lascivious thoughts are going through that pretty head of yours?"

"Wouldn't you like to know?"

"I...would...love...to...find...out..." Each ellipsis represented the make-out intervals between the inside of Terminal 5 and curbside.

"Where'd the car and driver come from, and what are you doing here? Of course, with that kind of welcome, I'm not complaining."

"My brother lent us his car and driver, and I'm here because after your Christmas surprise, I realized I wasn't *nice* enough to you."

"And how will you be *nice* to me?" He had that mischievous, bad-boy grin I loved. Because Max was the quintessential boy-next-door, I found the whole Harley Davidson rebel image he was portraying, *hawt!* Next thing you know, he'll come bearing a tattoo. That image was seriously doing things for me.

"I have a super fun few days planned. But tonight, there's a dinner at my brother's new place."

"Who's sleeping where?"

"Bold question, Mr. Davis. You, Nick, and Doug are on the twin beds and pullout sofas, and Laney and I are in the master bedroom. Not what you had in mind?"

He had that grin again. "Now that you and I are seriously pursuing this relationship, we need to further *every* aspect of this relationship."

I leaned over and whispered, "There are ears other than ours in the car. Why don't you sweet talk me later?"

Max and I met Nick, Doug and Laney at Fish Restaurant, and after rounds of beer and oysters, we decided to get our hands dirty and have the all-you-can-eat Maryland blue crabs.

"This is so much work for so little payback. I want to find a man who will shell an entire crab for me and hand it to me on a silver platter," Laney dreamed.

"Good luck. You'll be fortunate to find a man who can afford to buy you crabs, let alone feed you crabs." Her brother, the party pooper, burst her bubble.

"I want someone like Jake who will adore me and lay down his world for me. You guys didn't see him when he came to find Emily in Japan. He believed his life was over because she wasn't with him anymore. It was so sad and romantic at the same time."

"Jake's a wuss. He'd stay home and stare at his wife and kids all day if Emily would let him. He's such a goner. None of his buddies see him anymore unless they come visit him at home. I, for one, don't want to be so enamored with a woman. I'd like a life." Nick stated while shoving a mound of crab into his mouth

"Jake won't care what you say about him, but don't bring down Emily. He won't be happy," I warned.

"Nothing wrong with Emily. I love my new sister. It's Jake that's the problem."

"I don't care what you say, Nick. I want someone just like Jake!"

"Your family is wonderful," Max mused as we walked the High Line after a filling lunch, while the rest of our lunch mates went home for a nap. "You're very fortunate to get along with all your cousins."

This was finally my chance to ask Max about his family.

"Is your family not that close? I thought most families got along."

Max took a nervous pause and just kept walking for a while.

"You asked me once why I still had such strong feelings for Em."

Jackpot! I hit the mother-load with this question.

"My feelings for Em are not what you're thinking."

"Ok...what am I thinking and how is it not...?"

"You believe that I never stopped loving Em—that I still want her in my fantasy world, since in reality, your brother would kick my ass if I came anywhere near his wife."

We both gave in to a light chuckle.

"It's nothing like that. I still do love Em and will always love her, but it's a familial kind of love. My family is not the lovey-dovey, touchy-feely type of people. I didn't grow up with hugs and kisses and high praises for what I'd accomplished. My parents were militant about our upbringing. I think they reproduced only because it was the right thing to do. Though, they were disappointed that they didn't have the perfect family consisting of a mom, dad, son and daughter."

I pulled Max down onto one of the reclining wood benches and we sat with our coffees in our hands.

"My parents never told me they loved me, and my brothers and I pretty much raised ourselves."

"That's rough to have parents who are only physically there."

"So imagine my surprise when I met Em. She, too, was starved for love—for a whole different reason than mine—but whatever the case, she was the first person I openly loved. And boy, did she love me back in return. Do you understand now what Em means to me?"

"No. What you just said makes me even more insecure. How could you ever stop loving Emily if she was the first person you really loved?"

"Jane!" He was frustrated now. He always pushed his fingers through the front of his head when he was frustrated. "Emily was my first love, yes, but she was also family to me, and I to her. That's our bond—a familial one. I consider her my one true family member along with my brothers. Even though Em had a loving family in the past, and has a loving one now in the present, we love each other like...brother and sister. Em does nothing for me as a woman. At this moment, you, and only you, fill that position."

He moved over to my bench and put his face really close to mine. "You get it, now?"

"I get it. I don't know if I fully believe it, but I'll work on believing what you just told me. But for now, we need to pick up some tres leche donuts for Emily at Doughnut Plant and get over to their new home."

"So, why the home in New York? Are they planning on moving here?"

"Oh no. The entire Reid family would die if the twins moved. Since Emily likes this city so much, Jake thought it'd be nice for them to have a home here to visit, often. With the two kids, it's hard to go in and out of hotels."

"Maybe I should've gone into heart surgery. You're brother isn't hurting for money, is he?"

"You, who wants to go give free medical care to the poor in Africa, thinking about riches?" I kidded with him. "No, Jake and Emily aren't hurting, but they also don't have much to spend their money on. Their house was gifted to Jake by my grandfather, and outside of the new minivan Emily got, she never spends money. She's beautiful, and with that perfect frame, no matter what she wears—Stella McCartney couture or Stella McCartney H&M—she looks fantastic."

"She is that."

"She's what? Beautiful?"

"Yep, beautiful." Grinning, he knew I was jealous. "As Em is beautiful, you, my green-eyed monster, are stunning! Nobody can pull off this dark-hair sparkling blue-eye combo like you can. And for now, and maybe even for a lifetime, I prefer stunning."

Did he just say that??? Crap. That was hot!

Dec 31, 2012

New Year's Eve+Once+Masa+Alex Forrest+Sick Babies=Sex? Part 1

My morning got off to a titillating start. Since Max got here, we've been engaged in foreplay with absolutely no release (*all* puns intended). I walked into my bedroom as Max walked out with a skimpy towel wrapped around his well-toned body.

"Nice outfit."

"Yeah? You wanna see what I have on under?"

"Maybe..." I teased, giggling.

As he sauntered over to me, I wondered how we were going to pull this off with four other people in the house when I heard, "Hello everyone!" *Geez Louise!* Will anyone give us a little privacy?

Quickly closing the door, I greeted my parents, Uncle Henry, Aunt Barbara and the twins! We all flocked to the darling babies. "Hello cuties. What brings you here?" I asked, while grabbing Ellie. James got a similar greeting from Laney.

Ellie gunned straight for the diamond pendant on my neck—like father, like daughter. She tugged on it and wouldn't let go until I gave it to her and put it around her neck. She put the diamond in her mouth, which freaked us all out. Though it was on a long chain, I was keeping an eye on this troublemaker and making sure she didn't swallow the jewel.

"How'd the babies find emancipation from their parents?" Nick asked.

"Jake has a full day of surprises planned for Emily, so he asked that we babysit the twins today. We picked them up bright and early and went out to breakfast; and then we took them to the park. It's time for their nap and we weren't far from the apartment, so we thought we'd have them nap here."

"Well hello, beautiful girl and boy!" Max looked so natural taking James from Laney. Of course Ellie, the attention-monger, threw away my pendant and practically jumped into Max's arms. We had to do a baby swap. "You're so beautiful, Elizabeth," Max cooed. "You are an exact replica of your mother." She threw her head back and gave a dazzling laugh. "What's all this in your nose, young lady? You're a mess," he said, while looking into her nose.

"We've all tried to clean the snot out of both their noses but they won't let us get anywhere near them. They both seem to have a cold." Mom tried again to get near Ellie's nose, but she turned her face into Max's chest.

"Babe, can you get my toiletry kit?" *Babe...*I liked that.

By the time I got out some Q-tips, he had Ellie calmly cradled in his left arm. He then started explaining to her that he was cleaning out all the gook in her nose, so she could breathe. It looked like he was performing surgery up her nostril. Shockingly, this hyperactive girl just laid there listening to his soothing voice. Actually, we were all a bit mesmerized with Max's baby-whisperer techniques. James, who was worse off than Ellie, got the same care, but he opted to go lay in Mom's arms when Ellie threw herself back into Max's arms.

"Good work, Doctor." I tried to place my arms around Max's waist as Ellie stayed cradled in his arm, but this brat kicked my face not once, but several times, till I backed away. I swear she did this on purpose.

"You obviously have your mom's looks but your auntie's temperament." I was about to get upset and a bit jealous (of a woman who wasn't even in this room, and a baby who wasn't even nine months old yet—I know...I'm pathetic!) except Max pulled me in for semi-luscious kiss.

Family audience, be damned. Foreplay, begin.

Irritation gone, I happily called out, "Time to go nigh-nigh, Ellie. James is already in the room. You go join him, you flirt."

She dug her face into Max's body and put her chubby arms around his neck understanding that her time with my boyfriend was over. She kept shaking her head no and digging herself even deeper—if that was possible.

"You want me to put you down, beautiful girl? Come on, let's tell you a bedtime story and have you nap on Auntie Jane's bed."

"He's pretty dreamy, Jane," Laney said as we both watched Max carry Ellie into my room. "And he likes you so much!" Laney seriously needed a man. When I got back to work, I'd have to look around for a nice young lawyer who'd make her every dream come true. Though, she needed to lose most of those collegian ideals.

Because Ellie did everything in her power to keep Max away from me, we had to rush through brunch to make it in time for the New Year's Eve matinee showing of New York's hottest musical, *Once*.

Thanks to a generous Emily, we sat in a very cozy left box, perched adjacent to orchestra seats.

"My sister got us superb seats, huh?"

Max laughed.

"What's with the cynical laugh, Dr. Davis?"

"You call Em you sister when you're happy with her or if she does something that pleases you, but you call her your sister-in-law when the g.e.m. in you comes out."

"What's a 'g.e.m.?'"

"It's short for green-eyed monster."

"Not funny."

"But you are my gem—in every way. Speaking of, I have one more Christmas gift for you."

"You do?"

He nodded and pulled out a slim, elongated box from the inside pocket of his jacket. "Here. Open it."

A sparkling gold chain bracelet winked at me as I opened the box.

I turned to Max.

"I wanted to give this to you after I got here and created some memories with you. When I saw this charm bracelet, I thought of each link as a bond we will form; and each charm I add, will be a memory that strengthens this bond," he said while pulling out a Statue of

Liberty charm. "This is our first memory together, my stunning gem, New York City."

OMG! I was actually speechless. Even if I wanted to say something, it was shortcut by Max's kiss. It was the most electrifying, heart-stopping, toe-curling kiss, ever. He gave me one of those, two handed, thumbs by my ear, fingers woven through my hair while curled around the back of my head and parts of my neck, type of kiss. He literally devoured my lips over and over again. If someone had taken a picture of us, we'd look like a poster for a Nicholas Sparks' movie. The kiss was fanfreakin'tastic.

What was even more fanfreakin'tastic was that every time the actors started singing a romantic song, (which was about 95% of their songs since this was coined 'the most romantic musical of the year') Max turned and kissed me. He kissed me as if we were the hero and heroine of a Harlequin romance novel, like we were the only two in the theater, like we were just about to make love. He was as hot and bothered by these songs as I was. By the end of the show, both of us were ready to get a hotel room.

"Hold on, my phone just buzzed," I said, as we exited the theater. "... very cool! My brother says New Year's Eve dinner at Masa tonight."

"Seriously?"

"Yep! Let's go."

"You're late," my brother chided when we stepped into Masa.

"Sorry. We were watching *Once* and I had my phone turned off."

"Did you enjoy it?" My sister was beaming. I didn't know if it was because she and Jake had had such a good day, or because she was happy for me. It was probably a bit of both.

"We enjoyed it very much," Max answered while kissing her cheek. "Thank you, Em...ily."

Emily looked surprised by her new moniker and I was shocked, but thrilled, that he called her Emily.

"About time you stopped calling my wife by a term of endearment, Davis."

"Yeah...it is about time. And I don't think I've had a chance to thank you for this trip, Jake. It's opened my eyes to what a gem your sister is in my life. I don't think I've had a better time with anyone as I've had with Jane. No offense, Em...ily. Boy, all those years of calling you Em is hard to erase overnight."

"No offense taken." Emily, who was already seated when Max was talking to her, grabbed Max's hand and pulled his ear to her lips. She proceeded to whisper something only they could hear, then tenderly kissed him on the cheek. He smiled, took my hand, and led me to our comfortable high-backed stools.

I was in such orgasmic bliss (you get the teasing theme of this story?) with all that'd happened today, that the loving exchange between my sister and my boyfriend bothered me, *none at all*! Nothing could ruin my evening.

"Max!" a voice, no different from nails screeching on a blackboard, called out again, "Max."

"Joyce..." Max bit out.

Joyce? *What the hell???* What was she doing here?

Jan. 1, 2013

New Year's Eve+Once+Masa+Alex Forrest+Sick Babies=Sex? Part 2

S eriously, Woman?!? What the hell are you doing here?

"Hi! What a pleasant surprise. I didn't know you were coming to New York." She said while touching my man's arm. I was this close to slapping her hand away.

This Joyce woman was about my height, with blond, blond hair, some freaky greenish (cat) color eyes, and had on a tight, tight dress. She looked older, her nose was a bit crooked and she had those pouty Angelina Jolie lips people liked—if one was into those kind of lips. I personally found those lips to make her mouth look too big. She kinda had that "girls gone wild" look with the big boobs and big lips. Great, my competition could model for a "girls, girls, girls" poster.

"Um...I'm here with my girlfriend and her family. Jane," he looked at me a bit nervous, trying to gauge my reaction, "this is Joyce. Joyce, my girlfriend Jane. You know Jake, over there." He pointed my brother's way.

"Hi, Dr. Reid. And you must be his lovely wife, Emily. I've heard so much about you."

Kiss-ass!

With all the intros done, I expected her to skedaddle, but she had the gall to say, "Max, can you come with me? I'd like to introduce you to my family—of course, you already know my parents. They're excited to see you again."

"Um, okay." As reassurance, Max kissed me close to my ear and whispered, "I'll be right back, my precious gem." Of course, the double entendre was heavy.

If he hadn't been so wonderful to me all day, I would've called him a choice name or two.

"What the hell is she doing here?" I asked my brother. "Did you tell her we were all going to be here?"

"Don't yell at me, little sis." He warned. "It looks like she is here with her family enjoying a meal, no different than what we are about to do."

"This can *NOT* be a coincidence that she is at Masa of all places, on New Year's Eve." *Alex Forrest from Fatal Attraction in the house!* "You must have told her about it. And you," I accused Nick, "how do you know that psycho, and why are you so friendly with her?"

"Chill out, Jane." Nick was laughing at me. "Though, I do agree with her, Jake. That girl is a bit weird. Whenever I stop by the hospital to visit you or Max, she's always hanging around Max. In fact, right before you came back to LA, Jane, Max and I went to a bar to watch a game, and not long into the first quarter, this woman showed up and sat at our table. The weird thing was, it didn't look like she was meeting anyone else there."

"You see!" I yelled again, but not so loudly where Joyce and her family would know what we were discussing.

"Whatever. I don't care. The only one who knew my plans was my PA since she booked everything for me. Aside from her, it was all a secret."

"Nick, does this Joyce woman hang around Jake as well?" Emily asked.

"I don't know since Max and Jake are usually together when I go see them at the hospital. But, I don't think it's Jake that she's interested in."

"I don't want you getting too close to this crazy woman, okay?" Even now, my sister sounded so cute. By the smile on my brother's face, he definitely thought so too.

"You jealous?"

"No, but if you make me jealous for any reason, I'll make your life a living hell." Ooh...my sister had a bit of a don't-mess-with-me, bad girl attitude. There was a threat masked under that sweet smile.

My brother chuckled, saying, "My beautiful wife, you have no worries from me. I am in love with you, and only you, and will be the rest of my life."

"Good to know. Just stay away, okay?" She warned again. She then asked Chef Masa if he'd start the meal and did something so awesome, I could've kissed her right then and there.

She walked over to Max, who was still conversing with Joyce and her family, and said in her sweetest voice, "Excuse me...but our meal's about to begin so we need Max back at our table. It was nice meeting you, Joyce." Before Joyce could protest, Emily placed her hand on Max's arms and tugged on him, while ignoring her. If that wasn't a serious set-down, I don't know what is. *Go Emily!*

I saw my brother trying to mask his laugh as Emily walked over to her stool after depositing Max in his seat.

"Missed me?"

"No." I was as curt as possible.

Then he did it again! Right as the servers brought out our first course, he placed both hands on my cheeks and did that Nicholas Sparks' movie-poster kiss. He practically swallowed me whole in front of everyone. "I missed you," he winked and picked up his chopsticks.

"May I take this empty seat?" Psycho asked as she sat next to Max. "I think I'd like to eat the prix fixe menu at the sushi bar instead of the a la carte menu at our table."

Even before Max's saliva had dried on my lips, Psycho ruined the afterglow.

Laney, who was to my left, giggled and tried to break up the tension on our half of the sushi bar.

"Jake, Emily, I want to thank you for inviting me on this trip and for paying for my plane fare and for this extravagant meal. That's really kind of the both of you." Laney, no different from my sister, was sweet. Some man would be lucky to snatch up such a kind and pretty girl.

"I'm glad you're here with us, but I can't take any of the thanks. My wonderful husband planned this entire surprise. When he told me we were spending some time in New York, I had no idea I was getting so much more."

Nick and Doug chimed in. "Laney says she wants to meet a man just like you, Jake. We told her to meet a real man, instead."

"Shut up, you two. That's why you're still single. You need to take lessons from Jake."

"Why thank you, Laney, for setting those boys straight, and for the huge compliment. If I find someone just like me, I will send him your way. And as for your thanks, you're welcome, and I'm glad you could join us."

"Was there a special reason for all these surprises for Emily in New York?" She continued to ask.

"Well..." now Jake turned to Emily and we all knew group conversation was over. "The last time Emily and I were in New York together, I broke her heart. There are some memories I can't forget no matter how much I try, and that is one of them. I needed to correct this memory and create new ones for us—much better ones that'll wipe out what I did to her."

Emily, of course, had tears in her eyes. "That's why you've been doing all this? I haven't thought about that day since our night in Kyoto. None of this was necessary, Jake. You and the twins have given me a better life than I could've scripted."

"Love, I still need to make up for the Grand Canyon incident as well. Since I can't buy the Grand Canyon, I don't know how I'll rectify what happened there."

"Oh my gosh!" I breathed. "Way too heavy for a sushi bar. Either keep it between the two of you or let's table it for another time."

"I think that's so romantic, Dr. Reid. Your wife is such a lucky woman." Who invited Psycho into our conversation?

"So Max..." was how Psycho started every conversation in between courses. She kept throwing questions at my man so we'd have very little time for conversation ourselves. My man knew I was pissed! He pulled my stool right next to his and kept his left arm around my waist. Often enough, he threw playful kisses on my face—the wet ones behind my ear, being my personal favorite. I was appeased... somewhat.

Twenty-eight courses done, Jake informed everyone that he and his wife were leaving us early. He had one last surprise for Emily.

"What's the last surprise, Jake?" Laney asked. "Please tell us. I'm dying to know."

Jake held back.

"Please???"

"Why don't you tell Laney? I'll be surprised either way."

"I have a suite reserved at the Trump Hotel for the night."

"How cool!" Laney clapped like a little girl.

"Overnight?" Emily asked, not sounding too happy.

"That's usually how it's done with hotel rooms, Love."

"We can't stay away from the kids tonight—especially James. They are both not feeling well and they both had a rough night last night. James was up most of the night and Ellie got up a few times as well."

"What? How come I didn't know this? Why didn't you wake me up? I could've helped you."

"I didn't want to wake you. You had watched them for most of the day while I went furniture shopping."

"Emi, I don't want you suffering by yourself if I'm around to help, okay?"

"All right. But...is it okay if we go home tonight? As it is, the kids haven't seen us all day. It might be a rough night for them again."

"Anything for you, my love." He then got up with Emily, pulled out a key card from his pocket and said, "Davis—enjoy, but be safe!" and handed him the hotel key.

HOT DAMN! PRIVACY TONIGHT!!! *Take that, PSYCHO!*

Our grins were telling and I made sure I grinned Psycho's way. Emily kissed me on the cheek and whispered, "Happy New Year, Miss Jane!"

And a happy new year it will be.

Both of us wanted to rush to the hotel, but we agreed to walk the seventeen blocks down to Times Square to see the ball drop. By the time we got there, we were nowhere near the ball, but we were able to do the countdown and engage in an intense make out session. All that controlled lust from the past few days turned into unbridled lust knowing what was going to happen tonight.

"Geez, you two. You already have a hotel room. Go use it rather than making us queasy." Nick kidded.

Nick didn't have to say much more. We practically ran the seventeen blocks back up to Columbus Circle and our clothes were half-off by the time we got on the bed. After almost two years of indecision and a few days of serious foreplay, we were gonna have sex. Fumbling with snaps, buttons, and zippers, it wasn't easy getting undressed when your eyes were closed and your lips were locked.

Then it happened. Just like in the movies, our phones started ringing. First, mine rang and when we ignored it, Max's rang. This kept going till the room phone rang. We couldn't ignore it any longer.

"I think someone's looking for us." Max and I were breathing heavy.

"Somebody better be dying or I'm going to be seriously pissed." I got off the bed and answered the phone. "Yes!" I shouted, frustrated.

"You and Max need to come over here right away and watch the twins. Emily is very sick. I need to take her to the emergency room."

"Where's Mom and Dad?" Did I really ask that selfish question?

"Get your ass over here, now!"

"We gotta go. Emily's ill and needs to go to the emergency room."

"What?" Max jumped off the bed and got dressed, faster than a New York minute. Familial love, my ass. He still loved her as a woman, whether or not he thought he did.

"You okay, Emily?" Max asked as soon as we got to their apartment. "What's wrong with her?" He then turned the question to my brother.

"She's been throwing up nonstop since we got home. She failed to tell me that she's been throwing up all day." My brother was *un*happy!

"You had such a special day planned for me. I didn't want to ruin it with whatever I caught from the kids."

Shaking his head, Jake said, "I'm going to get her checked out and probably get some fluid in her. It may take a while."

"No problem. Take as long as you like." Max was a lot more understanding than I.

Why of all days did she have to pick today to get sick??? She never gets sick!!! I knew I was being a brat again, but I was *un*happy as well.

Of course, as soon as Jake and Emily left, both kids got up, crying. We walked in and the twins wailed even louder because they wanted their parents, instead. I picked up James, the easier one, and Max picked up Ellie. After performing "surgery" on her nose again, he held her upright and quickly got her back to sleep.

"How'd you do that so fast? Good thing you're going into pediatrics and not me. All this crying has James even more miserable. His snot is everywhere."

"Give him to me and why don't you go lay down. It's late. You must be tired. I'll get this little one down after I clean him up."

I followed Max's instructions and got to the sofa, and I must have fallen asleep. When I woke up, Max was nowhere to be found. I tiptoed over to the kids' room, careful not to wake them up. The light was off but I heard the light squeaking of a rocking chair and Max's soothing voice telling James a story. I got close enough to hear what he was saying.

"You know, James, you look just like your mother when you cry. Your mother has a tendency to cry often. I guess...I was the cause for a lot of those tears." He was quiet for a while—possibly contemplating his sins. "I loved your mother for many, many years." Now he made me want to cry. I didn't want to hear about his love for Emily, but I couldn't walk away. "She and I loved each other but when I let her go, she found your father and fell in love with him. It hurt a lot at first, but your father was the best thing to happen to her." He rocked some more before continuing his confession. "Once I realized this, I was truly happy for your mom and just a little while ago, I realized that letting go of your mom was best thing that happened to me as well. I think I may have found love again, but your aunt is a difficult one. We fight all the time, and some days I wonder if she's worth the trouble. But, as soon as I see your auntie Jane, I know she's the best thing to happen to me. We may one day be family, little one. Would you be okay with me as your uncle? I'd sure be proud to have you two as my nephew and niece. Sleep, little one. I'll rock you till your parents get home."

Oh...my...gosh...

What a happy new year this will be...

Jan. 7, 2013

Back to the Same Hummm

Drummm...

"Hey. Merry Christmas. How was New York?" Donovan popped into my cubicle of an office.

"Merry Christmas to you too. New York was fantastic. How was your Christmas? What did you do?" Regardless of my feelings for Max, Donovan still looked as yummy as ever in his sleekly tailored dark blue pinstriped suit. He reminded me of a cross between Bradley Cooper with the wavy hair and killer smile, and Henry Cavill with the sexy as hell aura. Looking at him hurt sometimes. *It's okay to just look, right?*

"My Christmas was crazy. My four sisters with their families came into town and two stayed with my parents, one stayed with me, and one had the good sense to get a hotel room."

"How are your sisters doing? I haven't seen them in years. The last time I saw them was at Becky's wedding, three years ago. I got a text from Becky right before she came into town, but this trip was so last minute, I didn't get to meet up with her. I miss her."

"Well, she and Al are staying at my place. Why don't you come by after work, tonight? In fact, maybe we can all meet up after work, sans enfants. I'm sure all my sisters would like to see you."

Donovan came from a huge family, but because he was the only boy in the family, he hung out at our house whenever he needed a testosterone recharge. His sisters ranged from ages twenty-seven to forty with Donovan being somewhere in the middle.

"Jane!" Someone yelled from right outside my door.

"Uh-oh...bitch alert." I moaned.

"Where's the Mitchell document? Why isn't it done and on my desk for review? You know that we're meeting with these clients in a few days and I need to make sure your work is without error..." Andrea bit out till she saw Donovan in my office. "Oh, hello Donovan. How was your Christmas? Your family got into town safely?" A total Dr. Jekyll and Mr. Hyde routine ensued. "Whenever you can get it done, okay?" She winked at me in a malicious kind of way. *Weird!*

"What was that?" Donovan asked.

"I don't know. I think she's got the hots for you, and is jealous that we're friends. She's always a bitch to me."

"Whatever. Lunch, later?"

"Sure."

Should I not have been so friendly with Donovan, especially after having had such an intimate time with Max in New York? I supposed I could rationalize it and say that we'd been friends for so long that it'd be silly to give up our friendship because Max might be jealous. But, I should also remind myself that Max and I were starting again and life was so good between us, I shouldn't rock the boat.

"Hello, my precious gem." A phone call during the day from Max was a rarity.

"Hello! It's 10:30am. How are you able to call me?"

"I missed you." I felt that warm fuzziness again. "You busy?"

"Yeah. The head lawyer for a case I'm working on has decided to make my life a living hell. She yelled at me this morning till she realized Donovan was in my office."

"Donovan...yeah...we never finished talking about him."

"Before you forbid me to hang out with a guy I've known *all* my life and work in the same office with, I have to tell you I'm having lunch with him in about an hour and will probably be hanging out with him and his sisters tonight."

There was a long silence on Max's end.

"Max...?"

"Yeah, I'm here."

"What do you say? Am I *allowed* to keep my friend?" The sarcasm was a bit heavy on my part.

"Max...we're all headed to the cafeteria for a late breakfast. Do you want to join us, or shall I bring something back for you?"

There was that nail-on-the-chalkboard voice, again.

"I'll be right there."

"I'll save you a spot."

"Sure."

"Max? Shall I hang up so you and Alex Forrest can go have breakfast?"

"Yeah. Why don't we hang up? We'll talk more when we're face to face. Bye."

Just like that, without letting me say goodbye, he hung up on me. *Jerk!* What was his problem again? *Aargh!* How can things go so well and then go so far south again?

I hadn't gotten any work done when Donovan stopped by to pick me up for lunch.

"An egg-salad sandwich?" God, he knew me so well.

"Yes." My phone rang as I was picking up my purse.

"Hey, Laney. What's up?"

"I brought your Kindle and I'm downstairs in the lobby. Can you come down?"

"Yep. See you in thirty seconds."

"Laney is here with my Kindle that I left in New York. She's downstairs."

"Well then let's go."

Even in fifty-degree weather, Laney was dressed in a tight, short dress with thigh-high boots, a stylish scarf and a matching hat. She looked good.

"Isn't that Emily's Chanel outfit from Paris? Why are you wearing it?" That comment came out a bit snarky because I'd wanted to borrow it, but Jake wouldn't let me.

"Yeah. Emily let me borrow it since I have a date tonight."

"How'd you get it past Jake?"

"Jake said I looked good in this outfit—though never as good as his wife."

Jerk! He had no issues with Laney borrowing this outfit, but wouldn't let his own sister wear it. Wait until he asks me for a favor next time!

"Hello, Miss Delaney Reid. My, you've grown up. How old are you, now?"

"Old enough..." she retorted.

"Bold words from such a youngin. Sassiness must run in the Reid family."

"Do I know you?"

"Laney, this is Donovan Taylor. He's Jake's best friend and he used to hang out at our house a lot when we were younger. You might be too young to remember."

"I don't remember, but hello Mr. Taylor. It's nice to meet you again." Our gentle Laney was unnecessarily hostile towards Donovan. Maybe she got up on the wrong side of the bed this morning.

"Here," she said handing me my Kindle. "I've got to go."

"Would you like to have lunch with us, Miss Delaney?"

"No thank you, Mr. Taylor. Bye Jane." Just like Max, earlier, she left without listening to me say goodbye. *Brat!*

"She's cute! Independent, spunky, and no fear...gotta love youth."

"Yeah, whatever."

"I texted all four Taylor sisters along with the two Reid brothers and we are all are meeting tonight at Jake's house. Why are Jake and Emily back from New York so soon? I thought they were staying there for a while."

"Jake didn't tell you?"

"No...what was he supposed to tell me?"

"I'm sure he'll tell you tonight. This news...it's HUGE!"

"Can't wait to hear it, then."

Jan 10, 2013

Unexpected Flight Plans

We had the best time the other night at Jake's house. It was like being a kid again and having a huge slumber party. Emily got along well with all of Donovan's sisters, even Kelley, Jake's one time long-standing girlfriend. But, before I rehash our fantastic night... the BIG news.

Jake and Emily are expecting! Yes, only after nine months, she is pregnant, again. That was why she was throwing up New Year's Eve, and that was why she ended up in the hospital. Jake and the rest of the Reids are ecstatic! Emily is in a bit of shock, but once that wears off, I'm sure she'll be happier than the Reid lot, combined. Though I was bitter the night Max and I didn't get to finish what we started in the hotel room, I could never trade what I heard outside James' bedroom—even if the jerk hasn't called me since our last conversation concerning Donovan. Max had such a chick side to him sometimes.

"Whatcha daydreaming about?" Hot man in another perfect suit, alert.

"Hey Donovan. I was just thinking about the other night at Jake's house. I had so much fun! I can't believe we all stayed up till the sun came out. I was so exhausted yesterday. I went home from work and conked out."

"Me too. I had a great time, but I can't do those all-nighters anymore. Emily was a good sport. Even as she was yawning away, she played the perfect hostess. I'm sure it was miserable for her to get up to the twins, only after a few hours of sleep."

"Yeah, but Jake called my parents right before he left for work and asked them to come over and help her. There's no better husband than my brother."

"I think Kelley was floored and jealous at the same time when she saw your brother in action. She couldn't stop mentioning how attentive he was to your sister-in-law. She said he was more attentive to Emily in those few hours of the night, than he was their entire relationship. I think she was a bit pissed."

"Funny. Yeah, Jake is a bit ridiculous where his wife and family are concerned. It's no wonder she's pregnant again."

"With their speed of progress, they may be at half a dozen kids before I even have one."

"I just hope it's not twins again. However, if Emily has twins, again, we'll all have a baby to hold. As you can tell, we are all a bit obsessed with those kids."

"I've noticed. I, too, find them adorable—especially that Elizabeth. She's quite a charmer, even at her young age. She must get it from her aunt."

Dear God, he was giving me one of those flirtatious, gorgeous smiles. What kind of defense can a girl have against such perfection like that? I ignored his comment and changed subjects.

"I was super glad we had the reunion. We need to get together more often."

"Yeah, I agree. By the way, when's your flight tonight?"

"Jane!" Ms. Biatch Lawyer was calling. "Oh, hello, Donovan. I just needed to make sure Jane was ready for our meeting with the Mitchell Group. She can be a bit messy with her work. You can't believe all the mistakes I have to correct whenever she sends me her finished documents..." While the Biatch was going on about my flaws, I stood behind her mimicking her witchy ways. Donovan did his best to hold back his laugh. "I'll see you on the 8:00p.m. flight!" She said whatever she needed to say, and walked out.

"Boy, you gonna be okay being with her for a few days?"

"No, but do I have a choice? I'm going to stay at the apartment rather than at the hotel with her, Mark, and Andrew. I don't even know why I'm attending this meeting. They really don't need me. Ms. Biatch is the head of patent law. She's only making me go so I can be her personal assistant and do all her grunt work."

"Have a good trip. I'll see you when you get back."

"Okay, see ya."

I contemplated whether I should give Max a call. He had no idea I was leaving for three days since he hadn't called me in about the same number of days. It served him right not to know what was going on in my life. Nevertheless, I missed him and knew I was being stubborn about not calling him. I decided to be the bigger person.

"Hello?" that scratchy, pain in my arse voice answered my boyfriend's phone.

"Max, please," I bit out in the most pleasant voice that I could muster.

"Is this Jane?" She was way too cheerful! "Hi!!!"

OMG!!! I wanted to throw the phone against the wall.

"Hold on, Max is changing out of his scrubs right now."

What the hell???

"Max..." She used a way too familiar tone when calling his name. "You've got a phone call."

"Uh, thanks. Hello?"

"You pretty much hung up on me the last time we spoke, it's been three freakin' days since you last called me, and Alex Forrest just picked up your phone and told me you were changing clothes. I think I've said all I want to say. Good-bye!"

"Ja..." Those were the last sounds I heard from the other line before I hung up. Boy, this relationship stuff was hard. Maybe I, too, need to find someone like my brother. Perhaps Laney was on to something.

I decided to call it a day and go home and pack for my business trip. I was mad as hell, but figured we'd work it out when I got back home.

"Jane. Pick up the home phone," Mom called from downstairs, as I finished packing.

"Hello?"

"Gem, my sweet, you can't just say what you want to say, then hang up on me. You gotta give me a chance to explain myself. And, what's with turning off your cell phone?"

"What do you want? I'm busy." Mean, I know, but I wasn't in the mood to play nice.

"I'm sorry I haven't called you. I was mad, I was busy, and I was an idiot." Okay...not bad. "Would it make you feel better to know that I've been miserable the last three days? I've missed you, my precious gem." Getting better... "Can we meet tonight? I'll do *whatever* it takes to make it up to you." That suggestive tone was doing things for me.

"I wasn't lying when I said I was busy. I'm leaving for the airport right now. I have a business trip up in San Francisco. But...you can make it up to me *all* you like when I get back...I'm gonna be *very* demanding..." I used my best phone-sex voice starting from the *But...* part.

"Is...Donovan going?" Max sounded insecure again.

"You really asking me this when Psycho answered your phone and told me you were naked?"

"She did not say that. She was just holding on to the phone for me when I went in to change. I didn't have any pockets. And, you're avoiding my question."

"It's me, Andrea, my boss from hell, and Mark, and Simon from M&A. Donovan is not part of this team, so no, he's not going. You know, you're a *G.E.M.* yourself."

He laughed. "How long are you gone for?"

"I think three days, give or take a day, depending upon how it goes."

"All right. I have exams the next few days so I won't be able to see you anyhow if it isn't tonight. This works out perfectly. When you get back, I'll have some free time and we'll tie up all the loose ends."

"What loose ends are we tying up?"

"Our conversation about your extra-curricular activities with other men, and our unfinished business from New Year's Eve." I could tell he was smiling on the other end.

"Sounds stimulating! Can't wait. I'll see you in a few days."

"Bye. I'll miss you!"

"I'll miss you too."

I was glad to have worked things out with Max before leaving for my trip. Sitting on the plane, I thought over our conversation and blushed at the thought of tying up our unfinished business from New Year's Eve.

"Whatcha daydreaming about, now?" Donovan asked, taking the seat next to me.

I just stared at him.

"Mark's wife went into labor four weeks early. I'm the replacement."

Uh-Oh!!!

Jan. 14, 2013

Circa 1814 Part 1

*I*f I'd known that being an associate lawyer of a big firm was no different than living the life of a first year medical resident, I would've picked a different profession. I would've gone with my first choice of becoming a writer. Then I could've sat in front of a computer screen all day and eaten bonbons, while coming up with scintillating story lines. Law school was the wrong choice.

We had been going back and forth with the Mitchell group for the past two days with no resolution in sight. Our client would not concede to any of their demands, and of course, the Mitchell group would not concede to any of our client's demands. In the past forty-eight-hours, I think I slept no more than ten hours. I felt like hell, I looked like hell, and there was no end in sight.

"How you holding up?" Andrea shot daggers with her eyes when she saw Donovan ask me this question while patting my hand to comfort me.

"I thought the New York office was bad. This case is the toughest one I've seen yet."

"Jane, don't be such a whiner. You're not the only tired one here," said the biatch who went to her hotel room at 10:00p.m. last night, and slept a full night's sleep.

What was *I* doing while Ms. Andrea slept the night away, you ask? As the least senior member here, it fell upon me to rewrite all the documents from the meeting. And of course, I'd have to rewrite them again tonight, because of all the changes that will occur by the time we are done today.

"Hello all. How are negotiations going?"

"Gimpy!!!" I jumped up to hug Sir Roland Hugh Ascot III. "What are you doing here? You didn't tell me you were going to be here."

Getting the chance to hug this eighty-four-year-old elderly love of my life was the highlight of this crappy trip.

"I'm here checking up on our employees. You working hard? By the circles under your eyes, I can tell you're not slacking off."

"Jane," Andrea admonished in her "kindest" voice, "you're being rude by not introducing us to this gentleman. Hello. I'm Andrea Kot, lead partner in the patent law department."

"Hello, Andrea Kot, lead partner in the patent law department, I'm Roland Ascot."

"Roland Ascot, as in Ascot, Ascot & Pemberly? *The* Roland Ascot, founding member of our firm?" Andrea was a bit tongue-tied. "And how do you know our Jane?"

Sure...now that she knew how well connected I was in this firm, I was *her* Jane? Whatever! Before Gimpy could answer, I introduced him to everyone else.

"Gimpy, this is Simon Han and you remember Donovan, Jake's best friend? They're both from the mergers and acquisition department."

"It's an honor to meet you, Sir." Simon was in awe.

"Nice to see you again, Sir." Donovan shook Gimpy's hand.

"You married, yet, Son?"

"Not yet, Sir."

"Hasn't Jake schooled you on the virtues of married life? He's a man in bliss, last I saw."

"Oh yes he has, and he definitely is a man in bliss. Unfortunately, I can't seem to find any girl who'll take me."

"Why don't you marry our Jane here. She's as stubborn as she is beautiful."

"She is that, Sir. I'd take her in a heartbeat if she'd have me." Donovan winked and squeezed my hand.

OMG! He couldn't have meant what he just said. "You're one to talk, Gimpy. When're you gonna marry Gram and make an honest woman out of her? I know you two are living in sin out in London." Gimpy burst out with that deep, rich laughter I so loved hearing. "She won't come back to us because of you, huh?"

"Young lady, you talk too much." He laughed again. "How about it, my Janey...you want me to marry you and Donovan right now?"

I blushed. "Gimpy, I have a boyfriend. I'll introduce you to him when you're in LA." I said shyly, not understanding why I felt so self-conscious.

"All right. Enough talk of marriage. I have a treat for you all. I know you've been at a dead end with this deal. I happen to know the old goat who owns the Mitchell Group. Let me deal with him today. You all can have a day off."

Everyone clapped. We were all so in need of a break.

"Donovan, let me talk to you privately for a second, and Janey, my dear, I will see you later." Just like that, he dismissed us all but Donovan.

I sat in the break room waiting for Donovan, ignoring Andrea's prying questions.

"Jane, let's go." Donovan quickly shooed us out of the break room before anyone got a chance to stop us. "We have a few things to take care of before seeing Sir Ascot again."

"Where are we going, and when are we seeing Gimpy again?"

"Surprise," he smiled and put us on the elevator as Andrea tried to follow.

"What's going on?"

He kept his mouth sealed and continued smiling.

"Donovan!!!" I whined. "A hint or two or three?"

"Okay. A dress, a tux, a horse and carriage. There are your three hints."

Oh my gosh, did Gimpy command Donovan to marry me? Didn't I make it clear that I had a boyfriend? What was going on and why would Donovan agree to such a crazy demand? And wait...why wasn't I consulted in this whole marriage decision? *What the hell am I talking about?* Nobody was getting married today...but why else would we need a dress, a tux, and a horse and carriage?

Ugh! *How* do I always find myself in these crazy situations?

Jan. 17, 2013

Circa 1814 Part 2

$\mathcal{M}$ y biggest guilty pleasure in life is reading Regency romance novels. You know the ones with the embarrassing book covers (front and back) where the woman has the long wavy hair that flows down to her empire-waisted dress, showing off her scandalously low décolletage, while the buff Fabio-looking guy has his shirt unbuttoned and is caressing her from behind? Every book title has a Duke or an Earl in it, along with words like "his wicked ways," or "how to marry" or "the pleasures of". Yes, I am one of those women who cannot get enough of the lofty Duke dallying with the scullery maid, but eventually finding true love with a high-spirited Lady, or the Viscount who falls in love with the high-born, but poor daughter of a Baron. I love reading the traditional Regency romance with the fine historical details, as well as the Regency historical romance that includes more love, more drama, and more sex. They're all delicious in my book (I seem to be rolling with the puns these days :P).

Well, I don't know how this happened, but somehow I was transported back to the 1800's as soon as I left our San Francisco office and stepped into the *Madame Claudine's Dress Shoppe—Your Modiste of Choice.*

"What is this place?" I marveled, touching all the gowns, hats, gloves, fans, and parasols.

"I told you. A dress, a tux, and carriage and horses. Go pick out the dress you want to wear tonight."

"What's tonight?"

"Why, Lady Jane. Don't you know? Tonight is *Le Beau Monde Ton Ball*, at Almack's," the shopkeeper told me. *How'd this gal know my name?* "It's a masquerade ball, so don't forget to pick out your dominos," she addressed the both of us.

"Donovan. What is going on? Why do I feel like a character in a Regency romance novel?"

"Your 'Gimpy,' as you call him, purchased tickets to this ball and he told me to bring you. There's a surprise waiting for you there. Everything you borrow and use is compliments of Sir Ascot, so borrow away."

"You're being serious? I'm going to a real, pretend *ton* ball?"

"Yes, Lady Jane. Now go pick out your dress," he commanded.

"I think the ice blue cambric gown would suit nicely with those fiery blue eyes, Lady Jane." *The* modiste of the shop came out in full Regency regalia. She had on a gorgeous muslin morning dress and spoke like a member of the ton—though in actuality, no modiste could be considered part of the upper class.

"Why Lady Jane, I think you would look exquisite in that dress," Donovan winked.

"I think I might go for the cyprian look." La modiste looked horrified. "I think she's about to suffer an apoplexy," I whispered.

"I'm going to be in a fit of apoplexy myself if I have to wear these tight breeches." He was holding up a pair of buckskin pants that looked a *tad* bit slim and fitting.

"Those skin-tight breeches are hot. You'd look quite the dandy, Donovan, Earl of Los Angeles. Beau Brummel, watch out!" I laughed. "Just make sure nobody gets you *hot*, if you know what I mean, or else, we will all know what *you* mean." I laughed even harder. "There's no room for error in those pants."

"Move along, doxy, before you get what's coming to you and I put a hand to your backside."

"Did you really say that? Oh my gosh, that was so funny. Where'd you learn that?"

He rolled his eyes at me. "I have four sisters. They loved this Jane Austen kind of stuff and read it to me regardless of my willing participation. I don't know what you girls find so fascinating about this era. We had those embarrassing novels all around the house. My mom loved them, too."

"Ok, Beau. Let's pick our outfits and get to the ball."

Our hackney dropped us off at the apartment and we proceeded to get dressed (in separate rooms, of course). I could see why Regency ladies all required a lady's maid. It wasn't easy putting on evening gowns without help. The drawers came first, then the chemise, then a tight corset over the chemise. The blue gown had so many buttons on the back starting from my rear end, I had to button up as many buttons as possible and step into my dress before asking Donovan for help with the rest of the buttons. As for my hairdo, there was no way I'd be able to do one of those ringlet coifs starting from the top of my head, so I left my hair down, but half tied back. For an era where men and woman didn't touch each other bare-skinned before marriage, the neckline, or more fashionably called, décolletage, was deep and plunging. Thank goodness I had somewhat of a chest to keep the dress up.

"I need help." I stopped dead when I saw Donovan in his evening breeches, (which were not as tight as I thought they'd be...*shucks?!?*), a perfectly starched shirt, cravat, waist coat, tail coat, evening dress shoes, and a great coat. He even had a watch fob. He looked devastatingly handsome!

"Aren't you a vision in blue!"

"Uh...um..." I was a bit tongue-tied.

"Is it my outfit that's put you at sixes and sevens or is it the quizzing glass?" I busted out laughing when he put the quizzing glass up to his right eye. He looked like a modern day Mr. Darcy. *Sigh...*

"I need help," I said, turning around.

"Why you, trollop, you. Are you asking me to button...or unbutton...?"

As soon as his hand touched my body, I felt that spark between us that shouldn't be. This was wrong. I had to have a talk with him. The friendly flirting had gone too far, and I *was* being a trollop.

"Let's talk." I faced him, serious in my demeanor.

"Not now, Lady Jane...I know the inevitable...just give me tonight..." was all he said as he turned me around and buttoned up the rest of my dress.

I suddenly felt bereft. All joking aside, Donovan was a dear friend and a one-time, long-time "love" of mine. After tonight, I knew I'd have to let go completely, and he, too would let go of me. *Sigh,* again!

Carriages lined the block and waited their turn in front of the stately mansion in Pacific Heights. A cotillion dance was already in play when we stopped at the top of a double curved staircase. We were announced by the butler as Lady Jane and Earl Donovan to the crowd. The ball was a crush, as the old English would call it, with hundreds of people crowding the ballroom, sipping champagne, dancing, and telling Banbury tales to one another. *Le Beau Monde Ton Ball* was magnificent. The earl and I visited the card room where ladies played whist and piquet. We tried our hand at *vingt-et-un* in the men's card room but had no luck winning a pound or a shilling.

"Come, I think your surprise is here." Donovan put my gloved hand in the crook of his arm and led me out of the card room.

The entire ballroom was in a tizzy, excited about the newest arrival. I looked up to the top of the staircase as the butler was announcing Almack's Patroness, Countess Estelle Cowper Reid—my grandmother!!!

I ran to her as soon as she got safely down the steps. "Gram! When did you get to America, and what are you doing here?"

"Hello, Sweetheart! I just got in yesterday. I was going to go straight to LA but Roland told me you'd be in San Francisco so we thought it'd be fun to see you at this Ball. Isn't it marvelous?"

Hugging her, I answered, "I'm so happy to see you. You've been gone too long. Didn't you miss us?"

"Of course I missed you and the family, but it's James and Ellie I missed most. If it weren't so hard for me to go back and forth on a plane, I would've come back sooner. I've kept in touch with Emily and the twins through video chat, but it's not the same as being with them and holding them."

"You heard the big news?"

"Yes. Emily was in a state of shock when she called me from New York."

"Hello? Where's my welcome, dear Janey? I'm the one who brought you your Gram and planned this surprise."

"Hey, Gimpy. Thank you for bringing Gram back to us."

"Hello, Grandma Reid. You look as lovely as ever." Donovan bowed over my grandmother's hand, then kissed it.

"Hello Donovan. So good of you to escort my granddaughter to the ball. Are you two enjoying yourselves?"

"We are, Gram. What a hoot to be at such a spectacle."

"My lovely Estelle, I hear the instruments getting ready for a waltz. Would you care to join me in this dance?" My Gimpy still had it. Even at his age, he was the charming English gentleman.

"You silly old coot. I can't do any revolutions at my age," Gram admonished lightly.

"Come on, Estelle. Let's pretend like we're back in Paris and you'd just accepted my proposal. Let's go back to that night, before that rogue of a suitor of yours stole you from under my nose."

Gram laughed. "I think it was you who stole me from under Jerry's nose. All right. Let's try it, but slowly."

"May I have the pleasure of this dance, Lady Jane?" Donovan graced me with the same charming ways.

"Well, I don't know, Sir. My dance card seems to be filled already, and your name is not on any of the lines."

"I shall have to usurp one of the dandy's turns. *I am an earl!* Who dares to challenge an earl?"

"Ah-hem!" The butler cleared his throat again for another arrival. "The Duke—Maximillian Arthur Davis!"

Max??? Where did he suddenly come from, and how did he appear in this fantasy storyline?

Waltz! Tango!! Foxtrot!!!

Jan. 21, 2013

Circa 1814 Part 3

" *I* believe this is *our* dance?" Max, looking every bit the English Duke, politely demanded a waltz with me.

Donovan held on a bit longer than comfortable, raised my left hand, and gently kissed the exposed sliver of skin on the inside of my wrist, where the edge of my glove met the edge of my sleeve. I wanted to swoon on the spot—first, because that was undeniably romantic and a ten on the hot-o-meter! And second, because I saw the ring of fire in Max's eyes. I quickly put my hands on Max, in waltz position, as Donovan conceded this dance.

"Are you mad?" I squeaked.

"...as hell," he said with a begrudging smile on his face. "You look stunning, my lady Jane—a little too fetching for public viewing." He pulled me scandalously tight into his body and whispered in my ear, "*This...*" Max's index finger started at my collarbone. "*Neckline...*" Then it slowly inched down. "*Is...*" It then lightly grazed over the top swell of my breast. "*Dangerously...*" And soon followed the curve of the swell. "*Low....*" Finally his finger reached where the heart-shaped bodice met—right at center point. Damn, talk about hot. *THAT* was off the hot-o-meter chart, hot! "And there seems to be too much clothing underneath this dress," he continued to whisper, seduce. This time, he used his hand to do a slow S revolution from the top of my back to as far down as his hands could reach. All of a sudden, I was weak in the knee. "You, my lovely, are truly a diamond of the first water. After this dance, I'd be honored to take you home." *Yes! Home! Bed!* Goodness, I was a trollop.

Somehow, by following the couple next to us, we did a decent imitation of the waltz.

"How'd you end up here, and how do you know the Regency lingo?" He held me tighter and didn't say anything else till the waltz ended.

"Where's Gram?" He asked while looking around the ballroom.

"Right behind you," Gram answered. "What an entrance you made, Monsieur Le Duc."

"Hello, Gram!" He gave her a warm hug and kiss on the cheek. "Did you have a comfortable flight here?"

"I did. Nice of you to join us, Your Grace. You came to keep an eye on your wandering beloved, I assume?" She winked at him.

"Wandering, being the key word, Gram. I'm going to have to keep a tight leash on this granddaughter of yours."

"You can always get leg-shackled to her, my boy. Then, you'll have no worries of cicisbeos stealing her from under your nose. That theme runs in this Reid family."

"Hello. You must be Sir Roland Ascot. It's an honor to meet you."

"And you must be the young man courting our Lady Jane?"

"I am."

"There appears to be more than one of you courting Lady Jane." Now Gimpy was putting me on the spot.

"I'm sure I don't know why this spinster is so popular," Gram uttered.

"Gram! Did you really call me a spinster?"

"At your ripe age, you'd be considered an ape-leader."

"Oh my gosh. I always knew Jake was your favorite, but I thought maybe I was your favorite granddaughter."

Both Gram and Gimpy laughed at me.

Max placed my hand in his arm. "With your permission, Gram? Sir? We'll see you tomorrow?" He was making me leave the ball already?

"Will you join us for an early breakfast before you go back to LA, Your Grace?"

"It would be my honor, Gram, I mean, Countess. See you in the morning."

I waved goodbye to Gram and Gimpy, and to Donovan who was walking towards them.

"Come on you light skirt. Let's get you home."

Max didn't have time to rent a carriage, so we took a regular San Francisco cab and were back to reality. My one night of living in Jane Austen's world was done. I should be grateful that Max and Donovan didn't get into fisticuffs, or worse yet, take out their dueling pistols to meet at dawn.

"What has you shaking your head, Lady Jane?"

"You and Donovan meeting at dawn with your swords or pistols."

"Oh yes, the minor earl. I believe I bested him in all ways tonight—the title, the property and money that assumedly comes with the title, the tempting woman. You, my lovely Jane, and I have a bit of unfinished business when we get back to your manor. I'd like to get you and our loose ends, all tied up."

Damn! The heat was rising and I was hot everywhere. It didn't help that I decided to be as true to this era as possible and wore a lady's unmentionable, or underdrawers, rather than underwear.

"What will we be tying up?"

"You...if you're lucky."

What the hell did I say to that?

"You're blushing, my fair maiden." Max pulled me onto his lap and we gave the cab driver a show. It wasn't indecent, but the tension that built up spoke of indecency to come.

"I'm really curious to know how you ended up in San Francisco today."

"Deuce take it! I'm trying to seduce you, and that's all you can think about?"

"You're so funny! How'd you learn this lingo? It's not like you had sisters who read this stuff."

"Your *sister* emailed me a copy of a Regency glossary and era description and told me to learn it before arriving in the city."

"Emily?"

"Yes, Emily. Who else? She spoke with your grandmother yesterday and I guess Gram told her about tonight. She called me immediately and forced me up here."

"How about your outfit and..."

"All Emily. In between suffering from morning sickness and throwing up, she reserved everything, down to the plane ticket, and told me to come up here and declare my intentions. She thought you might 'get swept away by the whole mystique of the night and romanticize Donovan as your true love.' Those were her exact words."

I was slightly pissed that Emily thought so little of me, but also a bit embarrassed that she was correct. I did get carried away like some ingénue chit.

"Cat got your tongue?"

"Only if the cat's name is Max." That made him laugh. Sassy tongue— that's me!

"Lady Jane, I want you to know that I was in the middle of exams while you were off frolicking with another man, and I still have one more exam left tomorrow. I haven't slept in almost three days, and memorizing all this Regency information on the hour-flight was worse than studying for medical exams. I kept nodding off, but couldn't fall into a deep sleep between Emily's voice in my head imploring me to know the information, and terrifying visions of your wayward ways." He broke into that beautiful smile. If Donovan had that Bradley Cooper / Henry Cavill good looks, Max could be liken to Josh Duhamel / Americana boy-next-door good looks. I was a lucky girl!

"Are you leaving tonight?"

"I will be no further away than right behind you, on top of you, and / or under you, in bed tonight."

Aieee! *Mamamia! Muy Caliente!* I am *en fuego!*

"But, I have to leave right after breakfast with Gram. My last exam starts at 8:00am, but your brother—forced by his wife—got me into a later exam that takes place in the evening. He was *not* happy about asking his colleague for a favor."

I laughed out loud. I'd have to pay my brother back, somehow. "What'd he tell his colleague?"

"Emily came up with the excuse of a family emergency."

"My sister's resourceful."

"She sure is. Now, let's get to bed, wench. We've got a lot of making up to do."

Rather than joining Max in the shower as he suggested, I took care of some business. I dug up all our devices and turned them off. No call, text, voicemail or ill baby, was going to disturb us this time. I also dug up all the candles from the kitchen. And lastly, I dug up a sexy negligee I purchased a long while back, but never got to use. We were going to finish what we started in New York. Once Max got out, I decided to jump in the shower, too, before jumping my boyfriend. After bumping into hundreds of people in that crowded ballroom and caking on the make-up and hair spray (yes, I know that they didn't wear make-up and hairspray back then), I felt gross. A happy whistle came out while I washed myself clean. *Woo-hoo!* I did a little jig in the shower thinking about all that was going to go down in bed. After blow-drying my hair, I walked into my bedroom and wouldn't you know it...

Candles to set the mood—lit

Boys to Men Acapella on iPod shuffle—on

Red naughty nightie—donned

My half-naked boyfriend—SNORING!

He was completely passed out.

LOL! Good night!

Jan. 24, 2013

Donovan and Who???

" Should we go watch a movie, then have a late dinner?" Max was off for a few days before his next semester began, so he called me at the office more than usual.

"You gonna fall asleep on me again?"

"How long am I going to pay for that?"

"Until my ego is pieced back together! Did you notice *any* of my effort?"

"You know I did. I tried to show you how much I noticed, but you stopped me mid-demonstration."

"Sure. Blame it on the girl who wanted to rush out to meet her grandmother for breakfast—especially when we were already more than twenty-minutes late! I don't think you even took a good look at the nightie. Did you even appreciate it?"

"Since I doubt that nightie was purchased with me in mind, I don't know how to answer that question. And for the 100th time, I'm sorry. I told you I hadn't slept much days prior, and if it wasn't for your wayward ways, I wouldn't have flown up and wasted valuable study time."

"Did you just tell me you wasted your time?"

"You know what I meant. Should I put *you* on the spot and ask why there was an indecent negligee in your possession when you had no idea I was coming up?"

"For your info, I bought that about a year ago when we were supposed to spend a weekend up north. But instead, we got into an argument and didn't see each other again till about a month ago. So there!"

"Well...then I guess it's my bad again, huh? Are we going to a movie tonight or do you want to get off the phone and not see each other again for a while?"

Jerk! UGH! I hate it when he corners me. This was reason #1 why I ended our relationship the first time. I never had the upper hand. He was somehow always right. Even when he was wrong, and we both knew he was wrong, he was right. When did I become the submissive woman?

"All right. A movie it is." I pouted on the phone. "Pick me up from home?"

"Ok. See you soon, my precious gem."

"Yeah, Sleepyhead. See you soon."

A few days ago, we wrapped up our deal with the Mitchell Group, and I flew home with Gram and Gimpy. They fought off Emily's insistence and chose to stay at my parents' place, arguing that Emily needed rest and privacy during her first trimester. Because she's been sick so much, we've had the twins over every day, and Gimpy and Gram are in *LOVE* not only with each other, but with the twins as well.

"Good afternoon, Sir, Gram." Max greeted.

"Good to see you again, Monsieur Le Duc." Gram teased. "Where are you and my granddaughter off to tonight?"

"Just a movie and dinner. I should have her home before midnight."

"You can keep her if you like. She's way too old to be living at home. Why at her age, I think I was already pregnant with my third child."

"Gram, are you trying to get rid of me?"

"Obviously, someone's going to have to try. You're too comfortable here."

"Aaah!" My niece belched out her enthusiasm while bouncing on Gram's lap. We needed to get out of here before she attached herself to my boyfriend...again.

She kept up the screaming and arm flailing, ready to jump regardless of Max's intention to catch her. Max didn't keep her waiting long.

"Elizabeth!" He hugged and kissed her as though she were his own child. To be fair, he put her in his left arm and took James into his right arm. It was like juggling two basketballs. "Hello James!" He gave him the same greeting. "I see you are both feeling well now. What have you been doing with your time?"

James, who was normally shy with most people and mostly an observer rather than a participant, must've bonded with my man back in New York. He gave Max a wide and bright smile and started babbling about who knows what.

"Is that right, Master James?" Max conversed back with him.

Ellie wouldn't be outdone. She too said a lot of gibberish.

"Why don't you start walking, and we'll take the twins back. It's time for their dinner and bath."

"Say bye-bye," Max encouraged.

They both waved their hands and said something remotely like bye-bye.

"You want me to take one?"

"No, I'm good."

"Da!!!!" Ellie's piercing scream almost took out my eardrums. "Da!" James joined in as they both saw my brother's car pull into their driveway.

"How do they know he's in there?" I asked, confounded at their level of comprehension.

"They must be smart like their aunt," Max joked.

"Shut up," I punched him in the arm, lightly.

Both kids jumped into their dad's arms and didn't give us a second thought. It was a serious love-fest between the three of them till Emily came out and of course, the twins wanted nothing to do with their dad and moved on to Mom. They were so fickle!

"Where are you two off to?" Emily called out in between accepting kisses from her babies.

"The movies, then dinner. You want to join us?" I asked.

"Possibly for dinner. Let me get the twins down, and if Laney is around, I'll see if she can babysit while they're sleeping. Text you later?"

"Sure." We called out.

We saw an early showing of Les Mis and it was phenomenal!

"What a great movie, huh? I didn't realize that Russell Crowe could sing."

"How do you even remember what happened during the movie? I think my eyes were shut more than they were open." I complained. "I had trouble seeing *and* breathing."

"Really, Lady Jane? I do remember someone insinuating herself on my lap soon after the movie started and getting very comfortable with me."

I laughed. "I guess those are the perks of watching a movie a month after its release date. Everyone else has seen it already."

"You and I need to consider getting different living arrangements. Aside from lack of time, we both have too many roommates."

"So what are you suggesting?"

"I don't have any solutions yet, but we definitely need some privacy."

A part of me was scared he might suggest we move in together; then another part of me was relieved he didn't mention it; but that last part of me was ticked off he didn't suggest it. I needed to let that one go for now.

"Tell me about your grandmother and Sir Ascot. What's their story?"

"I'll let Jake tell that story. He knows the details better than I. I see them waiting for us over there."

"How was the movie? I'd like to see it when it comes out on video." Emily looked happy to be out of the house.

"Emi, I'll take you to go see Les Mis if you want. You don't have to wait for the DVD version."

"A dinner *and* a movie with babies at home? Forget it. Too time consuming. I'll take dinner over a movie, any day."

"Laney babysitting?" I inquired.

"Yes." My brother answered. "Last we left her, Donovan was helping her study for a statistics final."

"Donovan?" Why was I a little bit upset that they were together?

"He came by to get Roland's signature on some documents and stopped by our place to say hello. I was helping Laney with her studies when he popped in so I put him to work." Jake looked triumphant for some reason.

"What'd you do that for? Laney doesn't like him."

"Could've fooled me. Emily just called home to check up on the kids and he was still there. They'd just finished eating dinner." Jake had that smug look I so hated.

"What?" Now I was more than slightly upset. I was almost pissed.

"Uh-oh. My gem is coming out, but for reasons I'm not too happy about."

"What's a gem?" Emily wanted to know.

"Acronym for green-eyed monster. My gem has a tendency to get jealous over stupid things."

I should've gotten upset with Max for telling my brother and sister about my jealous tendencies, but I couldn't stop thinking about Donovan and Laney.

DONOVAN and LANEY??? NO!!!

Jan. 28, 2013

Let's Get the Elephant Out!

*L*unch today?

No can do. I have a business mtg./lunch on the Westside. Dinner instead?

Sure.

Bowl of spaghetti bolognese and linguine in cream sauce with shaved white truffles?

You had me at white truffles.

No one can accuse you of being a cheap date.

Perhaps we'll go dutch, then it won't be a date.

Whatever. 7:30, Madeo Restaurant.

That was the text I started with Donovan, the moment I got into the office.

Is it okay if I have a friendly dinner with Donovan tonight?

Is this to grill him about Laney?
Is it because you're still attracted to him even though you are with me? OR
Is it truly a friendly dinner where you will tell him you are madly in love with me and you want him to stop harassing you? If it's #3, then ok.

Aargh! How does Max do this to me every time? And we're only texting!

I have no interest in him and Laney (plus he'll have no interest in Laney)
I am not attracted to Donovan (though I admit he's a tiny bit good looking)
I am not madly in love with you!

Uh-huh, keep telling yourself that (and that too)
You better not be (your admission gives me the freedom to find other women attractive)
Aren't you though?

My blood was boiling at this point. Max was seriously pissing me off.

Whatever
Whatever
I am not! Why would I admit to something you haven't admitted to yet?

Do you want my admission now?

No. I don't want to read about it in a text. That's worse than breaking up via text. If you have an admission to make to me, see me in person and tell me then.

Okay, my stunning gem. I'm going out with some of the guys after rounds. Have a good dinner.

That psycho better not be there!

Goodbye!

Geez, I've only been back at this relationship business for a little over a month and I can see why even super couples like Jake and Emily had problems before marriage. This relationship stuff was serious give and take. It would be so much easier if I could just take...and take...and take...

After a long day with the crazy boss lady driving me up the wall, I was ready for a good dinner and a nice Italian white to go with my white truffled pasta. Mmmm!

"Have you been waiting long?" Donovan rushed in.

"No. I got here a few minutes ago and ordered myself a prosecco. You want a glass?"

"Sure. Did you drive here?"

"Nope. Caught a ride with Simon as he was leaving for home and I figured you'd drive me home. Then, I can have a glass of wine or two with the promised truffles without worrying about driving."

"Good thinking. I have the company car again so we can both relax tonight." He smiled and kissed me on the head.

"Why do you always do that?"

"Do what?"

"Kiss me on some part of my head? I feel like a little girl whenever you do that."

"In some ways, I still see the little girl who used to follow me and her brothers around the house."

There was so much tenderness in that statement. Many times, Donovan just simply made me happy! He didn't stir any ugly emotions. He didn't make me see red. Instead, he always stirred up those girly emotions—like those you feel when watching a Disney princess movie. Just happily-ever-after happiness!

"What's the deal with you and Laney?" Brain-to-mouth filter was a bit off again.

He looked at me, mid-prosecco sip. "What about Laney?"

"Why were you hanging out with her the other night?"

"Why the sudden interest?"

"That's what I should be asking *you*. Why the sudden interest? She's like a decade younger than you."

"Miss Jane Sydney Reid. Do I detect a note of jealousy? I don't think you have any right to be jealous about what I do with my evenings when you can't even dance a waltz with me without your *bodyguard's* approval. How'd you get out tonight? He actually let go of you for a few hours?" Donovan laughed a mocking laugh.

"Okay, let's talk about the elephant in the room. If you are/were attracted to me, why haven't you asked me out in the past? Is it something that just developed when I came back to LA? I've told you that I've crushed on you since I was seven. I'm sure you and my brothers all knew even before I admitted it at the Laker game."

"Your moron of a brother wouldn't let me ask you out."

"Jake or Nick?"

"Jake, of course. Using my age as an excuse, he said he'd kick my ass if I asked you out when you first moved to New York, then the jerk went off and got engaged to someone exactly your age. I should've kicked *his* ass for being a hypocrite." He laughed another dry laugh.

"You were going to ask me out when I got to New York?"

Somehow he nodded his head yes while sipping his drink. "I was actually first going to ask you out when I did my internship at Ascot, Ascot, and Pemberly in San Francisco."

"That was like..." I counted back a few years to when Donovan lived in San Francisco for a summer. "Wasn't that the summer before my sophomore year in undergrad?"

"Something like that. In the few years I hadn't seen you, you went from being a pretty girl to a gorgeous one. You had my nerves going in all directions."

"Why not back then?"

"Your brother, again. He didn't want me trifling with his sister, who was only a sophomore in undergrad. And, I agreed with him at that time. Plus, I think you were dating someone."

"What'd you care what my brother thought? Why'd you listen to him?"

"Well, aside from the fact that he was my best friend and possibly a future brother-in-law, what he said made sense. Back when you were nineteen and I was twenty-four, I did find you striking, but young. Then when you were twenty-two and I was twenty-seven, you were settling down in a new state, finding your way through law school, and I was just about to move back to LA. I didn't want a long distance relationship and soon after I moved to LA, I ended up dating Kate, again. And now that I'm free, you are not. I guess it wasn't meant to be for us."

I sat and contemplated that one.

"And as for Laney, as you stated earlier, she *is* a decade younger than I am. I find her to be an attractive girl, but I'm not attracted to her. She's way too young for me. Plus, I get the feeling I'm not her favorite person."

I knew it! *You see, Max. I was right!*

"What's going on between you and Max? He's appears to be as territorial as they come."

I cracked up.

"He's not like that at all. You seem to bring out the alpha male in him. Emily tells me that he was always easy going and laissez-faire when they were dating. With me, we're always fighting and looking to one up each other. He drives me nuts all the time, and I suppose I do the same to him. But somehow, it seems to work. I..."

Was I going to admit for the first time that I loved Max...and to someone who wasn't Max?

"You and Emily are very different people. When I'm around Emily, she makes a man want to take care of her and protect her with all his life. She has that gentleness that brings out the good in people. Look at your brother. Look at what a mush pot he's become since meeting her. Who would've thought that playboy would become the model husband and father?"

I hated being compared to my sister-in-law. I could never win.

"But you, my vixen, make a man want to fight for you. You have that tigress personality that draws a man in and sucks the life out of him. He'll draw blood at dawn to have a chance to woo you."

"Is that good? I think I'd rather have Emily's description."

"Miss Jane, I'd rather date a vixen than a saint any day. Your sister-in-law, your cousin Laney—they both fall into the category of deceptively high-maintenance. A man would have to be near perfect to feel worthy of being with them. With you...what you see is what you get."

"Hmmm...the other description still sounds better. In any case, are we okay? Can we still be friends?"

"Have we ever been anything but friends? You know where I stand. Don't know how long I'll be standing here, but until you give me the green light, or until I move on to another pasture, we will stay life-long, good friends." He kissed me again on my forehead. This felt like our last supper, and that kiss was the kiss of Judas. "I see the server with our linguine and the white truffle isn't far behind. Let's eat!"

Jan. 31, 2013

Surprises All Around

Donovan and I were in a weird funk with our friendship, but fortunately, unless we sought each other out in the office, our paths did not cross too often. He worked in a different department and our floor was huge. And a lot of the times, he was on a different floor or out of the office for meetings, as he was a young but high-powered lawyer with Ascot, Ascot, and Pemberly.

It's been fantastic having Gimpy at work. Since he had first dibs on the company car and driver, I carpooled with him and he filled our long car ride with interesting stories about his life, his family and his love for my grandmother. I thought Jake and Emily had an intense love for one another—Gimpy had been holding a torch for Gram for sixty+ years. He loved the wife of his youth, but she passed on early and he never remarried.

"So you were the consummate playboy, waiting for my Gramps to die or divorce, so Gram could be yours?" I asked with a laugh.

"Divorce, beheaded and died..." he sang Henry VIII's song. "No, silly girl. I was not waiting for Jerry to die or for your Gram to get divorced. I figured if it was meant to be, it would happen again."

"How come you never married again? Didn't you want kids?"

"I suppose that's a big regret, but I was busy building my career and the law firm, and I didn't really have time to build a relationship. After Lauren died, I spent all my energy opening up the office in London. When my younger brother finally graduated from law school, he was a big help. And fortunately, he married a sweet gal who supported his workaholic tendencies. I guess I traded a family for a career. At the time, I also had no thoughts of trying to love someone again. It took me a long time to forget your grandmother. Why, I was almost thirty-five before Lauren and I married."

"It took you a decade to forget Grams? That's so romantic!"

"That's pitiful is what it is. But your Gram was and still is an unforgettable woman."

"What did you get Gram for Valentine's Day? You know it's only two weeks away."

"Wouldn't you like to know, young lady?"

"Come on, Gimpy. One clue."

"No clue for you. You're too smart. You'll figure it out on the spot. Did I ever tell you I always thought of you as my only granddaughter? None of the other Reid children caught my attention like you, Miss Jane."

"You mean Jake wasn't your favorite? He's everybody's favorite grandchild. Laney is a distant second. People are obsessed with her American Girl doll look with the shiny blond hair and those cornflower blue eyes. She really looks like a doll. She's also the sweetest of us all, though she's a bit stuck in her own fantasy world. It's like she never grew out of her elementary school dreams."

"It's always good to dream, Miss Jane. You're too realistic, which makes you a bit pessimistic. But then again, you chose law as a profession. What else can you be?" He chuckled. "No, I fell in love with you when you first met me as a three-year-old and couldn't decide what to call me. You already had Gram and Gramps in your vocabulary, and you knew that I was similar in age with your grandparents so you were rather stumped. Even though your entire family called me Mr. Ascot, you proudly informed us all at dinner one night that you were going to call me 'Gimpy.' That's when the name stuck, and that's when I knew you'd always be my favorite."

"*Finally!* I'm somebody's favorite!" I added much emphasis to those words. "It's crazy that you, Gram and Gramps stayed friends."

"I always did like Jerry. He was a capital fellow."

"I love the way you talk! Your British accent is so cool." I tried my best British accent but failed miserably.

Gimpy and I came home from work early, so I could help Mom get ready for Dad's birthday dinner. No doubt she had everything under control, but it was a nice excuse to get away from Andrea. The whole family was meeting tonight and we all looked forward to catching up on life.

"Where's Max?" Laney asked, while I was chatting with Susan and Samantha.

"He's at the hospital. He couldn't slip out of his rounds today."

"Bummer. It would've been nice to have him here..." she trailed then looked over our heads. "Who invited him?" All of a sudden, Laney went hostile.

"Hello pretty ladies," Donovan said while greeting me with a kiss on the cheek—the cheek now and not the familiar forehead. Was that a good sign or a bad sign? Did this mean he saw me no differently than all the other women he greeted with a kiss, or did he now see me as a woman and not a little girl? *STOP!* I was thinking way too deeply into a casual kiss.

"I didn't know you were coming. Are your parents here?" Both Sam and Susan were a bit starry-eyed with Donovan, but Laney had no interest. In fact, she was just about to walk away when Donovan stopped her.

"Hello, Delaney."

"Hello Mr. Taylor. What are you doing here? This is a family event."

"Your cousin Jake and your Aunt Sandy invited me, so I came with my parents. Since I practically lived in this house during my child-hood, I almost grew up a Reid. Who knows, maybe one day I'll marry a Reid and then we'll *all* be family."

I kinda panicked when Donovan talked about marriage. My feelings for this man were unclear, even to me, and in no way was I thinking marriage with this guy. Shoot, I hadn't really thought about mar-riage to Max—well...maybe I had thought about it once or twice.

"I don't think any of the Reid girls are available to marry you. Jane is almost married to Max, and you're too old for the rest of us." All this time, I thought of Laney as this sweet, even-tempered dreamer, but damn, this girl had some bite to her.

Donovan laughed at her comment. "Is that why you address me as Mr. Taylor, rather than Donovan? You think I'm too old?"

"You are too old. Anyway, I came here to tell you," she turned to me, Sam, and Susan, "that I've decided to defer film school and go live in London for a year, instead."

"Why?" Sam asked. "And why London?"

"I loved living in Japan, and I want to live away again for a while before I recommit myself to school. And as for why London? Because it's a fun city, and Gram has a home there, and I won't have to pay rent. Dad says he won't pay for anything other than schooling now. He says I'm too old to be supported by him."

"Then how will you survive out there?" It was Susan's turn to ask.

"I'll get a job. Maybe I can get a job at some publishing agency or maybe..." her eyes lit up, "I can get a job working at LK Bennet or Reiss or even Top Shop. I've always wanted to work retail."

"Don't you think that's a waste of a year, Laney? You'll be making six pounds per hour. That's like nine dollars. Is Uncle Henry okay with your plans?" What a complete waste of time, I thought.

"Dad says as long as I can support myself, he's fine with it. And it's not like I'm going to be a sales girl forever. I'm just doing it for a year. Think of all the traveling I'll do when I base myself in London. I can go visit every European country."

"On six pounds an hour, good luck! You'll make just enough money to ride the tube."

Gimpy was right. I was a pessimist.

"Why I think going away for a year is a wonderful idea. That's a year of creating memories you can't buy. But of course, we'll all miss you if you're gone that long." Donovan was always so smooth.

"Why would you miss me, Mr. Taylor? We hardly know each other." She then totally dismissed him and spoke to the cousins only. "That's why I came over here. I wanted to give you my big news."

147

Okay...

"Everybody...may I have your attention?" Gimpy called the room together with his fabulous accent. "First of all, I want to wish Bobby a happy birthday." Everyone cheered and clapped for Dad. "Second, I wanted to tell you the story of a beautiful young woman who graced my life many many years ago. This woman took Paris by storm when she got there and had every chap lining up to woo her." Gram was blushing. "When I first met her, she was sassy and witty and breathtakingly beautiful. I couldn't believe that her parents would let her out of their sights. I wanted to kidnap her immediately before too many fellows noticed her, take her to the nearest church, and marry her. However, fate had other plans, and her once-suitor came back and took this beauty away from me. Now, sixty-six years later, I have a chance to make her mine." He walked over to Gram who was sitting on the couch with James on her lap, and got down on one knee. "Estelle, my beauty, my love, will you do me the honor of living out the rest of your life with me? We may not have as many years as I would have liked, but I can promise you this—your last years will be the best years of your life. I've loved you since the day I met you. Please do me the honor of being my wife."

That was so freakin' romantic! Who would have thought that two elderly folks in their eighties would profess their love for one another and get married? Oh my gosh, this was true love.

Gram, of course, said yes, and when Gimpy got up to kiss her, he frightened James and all of a sudden, we saw him back off Gram's lap and wobble—and I mean wobble—his way towards his mother.

"Oh my gosh! James is walking. He's taking his first steps." Jake called out.

We all turned to James, then to a horrified but proud Emily, then back to James. It was a harrowing experience for us all as our bodies swayed with him every time he looked like he was about to take a tumble. I felt like a simulator driver in one of those car-racing games. We all breathed a sigh of relief when he made it to his mother and everyone clapped for him. Emily was in alt.

Of course, our little Ellie, not to be outdone by her brother, screamed for attention. Once her brother was safely in Emily's arms, Ellie kept screaming "Uh!" Not understanding what she wanted, we all stared at her. When she realized that "uh" was getting her nowhere, she raised both hands and called out, "Uh!" again.

"Jake...I think she's trying to say, 'up.' Pick her up and see what happens." Emily asked.

Jake did exactly that and Ellie was grinning like a Cheshire cat.

"Put her down and see what happens," Emily said this time.

My brother obliged, and as soon as her little tushy hit the ground, Ellie screamed, "Uh!"

Jake picked her up and kissed his little girl, and we all gave her a round of applause as well. This time, she had that cat who got the cream smile. She looked just like my brother!

What an eventful day! A move to London, a wedding in June, a walking nine-month-old and a talking nine-month-old—there is never a dull moment in the Reid family.

Feb. 4, 2013

He's Going Where?

You probably all thought I had no girlfriends, huh? I haven't mentioned any of them because I haven't had a chance to meet up with them since Max and I got back together. In my defense, I don't have much free time. Between work, family obligations (and with all the Reids having homes on this cul-de-sac, there's a stream of family functions), and Max—there's hardly time to sleep. But tonight, my girlfriends and I were putting on our LBDs and celebrating.

Growing up, I had three best friends. The four of us did everything together. Becky and I knew each other from birth because our dads were friends since med school. Evie and Ashley, I met in kindergarten. We all went to the same K-12 school, and then the four of us went up north to undergrad. Though we went to three different colleges up there, we remained the best of friends. Even now, with Becky in Chicago, Ashley in Texas, and Evie in San Diego, we try to meet for holidays and special occasions. Tonight was a special occasion! Ashley got engaged on New Year's Day, and she and her fiancé were in town for their engagement party. They'd had one already in Texas with his family, but Ash's mom insisted she have another one here as well. Tonight, the four of us were getting a little pre-engagement party going before the formal affair in a few days.

"Girlfriend, I'm the one engaged, but you're the one who looks smokin' hot!" Ashley and the girls oohed and aahed over my dress, that wasn't my dress.

"Where'd you get that dress? And where, may I ask, did those *tall,* white, patent leather boots come from? I need a pair of those. Al would go berserk if I showed up to bed in a dominatrix outfit and those boots."

"Eew!!! None of us needs the visual, and definitely not a play-by-play of your nighttime romp, Becky. Let's keep the domestic affairs, domestic." Evie, I'm-going-to-stay-a-virgin-till-I-get-married, was the one we made fun of most. She had the least experience with men and none of us thinks she'll get married before forty.

"Nothing I have on tonight, except for my g-string, belongs to me. The dress and boots belong to Emily. My brother bought them for her in the Chanel shop in Paris a couple of years ago. She's pregnant again and says she feels a bit scandalous wearing thigh-high boots while carrying a baby."

"She's pregnant again?" All three ladies called out simultaneously. "What about the twins? Are they even a year old yet?"

"They'll be one in April. They are all sickeningly beautiful and in love with one another. They are the picture of happiness."

"You think Emily will let me borrow those boots?" Becky asked.

"Don't know. Ask her yourself."

"So...what's going on with you and Max? You *are* back together?"

"Yeah, Ash. We're back together and this time for good, I think. I don't know how you and Becky finally realize a guy is *the* one for you. We are always arguing about the stupidest things. There's never a peaceful week with us."

"Maybe it's you...not Max." Evie butted in. "You're a bit on the argumentative side. And that's great if you're trying a case, but not the best thing when you're talking to your boyfriend." Now, how did a girl who's never really had a boyfriend understand my relationship so well?

"I don't know...I really like him and I think he really likes me too, but...in any case, all is going well as we speak. I think he's out with some friends, but he said he'd stop by to pick me up at the end of the night so he can meet you all. Of course, he'll be at the engagement party, too."

The night progressed with the four of us gabbing mainly about Ash and her fiancé, Jared. Ash brought pictures of her wedding dress, as well as pictures of our bridesmaid dresses. We had all promised one another when we were younger that we'd pick out knockout bridesmaid dresses. Becky picked out stunning evening gowns when she got married, and Ash picked out cute summery ones for her wedding. None of us complained.

We were talking about old times and old crushes when I heard that nail-on-chalkboard voice calling my name. We'd done a few rounds of tequila shots throughout the night so I thought I was hearing things when it happened again.

"Jane! Hello...Jane...over here..."

"I think someone's calling you." Becky, who'd had way too much to drink, pointed in the opposite direction from where the voice was coming from.

"Hi, Jane. How fun to see you here."

Gawd!!! It was Psycho! "Hey...Alex...I mean, Joyce. What brings you here? Are you here alone?"

"Oh, I'm meeting some friends. I must be the first one here."

Liar! It was some time around midnight. I doubted she was meeting anyone at this hour. What a psycho stalker. How the hell did she know I was here, and why would she stalk me instead of Max?

"I just left Max." As soon as she said this, I swear, it took every ounce of self-control not to pounce on this woman and beat the crap out of her. "We had a nice dinner after our shift at the hospital."

"Uh-huh," I gritted my teeth.

All my girlfriends, even the drunk ones, were wide-awake now. Both Becky and Evie were literally holding me back.

"You must be so sad that he's leaving in a few months." She gave me a seriously evil smile while saying this. "I'm sad, too, that I'll be leaving my family. I'm sure Max and I will keep each other company when we miss our friends and family back home. It's only for the summer, unless we choose to stay longer."

I had no clue what this woman was talking about, but I wasn't going to give her the satisfaction of knowing that I had no clue. Though, I was sure the confusion and hurt in my eyes gave me away. Max hadn't mentioned anything about leaving. Where was he going, and why was Joyce going with him? Stupidly, I was heartbroken that he was leaving me.

"Where is Max going?" Thank God for Becky. If she hadn't asked this question, curiosity would've killed me!

"It's a doctors without borders-type of program. We'll be helping children in need of medical care. Max and I found out a few weeks ago that we were accepted, and we'll be gone the whole summer. Oh, I think I see my friends. I'll see you around. Bye." The bitch ran off after purposely dropping that bomb on me.

"Who was that?" Ashley asked. "There's something wrong with her. And what was she talking about when she said that Max was leaving?"

"I don't know," I whispered. "Is Psycho still looking my way?" I had to put my head down because I thought I might cry. Maybe it was all the alcohol making me melodramatic, but I really wanted to cry. How could Max make such a huge decision without mentioning it to me once? "Ash, look for me. I need to call Max right now, but I don't want to do it if Psycho is watching me. I don't want to give her the satisfaction."

"She was staring at you for a while, but then she disappeared somewhere. I don't know where she is anymore."

"I need to call Max. Sorry."

"Jane...be calm before you call him. You don't know if that woman was telling the truth," Becky tried to comfort me.

"Sorry for ending the party."

"Our rides are coming anyway. Call him. Get this resolved." Evie also comforted me.

"Hello, my precious gem. I'm on my way to you up right now." Max greeted me.

"Max...I just have one question and I want you to answer me truthfully."

"Okay..."

"Are you going somewhere this summer?"

"Um...yeah, I am...well, I'm not sure if I am now..." He stumbled over his words.

"When were you going to tell me about this trip you had planned?"

"It's not exactly a trip, Jane. It's not as if I'm going on vacation. I haven't mentioned it to you because..."

"Let me get this straight. You never once mentioned to me that you applied for a program that'll take you away an entire summer, maybe even longer—not while applying for this program, not after you got accepted into this program, and not even now, while you are thinking about going on this program. Were you just going to say goodbye the day of your departure?"

"Jane, you're being overly dramatic about this. Yeah, it's true I haven't talked to you about my summer plans, yet. We only got back together a couple of months ago. I wanted to make sure things worked out between us before I made a decision about summer."

"Oh, so you wanted to keep both options open just in case one didn't pan out?" At this point, I was more mad than sad. It's almost as though he had been using me all this time. *What would be more fun and beneficial to me this summer? Hanging out with my girlfriend or going to save all the impoverished kids in the world? Hmmm.* Deep inside I knew he wasn't using me, but whatever. I was pissed—irrationally pissed! "I'm going home with Becky and Donovan. Don't bother picking me up!"

"Hello, Ladies!" Donovan greeted all of us, as I hung up on Max.

"Girls, I'll see you at the engagement party. Becky, Donovan, let's go."

I didn't know Max's eta, so I rushed the three of us out of the restaurant.

"Why the rush, Miss Jane? You being chased by someone?"

"Yeah, something like that."

"I take it I'm your ride home?" Donovan opened the car door for the both of us. Always the consummate gentleman.

"Can I crash at your place tonight, Donovan?"

"Is your boyfriend going to want to duel with me at dawn if I say yes?"

"No...he won't care," I whispered, blinking back tears.

February 7, 2013

Pain

I decided to call in sick on Friday and spend the day moping around the house, instead. I hoped for time to think about what had happened at the restaurant, and how I was going to deal with Max leaving me.

Donovan dropped me off first thing, and like a weird rerun of a bad sitcom, Max was waiting for me, at my doorstep, ready to battle. My attire didn't help the situation. I was in Donovan's shirt and sweatpants, and I was coming out of his car at 6:30 in the morning. Whatever...I didn't care at this point. I'd had such an exhausting night talking and agonizing with Becky, I didn't have much strength left.

"Uh-oh. You gonna be in trouble? You want me to tell him this isn't how it looks?"

"Are you laughing right now? 'Cuz if you are, I'm gonna put my foot to your backside."

Donovan started cracking up.

"Shut up, Donovan. I'm too tired for your stupidly morbid sense of humor, and I gotta prepare myself for a fight with Max right now. For all I know, we may end up breaking up."

"We've had this discussion already. You know where I stand, my vixen, should things go sour. Go get 'em, Tigress!" He rubbed my head and kissed it again. Why'd he have to do that right now and make me smile? I didn't want to smile in front of Max. I wanted to stay angry.

"Whatever. Go give Andrea a kiss for me, instead. Then maybe she won't make my life hell when I get back to work on Monday. Bye." With that, I shut the car door and didn't look back.

I walked up the steps and stood a few feet away from Max. He looked...upset? Angry? Sad? But, not remorseful!

"What are you doing with him again?"

"Donovan is the least of our problems."

"Jane." He tried to contain his anger by shoving his hand through his hair. "You cannot run to Donovan every time we have an issue. I am your boyfriend. Not Donovan!"

"You know, Max...a boyfriend usually tells his girlfriend when he plans to leave her for a while. A boyfriend may even consult with his girlfriend before making this decision. And usually, a girlfriend doesn't have to find out from another woman that her man is going away. Do you have any idea how I felt when Joyce triumphantly announced that you two were going away this summer? And do you also know how I felt when my best friends asked me what Joyce was talking about, and I didn't have any answers for them? I might as well have been a stranger to you, because at that moment when Psycho proudly announced your trip, I knew you about as well as my best friends did."

I caught a lone tear before it fell. I didn't want him to have the satisfaction of knowing how much he hurt me.

"Jane. This was something I applied for when we were still separated. I got the acceptance right before I met you and your family in New York, and have been mulling over what to do. You know this is what I want to do. You know that helping impoverished kids is my goal as a pediatrician. This can't work between us if you don't understand what I want to do with my life."

"There are many impoverished children in our own backyard. You don't have to get on a plane to help them out. If that's really what you want to do, then drive south about half an hour and do what you feel is your life's goal. I'm sorry that you've had to *mull over* whether or not to separate from me. I won't stop you from accomplishing your life's goal. Heaven forbid that I get in your way. Call me when you're done saving the world."

"Jane. Stop!" He held my hand right before I stepped into the house.

"No. You stop. Stop and ask yourself this—If going on this summer program is so important to you, 'a life's goal' as you call it, and if I'm important enough to you to be called your girlfriend, then why couldn't you discuss any of this with me? If you need to fly hundreds and thousands of miles to get away from me, from us, then go. Just don't use saving the world as your excuse."

"You know that's not what I'm doing."

"I don't know anything, anymore. I just know how I feel, and it doesn't feel good. Let's talk again, later, Max. I don't want to say anything out of anger."

I closed the door behind me, walked straight up to my room, and shut myself in for the day. As much as I wanted to, I didn't cry. I told myself that Max and our two-month relationship wasn't worth crying over. I laid on the floor, in fetal position with a pillow to lean on, and thought about nothing.

"Jane?" I woke up to a sweet voice. "Is it okay if I come in?" Emily walked in with a tray of food.

"Sure." I got up from the floor and wiped off the dry tears that had crusted around my eyes. I must have cried in my sleep, since I didn't remember crying when I was awake. "If you don't mind, can you just leave the tray on the table?" I didn't finish that sentence, but she knew I didn't want her here.

"Do you want to talk?" Emily cautiously asked.

"Not really. Even if I did, you're the last person I want to talk to since you were so close to Max at one point. It'd be a little weird."

Emily looked thoroughly hurt. Tears glistened her eyes immediately. "Okay...sure...I understand. Just know that I'll be here if you need me..." She quickly left the room.

I could be such a bitch at times. I'd apologize later but right now, I was in so much pain, I wanted to mow down anyone in my path.

I had bouts of extreme physical pain throughout the day—literally. It was the weirdest thing. Every few hours, my body would severely suffer an ache, a burn, an illness—everything combined—whenever I thought about this situation. I about keeled over when I thought about Max and Joyce intimately discussing their trip. The pain came on even stronger when I thought about us breaking up. Something like this had never happened to me before.

I'm no twenty-seven-year-old virgin. I'd had many boyfriends before, and two very serious ones before Max came along. When the relationships ended, sure I was sad, and sure my heart was broken, but I'd never been in so much bodily pain over a guy. What would happen to me when Max and I actually broke up?

This was how my day went. Out of sheer stubbornness and spite, I kept myself from crying over this guy. But, I couldn't do anything to stop the torturous onslaught that visited me every few hours.

"Jane? Honey, why don't you come down and have dinner with us?"

"No thank you, Gram. I'd like to stay in my room if that's okay. I'm sorry to be rude, but could you ask everyone to give me some privacy, today? I promise, I'll be back to my normal self by tomorrow."

"Dear, come down and talk to us. Your mom and dad are very worried about you. Let us help you."

"Gram..." I almost broke down. My stomach felt that weird tingle, my nose started clogging up, and the tears filled up fast. "...please just let me be, today?" I whispered.

Gram lost this battle and closed the door.

I, too, lost the battle and the floodgate opened.

I cried.

February 11, 2013

Brother (s)ly Love

Max has texted or called every day since that morning, but I haven't had the courage to talk to him. I wanted to talk to him, but I was afraid of how our conversation would end...if we would end. Today is the beginning of the week, and I have yet to return any of his calls. Chicken...I know! This is what went down last weekend.

We were on our way to Sam's birthday party when the phone rang again, for the third time.

"Will you put the poor guy out of his misery and pick up the damn phone?" Nick begged. "Never mind. I'll answer it."

"Nick, no!"

"Hey Max. This is Nick and you're on speaker because my sis is driving."

"Hey Nick. Jane?"

"Yeah..." I whispered.

"Baby, why aren't you answering any of my calls? You gotta talk to me. We need to talk about what happened the other morning."

"I know..." *Dammit!* I didn't want to cry but the tears automatically filled my eyes.

"Can we meet now? Are you nearby, somewhere?"

"No." I started wiping the tears off my face. I hated being emotionally crippled. "Nick and I are going to Samantha's birthday party in San Diego, and we're going to spend the weekend there."

"Do you want to meet us there today?" Nick asked without my permission. I punched him hard in the arm.

"I'd like to but I can't. Baby, can I come by and see you another day this weekend?"

"I'm not ready to talk to you yet," was all I could muster.

"Jane...it's been a week. This isn't healthy. We can't go on like this. You promise to talk to me when you get back?"

"Yes."

"If I text you, will you at least respond so I know you're there?"

I don't know if I'm really here.

"Gem...?"

"All right." I hung up the phone without a proper goodbye.

"What is wrong with you, Jane? I've never seen you so emotional. What did Max do to you?"

"I don't know why I'm like this either, Nick. I feel like a basket case, and whenever I think of breaking up with Max, I go into these bouts of physical pain."

"Are you guys breaking up?"

"I don't know yet."

"Max was worried about you when you stopped answering his calls, so he called me and told me what happened—kind of. He didn't go into details, but I got the gist of what went down. Was what he did so bad that you have to act like the world is ending?"

"It's *my* reaction to what he did, that's scaring me. I've never felt so devastated and betrayed and I don't like it. If it's over, I should be sad that it's over, but it shouldn't feel like my life is over."

"So...it's not that you're mad at what he did, so much as you're mad at your reaction to what he did?"

"Yeah."

"Seriously? Max is going out of his mind thinking he's committed the gravest sin against you, and you're upset because of *you* and not because of *him*?" Nick shook his head and closed his eyes in disbelief.

"He started this whole argument. If it weren't for him, I wouldn't be in this state." I argued against Nick's incredulity.

"Get a grip and resolve this already, will ya? I can't take your moping! And poor Max. He's miserable too. This is why I don't want a serious relationship till I'm at least forty. You women are demented!"

Samantha's party was a quiet affair, as quiet as it can get with all the cousins in one place. Jake came down with the twins, but without

Emily because she was still going through morning sickness. The babies were a joyful distraction.

"Hello my handsome nephew. How was the drive? Do you like being out in the ocean?" I held onto this newly walking nine-month-old for fear that he may fall off Uncle Billy's boat. He kept squirming, trying to get down and practice his newfound freedom. When Nick came around, James moved on to Nick in hopes that he'd let him walk.

Instead, Nick too, held on tight and distracted him with his best SpongeBob imitation while lifting him up in the air. "Hello, Nephew!" James started cracking up.

"Who lives in a pineapple under the sea? SpongeBob SquarePants..." Nick went on and on with this song.

James couldn't stop laughing. As soon as Nick started with the "Whooooo..." James would burst into a fit of giggles that was so cute. Seeing and hearing her brother laugh, Elizabeth somehow urged Samantha to bring her to Nick, and she wanted a part of the fun. She, too, would clap her hand and jump up and down in Sam's arms with glee.

"Uh!" She commanded Nick to pick her up. Of course, when the babies command, we all obliged. Nick and Sam swapped twins.

"How you doing?" Jake moseyed over to me.

"I don't know, Jake. I just hurt a lot."

"I know what it feels like to be hurt by, and to hurt the one you love. Just remember that when I took my time licking my wounds, the woman I loved thought I no longer cared and left me. Those were some of the darkest days of my life, not knowing when I would see her again, not knowing how she was doing. Imagine my misery and regret whenever I think about how I could have prevented both our heartaches. This woman, whom I loved more than life, left believing I didn't love her anymore. When I think back to that time, I can't believe how stupid I was. Though everything ended well for us, I still don't like feeling that sense of regret." Jake put his arms around me and enveloped me into his body. "Don't do anything you'll regret later. You can't ever take it back, and you don't ever forget. You understand what I'm telling you?" I nodded yes and let my big brother keep holding me.

Sandwiched by love from both bookends, today was one of the rare days I enjoyed being a middle child.

February 14, 2013

A Happy Valentine's Day?

$\mathcal{T}$he last ten days have been ugly! I went to Ashley's engagement party alone and stayed the entire time with a pasted
smile on my face. My girlfriends knew not to ask about Max's absence, but no one else seemed to have gotten that memo.

Andrea, my crazy boss from hell, yelled at me in front of the entire
patent law department for a small error I made in the brief I wrote
up. She yelled for so long and so loudly, that everyone in the firm
stared into the conference room. It was only when Gimpy walked
into the meeting that she stopped yelling.

"Is there a problem, Ms. Kot?"

"I'm sorry sir for causing any worry. Jane here made a huge error in
her brief, and I was chastising her a bit."

Lambasting was more like it.

"Ms. Kot, I don't know what my dear Jane could've done so wrong,
but I'd like for you to show a little grace and decorum. We do not
go into tirades regardless of the situation, and we definitely do not
bother all the other lawyers who are hard at work. Why, I could
hear you all the way from the conference room, down the hall. It

was embarrassing to step out of my meeting to see what was going on in here."

I didn't know whether to be brave and stick my tongue out at my boss, or to be deathly afraid of the tongue-lashing to come.

"I apologize, Sir Roland. I'll try to keep it down."

"Jane, may I have a word with you in my office?"

I gladly followed Gimpy into his office and sat on his plush sofa. After frosting his windows for privacy, Gimpy brought over a tissue box and a cup of water and sat in front of me.

"What's going on Janey? Why the long face? Your Gram and I have been worried about you the past few days. You've been dreadfully down, and I haven't seen your beautiful smile in a week. Trouble with the Duke?"

I told Gimpy about the other night and how I felt so betrayed that Max hadn't discussed this major event in his life with me. I also told him how sad I would be if we were to separate again.

"Missy. Have you talked to your young man? What does he think about all your concerns?"

"I haven't spoken with him in a few days. He was mad when he saw Donovan bringing me home the next morning, and I was mad at him for not thinking about me at all. That crazy Joyce knew what was going on in my boyfriend's life better than I did."

"Yes, I recall seeing you come home in clothes that looked like a man's clothing. I wouldn't have been too happy either if my lady were to spend the night with another man and come back wearing his clothes."

"But it wasn't like that, Gimpy. And plus, that's not the issue here."

"Regardless of what it actually was, many times, what it seems is a lot worse than what it is."

"Gimpy, were you happy after you let Gram marry Gramps? How did you let her go when clearly you must have been, and still, are very much in love with her?"

"Your grandmother never loved me like she loved Jerry. Once I accepted this, I eventually met another woman and fell in love with her."

"Did you still think about Gram?"

"From time to time, but I loved my Lauren. She was my rock until she passed away. You know, the four of us—Lauren, Estelle, Jerry and I—eventually became good friends. And of course, only recently did Estelle and I renew our relationship."

"Why is life so complicated, Gimpy?"

"It's only as complicated as you make it, my dear Jane."

None of the tissues had been used, but I felt so down and tired. It was sweet of Gimpy to be so concerned for me, even if I didn't feel any better.

"Roland, may I take my sister out for the day?" I jumped at the unexpected intrusion in the room.

Jake. What was he doing here?

"Go ahead, Janey. I'm giving you a pass today, but I want to see a smile on your face next time I see you."

"Thank you, Gimpy."

We stopped several times before heading into the elevator so Jake could greet my coworkers. Geez, how did he know so many of the partners in this firm?

"What brings you here?"

"Your sullen and sulking face brings me here rather than to my family, especially my wife, on this day of love."

"How's Emily feeling?"

"She's as sick as a dog all day physically, and sick with worry for you mentally and emotionally. Why she loves and cares for you so much, when you're such a brat to her, is beyond me."

I gave him an I-don't-know-what-you're-talking-about look.

"Don't give me that feigned innocent look. I wasn't born yesterday."

"Does Emily think I've been a brat to her as well?" Now I felt guilty because I knew I had been way more than a brat to my sister.

"I'm sure she does, but she hasn't mentioned it. Jane, you know my wife grew up lonely. She wants to be your friend and sister. Don't disappoint her with your pettiness."

Initially I felt guilty, but now I was getting defensive. "Is that why you're here—to berate me about my attitude towards your wife?"

"No. I am here because I am your brother, and Emily and I are both concerned for you. You've been severely depressed the past week, and Emily thought since you wouldn't confide in her, perhaps you may talk to me."

Okay, now I felt like a total bitch for shining off Emily.

"What's the real problem? Why are you avoiding Max? Is it the Donovan, Max, Jane triangle or is it the summer program that's eating you up?"

"Donovan is not a part of this equation."

"Oh he's definitely sixty degrees of this triangle right now. It matters not one bit to me whether you date Max or Donovan. In fact, I'd prefer Donovan, but he's not the right guy for you. You are both too cynical and jaded. Donovan needs someone more like my wife and you need Max. He is the one for you."

By this point in the conversation, we had walked half a block down to the Water Grill and sat at the bar. I chewed on Jake's brotherly advice, while our drinks were being poured.

"How do you know about the summer program?"

"I know because I sent him the application, and because he and I discussed it in length before he applied."

"It appears Max discussed this program with everyone but me."

"Little sister, you were not around when he sent in the application. But even then, Max worried about your reaction to this trip, if you two were to get back together. You do understand that he'll only be gone for a month? It's not like you'll be separated forever." Jake didn't exactly roll his eyes at me, but the tone of voice was no different from an eye-rolling. Yep, he was back to his pompous older brother role. I thought he had lost that pomp back on Uncle Billy's boat.

"It's not a matter of how long he'll be gone. Do you know he actually told me that he was 'mulling over what to do'? Not agonizing, not heartbroken, not torn, but mulling...what kind of stupid-ass word is that?"

Jake chuckled. "You remember when I saw Emily at your apartment during MLK weekend and I went outside to keep her from leaving?" I nodded yes. "You want to hear the asinine words I used?" I nodded yes, again. "After she told me that she had waited eight hours for me at the Grand Canyon, I asked her how stupid she could be for not realizing that I wasn't coming back. I think I won the idiot of the year award for that comment." I laughed. It felt weird to laugh. "We guys don't know what to say when we feel guilty and backed into a corner."

"What do I do, Jake?"

"Do you want this to work or are you giving up already?"

"I wanted it to work so badly, Jake. I wanted nothing more."

"Wanted? As in past tense? Is it done?"

"How come he didn't talk to me and tell me what was going on? He knew about this for at least a month. Why was I the last to know?"

"I don't know...but here's your chance to find out."

Jake stood up and waved his hand. I turned around to see Emily walking into the restaurant with Max.

"Hello, Sweetheart. Everything good?" Jake lovingly asked his wife.

"Yes," she whispered and they embraced. These two made life and relationships look so easy.

"Hi Jane." Emily turned to me. "I'm sorry but I butted into your business without your permission. You can be mad at me later, but only after you and Max talk." She then turned to Max and said, "Don't make the same mistake twice."

Jake and Emily both waved goodbye and we were left standing, facing off.

February 18, 2013

A Happy Valentine's Day!

"Hi." I was a mixed bag of emotions standing in front of Max.

"I've missed you, Baby," was all he said as he pulled me into him. He held me tight...he held me long. He really did miss me. Just like I really, really missed him.

"Take her, Davis. She's all yours." My brother almost pushed us out of the restaurant. "Don't bring her home till everything is straightened out. If you wanna drive straight to Vegas and take her off our hands, you have my blessing."

"Jake..." Emily complained. "Leave them alone."

"I'm trying to, but they won't leave *me* alone. Let's go celebrate Valentine's Day, Wife. I've a fun evening planned for us."

"Bye..." Emily called out to the both of us.

We drove in silence for a long while, but Max didn't let go of my hand. He held it while driving, and from time to time, would lean over and kiss me where he could. I was physically, emotionally and mentally exhausted from the last week.

"Jane...Babe...Wake up."

I woke up to darkness and snow. We were up in the mountains somewhere parked in front of a one-story log cabin.

"Where are we?"

"Happy Valentine's Day. When you didn't answer my calls and messages, I thought a grand gesture was in order. But maybe I should have asked first, if you'd like to spend Valentine's Day with me? I rented a cabin for us for the night. Are you okay with this? I can drive back home if you don't want to be here with me."

"There's no place I'd rather be. I missed you too...very much."

He held me again, but it was awkward to embrace in the car so we got our stuff and checked out the cabin.

"Emily?" I asked, pointing to my suitcase.

"Who else?"

Damn! I owed Emily big when I got back home.

"Should we eat first or talk first?"

"Is there anything to eat?" I hadn't had a decent meal in a while, and all of a sudden I was very hungry.
Max pointed to the rolling cooler and picnic basket.

"My sister?" *Shoot!!!*

"Could there be anyone else?"

"You think she did this more for you or for me?" That was a crappy thing to say. I put my head down, shut my mouth and laid the food on the table.

After polishing off a chicken parm, salad, and dinner rolls, we went straight through the dozen chocolate dipped strawberries with champagne. No doubt, Emily probably dipped these herself.

"You have chocolate all over your lips," Max said, leaning over and lazily licking and sucking the excess chocolate off. This put my hormones in overdrive and next thing I knew, Max was lying on top of me on the plush rug and clothes started magically disappearing.

"We need to talk..." I somehow murmured with his tongue in my mouth.

"Right. This wasn't why I brought us up here." *It wasn't???* "Let's talk. You want to go first or shall I?"

He stared. I stared.

"Okay. Let me start. Your brother sent me this application while you were still in New York and encouraged me to apply. He knew this was what I wanted to do, and he thought it was a good way for me to test the water. I told your brother that I wanted to go but that I was worried about us, even though there was no us at the time. If we were to get back together again, I didn't want to separate before we had a chance to establish a relationship."

"All right...that all sounds reasonable. If you were so worried about us, why didn't you say anything to me? Why not just explain the program and see what I'd say? I would have gladly sent you off and waited for you."

"In all honesty, I'd forgotten that I'd even applied. When I got the letter, things were so good between us, I had no desire to leave you. I was torn between feeling selfish, foolish, and apprehensive about separating from you."

"Explain."

Max collected his thoughts for a while. "Well, I feel guilty that after two months of having you as a girlfriend, I want to forget helping anybody—I only want to spend my time with you. For almost three years now, I've been studying for, and preparing my heart to go help kids in need, but every minute I spend with you, every kiss we share, I can't unglue myself from you."

Now that was a truly sweet sentiment. Maybe I was too hard on him, me, and us?!?

"Then, I felt stupid, foolish, even idiotic, for not being able to separate from you for a measly month. Being apart for thirty days wasn't going to be the end of our relationship, nor the end of the world, but I didn't think I had it in me to be apart, again."

Maybe all that drama *was* for nothing.

"And last, I'm apprehensive—maybe insecure is a better word—about us. I'm still not wholly sure about your feelings. Every time I think we're okay, I find myself challenging Donovan in a game of tug-of-war for your heart. After seeing you come out of his car, in his clothes, I have no confidence that I'm on the winning end."

Whewwww.... That was a whew expressed not out of relief, but out of frustration and discomfort. My heart broke when I thought about Max when he saw me with Donovan, again. I seriously had no sense of empathy. How would I have felt if I saw Joyce coming out of Max's apartment, wearing only his clothes? I probably would have dropkicked her down the stairs first for trying to take away my boyfriend, but eventually I'd be heartbroken.

"Let me clarify a huge misunderstanding. Yes, I spent the night at Donovan's and yes, I was in his clothes, but no, I did *NOT* spend the night *with* Donovan. I spent the night with Becky, his sister. She just happened to be staying at his house. If Jared, Ashley's fiancé, would've picked her up before Donovan picked up his sister, I would've gone home with them. I just wanted to leave before you arrived. I couldn't face you at that moment. Becky didn't exactly bring extra sleepwear so I went to bed in Donovan's shirt and sweatpants. It was nothing sexual. It was like a brotherly gesture."

He didn't look any more relieved. "Why didn't you answer any of my calls for ten days?"

"That morning when you saw me get out of Donovan's car and we had the row outside my house...something weird happened to me. I took the day off and stayed in my room all day, depressed. Every time I thought about what had happened, or if I thought about us breaking up, my body would be in so much pain. It wasn't just my heart that suffered, every part of me hurt. It was the most bizarre experience and it frightened me to feel so much."

Max just held me for a while, and kept telling me how sorry he was. "Are you still hurting?" His loving eyes bore down at me. "I'm sorry I did that to you. I never meant to hurt you, Jane."

"Every day, I hurt at times, but it isn't as often, or as bad as that first day." Once I saw the pain in his eyes, I felt guilty telling him about my overkill reaction to this situation. "Anyhow, I realized that I was more upset with my reaction to what you did to me, than to what had actually happened. This was why I didn't answer your calls. I didn't know what to think about these crazy bodily pains, and why I was in such agony over our fight."

"So...all this time, you weren't really angry with me? You were angrier with...*YOURSELF?*"

Uh-oh! "Hey, I was plenty angry with you!"

"Seriously, Gem? That was why we didn't see each other for ten days, and you had me going out of my mind with grief and worry—because you couldn't figure yourself out???"

What kind of Dr. Jekyll and Mr. Hyde routine was this? One minute he's practically debilitated, empathizing with my pain, and the next minute, he's bitter and churlish? Who's in the wrong here?

"I'll have you know..." My retort began in a most unsavory way.

Max finished that statement (and then some) in a most delicious way.

February 21, 2013

Hung Up on the Details

You all are probably wondering if we did the deed last weekend up in that cozy log cabin? Should I leave things *hanging*? I'm not one to kiss and tell but...before I get into the information you are all *hung* up on, let me tell you a few promises I made to myself and to Max (though I haven't told him about these promises, yet).

First, I'm not going to make Max insecure any more. This means, no more unnecessary friendliness with Donovan or any other man who may cross my path. Though, Max said that friendly lunches (preferably not dinners) are ok.

Second, I'm going to be less of a gem. This weekend proved to me that we are a solid couple, and we are both going to look at this relationship as a stepping-stone to the last step. We may not make it there, but we will try for the happily ever after. I'm also going to stop with the petty jealousy where Emily and Joyce are concerned. It's "unnecessary and totally uncalled for" my boyfriend tells me, and I believe him.

Lastly, I'm going to be a nicer person. I'll be nicer to Max (of course), and also to my siblings—Emily, especially! I've been nothing but a brat (or a bitch, depending upon the situation) to her. She's pregnant, she's ill, and yet she's still happily willing to take care of me.

Case in point, she bought me all new clothes, sleepwear, toiletries, and even a pair of comfy Ugg boots, for my weekend up in Big Bear. She even packed our weekend meals. Why, you ask, did she do this? Because a) she's a nice person b) she wants the best for me and Max c) she loves me. Yep, it's all of the aforementioned. I couldn't have asked for a nicer sister.

Here are some of the promises Max and I made to each other while on our mini-vacation. No more silent treatment was numero uno on his list of no-nos. We both promised to discuss any major happenings in our lives without reservation. I also encouraged him to go on his "mission," so he could test the waters and see if this was really for him. I didn't want him to ever regret and blame me for what could have been. Max wanted to think it over some more before committing.

Another huge no-no for Max was Donovan. Max said (in his sexiest, most alpha male voice), "This is the last time I will tell you—I do not want Donovan *ever* touching you again. No *brotherly* kisses, no innocent touching, no *nothing!* Next time I see him so much as casually bump into you, he and I will have serious problems. Understood?" That statement did things for me, and we ended up hot and heavy on the rug again. Then, I did my best alpha girl imitation and threatened to chop off his manhood if I ever had to talk to Joyce on his phone again while he was anywhere close to being naked. In fact, I told him if I never saw her again, that'd be too soon. That did things for his manhood and this time, we ended up on the bed.

Okay...I know, I know...you've been patient on matters of the body (and so have I, for that matter!). The raw truth? I did not get to experience the *hung*ness of my man, completely. I saw it, I felt it, but I didn't *feel* it. Why, you ask? Because a) neither of us came (literally and figuratively) prepared! (Don't all guys carry their best friends in their wallets? Apparently, my man does not. Is that good or bad? This past weekend, it was definitely bad.) b) He didn't want to "take advantage of me" while I was in a "fragile" state. (When has he ever known me to be fragile? Though, I get what he's saying.) c) He said as much as he considered it, since he thought we were over, he felt like a "douche-bag" thinking about having sex with me when I was heartbroken over what he'd done to me. (Damn! I did over-react to this situation.) Though believe me, there were moments when both of us considered driving an hour in the dark, down the dangerous mountain road, to the nearest grocery store. As much as I tried to convince Max that this was not the right time of the month for me, and that conception was not possible, he wouldn't go for that logic. Actually, he was vehemently against that method. Odd...but whatever...

So what'd we do while we were high up in the mountains? We did things that couldn't be done because both of us lived with too many roommates. We spooned on the couch and watched a movie. We cooked (or reheated), and cleaned together. We made out on just about every warm surface—okay, we did a bit more than just make out. I think we covered every base but home—but those details are for another day when I can tell you about *everything*. We laid in bed and talked forever! Laying in his arms and talking—uninterrupted for hours—erased any bad memories of the last ten days for the both of us. We'd never had this kind of freedom to open up to one another.

Max and Jane. Jane and Max! We are a couple now, and nothing is going to get between us and our goal of striving for a solid relationship.

As a thank you and an apology to the ladies in my family for my atrocious behavior the past few days, I offered to take everyone to the Montage Hotel, Saturday night. Spa treatments and lunches by the pool, compliments of Jane Sydney Reid. The boys were going to do their own trip up at the ranch, Max included. I can't wait to get away and spend some quality time with the Reid ladies. It should be a totally relaxing trip. What could possibly happen on a family overnight in Laguna Beach, right???

February 25, 2013

Who Wears a Bikini in February?

om, Gram, Emily, Ellie (yes, Ellie too, since she is a girl and she is a Reid), and Laney got to the Montage Hotel late Saturday morning for brunch. Originally, Laney wasn't part of the plan but since Uncle Henry and Aunt Babs were out of town, and since the boys had invited Doug up to the ranch, I didn't really have a choice but to invite Laney. Mom and Gram shared a room. Emily, Ellie and I were supposed to share a room, but with the addition of Laney, I had to get another room (an additional $695 for the room + spa treatments...*GROAN!*), so Laney and I shared a room instead.

"This place is so beautiful, Jane! Thanks for inviting me. I could've stayed home, but I'm glad Emily convinced me to come."

Yeah...mooch...you've been invited on too many get-aways lately at our expense. And thanks, Emily! "You're welcome and yeah, it is nice here. Let's get out and go to our first treatment."

Emily opted out of all the treatments saying she wasn't comfortable laying on her back for so long. Instead, she and Ellie went to the kiddie pool. When we got back, we found Emily reading a book and Ellie sleeping like a baby on the lounge chair next to her.

"She's knocked out!" I stated.

"Yeah. The pool really wore her out. You know how much both kids love the water. She wouldn't get out even though she was tired and getting cranky. I finally coaxed her out with watered-down apple juice."

"Ooh! You actually gave her some juice?"

"Yeah. I gave in. How were the treatments, Gram?"

"Lovely. I think this is one of the loveliest resorts I've been to in a while."

"You've been out in London too long, Gram," Laney said. "We've missed you. We are all glad you're here." She hugged and kissed our grandmother. Okay...so Laney isn't so bad....

"Thank you, Sweetheart. I'm happy to be back home, too." She answered her granddaughter and squeezed her hand. "What time shall we all have dinner? I'd like to rest until then." She addressed all of us.

"Good question, Estelle. I'd like to go up with you and take a nap. All this pampering is exhausting!" Mom laughed at her own ridiculous statement.

"I have an early reservation for us at Studio at 5:30p.m., since we have Ellie as well."

"All right. Your mother and I will see you then."

"Is it okay if I step out for a little bit?" Laney hesitantly asked.

"Sure." Emily answered. "Where will you be, and will you be back in time for dinner?"

A sudden blush colored Laney's face. She really looked like a doll now. "William drove down here hoping to spend a little time with me...if that's ok? I know it's a girls' weekend and I didn't know he was going to make the drive down to see me...he left me a voicemail while we were in the spa and I just got the message..."

"Of course it's okay, Laney. I'd love to meet him if he's willing to come in and say hello. Maybe he'll say hello when he drops you off?" Emily suggested with the kindness of an older sister or a mother watching out for her daughter. Though Laney was only four and a half years younger than Emily, Emily saw herself as my cousin's protector. The two women were similar in temperament and outlook on life.

"I'm sure he'd love to meet you, Emily. And you too, Jane."

Good for Laney. Maybe I didn't need to find her a man after all. She'd gone and found one herself. This was a first. I couldn't recall Laney ever having a serious boyfriend in her twenty-two years of life.

"Oh!" Laney jumped. "There he is."

Walking toward us was the sweetest looking boy. Literally, he looked like a sweet-looking high schooler. He had those puppy dog eyes that zeroed in on my cousin and his smile was bright and wide as soon as he saw her. It felt like I was watching some high school Bella meets Edward for the first time, and it's love at first sight/bite.

"You got here earlier than you said you would."

"Yeah," he shyly gave Laney a semi-hug. "There was no traffic."

"Hello." Emily put out her hand and smiled wide and bright, herself.

"William, this is Emily and that's Jane."

"I've heard a lot about the both of you. It's wonderful to finally meet you."

"It's nice to meet you, too. I do hope you'll come and see us some time so we can get to know one another?" Emily was the Reid spokesperson today.

"Of course. I'd love that." And he truly looked like he wanted to get better acquainted with all of us. The "kids" looked perfectly suited for one another.

"Mmmmammmmammma," we heard an excited shout. A portly body, with Nick's six-foot frame holding his hands from behind, came "running."

"James!" Emily got up to greet him. She picked him up, and they hugged and kissed each other like they hadn't seen each other in days. Geez! They'd only been separated for a few hours now. Behind James and Nick, came the cavalry. My handsome boyfriend, with his lazy grin, and my kinda handsome brother, walked over to us.

"Why are you guys here? I told you that this was a girls' weekend."

"Now what kind of welcome is that for your boyfriend and brothers?" Max pulled me in to him and kissed me too openly. We had to stop this PDA in front of my family. "Hello Gem," he whispered. Ooh! I liked that whisper—so many hidden promises.

"Hello, Beloved." My brother tried to give Emily the same affectionate greeting, but she shied away just before it became PDA.

"What brings you here? I thought we were spending the weekend apart." Emily tried to push her non-budging husband away.

"What would convince me to sleep alone?"

"Well, you wouldn't have been alone since James is with you, big brother. This is a women's retreat."

"Just because you enjoy sleeping alone does not mean I enjoy sleeping alone. I do not separate from my wife."

"Minors listening," Emily giggled. "Jake, Max, and Nick—this is William. He's wooing our Laney."

Once the "minors" got over their embarrassment, they greeted everyone. Jake announced that Dad and Gimpy were not far behind them. The good news—the three respective couples were getting and paying for their own rooms. The bad news, because of our awkward set-up—Max, me, Laney and Nick—we had to split into a girls' room and a boys' room. Another missed opportunity!

As soon as Ellie woke up, William and Laney appointed themselves as babysitters and hung out with us. We were all having a grand time. And then...I spotted *her*. Like Aphrodite appearing from sea foam, this gorgeous, confident, self-assured woman appeared out of nowhere. I felt like I was in a movie where everyone stopped what he or she was doing to watch this beauty walk by. She was so noticeably eye-catching, eye-popping, mouth-wateringly attractive. Stunning! She was absolutely stunning! You know those rare women who ooze so much sex appeal that even though you don't bat for the same team, you can't help but stare and admire? Well, she was one of those women. She looked like she could lead the congregation.

It was no more than 70 degrees, end of February, and she wore a gold, almost string bikini. She was a dead ringer for an old Chanel print ad with the tanned bikini model lying poolside. Her hair was wet, slicked back and her body was perfect. She wore spiky high heels that very few women could pull off, poolside. Louboutins? Manolos? Jimmy Choos? Damn! I needed a pair of those shoes.

Maybe I'd ask her where she bought them. I couldn't get past the outfit when I heard Jake's surprised voice.

"Kate...! You're back...." Jake greeted the goddess by giving her a kiss on the cheek.

Uh-oh. I hoped this wasn't one of Jake's old girlfriends. Emily looked like she was in a state of perturbed admiration, if such words co-existed. Of course, Emily had not a thing to worry about where my brother was concerned. He was the exemplary family man.

"Hullo Jake," the goddess spoke...

February 28, 2013

"Laters, Baby!"

"Are you back for good?" Jake had one arm around his wife and his other arm cradling James, while Ellie sat in both of Emily's arms. "When did you get into town?"

"I just got in this week and for the time being...I'm back."

"Hello," Emily introduced herself with a little less welcome than usual.

"Sorry. Emi, this is Katherine Beauvais. Kate, my wife, Emily Reid and my children, Elizabeth and James."

"Hullo. A pleasure to meet you. I'd heard Jake got married, but I didn't realize he had a complete family already. What a foursome you make. Your Christmas card must represent America at its best." This goddess spoke a sensual English accent with a French overtone. Forget the shoes. I needed to get one of those accents.

"Thank you," Emily called out as nicely as possible.

I thought I saw Jake's body twitch with a chuckle. His face showed no sign of laughing, but his body couldn't completely hide it.

"So, what will you do while you're here?"

"Oh, you know...the same old, same old..." That cryptic remark didn't help my sister any.

"Would you like to join us for dinner tonight?"

I saw Emily freeze instantly with that question.

"Jake," I interrupted. "We have a reservation at Studio for 5:30p.m., already."

He flat out ignored me and instead, asked William if he'd like to join us as well.

"7:30?" He didn't ask any of us if the time was okay. He only addressed this Katherine or Kate woman. Emily was not happy. "The same old, same old?"

She nodded. "Thank you for inviting me to dinner. I'll see you at 7:30," she said and walked away.

We all dispersed to our respective rooms. Since Laney went out with William, Max came and hung out with me in our room. I tried to tempt him to hop in bed with me, but with the possibility of Laney walking in on us at any moment, he abstained, *again.*

Since I wasn't seeing any action in the hotel room, I decided to go shopping, while Max lounged around watching ESPN. With the addition of Sea-foam goddess at the dinner table, I needed to look good! Just because she had a better body, sexier accent, and probably more money, didn't make me inconsequential, right? She was just a woman.

"You look enticing, Jane." I tilted my neck to give Max better access while getting dressed. I couldn't understand what had changed, but since I walked back into the room, Max couldn't keep his hands off me. "Are you naked under this dress?" There was no need to ask as his hands did a naughty policeman frisk.

"Um, no," I giggled from the assault on my neck.

"I don't want anything under your dress. I want easy access." It sounded like there was a smirking tone in that comment, but I couldn't tell since his words were muffled by my neck that was well...being...muffled!

"I am not going to dinner with my family with no bra and under-wear. I'll be self-conscious the whole night."

The protest didn't go too far once I felt his hands unzip the dress, then unclasp and take off the bra. After zipping it back up, he went the other way and lazily searched for my underwear, but didn't play there long enough for him to lose control or for me to feel satisfied. *Damn!*

"Shall we forget dinner and get in bed?" The hell with dinner—we had an empty room and a large bed. Who wanted dinner?

"No, let's go." He abruptly stopped his play, grabbed my hand and led us to the cozy Arts and Bungalow style restaurant. *Seriously???* Looking nonchalant, he seemed to recover much faster than I did. I *know* my face was still flushed when we walked in.

My brother never ceased to amaze me. Even on such short notice, he had us sitting at the chef's table tonight. In order to get to this private room, we walked through the kitchen on immaculate hard-wood floors and sat at a table which seated ten. Through the windows in this room, you could see the Pacific Ocean, and once seated, you could look into the gigantic kitchen outfitted in dark wood, marble and copper. Jake and Emily sat facing the kitchen, Sea-foam goddess sat next to Emily—chatting amicably, and William awkwardly waited for Laney. We joined the party and I sat on the other side of the table, facing Jake, and Max sat facing Emily. I listened to Sea-foam talk about her life in London, Paris and New York when all of a sudden, she broke into a blinding smile. After excusing herself, she stood up to greet none other than...Donovan!

"Donovan..." she caressed those seven letters like a silk wrap around her body.

Goddess and Donovan? *Wha...???* I looked to my brother, who did not look back at me, and then to Emily, who nodded a barely-there yes. The two of them greeted each other with a brief kiss that somehow lingered. I know it sounds like a paradox, but I swear, that kiss went on and on even though their lips separated as immediately as it joined. It was *way* more than a kiss on the forehead, that's for sure.

"Laney," William stood up and walked a short step to her. "You look beautiful tonight!" William was mesmerized by Laney's surprisingly sexy blue dress that showcased her body and her eyes perfectly. Sexy was not a word I associated with my little cousin, but tonight, she was a bombshell. Now, I felt underdressed (and naked!). I hated feeling underdressed!

"I didn't realize I was dining with the Reid crew tonight." Donovan walked over to shake my brother's hand and kissed Emily on the cheek. He gave a curt nod to Max—who nodded back just as curtly—and introduced himself to William. "You must be the lucky man escorting our Delaney."

"Yes Sir, I am the lucky one." Laney looked a bit apprehensive and somewhat unhappy.

Our conversation followed the ebb and flow of dinner service. At times, we were all animatedly talking about some topic, and at other times, we all went into our own private conversations. *Our conversation was a debauched one, expressed more with our eyes and our hands than with words. Since that brief make-out session back in the hotel room, Max took up where we left off, here in the dining room. It started with a casual holding of the hands. Then it progressed to his arm draped around my arm, with erratic and incidental caresses behind my back. His fingers made continuous brushstroke-like sweeps along my neck. And the butterfly kisses on my head, side of my face and neck almost became sensory overload. It was as though he was marking his territory in front of Donovan. Not that it was necessary, as Donovan didn't give me a second look. His attention was solely focused on Sea-foam, and from time to time on Laney, since she sat directly in front of him.

My boyfriend was raising my temperature in the already hot dining room.

"Back in undergrad, Donovan and I used to drive down here often and eat in the kitchen. The chef created a small bar area in the corner for us, and while everyone was busy cranking out meals, the three of us drank and ate like kings and queens," Jake explained to Emily, while the rest of us listened in. "I think we must have spent almost every weekend here, our senior year."

"So you've all known each other for a while," I added.

"Yeah, you could say that..." the three of them—Jake, Donovan and Kate—laughed.

"How could you afford to eat and sleep here every weekend?" Emily inquired.

Both men stared at Kate. She voiced a stirring laugh. Even her laugh was hot. "These boys, or at least at the time they were boys, stayed at my place. I have a residence here."

Emily didn't look happy with that info, and I, too, might have not been happy, had I not had other things on my mind. At this point, Max has his hand on my thigh, just under my dress and his long fingers were exploring. I took great pains to quietly scootch my chair in, so no one would notice our bawdy behavior at the dinner table. His chuckling eyes met my pleading ones.

When I looked up to see if anyone noticed our 50-shadiness, Jake was busy whispering into Emily's ears—no doubt reassuring her that he wasn't as much of a playboy as he appeared (good luck with that!), Donovan and Goddess were in an uber-serious conversation, and Laney...oh Laney...she did not look good. Her face turned pale white (if that was possible on her already milky white skin) and William looked worried.

"I'm okay, William. I think I'll just go outside for some fresh air."

Her abrupt statement stopped Max's finger-play. *Aargh!*

"I'll go with you," he stood up, immediately.

She kind of ignored him and just walked out. Emily got up and followed her, while Jake reassured William that his fairy princess would be fine.

"William, would you like more wine?" Jake played host.

"Oh, no thank you. I need to drive back home tonight. I'll stop at this one glass."

"Speaking of, don't you think you're drinking too much for someone who has to drive home tonight?" I sounded like Donovan's mother.

"Who says I'm driving home tonight?" Donovan challenged me to counter that statement.

Okay...that shut me up.

Jake moved over to Emily's chair, and the threesome had a lively conversation about their college days. William took off to see if he could find Laney, and Max and I were left in our corner, alone. Max turned his back towards the threesome and paid sole attention to me. With wicked eyes laughing, he replayed the elevator scene from 50 Shades. You all know what I'm talking about? Yep, that scene where Christian takes Ana to a celebratory dinner at his club and commits a public indecency in the elevator? Well, for us, it was under a dinner table, and though it was short-lived with Emily and William walking back in sooner than we'd hoped (damn you two!), Max had had his finger on my pulse!

Dinner done, we all separated for our respective rooms. I was so hot and bothered by the play-action under the table, I could care less which direction Donovan and Kate went. I just needed a room...a private room. I truly contemplated shelling out another $695 so we could be alone tonight, or maybe begging Nick to room with Laney for one night.

"I guess it's goodnight, sleep well?" I asked in front of my room.

"We're not sleeping tonight," was the answer I got as he opened my door. "I moved Laney into the other room earlier today. We have unfinished business..."

Is it plagiarism if I leave you with, "Laters, Baby!?!"

March 4, 2013

Deed...DONE!

A married girlfriend once told me that she complained to her husband about the fact that he wasn't Christian Grey. Her exact words, "Why can't you be more like Christian Grey? He can go 4-5 times back to back!" Her husband's response? "That's why they call it fucking fiction!"

I laughed at her and thought honestly, can anyone—man or woman—possibly go at it that many times? Wouldn't the girl be sore? What about UTI's? Well, to my delight, I got my answer this past weekend at the Montage. I take it I have your interest?

When I last left you, Max had pushed Laney into the other room upon learning that Nick was spending the night with a friend in San Diego. Unbeknownst to me, Max was doing more than watching ESPN while I went shopping. When we got back into the room, chilled champagne, soft music and even dessert were waiting for us—not that any of it was necessary.

"I believe this night is long overdue?"

Hell yes!

"I hope you're well rested because I plan to see the sunrise with you."

"You sure you're not going to fall asleep?" No...I didn't say this aloud. It was only a question in my head. *Do you think I'm stupid?*

We immediately got busy and were unevenly clothed as it only took one short unzipping to get me *nekkid.*

"You're gorgeous," said the lust-drunk man.

"And you're fully clothed," said the happy to be the object of a lust-drunk man, woman.

I know you've heard me say, "What happened next was straight from..." before, but I swear, what happened next was straight from that little known novel with the number 50 in it. To be positive that I wasn't imagining our first time to be almost a duplicate of Christian and Ana's first time, I went back, read, and reread those scenes.

You all remember Ana's first night at Escala? Remember how her first *explosion* happened in what I thought was a not very believable way? Well was I wrong! I had no idea that my *girlfriends* were so sensitive.

Here is the first weird parallel that had me moaning and gasping, but also thinking that somehow, I was cast as Ana in the upcoming movie, and Max was cast as CG.

"You're so beautiful, Jane," he mouthed as his fingers, hands, and mouth were all over my almost C cup and he was relentless in getting his fill. I would definitely say he was a boobie man. Not long into his demonstrations, Ana's words of *"Oh, please"* were on the tip of my tongue when in a very CG voice, Max says, "Let it go, Baby!"

If I hadn't exploded at that moment from sheer shock of his alpha-maleness, I would have died laughing at his CG imitation.

He didn't give me more than a second of recovery time when the elevator scene resurfaced and his fingers began their exploration, and the words *"Oh, please,"* came back to the tip of my tongue when my tongue wasn't tied up with Max's. Max kept telling me how I looked beautiful while in the throes, and I didn't pay much attention to it until he said, "You are so beautiful, I can't believe you're mine." That would have freaked me out, once again, but the tidal wave was about to come crashing down and I didn't want to miss it.

Right as things were about to get even better, he took away his finger and left me hanging. But no sooner did the finger leave, another body part stood tall, ready to take its place. I don't know when all his clothes had come off, but somehow, like movie magic, he was about to enter my sanctuary when I uttered something that never should be uttered while having sex with a man. I mentioned another man's name while in heat.

"Oh my gosh, you're just as good as Christian...maybe even better," I moaned.

"What???" Max stopped dead in his tracks.

Uh-oh! Oh, um...I meant that as a compliment???

"Did you just compare me to a past lover while I'm about to make love to you?"

Crap! "No, no, no...you misunderstood..."

"I don't think so. I specifically heard a man's name and it wasn't mine." Max pulled himself off me and started getting dressed.

"Max! No! I..." What I did next was even stupider than calling out Christian's name in the middle of our lovemaking. I laughed. OMG, I laughed so hard at my ridiculous situation while Max was pissed and half-dressed.

"I'm going home," he briskly said.

"Come here," I grabbed his arm and pulled him back on the bed. "Let me explain."

Initially he wasn't too obliging, but he grudgingly sat while I went to get my Kindle. I turned to the middle of chapter eight and started reading the passage to him starting from the good part where Christian begins to undress Ana, and then gets busy.

"You see...Christian Grey is a character from *50 Shades of Grey*, and he's this BDSM sex god that just about every woman fantasizes about. The ways you've pleasured me so far, and some of the things you've said have been textbook 50. I thought maybe you'd read the book and were taking a page from CG." I tried to contain my laugh.

Somewhat chuckling, Max just stared at me. "A BDSM sex god, huh? Is that what you've fantasized about all this time while you were with me?"
*Generally I fantasize about CG when you aren't with me...*but I wasn't going to tell him that either.

Max slapped me hard on my rear end and pulled me on top of him in bed. "Read me more of that book. And I only want the good stuff."

And so the night flew by as we role-played Christian and Ana.

The first time sex scene—Yep! Did that. And in the same order.

The first bathtub scene—Yep! I got an A on that one. My CG said that I performed even better than Ana did.

The tit-for-tat scene right after I earned my A...*Oh yeah!* He got an A+ for that scene. I had to give him an A+ because he didn't stop after the first time, but he went on and on and on till I cried mercy.

For good measure, Max threw in a few *"You smell so good"* and *"Come for me, Jane,"* for laughs.

We did end up "chasing the dawn" together between laughing, making love and talking.

"Baby, I want to tell you something."

"What?" I asked while shamelessly wrapped around him.

He pulled us apart a bit, and gave me that serious Max look.

"I love you, Jane. I love the way you make me feel—happy, joyful, grateful for life, and even the crazy, ugly, bitter feelings, too. You make me feel alive. We could be together daily and I'd still crave you. I'd truly move heaven and earth to spend a moment with you, my precious gem. I love you."

Before I could respond, he put both his hands on my face and gave me a kiss that made me think, *"Ana Steele, eat your heart out!"* The kiss was raw, sentimental, and filled with affection. Not only did this man love me as a woman, but he also liked me as a person and as a friend.

"I love you too," was the last thing I remembered saying, before I dozed off in the morning.

"You're late!" Jake scolded with a chuckle as we shuffled to the brunch table.

"What are you, the time keeper?" Max retorted while giving Emily a squeeze on the shoulder, and kissing my grandmother and mom on the cheek. His attention eventually went to Ellie because James was already playing on the grass with Laney.

Ellie used her only word, "Uh!" and got Max to pick her up and take her with us to our spot at the end of the table. Surprisingly, Kate was seated, without Donovan, chatting with Gimpy.

"Emily, by the mound of food on your plate, I see you're feeling better?" I asked, showing that I *do* care about my sister.

"I'm back!" She answered with a grin. "I'm sure you were too occupied to notice last night, but I did eat every bite of what the chef sent out." She grinned some more.

Shoot! Were we that obvious? I looked to my boyfriend and he had the same silly grin. *Whatever.*

"Were you ill?" Kate asked in that same sexy voice. I guess morning, noon or night, she sounded sultry.

"My wife is almost five months pregnant, carrying our third child," Jake proudly announced.

"Almost five months?" I asked super surprised. "When did all those months pass by, and how did you not know till just recently?"

"I was still nursing the twins and my body wasn't back to normal, so I didn't notice any of the signs till I got sick. And maybe because I'm not carrying twins this time, my morning sickness died down earlier than before."

"Are you sure it's not twins again? You're eating for twins and then some." Perhaps that wasn't the most sensitive thing to say to a pregnant woman, but I knew my sister wouldn't mind. "And if you're almost five months prego, where's the belly?"

"Right here." She traced her burgeoning belly over her dress. Even pregnant, Emily looked darling, and by that stupid grin on my brother's face, he too knew she looked darling.

"Since you already have a boy and a girl, is there a preference?" Kate was more interested in our conversation than I expected her to be. She looked to me like a glam woman who would never sacrifice her gorgeous figure to have babies.

"No preference. I would eventually like a sibling for each child, but beyond that, I'll take healthy."

"Good morning, everyone." Geez Louise! Donovan was in workout shorts, a fitted top, and he was sweaty. His wavy hair was wet, sloppy, and curly, and he was still slightly panting from a run or whatever he did. Hey, just because I have a boyfriend doesn't mean I can't look and appreciate. I'm taken, not blind and dumb!

Whatever I thought or felt didn't matter. After greeting my grandmother, my mother, and then Emily, he went straight to Sea-foam and gave her a longer than we're-just-friends kiss. *Uh-huh!* I guess someone else got some last night as well. He *finally* got around to saying hello to me.

"Foreign pasture?" I purposely asked ambiguously, referring sarcastically to his grand statement of "...*you know where I stand. Don't know how long I'll be standing here, but until you give me the green light, or until I move on to another pasture...*" Still standing, my ass! He ran faster than Usain Bolt when Goddess showed.

"Wasn't welcomed on home soil..." was his riposte. *Jerk!*

I was about to make another unnecessary comment, but Ellie interrupted us when she screamed her one word and jumped from Max to Donovan. She then pointed to her brother, and Donovan carried her over to James and Laney.

"Everything good?" Max asked, bringing me back from watching Donovan symbolically walk away from me.

"Everything's great!"

Right??? What else can it be but great? I'm with the man I love, the man who adores me, and the man who can give Christian Grey a run for his money. If there are some of you who have no idea what I was talking about when comparing my man to Ana's man, I guess you'll have to go look up that book that starts with the number 50. Oh brother, just what E. L. James needs...another book sale!

March 7, 2013

Quote (s) of the Day

$\mathcal{T}$he rest of the week was really quiet at work, but home life was thrown into a complete tizzy. Gram and Gimpy decided to get married this weekend rather than waiting till June. From the words of my sagacious grandmother, "At our age, we could be dead tomorrow...so why wait?" Of course, Gimpy put a romantic spin on things as he said, "I've lived without your grandmother my entire life, minus those few blissful months in Paris. We've wasted enough time apart. I want my forever with her now." My Gimpy was the epitome of *HAWT* for a senior citizen.

Mom, all four aunts, Emily, and a few cousins were busy planning the wedding. It was to be a small affair in our backyard with mostly family, a few friends, and some work colleagues. The rehearsal "dinner" was set for an English Tea Party theme on Friday, and a wedding breakfast would be served after the wedding on Saturday. If you'll all recall, Aunt Babs is fond of themes. I say "dinner" because it's actually a late afternoon tea. Since Gram and Gimpy don't stay up too late, a 4:00 p.m. tea was the compromise. To quote Aunt Babs, "Come in your finest English Tea attire!" Boy, there was a lot of English in my life these days.

"You ready to marry my grandmother?" I asked Gimpy over lunch.

"My dear Janey, I was born ready. She is my sun, my star, my moon, my everything." Damn, that was smooth!

"Gimpy, you make all men, young and old, look bad." We laughed together. "Speaking of young men, where's Donovan these days? I haven't seen him in the office all week."

"Donovan is doing some work for us in Orange County."

"New client?"

"You could say that..."

"Gimpy, you holding out on me? What's going on?"

"Donovan is trying to woo Kate Beauvais to come work for us."

He's still with her??? Woo my ass. He's not wooing her, but I'm sure he's doing something that rhymes with wooing!

"Who is this woman? Why do we want her with us? Is she a lawyer?"

"Not exactly. She started with a law degree, but went into hedge funds instead. She was a successful hedge fund manager for a while, then set up her own company with two partners and has done extremely well. She just sold her share of the company and is in a semi-retired state."

"Isn't she a bit young to be retired?"

"Yes, she's only forty. She shouldn't waste that kind of brilliance lounging at the beach."

"She's forty???" Damn, I knew she was older than I, but I thought she was maybe mid-thirties at worst. How can someone her age look that young? "What's the story with her and Donovan?"

"I'm not sure, but from the looks of it, if anyone can get her into our office, it's him. I gave him a week to bring her in."

"Shoot, that means I gotta see her every day."

"Be nice, Janey. You have a wonderful young man in Max. Don't covet what you don't really want."

I didn't realize I'd said that aloud. "I'll be nice…" I murmured.

Max and I planned to have dinner tonight, so I rushed home and primped before meeting my man.

"Hello, my precious gem." He gave me an open-mouthed kiss as he sat next to me at the bar. "Should we just dine here or do you want to get a table?"

"We can sit here. They'll serve us dinner at the bar. How was your day?"

"Uneventful. Not much happened. How was yours? Is the house in an uproar with the wedding?"

"Yeah. Mom and all the aunts have now forbidden us from helping because all of us have too many opinions on everything. Emily's the only one who can help, but she's got the twins, and the aunts won't let her do much of anything because of the pregnancy, so it's basically the five daughter-in-laws."

"What do you get for a senior citizen couple who have more money between them than all of us combined?"

"They are not accepting gifts. They have asked for a donation to the hospital instead."

"Ok. So I've been thinking…"

Uh-oh. What have I done lately that may get me into trouble? With Donovan gone wooing Miss French-English, I'd been a good girl, or better said, I hadn't had a chance to be bad.

"What's going on in that head of yours? It scares me whenever you say, 'I've been thinking...'"

"After the Montage, I can't get you off my mind, not that you were ever very far," *Awww!* "and I can't come up with too many ways for us to be alone, so..."

"...so...?"

"My lease is up in June at the apartment. I have one year left in med school, then I'm unsure where I'll be after that. If we..."

"Just spit out your damn thought!" This native was restless!

"You want to get an apartment together? I'd love for us to live together that last year, then we can decide where this will go once I finish med school and...never mind. I'm getting ahead of myself."

"Never mind the getting an apartment together or never mind the thought after that?"

"I told you this weekend that I love you, and I mean every word. I have these visions of seeing you asleep in our bed when I come home in the wee hours of the morning, or of making dinner together then doing the dishes, and I definitely have vivid images of coaxing you into morning sex when you're still drugged with sleep. Do any of those thoughts sound tempting to you?"

Yowza! That was freakin', freakin' hawt!!! I'm going to frame that last sentence, "*...and I definitely have vivid images of coaxing you* *into morning sex when you're still drugged with sleep,"* and put it on my nightstand.

"Um..."

"You don't have to answer now. Think about it and tell me later. We still have a few months before looking for a place together. But..." he went for the kill and put both his hands on my neck, thumbs by my ear, nose touching nose, "I'd love to fall asleep and wake up to your beauty every day," and of course he kissed me—hot, heavy, and in public. There was another quote I'd put on my nightstand! *"I'd love to fall asleep and wake up to your beauty every day."* Goodness, I was dating a modern-day Shakespeare.

After that kind of kiss and those tender but erotic words, there was no need to think about whether Max and I should be roommates. I wanted to say yes immediately, but thought it wise to sit on it for a few days. We had some time before apartment hunting happened.

"Hannah!" Max dropped his hands from my face, and called out in surprise.

"Max!!!" This cute, redheaded college senior, cheerleader-looking girl ran over and hugged Max like he was her long lost brother. "I can't believe you're here. I was going to call you tomorrow to see if we could meet."

"What are you doing here? Why aren't you in Michigan?"

"I got tired of the cold and I just got laid off, so I'm staying at your house for the time being till I can get my life together. Mom and Dad, I mean, Mr. and Mrs. Davis have generously offered to put me up, or better stated, put up with me for a few months."

Hello???

"I'm sure Mom and Dad will love having you in the house. You were always the daughter they wanted but couldn't have."

"Your mom and dad are going to be here any minute now. We're meeting here for dinner."

Um...earth to Max...your girlfriend is being ignored...and oh my gosh, I'm about to meet your parents...why haven't I met your parents in all these months???

"There they are," this Hannah girl pulled Max off the barstool, and they both left me, with not even a second thought, to greet his parents.

I was a bit taken aback by the way his parents looked. Max was about six feet tall, well-built, and very good looking. His parents were both short, a bit heavy, and stern looking. They didn't break into a smile when they saw their son, nor did his mother hug him or embrace him as a greeting and show of love. Max wasn't kidding when he said his parents were not the touchy-feely type. Their conversation was brief and Max soon brought everyone my way.

"Jane, this is my mom, dad, and Hannah, a family friend. Mom, Dad, this is Jane, my girlfriend."

"Hello!" I did my best Emily welcome. "It's so nice to meet you."

All I got was a brief, "hello" from his parents. Hannah was a bit more welcoming. She acted as the spokesperson for the Davis family.

"Hi Jane. It's great to meet you. Mom and Dad didn't tell me Max was dating someone."

Why did this girl call Max's parents Mom and Dad?

That was a question for later.

"We didn't tell you about Max's girlfriend because Max hasn't really told us about her," his mom stated matter of factly.

"It's not as though you showed any interest...." The tone of Max's voice changed to a mixture of anger and hurt. I got a glimpse of how he must have grown up all these years. My heart broke a little when thinking of Max making every life decision without the approval and support of his family. My family and I'd have to give him some extra attention to make up for all his lost years.

"Well, if that's what you think, why don't we change that then?" His mother gave Max a stoic and harsh look, then softened a bit as she faced me. "Jane, would you and Max like to have dinner at our place this weekend? Does Saturday work for you?"

"We have a family wedding on Friday and Saturday, but Sunday is all right, if it's all right with you."

"Sunday is fine. We'll see you at 6:00 p.m.?"

"Sure. Thank you for the invitation."

There was a brief nod, and that was that. They invited me to dinner, I accepted, they nodded, and then they left for their table. No goodbyes, no nice meeting yous...only a nod.

Hannah put her arms around my boyfriend's waist, her head on his chest and hugged him longingly. "I'll see you Sunday," her words trailed, and she eventually let go. I got chills watching her turn back to take one last look at Max. To misquote Marcellus from Shakespeare's *Hamlet*, "Something is rotten in the state of California."

March 11, 2013

(Almost) Shocking Confession!

*W*hat a weekend—a rehearsal tea on Friday, an English wedding breakfast on Saturday, and dinner with the monster-in-laws on Sunday! The secrets revealed to me this weekend could be classified as shocking!, shockinger!!, and shockingest!!! Of course I know that last two aren't words in the Merriam Webster Dictionary, but by the time you read about these confessions, you will agree that no girl should receive these kinds of surprises without any warning. Just to give you a glimpse into what's to come in the next three, maybe four, posts—Max confesses a deep dark secret to me after the tea party, Donovan confesses an even deeper, darker secret to me after the wedding, then the deepest darkest secret to rival the deepest darkest secrets, awaited me at Max's family home on Sunday.

Friday—I woke up to a complete zoo in our house and backyard. It was worse than Emily's wedding because this was even more short notice than the three weeks Jake gave Mom. There seems to be something about shotgun weddings and the Reid family.

"Will you make it to the tea this afternoon?" I called Max, on my way into work. Gimpy and I were taking a half day. Gimpy had no reason to go in today, but he said it'd be much easier to work than to watch the chaos at home.

"Good morning my precious gem. Yes, I'll make it. I switched with a buddy, so he'll do my rounds and I'll take his late night one. What time should I get there?"

"I'll be home by 1:00, so come as soon as you can. We can hang out till the tea begins."

"So what happens at one of these rehearsal dinners?"

"It's always done in some sort of theme. When Jake and Emily got married, Aunt Babs turned her backyard into a Moroccan paradise with food, belly dancers, and music to harmonize with the theme. Today, in honor of our ancestors, we are going to be in an English garden with scones, sandwiches, clotted cream and chocolate fountains. And since it is a late afternoon party, I'm sure there will be heavier dinner items as well. After the food and entertainment, Gimpy has to follow tradition and get Gram something from the..." I stopped mid-sentence and turned to Gimpy to ask, "Whose tradition do you follow? Jake's, Uncle Henry's, or my grandfather's?"

"I may start my own tradition," he gave an evil laugh, then added, "I'll definitely outdo your brother's paltry earrings."

"Geez Gimpy, you and Jake are going to scare away any of our suitors with your high-rolling gifts."

"Max, you can find out for yourself what the entertainment is. I don't want to frighten you off. I'll see you this afternoon?"

"Definitely. Love you, my beauty."

"Love you too." I blushed saying this because Gimpy was giving me his English smirk.

"He's a good man, Janey. Take care not to scare him off."

"Scare him off??? Gimpy, you have so little faith in me."

When Gimpy and I got home, the backyard had been magically transformed into an English garden. Normally, our backyard is a huge parcel of grassy lot with a play structure for the twins, a gated pool in the furthermost back part of the lot, and a tennis court off to the side. Today, the play structure disappeared to who knows where, and a small pond sprouting irises, daylilies and other greeneries showed up in the pool. The gate protecting our little ones from the pool also disappeared. How they transformed a pool to look like a "pond" with flowers and green shrubbery, I could not tell you. There was a beautifully rustic wooden bench facing the "pond," and there were several swinging benches under wooden gazebos, off to the side. The tennis court was overflowing with tables ready to accommodate the catered food, and cute round and square four-tops with garden-themed chairs filled the middle of the yard.

"Wow, Gram. This looks beautiful!" Emily commented, while walking with her two little imps in tow. The imps were pushing a shopping cart into the house and "running" as fast as they could. Since James was pretty adept at walking, he led the way. Elizabeth wouldn't lose out to her brother and did her best to keep up, even though she kept tipping over. The mean aunt that I was, I laughed every time she fell over.

"This reminds me of our country home." Gram commented.

"You have another home?" I asked. "How come we've never been there?"

"It was a childhood home. My parents sold it."

"Shall we get the show on the road? I think tea is about to begin." Gimpy put out his arm so Gram could walk out with him.

"Is Max coming?" Emily asked.

"He should be here any minute now. You need help corralling the two outside?"

Emily only smiled as she gazed at the beautifully dressed boy and girl who pushed as fast as they could to catch up with the senior citizens.

"Hello, Love." My brother came over and greeted his wife with a tender kiss. "How're you feeling today?" He rubbed her barely-there stomach.

"I feel fantastic. No more nausea. I hate feeling nauseous. Did you see our babies?"

"Yeah. They clean up nicely, huh?"

"They sure do. They're so sweet when they play together, though I think we need to make sure they don't fall into the pond/pool."

"With all my cousins chasing after them, I don't think we have any worries, Love. You can relax tonight. I'll ask Laney and Nick to be in charge of the babies."

"Hey, big brother. I'm standing right next to your *Love,* but you've yet to greet me."

"Hey there, Brat. Where's Davis?"

"Right here. Hello, Gem!" He kissed me, both hands on my face, hot and heavy on the lips.

"You two need to get a room. That's disgusting."

"No it's not, Jake. I think it's sweet the way Max shows his love for our sister. I've always wanted one of those romance novel kisses." Emily said in a dreamy but teasing voice. "Max, you've changed since we dated." She giggled this time.

"Em..." he exaggerated the name Em. "Come here. Let me show Jake how it's done."

Max put out his arms and Emily did not waver in walking towards him. Of course my brother hooked his right arm around her stomach and pulled her back to him. Max laughed. Emily laughed. Even I laughed!

"You want one of those kisses? I'll give you one of those kisses." The love in my brother's eyes for his wife was almost sickening to watch.

"Let's get out of here. I don't think I can stomach this before we eat." I pulled Max out of the kitchen, but before Max left, he squeezed Emily's arm and gave her the sweetest I'm-happy-for-you look. I must be growing up because this entire exchange made me dizzy with joy. Gram and Gimpy will finish their lives loving each other, Jake and Emily worked through their struggles and would live a lifetime of happiness, and I was with a man who was capable of loving deeply. No matter the environment he grew up in, his tenderheartedness always shined when he dealt with his close circle of friends. Lucky girl—that's me!

We went outside, chatted with the family, played with the twins, and got our meal. "The ladies in your family are incredible! How did they get this done so quickly and beautifully?" Max and I decided to sit on the lovers' swing under the gazebo. "It feels so authentic."

"You should have seen Jake and Emily's rehearsal dinner. Aunt Babs has a thing for themes. She's obsessive about getting every detail on the mark."

"So...have you thought more about getting a place with me, come June?"

"Yeah..." I smiled.

"And?"

"I'd love to live with you, but...what about your plans to go away this summer?"

"Crap! I forgot about that."

"Are you going?"

"Would you be okay with me leaving you for a month?"

"Max. I was dead serious when I told you that I didn't want you to miss out on any opportunities. I will be a good girl and wait for you to return, hale and whole."

"I don't want to leave you, but I'm leaning towards going. It's only a month and I figure it'll be good for us to miss each other."

"I think you should go and help as many children as you can. They need you. But, make sure you come back to me because I need you more."

That sweet remark earned me a serious make out session under the gorgeous gazebo.

"Ladies and gents! Let's all gather around the stage. Grab a chair and we'll see what surprises Roland has for our beloved mother and grandmother," Uncle Henry called us all to the main event. "I think everyone here knows about our wedding tradition. If you don't know—i.e. Max Davis—ask your neighbor." Everyone chuckled. "Roland...take it away!"

Gimpy walked up to the stage while Nick and Doug trailed right behind him carrying a beautiful pirate treasure chest.

"When I approached Estelle's five sons a few months back and told them about my intention to marry their mother, they told me about the long-standing tradition you have in the Reid family. Though I'm not a Reid, I was told that I couldn't marry Estelle unless I agreed to honor and continue this tradition. Now, I don't quite fit into any category since I'm not the first child of any of your generation. Jerry picked the tradition of something old and started with a pearl necklace. Henry, the cheap bastard..." we all died laughing when Gimpy called out Uncle Henry, "picked something blue and gave his wife a blue garter. Jake, with the help of his gracious grandmother, gave his lovely wife not only the prize ring, but also a pair of diamond earrings." Of course my brother gloated and waved Emily's hand in the air to show off the stunning ring. "Since I needed to *best* the young man who robbed the Reid family coffer, I brought the Ascot family jewels to refill what's been plundered."

Nick and Doug carried the table that the chest was sitting on, front and center, and opened the surprise. There were *aahs* and *oohs* and whistles galore.

"You Reids don't kid around with this whole family tradition, do you? I don't think we'll ever be getting married if I need to follow after Roland." I think Max was kidding?

"Many of these jewels date back to more than a century ago, and many others were added since. Some are expensive, many are not, but they are all a piece of my family history and precious to me. What your grandmother and I decided to do was to allow each female member of this family to come up and pick the jewel of their choice."

That announcement got Gimpy an even grander standing ovation than Jake got when he gave Emily more diamonds. Jewelry was not my thing, but if you'd seen all that glittered in that chest, any girl would have been tempted.

"We're going to go from oldest to youngest, starting with...Elizabeth."

What??? Why did that imp get to choose first? She's barely a girl.

"Yes, Elizabeth is a female member of this family, and since she has no idea what she's choosing, Estelle and I thought she should go first."

Jake strutted up to the stage with his daughter and had that annoyingly smug grin. "Princess, which jewel would you like?" Jake placed his daughter on the table in front of the treasure chest and she, just like her father, was in heaven with all the sparkly toys. "You can pick any one you like," he encouraged her.

She stood up on the table with her hands on the chest, and Jake caught her a split second before she fell into the chest, head first. That brought about a horrified gasp from the ladies, and a light chuckling from the men. When her head came out of the chest, little Ellie had chosen her prize.

"Damn! That girl picked the most expensive thing in the chest," I muttered.

In her hand was a glittering diamond tiara. Who the hell wore a tiara in this day and age unless you were royalty? Father and daughter had identical smiles as my brother crowned the tiara on Ellie's big head.

"Leave it to Jake's child to grab the grandest treasure in this chest. Well, done, Elizabeth!" Gimpy announced.

Everyone clapped for Ellie who showed her dimples, her two front and bottom teeth, and lots of gum surrounding the teeth as she smiled. I clapped too, kind of.

"Hey," Max whispered to me after I chose my cameo pendant, "I have a surprise for you. Let's get up to your room for a few minutes."

Ooh...I liked the sound of that.

There was an Amazon box waiting for me on my bed, and I had no qualms about ripping it open. What I saw made me blush—and I'm no blushing-type.

"What on earth? How'd you know about these? Did you read the book?"

"Hell no. Do I look like I have time to read erotica? Since you seemed to be so into this naughty-girl sex, I thought I'd be obliging and buy you a few toys. Shall we give it a test try now?" he said while taking out Mr. Ben Wa from its packaging and walking into my bathroom to wash it clean. "I believe Google told me to take each ball and insert it into *your* treasure chest?"

I was getting so hot and bothered; I started doing a little hop from one foot to another.

"Gem, I can't insert these into you if you keep hopping around. Now stay still," he ordered and slapped me in the ass.

This is the only man *ever*, to put his hand on my rear end with the intent to hurt (or pleasure). And damn, did it pleasure. He put both balls deep inside me and his fingers made sure (many times over) that they would stay there. Of course we couldn't just stop there, even with a huge party taking place underneath my bedroom window. There was no time to get undressed so Max lifted up my skirt, I unzipped his pants and gave the wall a thorough wipe down from my backside.

"I can't believe these balls stayed intact while I was having vertical sex."

"Did it do anything for you?"

"Don't know. The jury's out on this one. I'll let you know after we try it a few more times." We rushed to right ourselves before rejoining the Reid family. "I have a question for you..." I cringed at whether or not I should ask him this personal question, but I was curious.

"Yeah?"

"If you and Emily never had sex, was Jennifer your first?"

"Um...no..." He wouldn't expound.

"Then...who...was...it...?"

"Do we have to talk about this? Do you really need to know?"

"I don't *have to* know, but I'd like to know." *Now that you're evading the question, I MUST know.* "Why do you hesitate telling me who it was? I'll tell you who my first was if you're interested."

"I'm not interested in knowing the name of the man you lost your virginity to..."

"Well, I am interested in knowing the name of the woman you lost *your* virginity to...just tell me!" Then it dawned on me as to why he couldn't spit out a name. "Do I know this woman? Is that why you're so cautious about giving out a name?"

Max sighed. "Yeah, you know who she is. It was…"

March 14, 2013

Shocking (er) Confession!!

"Did you just tell me you lost your virginity to Hannah??? The girl living in your parents' house right now. The girl who hugged you back at the restaurant like you were the greatest thing since sliced bread, Hannah?"

"Yes."

"How old were you? You met Emily when you were eighteen or nineteen, as a freshman in college."

"If you must know, Hannah and I were high school sweethearts and she and I started dating when we were sixteen."

"And...?"

"Gem, is this really necessary?" Max was super uncomfortable talking about his horn-dog teenage years. I was willing to wait it out the whole night to hear this story.

"Oh yeah, it's necessary, Buddy. You need to tell me all about you and Hannah."

He sighed some more. I didn't know what the big deal was. Lots of kids had sex in high school—not that I would want my high school son or daughter experimenting at that age.

"We had sex for the first time when we were in our junior year of high school."

"That's it?"

"Yeah, that's it. What else is there to say?"

"What happened to her after high school? Did you drop her for Emily?"

"No. Her family moved away to Michigan the summer before our senior year and we just grew apart. By the middle of our senior year, we broke up."

"And that's it?"

"What else do you want me to say?" Now he was sounding upset, though I had no understanding as to why.

"All right. I'll drop it...for now. Let's get back to the party."

"Jane, I don't want you to bring up Hannah and our past relationship again, okay?"

Geez...what's got you in such a snit? "Okay," I agreed reluctantly.

Max left for the hospital, and the party died down early as our eighty-year-old lovebirds needed their beauty rest before their big day tomorrow. I thought more about Max and Hannah and before I fell asleep, I couldn't help wondering why Max was so agitated with me knowing about him and Hannah.

Saturday morning was glorious! The sun smiled on Gram and Gimpy as they said their vows, and the wedding breakfast got underway. We had more of an American wedding breakfast with lots of traditional English food items as well. We had biscuit cakes, scones, English pancakes, croque monsieurs, bread puddings, as well as frittatas, eggs benedict, and an omelet station. About 100 family members, friends and law associates attended the celebration.

"Hullo Jane. It's nice to see you again." Sea-foam goddess looked regal in her garden-cum-knock 'em-dead dress, and matching hat. "Your grandmother and Roland are divine together."

"Yep. Divine...that's them." What a stupid answer! "Has Donovan convinced you to join our firm?"

She gave a hearty laugh. "Yes. Donovan was convincing enough...I believe I'll join the firm for the time being."

Yeah, slut! I'm sure Donovan convinced you plenty.

"There you are," Donovan called out to Kate. "The partners would like to speak with you. They're over with Roland right now."

"If you'll excuse me?"

I watched Kate walk away from us and was at a loss for words. How would I handle watching the two sex-gods working together?

"So Gimpy told me it was your job to bring Kate into our firm. I see you've succeeded."

"I guess you can say that."

"What's the story between you and this woman? You seem awfully chummy with someone who appeared out of nowhere. I don't think I've ever heard you or Jake talk about her."

Donovan smiled. I don't know how I didn't notice till this moment, but Donovan came dressed to the nine. He looked...dear God...he looked dazzling, delicious, debonair, James Bond-like, David Beckham at Wills and Kate's wedding-like, OMG-like! He had on the dark suit with a tail, a cream-colored ascot cravat with a pin in the middle, a dark colored brocade vest, and even a top hat.

"Who the hell dresses you every morning?" I blurted out.

Donovan smiled again. This was a smile that could make us all forget our spouses and significant others.

"Why...you applying for the job? I promise not to be too demanding if you choose to fill in as my valet."

"Shut up," I laughed. "I can't get over how good you look." What a stupid thing to say to a man.

"Why thank you Lady Jane. You look just as delicious," he flirted. *How'd he know I thought he looked yummy?*

"Should you be saying stuff like this to me? If my boyfriend doesn't kick your ass already, it may be Sea-foam who'll finish the job."

He gave me a confused look. "Who or what is Sea-foam? Never mind...I don't want to know. You asked about Kate? If your *boy-friend* will allow you to sit with me, I'll tell you about her."

Luckily, Max was occupied dancing with Ellie and James, so I freely plopped myself down looking forward to hearing about the goddess.

"Kate and I've been together, on and off, for about ten years."

What the hell? Why didn't I know this?

"We started seeing each other my junior year in undergrad, and by the end of my senior year, I'd practically moved in with her and had asked her to marry me."

What the HELL?? Where was I during all this?

"What'd she say when you asked her to marry you?"

"She laughed at me and told me to finish law school, then get a job."

I didn't know how to respond to that comment.

"Kate was in her early thirties at the time, and on the fast track to success and stardom in the hedge fund world. She didn't need a strapping young buck holding her back. So we broke up, I went to law school, got a job, and we've been picking up where we left off ever since."

"In the young buck department?"

"Funny! I love your sense of humor, Jane."

"So she's back to pick up where you left off again? Are you so in love with her that you drop everything and anyone whenever she's back in town?"

He raised one eyebrow at me and my accusation. "She came back to ask me to marry her, if you must know, my curious Jane."

WHAT THE HELL???

"I see I've finally shocked you into silence."

"You gonna marry her?"

He shook his head no. My body shook in relief!

"I don't love her anymore, though the attraction is still there. Maybe what I felt for her back in college was a young buck's fascination, adulation, obsession. I don't know if it was love. Plus, there's somebody holding me back from wanting to explore anything with anyone new." My body now shook in expectation and fear. "I know you're with another man. I'm not going to take what's not mine. But I can't help wonder what it would be like to be with you...to laugh with you...to love with you.... A chance with you is what's holding me back from moving on.... There's my confession for the day. And now, I better get out of your *boy*friend's seat."

Waltz...Tango...Foxtrot...!

March 18, 2013

Shocking (est) Confession!!!

"You nervous about meeting my family?" Max asked while we drove together to his house.

"A bit?" I think I was more nervous about seeing Hannah again. No matter how many times Max told me Hannah had moved on since their high school relationship, it did not look like it from where I stood.

"You have nothing to worry about. They'll all love you. Just remember that my family is not as jovial as yours. If you keep that in mind, all will be okay."

"All right."

Max's family home was nice, really nice. Looking at his home, I realized how much he downplayed his family's wealth. It was a wonder why he was living on student loans rather than asking his parents for help. I suppose that was another question for another day...

"Hello," Max's mom and dad greeted us.

"Hello Mr. and Mrs. Davis. Thank you for inviting me. These are for you," I said handing them a bottle of wine and an orchid plant. "You have a lovely home." Now I sounded just like Emily.

"Thank you," Mrs. Davis answered politely. "Hannah, could you put these away for me?" She passed off my gifts without much thought.

There she was—the girl who popped my boyfriend's cherry, metaphorically speaking, of course.

"Hi Jane. Welcome to our home."

Last I checked, this wasn't your home but whatever...

"Thank you. Can I help with anything?"

"No, dinner's set. Let's all sit down and eat." His mom led the way to the dining room.

No cocktail hour, no conversation over a charcuterie platter, no get-to-know-you time...straight to dinner. Okay...

"Hope you like chicken. That's all I know how to make," Hannah said with a smile.

I hoped she didn't poison my plate.

"You made your baked chicken dish?" Max asked with a smile.

"I know how much you liked it in the past, and I thought you might still like it?" She gave my boyfriend a lovey-dovey look that I'm sure he didn't notice, but I sure did.

"It's been a long time since I've had it. I'm sure it'll be as delicious as always." He gave her a side hug. I totally felt like the outsider at this dinner table.

"Hello!" Two young Max look-alike men greeted me. "You must be Jane. I'm Garret, Max's younger brother, and this is Josh, the youngest of us all."

"Very nice to finally meet you."

I sat next to Max and his brothers, while Hannah sat on Max's other side with his parents. While Mr. and Mrs. Davis didn't say much, when they did, it was a question that led to a conversation between them, Max and Hannah. There was no room in their conversation for me. Max's brothers were cool. Catching on to what was happening on the other side of the table, they started a conversation that involved the three of us.

I learned that Garret was studying to be an architect and Josh was a dreamer.

"So Josh, you're going to take off for a year and live in Italy so you can paint?" I asked, a bit flabbergasted.

"Yeah. I've earned enough credits to graduate early so I think I'll use that time to explore my artistic side."

"That's kind of cool. Crazy, but cool," I commended. "No one in my family is that brave. My younger brother took a year off to decide which graduate school to attend, but he was working in a bio-chem lab in the meanwhile. My older brother went from undergrad to med school, I went from undergrad to law school—we're all pretty dull people. So where will you stay in Italy?"

"I don't know. I may go hang out in London for a while, then Paris, then eventually make it into Italy."

"My cousin Laney will be living in London as of June this year. You should befriend her and hang out."

"That'd be cool."

"You good?" Max whispered in my ear.

"Yeah," I whispered back, and was tempted to give his lips a kiss. "I just want to know what the hell this is that we're eating."

Max busted up laughing. "Hannah, Jane would like your baked chicken recipe."

Hannah broke into an uneasy smile that made me feel bad. "Oh, it's a chicken breast stuffed with Rice-a-Roni, smothered in Campbells' cream of mushroom soup, then baked for forty-five minutes. This used to be Max's favorite meal."

"I'll try and remember to make it for him next time he comes over. Thank you," I grunted, trying hard not to laugh.

"So Jane, you're a lawyer?" Max's mom asked. "And your brother is a doctor?"

"Yes. And my younger brother is in med school with Max."

"How did you and Max meet?"

How to answer this one.... There was really no un-awkward way around it.

"My brother Jake married Emily Logan."

"No way!" Garret called out. "I wanted to marry Emily Logan when Max broke up with her."

"Me too!" Josh added. "Who wouldn't want to marry such a pretty and sweet girl? I always thought Max was crazy to break up with her."

"Well, Max's loss was my brother's gain. They are blissfully married with twins and another one on the way."

"I'd like to see Emily again." Josh said with Garret nodding his head in agreement.

"Why don't you guys come over with Max one night? Emily and her family live across the street from my parents' house. You can meet my brother and their beautiful babies. Maybe next weekend?"

"Could I come too?" Hannah added.

"Of course," I said. Though I was unsure about Hannah, she did seem like a perfectly nice person. She appeared to be sweet, Max's family liked her, and there was no awkwardness between her and Max. So maybe I was making something out of nothing. With her living here, I'd have to get to know her whether or not I wanted to get to know her.

"Hannah. Tell me what brought you back to California."

"Oh Max, it's a bit of a long story, but to make it short, I lost my job, my parents are going through an ugly divorce, and I happened to email your mom about a job at her company, and she graciously invited me to live here. I'm sorry that I've taken over your old room. I hope that's okay," she treaded cautiously.

"That's fine." Max didn't sound like that was fine. By the surprised look on his face, I could tell Max had no idea his room was given away. It wasn't very kind of his parents to do this without his knowledge and to take away Max's place in his home. Max wasn't showing any outward signs of hurt, but I could feel it.

"Well, we thought that we owed it to Hannah," his mom answered cryptically.

"Oh Mom. You don't owe me anything. I'm so grateful you've allowed me to stay here rent-free while I try and figure out my life. And it's wonderful to reconnect with Max, Garret and Josh."

"Hannah, we owe you more than a roof over your head." Max's dad finally spoke.

Max and Hannah were both looking uncomfortable. *Gawd...will someone explain to me what's going on?*

"We should never have disapproved of your plans to get married," Mrs. Davis said calmly, while I was about to jump out of my seat.

Marriage???

"MOM!" Max raised his voice in anger.

Max's mom could care less. She gave her son a not very kind look and continued, "Your father and I blame ourselves for the loss of the baby."

BABY??? What BABY??? Why won't anyone tell me what's going on?!?

"If we hadn't been so adamant about you finishing high school before getting married, Hannah might not have miscarried your baby. We've always thought that our censure and criticism of you getting Hannah pregnant caused her undue pressure and stress. You two could've married right away and made a lovely family by now."

"DAMMIT MOM!" Max roared. "Is this really necessary?"

I don't know what happened from here because everything kinda went dark...

Indelible Lovin'
Max & Jane's Story
d. w. cee

March 21, 2013

Fuck! Did That Just Happen?

"**A**re you sure you're feeling all right? I don't need to take you to the hospital?" Max asked, very concerned for my welfare.

"No. You checked me over. I'll have Jake check me over. I'll even go see Uncle Henry if necessary. You can just drop me off now." I opened the door, trying to escape without talking about anything. I pretended to still feel faint during the drive home after the dinner from hell.

"Jane." Max grabbed my arm. "Hear me out. Let me explain. I don't want you going dark on me again."

I paused for a while, and just stared off into space.

"I got the gist of what happened between you and Hannah, thanks to your mother. Give me time to process, evaluate, accept...and whatever else I need to do. I promise I won't go dark, but I probably won't call you or answer your calls for a few days."

"I'm sorry, Jane. I'm sorry how that all came out. I'm sorry my mother acted so cruelly. And I'm sorry I'm always disappointing you."

That last sentence broke my heart. "I don't think I'm disappointed in you because of what happened in high school. I'm upset because... Max, I need to gather my thoughts and think through what happened tonight. I don't want to say anything that will hurt you even more than you are hurting already. I'm sorry I can't be here for you right now when you're struggling, but I need to take care of myself first."

Was that selfish of me to want to nurse my confused heart, first? Max's face truly broke my heart. I could feel the tears wanting to form, but I wasn't going to give in to them.

"All right." He said in a defeated and somewhat angry voice. "Call me when you're ready to talk."

His body turned back to the steering wheel and it was as though he was dismissing me. How dare he dismiss me? That pissed me off so badly, I slammed the door and didn't look back. By the sound of the car peeling out of our cul-de-sac, I wouldn't have had time to even look back. *Jerk!*

I walked straight to my brother and sister's house to get some answers.

"Is it too late to come knocking?" I was an uninvited, unwelcomed intruder in my brother's opinion, from the moment he let me in.

"Yes," Jake answered. "We were in the middle of a movie."

"Jake," Emily warned. "How'd it go tonight?" She patted her hand on a cushion telling me to sit next to her on the gigantic sofa. I chose to sit in an armchair across from them.

"Emily, do you know who Hannah is?"

Emily shook her head, no.

"Max dated her in high school?"

Emily still shook her head, no. "Max never told me about a Hannah. I just know about Jennifer, the girl he dated after me."

I relayed the Davis family story hour and Emily's eyes bugged out with each layer of drama.

"You need me to check you over? I can't believe you fainted." I actually shocked my brother.

"Me neither, but I feel fine right now, I think. It was a good thing Garret was right next to me when I did my head plop. I've never fainted before. From what Max told me, I was only out for like a minute. Once I woke up, Max did a thorough check-up and drove me home."

"Did you ask Max about him and Hannah?"

I shook my head no to Emily, and just sat there for a few minutes.

"I'm not upset about Max getting Hannah pregnant. It was stupid but whatever.... What upsets me is that we talked about Hannah and their relationship on Friday, at the rehearsal tea. Max didn't want to talk about it, but I forced some information out of him and not once did he hint at the fact that Hannah was a huge part of his life. That's what upsets me. He lied to me."

"Jane, I don't think he lied to you. It's not easy to tell anyone, especially your girlfriend, that you knocked up a girl in high school." My brother was actually defending Max. That was a change.

"What else would you call someone who doesn't tell you something that important?"

"How long have you two been dating?"

"Three months."

"And have you told him everything about your past?"

"What's there to tell? If there's anything important, I have no issues telling him." I didn't know why Jake was picking on me. I wasn't the one who knocked up a former girlfriend and didn't tell his current girlfriend about it.

"So you've told him about the loser that you practically lived with in law school?" Jake challenged me. "That same one whose ass I had to kick to the curb when we figured out that he was stealing from you?"

"That's hardly the same level of secrecy. Plus, I wasn't trying to keep that a secret. It just never came up."

Jake was doing the quirking of the eyebrows. "And you told him about the other loser you dated in undergrad? The one you almost got married to in Vegas, but came to your senses at the last minute? That one too...not the same level of secrecy?" He imitated my voice.

Now my brother was just irritating me. This wasn't about me. It was about the fact that Max purposely kept Hannah from me even though she was back in his life. He should have chosen to tell me all about his past.

"NO! It's not the same as not telling me about a baby."

"Don't be a frickin' hypocrite. I know Max wasn't your first. You could've ended up pregnant just like Hannah. You just happen to have been more careful, or maybe just damn luckier. Give the guy a break. He's got a bitchy mother, an almost mother-of-his-child ex

248

who jumps back into his life, and a girlfriend who won't give him any peace. Give it a rest, Jane!"

I just stared at him, dumbfounded. How did I go from indignant to admonished all within a few minutes?

Emily tried to soften Jake's blow by adding, "Max was such a lost and private person when I met him in college. He rarely talked about his parents, though he adored his brothers, and he didn't go home unless he had to go home. I was always happy to have him with me, and a part of me thought he stayed around for my sake, but deep inside I knew something was terribly wrong with his family life. The few times I spent the holidays with the Davis family, I thought I'd go bonkers with all the tension between Max and his parents. If it weren't for Garret and Josh, I don't think I could've withstood those holidays."

"I hate the fact that you were alone for so long, Emi." There goes my brother. One minute he's berating me, and the next he's waxing poetic about his wife, when his sister was the one alone right now. *Hey brother! How about some love for your only sister?*

"I wasn't alone. I had Max and Sarah and Charlie. They were my friends and family till I got my chance with the illustrious Dr. Jake Reid," she laughed.

Even in the midst of my pain, Jake and Emily were...being Jake and Emily. I had to laugh and roll my eyes at them.

"Ahem...hello! My issues...not your past issues, please!"

"Sorry." Emily pushed herself away from my brother's embrace. "Max hides a lot of pain in his heart, and he'll keep it hidden away till he's confronted and has to fess up. But, he loves sacrificially and unconditionally. You must know this by now, Jane. Look at how he broke up with me. Of course he didn't tell me at the time why he broke up with me, but he did it to send me off to a better life. He was so lost in undergrad that he didn't want me to wander through life with him, searching for his meaning in life. He thought I'd suffered enough with the loss of my parents. If it hadn't been for his sacrificial love, I would've never met your brother."

"Max sacrificed for you, but I don't see that same kind of love for me."

"Really Jane? Come on. Do you not see how patient he is with you? Do you really not see how much he's trying to make your relationship work? Do you think he likes seeing you waver between him and Donovan?"

"How'd you know about that?" *Are there any secrets around here?*

"I see the way you look at him. And I, too, admit...he's a handsome man—especially when he dresses up, like he did for Gram and Roland's wedding." I could see Jake's body stiffen. "Max sees it too."

"If he sees it, does that mean he doesn't care enough to confront me, he doesn't have the balls to confront me, or he just figures let life fall where it may?"

"He's never confronted you?" Emily questioned.

"Okay, he has confronted me a few times...I guess I keep breaking my promises to him." I confessed. "It's not like anything happened with me and Donovan."

"I think Max loves you, despite your faults and if you told him you wanted to go to Donovan, he'd probably let you go if he thought Donovan could love you more and give you what you needed, better than what Max could give you. This unconditional love that he has for you is not a weakness. I think it's his strength."

"Listen to Emily, Jane. She makes sense and if anyone knows what's going on in Max's head, it's probably your sister—though it doesn't thrill me that she knows another man so well." He turned his wife's body towards him to address his next beef. "What did you say about my best friend? You find him *attractive*???" Jake emphasized the last word in horror. "I'm gonna go kick his ass the next time I see him dressed up."

"Perhaps you should go shopping with him," Emily teased. "That outfit he wore to Gram's wedding was pretty hot."

"Damn it! Don't ever look at him again, Emi."

Emily placed her hand on Jake's cheek and gave him an adored look.

My brother and sister gave me a lot to think about and everything they said made sense. The last look on Max's face still haunted me, and it was wrong of me to leave Max to nurse my own pain, when his mother had purposely hurt him so viciously. It was late, but the call was overdue.

"Hi," I cautiously said when Max picked up his phone.

"Hey." He sounded cooler than I would've liked.

"Can we talk? I'd like to talk tonight if that's all right with you."

"I can't tonight."

What?

"Why not? You just left here saying you wanted to talk to me, and that you didn't want me to go dark on you."

"Yeah, but I'm busy right now."

I had a sinking feeling I wasn't going to like the answer to the question I was about to ask.

"What are you doing that makes you so busy at midnight?"

"I'm with Hannah right now."

Shit! Shit, shit, shit! I calmed myself down before uttering another word.

"That's where you went after you dropped me off?"

"Jane." Now *he* had the gall to sound exasperated. "You didn't want to talk to me." He stated simply. "I tried to explain my side of the story, but you told me you needed to take care of yourself first." The asshole was using my words against me. "I'm letting you take care of yourself, *first*. I'm here with someone who's willing to share in my pain. As you said earlier to me, 'I won't go dark on you but, I probably won't call you or answer your calls for a few days.' I'll be in touch later." He hung up.

SHIT!

March 25, 2013

Aaargh!!!

$\mathcal{M}$ ax, the jerk, did not call me or answer my calls for the last few days, as he threatened. Sometimes I hated myself for saying things that came back to haunt me. I was a ball of nervous energy since my last conversation with my boyfriend, if he was still that. I finished all the documents that needed to be finished before my psycho boss asked for them, I cleaned out my cubicle of an office, and I even went home and cleaned out my entire room. I also started looking in the papers for a place to live. I was twenty-seven and living at home. Enough was enough. It was time to fly the coop.

"Any word from Max?" Emily asked when I went over to her house after work.

"No," I answered while helping her seat Ellie and James in their bath chairs.

The twins were seated in this contraption that looked like a low-seated chair that suctioned into the farmhouse sink in the kitchen.

"I have to do it this way because of my burgeoning belly," Emily explained as she turned on the space heater, created a gigantic bubble bath in the oversized porcelain sink, then proceeded to strip each child and place them in their seats.

"Which seat belongs to which child?"

"James always likes to be on the left side, closer to the door and Ellie prefers the right seat."

Weird!

"Dadadadada..." James called out calmly as he saw my brother's car fill into the driveway. Ellie didn't catch on till Jake actually walked through the door.

"DA!" She screamed.

"Does this girl have only one decibel?"

"Hello my precious babies!" Jake called out, kissing and blowing raspberries on each child. The twins were in heaven.

Ellie kept calling out "Mmmmm."

"What's she saying?" I wondered.

"I think that's her way of asking for more." Emily told the both of us.

"You want more?" The babies giggled and hollered with glee, as Jake kept kissing and blowing raspberries all over their bodies.

"Are you home for good tonight?" Emily asked her husband when he finally got around to kissing his wife.
"No. I only came home to put the kids to sleep since I didn't see them this morning, and then I've got to go back out," he answered Emily then turned his attention to me. "What are you doing here little sister?"

"I'm just trying to fill time; I came by to see my niece and nephew; and I came by to hang out with Emily."

"Why don't you go to the hospital with me after this is done? Max gets off in a couple of hours."

"I think I'll just wait till he calls me," I answered sadly.

"Be ready to leave in 20 minutes. The twins go down pretty quickly after their bath," Jake commanded.

Jake gave me lots of brotherly advice during the short ride from home to the hospital. I was more nervous than I thought I would be about facing Max.

"He's up on the fifth floor in pediatrics. Go make up with him. Apologize and tell him that it was wrong of you to leave him the way you did. Trust me when I say this is the man for you, Jane."

"All right," I answered reluctantly.

I walked along the hallway of the fifth floor and headed towards the student lounge area. That was where I was told I could find Max.

"Jane, what a nice surprise!" Psycho greeted.

"Hello Joyce," I answered politely.

"How are you?"

"Well, and you?"

"I'm super!" *This woman was so mental!* "I assume you're here for Max?"

"Yes." *I'm definitely not here to have a conversation with you!*

"He's been in the lounge area with a friend from Michigan for the past half hour."

Crap! She was here. What is she doing here? I didn't have a very good feeling about what was going on between Max and Hannah.

"The lounge is over there," she said as she pointed down the corridor.

"Thanks..."

When I got to the door, I was afraid to open it. What if they were in some compromising position? What if he had been leaning upon her the past few days rather than calling me? Aargh!!!!

I opened the door to find Max and Hannah seated next to each other, but in a perfectly acceptable situation.

"Jane." Max looked surprised to see me. "What are you doing here?"

What the hell do you think I'm doing here? No, I did not say that. I was good and I just gave them a nice smile.

"I was hoping to talk to you?"

"I'll leave you two alone," Hannah said, and got up very quickly. "I'm very sorry about the other night Jane. It shouldn't have come out the way it did. I hope you're not too angry with me or Max."

I didn't answer her, but I gave her a nice smile as well.

"I'll see you later?" Hannah gave Max an affectionate touch on the arm.

"Sure. I'll see you soon. Don't worry, Hannah. Josh, Garret and I will help you bring back all of your stuff."

"All right..." she looked at him one more time before heading out the door.

Max stared at me expectantly and waited for me to start.

"Hi." I said softly.

"Hi." He answered back, with very little enthusiasm.

"Are you done with rounds? Can you talk?" He nodded his head, but didn't speak. "Do you want to talk?" I actually stood in fear of his answer.

"I don't know Jane. I don't know if I'm done taking care of myself first."

Fine, Jerk! Go ahead and hold a grudge. I felt my freakin' nose tingle, my stomach did a little unhappy flip and the tears were forming behind my eyeballs. I quickly turned around. I wasn't going to let him see me cry over him. I ran to the door and pulled it open as quickly as humanly possible.

"Get back here!" He grabbed me around the waist and pulled me into him.

I struggled and pushed him away. If he didn't want me, I didn't want him either. I was no crying missy waiting for her man to come back to her. I'd walk away first before I let him walk away from me.

"Do I actually see tears in your eyes?" Max started with a small chuckle, but soon grew into a guffaw. "Are you crying over *me*?" He severely exaggerated the *me* part, while putting his hands over his heart. That gesture gave me the chance I needed to get the hell out of here. "I told you to get back over here, Jane! You leave this room, I'm not coming after you. Our relationship, as we know it, will be over!" Was that a freakin' threat? Unbelievable...but, kinda hot! (What was wrong with me? In this uber piss-me-off situation, I still got hot and bothered by Max barking out threats. Loser—that's what I was!) Back to being mad—who the hell did this guy think he was, ordering me around? So what if he held the title, *"Boyfriend."* No boyfriend treats his girlfriend the way he treated me just now.

I pulled the door open but wavered. Do I go...? Or do I stay...?

March 28, 2013

Dem Bones

"Are you staying?" Max taunted.

"No, Asshole. I'm not!" I yelled and opened the door, only to be bounced back into the room by my brother Nick.

"Sister! I can hear your damn voice all through the hallway. The kiddie patients are ringing in their complaints to the nurses' station as we speak."

"Shut up Nick, and get out of my way."

I tried to push him away, but Nick grabbed me, turned me around and pushed me over to Max. Max then turned me around and pushed me back to Nick. They might as well have been singing, *red rover, red rover, send Janey on over.*

At this point, not only was I seeing *RED*, but I was also incredibly hurt that Max shooed me away. "Stop! I get it. You don't want to have anything to do with me. You didn't have to push me away like that..." The tears fell and I ran to the door.

"Come back here," Max grabbed me and hugged me before I could get out. "God only knows why I love you so much when you drive me nuts 95% of the time. I love you sweet Jane and I'm sorry I made you cry. Your brother and I were having a little fun. I wasn't pushing you away."

"Ah Janey, did we hurt your girly feelings?" Nick walked over and sandwiched me from behind. "We're sowry," he said in a three-year-old voice.

"Shut up Nick, and get off me. I don't want your hug." I tried to shrug him off. He only held on tighter and laughed.

"Enough drama. Let's go eat." Nick pulled away, but Max kept his arms tightly around me. "Geez, Max! What do you keep doing wrong? My sister's been royally pissed with you twice in one month. Tread lightly or you may get the ax." Nick whispered the word "ax" while motioning his right hand across his neck.

Max and I cracked up.

"Have you had dinner?" Max asked, while kissing me by the ear.

I shook my head no. "I was going to have dinner at Emily's, but Jake brought me over here before I could eat anything. We should probably see if Jake wants to come as well. He hasn't eaten either."

"Nick, can you make yourself disappear for ten minutes? Go find Jake and ask him to have dinner with us."

"That's *all* you need? ten minutes? You're giving us men a bad name, Davis," he said jokingly as he walked out.

Even though Max started the apology, I decided to get this guilty conscience off my mind, first. "I am truly sorry about Sunday night. I was in such shock. I feel *really bad* that I left you to deal with your mom by yourself. I should've been there for you." There. It was done.

"Really bad?" He mimicked my words while kissing my lips, Max-style, with both hands on my face. "How *badly* do you feel?" This tone was doing things for me now. We'd stepped beyond what was proper in a public staff lounge.

"Very bad," I joined in the banter. "I've been a *really* bad girl..." Oh, let the fun begin!

He backed up against the door for assured privacy, or at least a chance to stop what we were doing before anyone could completely open the door.

"You're going to have to be punished." *Damn! Did he seriously say that?* "Come here and kneel." *Hot damn!! He did seriously say that.*

"Yes Sir," I answered submissively, but smiled wickedly.

Less than ten minutes later, "Jane...what the hell?" Max barked, as I left the room for him to deal with his not so happy ending. You didn't think after all those days of making me wonder what the hell was going on between him and Hannah, that I'd simply *kneel* back into his life, do his *bidding,* and all would be hunky-dory, did you? We're on the right track, but there needed to be a little pay back, Jane Sydney Reid-style!

"What are you cackling about?" Nick asked, trying to open the door to the lounge.

"I wouldn't go in there if I were you," I warned. "Let's go to the restaurant." I curved my arms around both Nick and Jake's arms and pulled them toward the cars.

"What about Max?"

"Don't worry, Nick. I'll text him the location of where we're going."

With a strawberry margarita in hand, I laughed with my brothers as I told them how James was trying to feed himself a pea tonight, but ended up shoving it up his nose instead.

"We should have invited Emily, tonight. Shall I call her and see if she can come out?"

"I doubt it, Nick. She's been dog tired these days since James started walking. Now she's chasing after a baby, while carrying one in her arms, and another in her stomach. It's been tough on her. In fact, I feel guilty being out with you guys, tonight." My brother so loved his wife. "There's Davis over there," Jake pointed.

"Hey," everyone called out to one another.

"Hello, Jane." Max said coolly, with a hint of a threat.

"Hello, Max." I answered back with laughter in my voice. "Everything, okay?"

"No!" he whispered, curtly.

I whispered back, "You seem grumpy. Couldn't you finish on your own?"

"Why should I when I have a girlfriend who'll finish me off?" He added suggestively but resolutely.

"Am I still your girlfriend? Last I checked, there was another girl sitting by your side." I questioned his beliefs.

"You two gonna whisper to one another the whole night?" Nick pretended to be annoyed with us. He could be such a pain in my ass at times.

"Later." The sound of his voice and the look on his face was definitely contrite and penitent.

After an enjoyable dinner, the four of us headed back to my house. Jake came in briefly to say hello to Gram and our new Gramps, who were back from their mini-honeymoon in Carmel. But he soon went off to his own family. Max, Nick and I sat with the elderly folks and enjoyed talking to them.

"Where will you set up house, Gram?" Nick asked.

"I think we'll stay here till Roland and I decide where we will live."

"What do you mean? You're not living in LA?" I asked, shocked that they'd even consider living away from us.

"Roland still has to show his presence in London since his home office is there. I don't know. We shall see, Janey." She then turned to Max, "Will you be spending the night, Monsieur Le Duc?"

"No, Gram. Jane and I need to discuss a few things, and then I'll be gone. I'll see you again, soon?"

We said our goodnights to everyone and Max and I went into my room.

"Shall we talk?" We sat on the chairs because we knew the bed wouldn't be the best place for a talk.

"Sure."

"Let me go first?"

I nodded yes.

"I've told you about my parents and how I felt that they never loved me enough. Hannah came from the opposite where she grew up in an overprotective home. Her parents hovered, helicoptered, and got in her nose about everything. We were both ripe for rebellion."

Max pulled me onto his lap and continued his story.

"We were young, we thought we were in love and we were definitely stupid. We started having sex on my seventeenth birthday, but didn't protect ourselves every time. We thought it wouldn't happen to us, and a few months into being sexually active, Hannah got pregnant. I was scared shitless. We tried to hide it from her parents, but she got so sick every morning, her parents figured out what was wrong and demanded we get married immediately."

"Oh Max..." I felt so scared and sorry for him.

"My parents refused to allow me to get married at seventeen, Hannah's parents practically forced us to the altar, and somewhere during that time, Hannah miscarried. What my mom said was true. She, my dad, and Hannah's parents overwhelmed us—especially Hannah—and she lost the baby."

Max stayed silent for a long while. I just sat and held him.

"I was so relieved; I didn't have time to be sad that a baby died. I didn't think of the baby as our baby. I just thought of it as a nuisance and a halt to my future. But Hannah thought exactly the opposite of what I thought. She looked at me and the baby as her future, and she went through a bout of depression when she lost the baby. I tried to comfort her, but in all honesty, I was too relieved to empathize or sympathize. Shitty of me, huh?" He asked quietly.

"Max, you were seventeen. Who wants to be tied down at that age? What you felt was normal. I would've felt the same if that had happened to me. You can't blame yourself for being honest."

"I blame myself for pulling away from Hannah when she needed me most. After she lost the baby, I tried not to be, but I was a bastard, and I shirked away from my responsibility as her boyfriend. Her parents saw my actions as a blessing in disguise and they uprooted their family to Michigan. That's how it really ended for us."

"Poor Hannah."

"Baby...please don't be upset with Hannah. She's a sweet girl, and she's down on her luck right now. I'd like for you to be friends with her, if you can, and treat her like a sister or a cousin. You'll like her."

Just what I needed...another one of Max's ex as a sister...GROAN!

"I was really lost when I got to undergrad. I think the pregnancy scare along with my parents' severe disapproval from that point on, sent me into a senseless rebellion. If it wasn't for Emily, I would've been a serious lost cause."

"Is that how you stayed a 'virgin' with her for four years? I always wondered about that fact."

"Yeah. My brothers called me a born-again virgin." We both laughed. "As much as I wanted to further our physical relationship, I was relieved more than anything when she told me she wasn't going to have sex with me."

I gave him a skeptical look. "You mean to tell me you never tried to get Emily in bed with you?"

"Well, I didn't say that...in any case, let's not talk about a woman who's your sister, a mother of three, and Jake's wife. If he had any inkling of this conversation, I'd probably end up hospitalized." That brought out another round of laughter. "I woke up and grew up after I let Emily go. That reality check was like an ice bucket to my face. It was then that I decided to go to med school, study pediatrics, and help kids who didn't have any help. I guess this is my way of apologizing to, and paying penance toward my unborn and unwanted child."

"Okay, I understand and accept what happened to you in high school, but what was the deal with you going straight to Hannah after you dropped me off here on Sunday?"

Max's snickering did not sit well with me. I stood up from his lap, only to be pulled back into his body.

"Sorry. I was being a bit of an asshole to you that night. You turning away from me that night hurt, so I wasn't exactly truthful about why I went to go see Hannah."

"Oh..." Guilty feelings got to me again and I hid my face in his chest.

"It's all right, Babe. I understand why you ran out of my car as quickly as you could. I wasn't honest with you from the start, the atomic bomb my mom dropped on you was beyond acceptable, and you just needed time to process all the information that was handed to you in one night. Once I cooled down from being pissed at my mom, I saw the light and understood why you did what you did." He put his arms around me and held me tight, showering kisses upon my head.

"And Hannah?"

His chuckling reverberated from the bottom of his chin to the top of my head. "Of course...Hannah. My green-eyed monster wouldn't be my gem if she wasn't most curious about another woman. I went to see Hannah..."

He stopped and made me wait...made me super nervous.

"Hannah...!" I got impatient.

"I went to see Hannah for several reasons. I wanted to make sure she was okay after what happened at the dinner table. She was probably just as surprised as the rest of us. Once she told me that she was all right, I proceeded to clear the air with her about her and me, and about you and me."

I stared at Max expectantly.

"As for her and me, I explained that there was no her and me. We ended back in high school. I didn't rehash the past, but I did explain about my future." He paused again. I think he was doing this for effect. *Asshole!* He knew I was pissed again. He laughed briefly, then stole a kiss from an unwilling me.

"I told Hannah that you are the reason I smile these days, laugh these days, argue these days, want to tear my hair out these days, and want to lock myself in a tug-of-war in bed with you these days."

"You did *not* say that last part, did you?"

"No," he chuckled. "Just because I didn't say it, doesn't mean I don't mean it."

"In so many words, I told her that you are my *everything* these days."

"Your *everything*, with whom you can go days without resolving these issues?"

"My *everything*, with whom I was embarrassed to have to explain about my dysfunctional family. Your family is ideal. How could you possibly make sense of mine? That's why I stayed away. If you want to know about my mom and dad, I'll tell you, but it's not pretty, and it's not something I enjoy explaining."

"We don't have to talk about your parents if you don't like talking about them. After Sunday, I can see why they've never been a topic of conversation. But...this *everything* wants to know why you threatened to let her go, back at the hospital."

"You couldn't just be happy with me telling you that you were my everything, could you? You had to bring up my threat. A threat that I wouldn't have been able to keep because there was no way I was going to let you go, my precious gem. Do you still not understand what you mean to me?"

"Everything?" I questioned, still uncertain.

"EVERYTHING!" He answered without hesitation.

"So we're all good?" I still questioned.

"We're all good. That's my life in a nutshell. I promise, no more surprises from the past. The entire skeleton is out."

I finally got *everything* from him, I think...

April 1, 2013

Flashback

I'm about to get on the plane, but I wanted to text one last time and say goodbye. I'll miss you.

I'll miss you too, my precious gem. Don't work too hard.

Like there's a chance of that NOT happening. Once again, I'm the least senior member of this legal team. All the grunt work will fall on me.

Baby, I gotta go. Everyone's waiting for me. I love you. Have a safe trip.

Wait!

Yeah?

Is...I mean...will Hannah be riding on the Harley with you...?

Maybe...

If you love me, you will NOT have any other girl riding on the back seat of that bike. YOU UNDERSTAND ME MAX DAVIS?!?

We'll see…

JERK!

Once again, I love you. See you in a week.

"Time to board," Donovan called out. "Put away your phone and turn that frown upside down. We're going to paradise. Why in five hours, you'll be sipping cocktails and sitting on the beach."

"No, *you'll* be sipping cocktails, and *I'll* be writing up documents!"

"Sucks to be an associate…" Donovan chuckled his way onto the plane.

Within the course of two days, I went from working late on a Saturday with Andrea and all the other associates from our department, to a Monday business trip with Donovan and Kate. Kate is now fully on board with our law firm and though she's technically not a partner, she has higher ranking than most members of our firm—not to mention the awe and respect of everyone. From the moment she stepped into the office, she brought in a huge hedge fund client who wanted to invest in, and merge a biochemical and pharmaceutical company from Taiwan. Because of the long flight for either party to visit one another in their respective countries, Hawaii was chosen as the midpoint. And, since there was some pharmaceutical trademarking involved, and because I was Gimpy's favorite (step) grandchild, I was chosen to go on this trip with Donovan and Kate.

Oh…and did I mention? Practically my entire hood is coming with us.

"Aw, come on!" I complained when I saw Jake, Emily, Kate and Donovan turn left upon boarding the plane, while Laney, Doug,

Nick, and I were herded to the right of the plane. "That's not fair. I can't believe the firm put us in different classes."

"Sucks to be an associate!" Donovan called out again, while sipping his mimosa at 8:00am.

"Hope you choke on your champagne!" I yelled back. There was laughter that ensued from the four fortunate ones up front. The rest of us put our carry-ons away and sat in our seats.

How, you ask, did the five other Reids end up on this trip with us? Well, sit back, think wavy screen on a television set and...flashback.

"Emi, we need a vacation—just the two of us—before the baby arrives in August," Jake lamented.

"We just had a vacation in New York. We don't need to go away again. And plus, I can't go anywhere without my babies. What will they do without me? Shoot...what will I do without them?" She giggled.

"How about you will spend time with your husband and your husband only. We don't have to go far—just far away enough where if I want your attention, I don't have to pass it by two mini despots before having you to myself."

"I don't know, Honey. I just weaned them. I don't want them to think I'm abandoning them as well."

"EMILY! I beg of you...a few nights away and a few mornings of sleeping in."

"Only a few nights? And not too far away?" She pleaded.

"Only a few nights and not too far away..." he agreed.

"All right. Let me go talk to Mom and see if she can watch the kids."

Emily took both kids up to their room to start the whole bedtime routine. I offered to help but she said she needed to take care of the first part (whatever that was) and she'd call me when she was ready for me. Whatever...

"Too bad you can't join me in Hawaii. Donovan, Kate, and I are going there on a business trip all next week."

Next thing I knew, Jake whipped out his phone and called his best friend. All I heard was a bunch of uh-huhs after he asked Donovan for our itinerary. Then he went online and booked himself and Emily two seats on our flight and a room in our hotel.

"I thought Emily said close by," I reminded him.

"It's only a five-hour flight." Jake shrugged.

"It's thousands of miles away," my voice got a bit louder, aggravated for Emily.

"Little sister...close is a relative word. It's not like we're going to Australia."

"Whatever...I'm going up to give your wife the good news."

"You do that. And while you're at it, tell her I'm going back to work till it's time for us to board the plane," he chuckled.

"Hey Jane. Scoot over. Let me have the aisle seat." Nick held up the flow of traffic.

"Nick, you scoot in. I hate being squished."

"But I have longer legs than you. You scoot in!"

"Nick, why don't you take my seat and I'll sit next to Jane? I don't mind the window seat," Laney smiled and got up from behind us.

Nick and Doug were acting like buffoons, excited to be doing something during their spring break, rather than helping Mom and Dad watch the kids. Of course, we all loved the little buggers, and of course, there will be plenty of attention given to them between the grandparents, great-grandparents, and all the grandaunts and uncles popping in throughout the week. But, in all honesty, would you rather be in Hawaii or babysitting your niece and nephew? Yep, I thought so!

"This is going to be so much fun. Did you check out where we're staying? I looked it up online. It looks badass! I don't think I've stayed at any place as nice as the one we're staying at, on the Big Island." Doug sounded like such a moron sometimes.

"And to think...it's all FREE!" Nick joined in on the meeting of the morons as they high-fived each other more than once, practically howling at the moon.

How, you ask, did these buffoons end up on this trip with us and *HOW*, you ask, are they staying in the most luxurious resort for free? Again, flashback...

"Jake! You seriously booked us a flight to Hawaii???" Emily was not a happy camper.

"You'll wake up the babies, Love. Don't yell," Jake tried to coax her from her ire, but it wasn't working.

"You promised no place far and you promised only for a few days! And we've already been to Hawaii. Why do we need to go back there? Can you cancel and get your money back?"

"It's only a five-hour flight," he said, pulling Emily into his arms, "it's only for a week," he started kissing her face, "and we've been to Maui, not the Big Island." He kept kissing her till she melted a little. These two were iconic lovers! "Plus, everything is booked, paid for, and no, we cannot get a refund. I know you don't want thousands of dollars going down the drain, my thrifty wife." Jake kinda chuckled as he knew he'd won this argument.

At this point, the two buffoons I had mentioned earlier, came over to share in the chocolate cream pie Emily made—we all did that from time to time, bummed off their food—and asked, "what's booked and paid for with no refunds?" Nick took a finger-lick of the pie before it was sliced.

"Emily and Jake are joining me, Donovan and Kate on the Big Island. They will be vacationing without the kids, while the rest of us work."

"That's so cool! I wish I could go somewhere this spring break." Doug sounded bummed. "Maybe Nick and I can go hang with Sam in San Diego for a few days."

At that unfortunate moment, Donovan called the house phone for some reason and Jake put him on speaker.

"Donovan, you're on the house speakerphone, and Emi, Jane, Doug and Nick are here. What's up?"

"What up Reids? You all enjoying Emily's cooking again? Emily, how come I never get an invite?"

"I always tell my husband to invite you. I guess your invite got lost in the email?!?"

"That's a dogged way of treating your children's godfather."

"Oh...do our children have a godfather, Jake? I haven't seen him with the kids since the birthing room, I think." Emily laughed silently.

"Okay, Mrs. Reid. I promise to come by and play with my godchildren and impart as much of my knowledge as possible."

"Well, thank you, Donovan. That should give me all of ten minutes? twenty minutes of freedom while you impart all your knowledge?"

We all started choking on our pie.

"You wound me, Madame." Donovan laughed with us. "Hey, Jake. You booked everything already?"

"Yep! Signed, sealed and delivered via email."

"There's going to be an extra room at the hotel. Why don't you cancel your room and take mine? Our clients are paying for it, but it'll be unused."

"I've already booked our room with points. I don't think I can change it now."

"Can we take the room?" Doug asked, while Nick nodded his head like a bobble-head.

"Sure. The more Reids the merrier. You boys can have my room as long as you can get yourself a plane ride over to the island."

His room? Where the hell was he going to stay? Like I really needed to ask. Whatever...

"Laney," Sea-foam called out in her classy British accent, "I have a bit of a change in plans and I need to catch another flight. Why don't you take my seat up in first class?"

What? Why her??? Laney wasn't even supposed to be here!

"Where are you going, Kate?" Laney asked.

"I have an emergency meeting right now, so I'll catch a later flight. I just got the memo."

"Does that mean Donovan is leaving too?" Nick presumed there'd be another empty seat.

"No, Nick. He's staying. Sorry." Sea-foam smiled at all of us, but motioned for Laney to get up and get her bag.

"Thank you, but that's all right. I'll stay back here with my cousins."

"When I got the call, you were the one unanimously selected to join the elitists up in first class," she smiled. Geez Louise, this woman even had a sense of humor. Is there anything she couldn't do?

"That was nice of Jake and Emily but I don't think..."

Kate didn't let her finish the sentence. She grabbed Laney's bag and started walking back up to the front of the plane. Laney shrugged her shoulders and followed.

Since today's theme is #fbf (that's flashback Friday for those of you who don't Instagram), I might as well finish explaining how Laney ended up on this trip as well.

"What about Laney?" Emily asked.

Emily always asked about Laney. Why??? Who knows!!! It was like she was her guardian angel or something. Next thing you knew, Emily would ask if Laney could room with me...ugh! Emily turned my way as though she knew what I was thinking.

"Since Jane will be working," Emily said to the boys, "maybe Laney can room with you two?" She asked, but it was more like a command. "It would be sad if we were all in Hawaii and she was here alone during spring break. Doug, will you buy her a ticket?"

"Heck no! She has more money than I do. She makes good money editing college papers. I'm a poor MBA student."

"Oh, quit your whining!" Laney walked in and slapped her brother in the arm. "I don't need you to buy me anything. I'll buy my own ticket." She harped at her brother then quickly asked, "Emily, what am I buying tickets to...a show? The movies?"

"Hawaii!" We all called out in unison.

And that's how these three goons ended up on this business trip with me, and now this brat of a cousin of mine was about to sit up in first class with the other three brats.

"By the way, why's Max going to Arizona today?" Nick interrupted my woe-is-me thought.

"He's helping his high school friend move her stuff from Arizona to his parents' home."

Nick and Doug gave me a quizzical look, so I explained about Hannah, minus the whole prego stuff. When Hannah moved from her home in Michigan, I was told she went to a friend's in Arizona, first, and then ended up in LA, soon afterwards. Hannah left most of her belongings in Arizona so Max, being a good friend—*aargh!*—offered to help her move everything here. And that's why I was dreading Max and Hannah on the Harley. They were supposed to spend a whole week together. Luckily, Garret and Josh were tagging along to help with the move. On a brighter note, Max was very happy to be able to spend some time with his brothers.

By now, you all must know me well enough to know that I was *NOT* the type of girl to allow her boyfriend to spend a week with another girl—especially not an ex-girlfriend who almost had his child! So...I did a little scheming of my own.

"I'm going to have Laney move into my room as of Wednesday and I need you guys to accommodate a few more guests."

"Why, who's coming?"

"I used up all my miles, and bought tickets for Max and his brothers to join us in Hawaii."

"I thought it was a little odd that you were so calm about Max spending a week with his ex," Nick chuckled. "Brilliant, Jane!"

"Devious, Jane!" Doug chuckled, too. "It'll be cool to meet Max's brothers. What do we care who else bunks with us? It's not like we're paying for the room. One generous turn deserves another."

"Max didn't mention coming to Hawaii when I talked to him last night."

"No, Nick. He has no idea." Now, it was my turn to chuckle. "I worked it all out with his brothers."

"You guys have no objections to going back and forth from LA to Phoenix in a rush?"

"Hell no!" Josh answered with a grin. "You can take us to work with you any day, Jane."

"Just make sure Max has no idea what's going on. I wish you could video tape the look on his face when you take him to the airport.

He'll be so shocked! And also, you guys will be a bit squished with my brother and cousin in the room. I hope that's not a problem."

"Jane. You worry too much."

"I just want everything to be perfect, Garret."

"Leave it to us, Jane. We'll take care of everything...!"

"Remind me never to underestimate you, Sis." Nick was either scared of me or proud of me. I wasn't sure which way he was leaning. Then he added, "Wicked, Jane. Wicked!"

Yep! I thought so too. You all didn't think I'd let Max have a week of quality time with Hannah now, did you? What do you think this is... April Fools?

April 4, 2013

Aloha from the Big Island

I finally understood the importance of being a VIP. When we landed at the tiny lavarock-filled airport, there were two cars waiting for us from the hotel. One had my brother and Emily's name on it and the other had our company name on it. We all easily fit into two cars, and we made a fairly quick drive to the hotel. Now, I always think Hawaii is paradise. It's like no other place in America. When I first visited the Big Island, I wondered how this place could be a part of the U.S. of A. It was gorgeous, lush, and peaceful—with serenity calling your name at every corner.

Bubbling over with exuberance, we rolled into the hotel, and I was blown away! Gorgeous was an understatement. Our family has stayed in some nice places before, but this was "champagne wishes and caviar dreams," nice. My mom was fond of Paris, so we stayed at The Ritz every spring for a while, and I've been to many parts of the world in my short twenty-seven years of life. And, we've even stayed at "nice" places on the Big Island in the past, but it was never this nice!

"How did you work this miracle?" I waved my hand to the beauty around us, while posing Donovan this question. "I can't believe I'm here to work."

"I didn't do a thing. Our clients picked the location, and they are paying for everything. Wait till you see Kate's room."

We took a long walk around the property and eventually got to the Presidential Villa. This place was as big as Jake's house and only one story, so it seemed even bigger. *Who can afford a place like this?*

"Our clients are paying for this?" Once again, I waved my hand to the entire villa. "Now I feel gypped!"

Donovan laughed. "The hotel upgraded her as soon as I showed them her hotel membership card. She must belong to some vacationer / hotel group. I don't know. I'll ask her when she gets here."

"Hey!" My brother called us from outside. "Can we come in and visit the palace?"

"The door's wide open. Come on in." Donovan called out to the three waiting outside.

"WOW!!!" The three Reids were as amazed as I was with this "room."

Nick joked, "Not that I'm complaining but...it seems hardly fair that you and Kate are in a three bedroom—especially since you'll only use one bed—while the three of us are crammed in one room."

"One of you want to stay here with us?"

Nick and Doug immediately answered, "Yes!" Laney stayed silent.

After a leisurely stroll through all the pools, we found my brother and Emily lounging on the beach sipping pineapple-infused water, while being sprayed by the hotel staff with Evian misters. What a crack up! Who goes around with Evian misters spraying hotel guests? Before this was over, I'd have to find out how much these guests were paying per night to stay in such luxury. I, for one, was grateful I was not paying for this trip.

"Is that Laney who just finished the ocean swim?" Donovan asked.

Doug replied, "I think she just did the beach run and the swim. She's a nut sometimes when it comes to exercise."

While Donovan and Doug were checking out Laney, I had to check out Donovan's beach attire. He was in a pair of your classic Burberry check swim trunks with a white polo shirt with the Burberry check-lined placket. From the way he filled out the outfit, Donovan took good care of his body. He was well built, with no misplaced bulges, and muscular by the looks of his arms and legs. I've never seen Donovan with his top off so I kept staring at him in hopes that he'd take off the shirt. I felt like one of those women in a department store commercial who kept blinking her hands begging for the store to "open, open, open!"

I was brought back to sanity with Laney's jubilant voice. "Oh my gosh, that was so wonderful!" She said as she came out of the ocean bouncing from all the extra energy.

Since I've been checking out everyone else's swim attire, I did the same with Laney. She had on a really cute teal swim bottom and matching rash guard. I don't know where I've been all these years, but Laney had grown into quite a woman. She filled the rash guard generously, she had long lean legs, and I just realized that this girl was at least a couple of inches taller than I was. I wasn't the only one appreciating her figure. Doug didn't look too happy with her attire, Nick grinned at Doug's chagrin, and the rest of the men who were not related, appreciated her gorgeous self.

"Don't you think your outfit is a little skimpy for a run and swim on the beach?" Doug was really irritated.

"I'm wearing a swim bottom and a rash guard. What do you mean skimpy? What else am I supposed to wear on the beach?"

"How about board shorts and a rash guard...no, make it long board shorts."

"Yeah?" Now Laney was the one who was irritated. Next thing you knew, she took off her rash guard somehow, without spilling out of her bikini top, threw the rash guard at her brother and said, "Why don't you go buy me a pair of long board shorts while I'm paddle boarding with Nolan."

"Who the hell is Nolan, and I want you to put this top back on, Laney! I'm not kidding!!"

Laney could care less what her brother said as she ran off to meet her new friend. We all laughed at his plight.

"Doug, leave her alone. I think she looks adorable. If you can't show off your figure when you're twenty-two years old, when can you show off your figure?" Emily was always Laney's champion.

"I didn't realize your sister was so athletic in water sports." Donovan also admired my cousin's physique.

"She is not at all what she looks. She is athletic in just about every sport she picks up." Now my brother was championing Laney. "I bet she can beat you in golf, Donovan."

Donovan gave my brother the rolling of the condescending eye. "You do know I have a 2 handicap? There's no way that little squirt can beat me."

"Do I hear a bet coming on?"

I said, "You can't bet for Laney when she's not here."

"Hey Laney," my brothers yelled over to my cousin who was about to go paddle boarding. "Come here for a sec."

"Yeah, Jake? What did you need?" She ran over with her Hawaiian friend trailing behind.

"I told Donovan over here that you could whip his ass in golf. You want to challenge him?"

Laney let out a devious laugh. "You want to challenge me, Mr. Taylor? You think you can beat me?"

"I have a 2 handicap, little girl. You think you can beat me?"

"I have yet to lose to any of the Reid men. Bring it on if you're not too afraid."

"Trash talking already...okay you're on!" Donovan was smiling, but he should've been really scared. Laney was an excellent golfer. "What are we betting on?"

"If you lose, you need to take me on the three-hour hike to go see the lava flow at the volcanoes in Kilauea. Nobody will go with me, and Doug says I can't go by myself."

"Deal. And if you lose, Miss Delaney Reid, you need to stop calling me Mr. Taylor. You will call me Donovan from the moment you lose till the day you die."

"Not likely...because I won't lose!"

This good-looking Hawaiian guy finally caught up with Laney. "You ready to go paddle boarding?" He had a sexy, lazy smile.

"Hey, my name is Doug, I'm Laney's brother, and you are...?" Doug was a bit more hostile than he needed to be. This guy seemed like a perfectly nice guy.

"Aloha! My name is Nolan. I'm Laney's paddle boarding partner. Would you like to join us?"

"No! He's not welcome to join us." Laney glared at her brother, then turned to Donovan. "You going to get the tee time for us?"

"Laney, you want to golf...you know *how* to golf?" This Nolan looked even more impressed with our Laney. In fact, he looked quite smitten with her.

Laney smiled and nodded her head yes to him. They looked super cute together.

"Can I join you two if you are planning to golf tomorrow? I'm the head golf pro here and I'd be happy to get you a tee time if I'm included."

"Sure! The more the merrier. See you at the crack of dawn, Mr. Taylor!" Laney teased Donovan one last time before heading off into the sunset in her skimpy teal bikini with her handsome Hawaiian golf pro.

"When did our Delaney grow up?" Donovan asked with a funny smile on his face, while appreciating her backside.

"What's with you calling her Delaney? She hasn't allowed any of us to call her Delaney since she was like ten years old. Why does she let you call her Delaney?" Doug sounded irritated again.

"I have no idea. She seems to play games with my mind where names are concerned. Look at how she refuses to call me Donovan. I feel like an old man whenever she calls me Mr. Taylor. As of tomorrow, Mr. Taylor will be no more!"

Jake laughed in the background. "I wouldn't be so cocky if I were you, Donovan. She wasn't lying when she said none of us have beaten her."

"Yeah, but can any of you boast a 2 handicap?" Donovan laughed at his own cockiness.

It turned out that our two Taiwanese clients wanted to golf as well, so the five of them were set to golf at 5:00am! I, for one, was glad not to be golfing. I'd be able to sleep in and lounge around until our meeting began in the afternoon. Although in reality, I'd have to get all the documents ready before the start of the meeting, which meant there was no lounging around for me. At such a luxurious resort, it was hard to make myself understand that this was not a vacation.

But, reality did set in and I wrapped up my (gigantic) share of the work before meeting my family, Kate, Donovan, Mr. Hong and Mr. Wang for lunch at the beautiful hotel restaurant. I saw a very happy Taiwanese twosome, a bubbly Laney and a surly Donovan walking in to join the rest of us.

Jake, Nick and Doug started cracking up the moment they got a glimpse of Donovan.

"I think she beat him," Nick announced.

"Of course she beat him. Look at his pout." Jake was loving it. "What was the score, Laney? I assume you won?"

"Did you ever doubt?" She giggled.

"Nope..." Jake walked over and kissed her on the cheek, then greeted Donovan. "Hey there buddy!"

"Yeah, yeah, get your laugh in now. For the record, Delaney cheated." I had to say Donovan made an extremely cute surly man as well.

"I did not cheat! You are such a sore loser!"

"How did my cousin cheat?" Jake inquired.

"That golf pro of hers kept giving her pointers on every hole. He knew the golf course like the back of his hand."

We all laughed at Donovan's tantrum.

"So what was the final score?" Nick asked.

Our Taiwanese guests told the story from here on out. "It was a great match. At every hole, the lead kept changing. Donovan would be up at one hole then Laney was up the next hole. I've never seen such a good female golfer. They were tied at the last hole, and we went to sudden-death three times. Finally, Miss Reid shot one under and won the hole."

Our entire table clapped for her. The Taiwanese men clapped most enthusiastically.

Donovan argued, "The golf pro whispers something in her ear, then next thing you know, she sinks an 18-footer. It was ridiculous how good that putt was." Donovan pleaded his case, but by the smile on his face, he was proud of my cousin.

Laney's happy expression all of a sudden changed. She suddenly conceded, "All right, Mr. Taylor. You win. You don't have to take me to the volcano. I'll see it next time." After that dramatic show, she just walked away.

"Laney..." Everyone (is it mean that I was not a part of this every-one?) called out her name with some form of an empathetic tone.

She turned around and said, "Enjoy your lunch. I'm going to shower and change before my lunch date."

She ignored all the calling out, and walked away. Emily stopped Donovan from chasing after her and once we started lunch, the whole Laney incident was forgotten.

I noticed that all this time Kate had not said a word during lunch. She and Donovan were cool to one another. Was there trouble in paradise? Once again, was it mean of me to enjoy the fact that Donovan and Kate were not getting along? Yeah, okay...it's mean, but oh well...

"Laney, you are back." Both our clients stood up to talk to her.

Laney, once again, looked stunning. I don't know how I never realized that she was a pretty girl. She was wearing one of those Hawaiian one-piece sarongs that turned into a dress or a skirt depending upon how you shaped it. She had put it on in such a way where she looked like she was wearing a flowy Grecian dress. Her brother did not look too happy with her again. With an easy flick of the wrist, her dress would fall apart if unknotted from her right shoulder.

"You will join us on our hike tomorrow morning to the volcano? Donovan said he would get us a driver and a guide. We are going to finish all our business today so that we can spend the day with you again tomorrow. Please don't say no."

Laney quickly glanced over at Donovan, and then smiled at our clients and said, "I would love to spend the day with you as well. Thank you for the invitation."

"Laney, after your lunch date, you want to go shopping with me and Jake?"

"Sure Emily. See you later," she whispered, and walked over to her table and her date.

"Is he her boyfriend?" Kate whispered to me, while giving Laney a piercing look-over.

"No. He's just somebody she met on the island today."

"Men seem to be silly putty in her hands." Was this Sea-foam goddess kidding me in her Chanel dress and Valentino slip-ons? She thought our little Laney was alluring? Did she actually find Laney a threat?

Hmmm...something weird but interesting was going on. Shall I coin it The Young and the Restless? The Bold and the Beautiful? Whatever it was, I couldn't help thinking that Kate was threatened by the wrong person. It wasn't Laney who was making Donovan doubt his relationship with Kate. I know, I know, I have a great boyfriend in Max. I'm just saying...the threat is sitting right next to you, not the table over. What's the old saying? Keep your friends close and your enemies closer? Well, your enemy can't get much closer than where I'm sitting. He He He!

April 8, 2013

Aloha (and coitus) Interruptus

I kept myself hidden from view when I saw Max's plane touch down. I was so excited to see him. I purposely avoided all of his calls and only texted back saying I was super busy and that I would get to him as soon as I could. By now of course, he knew he was coming to see me. Could it be that he was upset that I cut his week short with Hannah? Nah!!! What a ridiculous thought!

"Surprise," I whispered in Max's ears, sneaking up from behind while he was picking up his luggage from the one conveyor belt baggage claim.

"Gem." He crooned in the sweetest voice while dropping his suitcase and holding me closer than close. We immediately gave his brothers a show.

"Geez! Get a room. You're going to be arrested for indecency." Josh said with a chuckle.

"Hi Josh! Hi Garret!" I hugged both Davises simultaneously. "Isn't this island amazing? You been here before?"

"No," Garret laughed. "And thank you for including us in your work, vacation, whatever this is. That was really cool of you. Josh and I decided you've replaced Emily as our favorite girlfriend."

"Fanfreakin'tastic! I've never usurped Emily's reign in any category. That's all it took, huh? A free ticket to Hawaii? Wait till you get to the hotel. Once you get a load of our lodging, I will forever be your favorite."

"We'll see. We can be fickle." Josh and Garret had such an easy going charm about them. They were going to charm the panties off of some unsuspecting women if they weren't careful.

"WOW!!! You will definitely be the undisputed queen in our minds from today till the end of time." Josh declared when we got to the hotel. "This place is the bomb!"

"Babe. You sure we're in the right place? This place is amazing."

"I know, isn't it? And to think, it's all on someone else's dime." I squealed like a little girl.

"Why aren't you working today? Or are you still working and we're holding you back?"

"Long story, but thanks to Laney, our clients were agreeable to every point we brought up and they insisted we finish the business all in one sitting. We were done right after dinner last night."

"Sweet." He kissed me again. "Where is everyone?"

"They're waiting for us at the infinity pool. Let's get you guys settled and we can meet them for a late lunch."

"EMILY!" Josh and Garret hugged my sister as though she was their long, long, long lost sister. I was a bit annoyed with the attention they were giving her.

"It's so good to see you guys! It's been too long. How have you been doing? Max told me you're going to be an architect?" She addressed Garret first. Then she turned to Josh, "And you're going to roam the world, expressing your talent through art?" Her eyes creased and made a crescent shape while she smiled.

My brother pulled Emily away from the two men who were still holding some part of her and brought her back into his hold. It didn't matter who they were, Jake didn't like his wife in the arms of any other man.

"Hello, Gentlemen. I'm Emily's husband, Jake. You must be Garret." Jake shook his hand. "And you're the youngest, Josh?"

After the Davis boys did their duty, they turned their attention to Emily, again.

"I thought you said you'd marry me if it didn't work out with Max. Why'd you go and marry this guy, instead?"

"Hey," Garret pushed Josh out of the way, "Emily said she'd marry me before she'd marry you."

Emily giggled with the rest of the Davises. "Well, when your brother dumped me, I thought about the both of you, but Garret was still in college, and Josh, you were still in high school. Garret, you were in the East Coast, and Josh, you just started driving. What was I to do? So I went and got myself married to the next available guy." We all busted up laughing. We all, except Jake.

"Maybe in the next life?" Josh asked.

Before Emily finished her "maybe," Jake interrupted and said, "not in any lifetime, ever."

Walking to lunch, I gave Garret and Josh the evil eye and complained, "What was that all about? I thought you said I had beaten Emily in the favorite girl category!"

"I warned you we were fickle." Garret laughed.

Josh joined in, "You're our favorite...right after our absolute favorite."

Great!

"You are my absolute favorite, in any lifetime, Gem." Max whispered in my ear. "You don't need anyone else's attention but mine."

That earned my boyfriend serious brownie points...to be rewarded later...! Lunch was a happy affair.

We got a call during lunch, and were invited to join Donovan, Laney, and our clients for an outing on a green sand beach in the southernmost tip of the island. Emily and Jake decided not to come with us and since Kate didn't join us for lunch, I didn't bother suggesting we invite her. Oddly, she's been more than aloof during this whole trip and I felt kinda happy—okay...really happy—that she and Donovan looked to be having issues. Once again—mean, I know!

The six of us got in a rented van and chatted most amicably during the ninety-minute ride. When we got to the beach, we met up with the other four, and we loaded up into one monster truck—inside the truck and outside on the truck bed—owned by a local guy, as he escorted us another ten minutes to the exact location of the green sand beach. This beach was a small alcove in what looked liked the middle of nowhere, where the waves were huge and the sand was a shimmery olive green. The setting was gorgeous.

"More Davises," Donovan jokingly groaned while shaking Josh and Garret's hands. He even opened up his palm to Max and both men played nice today.

"Shall we grab some boards and head into the ocean?" Max started taking off his shirt and handed me the sunscreen for his back, and front. Once I lathered his back, I took a bit longer than necessary rubbing the protection to his front side and that earned me a wet, almost sloshy kiss with lots of tongue. I stopped us before anyone complained.

"Who taught Delaney how to surf?"

"Donovan, we weren't lying when we said she rocks in just about every sport. As Paris was to Nick's family, Hawaii was to ours, growing up. Our little Laney's been surfing since she could swim. Let's all go in and join her." Doug motioned for all of us to go into the ocean.

We were almost in the water when we saw Laney wipe out and possibly get hit on the head with the surfboard.

"Shit!" Donovan swore out loud and ran into the water. Doug, Nick, and then rest of the Davis brothers jumped in to save our *princess*. Within seconds, Donovan carried a protesting Laney out of the ocean.

"Put me down. I'm okay." She tried to jump off.

"Stay still, Brat." Donovan held on even tighter, if that was possible. He had her cradled into his body and she fought him every step of the way. "You have been a pain in my ass all day today," he yelled at her.

She hurled her body away from his, and Laney ran as fast as she could up the steep steps back towards the monster truck we came in.

"You should go after her, Gem."

"She'll be all right. Laney and Donovan are not the best of friends and they've spent the last two days together. I'm surprised it's taken them this long to get into a fight."

"You sure you shouldn't go over there with her? Should I go and see if she's okay?"

"I'll go see if she's okay," Josh declared.

"You don't even know her. She doesn't know who you are."

"Sure she does. We were introduced back at the truck." Josh had a grin a mile wide.

Could it be that our little Joshie has a crush on our little Laney?

"Let's go swim, Babe. Let Josh work the Davis magic." Max laughed and held my hand and ran me into the ocean.

I was tempted to have sex in the ocean after that thank you for the rubdown kiss, but this beach wasn't very big, and there were too many people around, so we fooled around for a while, but didn't take it too far. I figured we could skip dinner and take care of business when Laney was out of the room.

When we got back to the resort, my brother had made other plans. Of course my moronic older brother had booked us all to a luau without asking if we had plans, so a pre-dinner romp was out of the question. I was wondering how we were going to get some alone time when a beautiful opportunity presented itself.

"Laney, I think you should stay with us tonight. You have a bump on your head, and I'd like to make sure you are okay throughout the night. Someone needs to wake you up every few hours or so," my ingenious older brother suggested.

"Jake, I'm totally fine. I don't need anybody waking me up. With the exception of a slight headache, I feel fine." *Brat! Take the offer!*

"Why don't you stay with us, and we will all take turns waking you up every few hours," Josh suggested.

Donovan didn't look happy with that suggestion. "There are five of you in that room. How is Laney supposed to get any rest with so many bodies in one room? Where will she sleep?"

"She can sleep next to me," Josh chuckled. "I promise to check up on her every hour."

Boy, when Josh wanted something, he went after it with gusto. "Our little Joshie has a crush on Laney," I whispered in Max's ear.

"It appears so," Max laughed.

"Why don't Kate and I take Laney tonight? We have two extra bedrooms and I can check up on her throughout the night."

"Thanks Donovan, but I'd feel much better if she stayed with us." My brother wasn't giving up on this idea. God bless my brother!

"You guys are here on vacation, and I'm sure you're tired of getting up throughout the night with the kids. Why don't you and Emily sleep peacefully? You only have a couple more days left. I'll take good care of her, Jake. I promise."

Emily lightly nodded her head yes, and Jake gave in and let Donovan be the keeper of my cousin tonight. God bless everybody!

The only person who wasn't happy about this agreement was Laney. She pouted and shook her head no, but she couldn't overrule my older brother.

"You do know that this means you and I have the room to ourselves tonight. And I'm sure you came prepared?" I asked suggestively.

"By prepared, do you mean handcuffs, whips, chains, and gags? Those all got confiscated when I was going through the TSA check in, but I did come prepared in other ways. I've been prepared since the moment I saw you at the airport." We both giggled and waited for the stupid luau to be done. *Why was this show so long?*

Laney grumbled the whole time she was packing her stuff to go to Donovan and Kate's villa. I couldn't wait for her to leave, but I tried hard not to show too much teeth with my grin. I was going to walk her to the villa, but Josh showed up with Max, so even that was unnecessary. *Hot damn!*

I had my negligee all ready, but Max didn't give me a chance to do any prep. I was thrown—literally—on the bed, and he jumped right on top of me.

"Should we shower together first? We still have sand on us," I complained.

"That'll be round two," Max explained.

"How many rounds will there be?"

"12, like a boxing match, unless one of us gets ko'ed."

My boyfriend started kissing me behind the ear, and soon it turned to sucking down my neck. He started sucking hard enough where I feared a high school hickey coming on. Then the sucking progressed south and he latched onto my right breast right over the T-shirt (lost the bra before Max showed up) and I practically jumped off the bed. There was something freakin' arousing about that thin barrier between his suctioning mouth and my breasts.

"Did you let Hannah ride on the Harley?" *Where the hell did that question come from?* Sometimes I just couldn't help myself. "Did you?" I kinda asked again.

"You really want to talk about this when your sweet nipples are in my mouth and I'm about to give you your first orgasm of the night?"

"You can keep going. I just need a yay or a nay," I answered between moaning and grabbing onto the bed sheet for dear life. How had I never known in my twenty-seven years of life that my girlfriends were so sensitive?

"Yay." Max whispered just loudly enough.

"What? I told you I didn't want her riding on the bike. I don't want anyone else getting that close to you."

He stopped sucking (which was not what I wanted) and he was about to say something, but thought better of it.

"What?" I goaded him.

He pulled himself off of me (which was something I really didn't want him to do) and thought a few more seconds before laying it on me. "I've seen Donovan touch you, hold you, and kiss you way too many times on that forehead of yours, but haven't made an issue of it. But you're going batshit crazy over Hannah asking for a ride on the bike?"

Uh-oh...I shouldn't have started this, but now I had no choice but to fight back and win the argument.

"I am not going batshit crazy! It was just a question."

"If you're making me use my mouth arguing rather than giving you orgasms, you are certifiably batshit crazy."

He and I had a bit of a staring contest, then both of us started howling.

I was a moron. Was I going to admit this to my boyfriend? Hell no! But I admit it to myself. I bring unnecessary grief to all those involved with me.

"Did you say the words mouth and orgasmssss, as in plural?"

"Yes, GEM! Orgasmsss as in plural—of the oral kind." He grinned an evil grin.

I pulled his body back onto mine. "Well then, what are you waiting for...an invitation?"

"I don't want to hear one word out of you that isn't related to sex. You got that?" Ooh...the dominant Max is here now. My Dom!

After making quick work of both our clothes, Max told me he was going bottoms up this time and he trailed his kisses *EXACTLY* where I wanted them trailed. I could feel his breath getting oh so close to my happy place. He blew on me a few times then I felt his lips, his tongue so close to that sweet spot when...

"Max, Jane, open up! This is an emergency!" This time the culprit was Josh.

I try not to drop the F-bomb too often in my life. I *so* try not to be a potty mouth, but this was an instance where I had to shout, "Dammit all to hell! Leave us the fuck alone!"

There was a male audience outside laughing at my misery.

"WHAT???" I yelled opening the door.

"Eew! Get some clothes on." Nick complained at my Max's t-shirt attire.

"What's the emergency?" Max came to the door wearing the other half of our outfit.

"Have you seen Laney?" Josh asked this question half a second sooner than Nick.

"What do you mean, have we seen Laney? Isn't she staying at the palace?" I snapped at both our brothers.

"She left without telling anyone where she's going, and we're all worried about her." Josh really did look worried.

"What do you mean she left?" I asked with more exasperation than I could possibly explain. "Where could she have gone?"

"Nobody knows..." Nick added.

Shit. Why me???

April 11, 2013

Aurora aka Briar Rose aka Sleeping Beauty

"How can we help?" My kind and understanding boyfriend squeezed my hand as an empathetic gesture, as well as a warning.

I knew this wasn't the time to complain, but why did Laney have to get herself lost now?

"We're all meeting in Jake and Emily's room. Come over as soon as possible." Josh instructed us.

After an all too quick and dreamy Max kiss, we got dressed and assembled at my brother's room. Emily was a mess. She looked frightened and worried. I guess this was the difference between her and me. I figured Laney was a grown adult, and she'd come back when she felt like it. She wasn't exactly lost. She just didn't want to be found. For Emily, it was as though she'd lost her own child. She looked sick with worry.

"Emily." My boyfriend, of course, felt her pain and went over to give her a hug. "It's not good for you or the baby to be so worried."

"But what if Laney's hurt? What if someone took her? Where can she be, and why would she purposely do this to us? She must be in trouble somewhere," Emily said frantically.

"Nobody took Laney and she's not hurt. This is one of the finest hotels on the island, and I'm sure she's out doing something and forgot to tell us that she had plans," Max held her some more.

GROAN...!

Jake slowly unweaved the two of them (you go big brother!), and brought Emily back into his arms and kissed her forehead. Now that was a sight I preferred watching. I pulled my boyfriend back to me and placed my arms around his waist.

"Love you, Gem," Max whispered and held me tight.

"What happened, Donovan? Can you go over it one more time?" Jake asked.

"Shit. It's all my fault. I shouldn't have insisted she come and stay with us." I don't know what happened between those two, but Donovan looked upset! "She got to our villa and started mouthing off to me, so I took her into her room and had it out with her about what happened today."

"What did happen between you two today? Why were you both so angry with one another?" Doug chimed in.

"It's not any one thing. I got upset with her for flirting with our clients, and she got upset with me for...they're all stupid things, not worth mentioning. It's not worth bringing up and it won't help with our situation."

Now Josh added to our conversation. "I don't think they were stupid to her. When we chatted in the car, she was pissed at you and said she'd be happy never to see you again."

The glares Donovan and Josh gave one another were comical. Donovan gave him a *who the hell invited you into this conversation* look, and Josh gave back a *I don't give a rat's ass if you want me in this conversation or not*, look.

Max felt my body shake from wanting to either laugh or add my two cents, and he held me a bit tighter and whispered, "Don't...only if you can help..." I was going to retort, but I felt a loving kiss to the backside of my head and a sweet caress to add to it, so I stayed still in my boyfriend's arms.

"*Anyhow*," Donovan stressed—more to get Josh to butt-out of his conversation—"after Delaney and I talked, Kate and I got into an argument, and when I went to check up on Delaney, she was gone."

"Did she take her stuff?" I had to add something to this discussion.

"Yeah, she took everything she brought."

"Why would she leave because you and Kate were arguing? What did you and Kate argue about?" Another great question by...me!

Donovan wouldn't give us an answer until he saw how torn Emily was about this whole situation.

"Kate and I have been having some issues (*I knew it!!!*), and she was not happy about having Delaney in our room. But it's not Kate's fault, and she feels terrible about what's happened." (Now why'd he have to go and defend her if they were having issues?)

"Donovan, would Kate mind if we went back to your place and looked around a bit? Perhaps Laney left a note telling us where she was going?" Emily was practically out the door before she even finished this question.

Kate—unlike her usual glamorous self—looked like hell. Was it wrong of me to feel giddy that this perfectly groomed woman wasn't so perfectly groomed tonight? I think E L James was onto something with this inner-goddess stuff because my inner-goddess was breakdancing right now.

"We're sorry to all barge in. We were hoping to see if Laney left anything behind?" Emily said, oh so kindly.

"No bother at all. Please feel free to look around."

All nine of us went into the room, and while the men looked at the obvious places, Emily and I looked in between the crevice of the mattress and bed frame.

"I found it. Here," I handed the note to Donovan, "addressed to you."

Dear Mr. Taylor,

I'm sorry to be such a nuisance in your life...no, scratch that...'a pain in your ass' as you told me earlier. Please apologize to Kate for my brief intrusion. I will be getting my own room. PLEASE do not alarm my family and make a bigger deal out of my leaving your room than it has to be. I would like some privacy of my own. Yes, my head hurts, but no, there's nothing wrong with me. See you tomorrow—or maybe in another lifetime, if I can help it. -Delaney Reid.

You see! I told you she just didn't want to be found. Geez Louise! All this for nothing!

"Let's go to the front desk and get her room number to make sure she's okay." Jake commandeered the lot of us.

"What for?" I said a little too loudly. Everyone stared at me so I shriveled back into Max's shelter.

The front desk, of course, wouldn't give us any information, so Jake had them call Nolan the golf pro, hoping to enlist his aid. Nolan couldn't get much more information out of them except that another Reid was staying on the property, and the registered name wasn't Delaney nor Laney. Nolan vaguely hinted to Jake that if we could figure out what name she was registered under, he'd work the back channel and find a room number for us.

"What name could she be using?" Emily asked me specifically. "Were there any other nicknames Laney used to go by when she was younger?"

"Emily, that girl had so many imaginary friends and she pretended to be so many different characters when she was younger, if we went through them all, we'd be here all night," I said, until a light went off. "Oh my gosh! I know!!! Who has a cell phone?"

Donovan handed me his.

I did a quick Google search and told Nolan, who was still on the line with Jake, to look up Aurora.

"Who the hell is Aurora?" Nick asked.

"Nolan says no Aurora."

"Donovan, let me have your phone one more time." This search took a bit longer, but I had my answer. "Ask him to look up Briar Rose."

Jake quickly gave Nolan the name and bingo! We had a room number.

"Who, or what is Briar Rose?" Doug asked, totally confused.

"Don't you remember when we were little, Laney always wanted to play Sleeping Beauty? She always had me cast as Maleficent, the evil one, Nick was always Prince Phillip, and you took turns playing Flora, Fauna, or Merryweather?"

All the men started sniggering.

"I did *NOT* play a fairy godmother!" Doug argued.

"That's right!" It dawned on Nick now. "We did play Sleeping Beauty all the time."

"So who's Aurora and who's Briar Rose?" Nick was about to answer Donovan's question, when I butted in again.

"Seriously??? You have four sisters! You mean to tell me you've never watched Sleeping Beauty, or you never role played this fairy tale?" I rolled my eyes at him because I knew he was lying.

"I don't have time to go strolling down memory lane, Maleficent." Donovan said that in a mean kinda way. "I can see why Delaney cast you as the evil step-mother."

"Queen! Not step-mother! Get your fairy tales straight. We're talking Sleeping..."

"Enough, you two!" Jake cut us off and continued walking to the next building.

I was pissed with both my brother and Donovan, and so Emily finished the story for the rest of the crew. "Sleeping Beauty's given name was Aurora, but when she went into hiding with her fairy godmothers, they renamed her Briar Rose so no one would know her true identity. Very clever of our Laney to call herself Briar Rose."

"Clever, my ass!" I whispered, but my boyfriend caught on and gave me a chuckling warning.

We got to Laney's room, and Jake knocked on the door. A groggy Laney opened the door looking nothing like Sleeping Beauty when she woke up from her 100-year nap. Her hair was ratty, her eyes clouded, and she was wearing only a t-shirt with her perky nipples showing through. Emily quickly hugged her, then closed the door and asked us to stay outside for a moment.

"Delaney, are you okay?" Donovan was the first one to speak once she reappeared with Emily.

"Yes I'm fine. I'm sorry to have caused you guys any worry." Then she looked over at Donovan slightly upset. "I told you not to tell my family that I left."

"Jake, can I have a word with Delaney, alone?"

"Donovan..." Jake warned.

"Please...she'll be okay..." Donovan said to Jake and Emily. They nodded their heads in approval.

Ten minutes into the twiddling of the thumbs, I felt I had been patient enough. We had places to go (our room), people to see (each other), and things to do (well...you know...). I was almost about to announce our departure when Donovan opened the door. He came out, closed the door, and headed toward his room with Emily and Jake in tow. That was it! No, "she's all right," or "we had a good talk," or "Laney and I decided...." *What the hell?* After all that, I have to stay in the dark?

The rest of us stared at one another for another few seconds, then split. I'm sure you're all wondering what happened behind closed doors. For sure, I will ask the three of them later on, but for now, it's a mystery to us all. And very possibly, you will never get any information from me, because I won't get any information from them. The best I can say is maybe you'll be able to read it in another post from someone else's point of view, because this point of view has somewhere to be (in bed), someone to be with (my honey), and something to do (Mmm-hmm!).

April 15, 2013

Tête-à-Tête

After a busy morning packing, we all made it back on the plane safely and everybody broke off into their own private conversations, or they fell asleep. Garret, Nick and Doug each took up three empty rows and slept the plane-ride away. Laney and Josh were in the corner talking, and Max and I were a few rows ahead of them having our own quiet time. Soon after we took off, Donovan headed our way, but went straight to Laney.

"There's a seat up front with your name on it," Donovan said sweetly. Boy, he must've done something *really* wrong to Laney, because he was super nice to her today.

"Thank you, but I think I'll stay back here, Mr. Taylor."

"Are you still upset with me?" He questioned with a wrinkled face. I had to admit, even that was pretty hot-looking on this guy.

"No I'm not upset. It's nothing like that. I think I'll just hang back here and chat with Josh."

Now disgruntled, Donovan walked back to his seat.

Laney and Josh were darling together. They were the same age, both idealists, and they had a unique way of looking at life. They were totally happy-go-lucky people, and if they were to get together, I didn't think they'd have too many issues. I hope they'd consider dating, and then we'd have another Davis-Reid match made in heaven—or at least a match made in Hawaiian paradise.

"What are you smiling about, my precious gem?"

"Your brother and Laney." I smiled some more. "Don't they look cute together?"

"They do look cute together, but I think Laney's heart is somewhere else."

"I don't think it was anything serious with the guy back on the Big Island. Plus, he lives thousands of miles away. How are they going to have a relationship? I wouldn't worry about Nolan."

"I don't know, Gem. Josh is going away next year. I don't know if those two can have a relationship being thousands of miles apart, either."

"But that's perfect! Maybe he will base himself in London, and Josh can go back and forth between London and Rome. They can have a European relationship. How romantic!" Max only smiled and kissed me lightly on the lips. "By the way, can I ask you a question?"

"Sure," Max agreed.

"It's kind of personal...very personal...are you sure it's okay?"

"Gem, if I find it to be too personal, I'll let you know, all right? Otherwise, I want to share my life with you."

That earned him a brief make out session on the plane.

"From watching you with your money, and from what Emily has told me, I thought your family was not too well off. But after seeing your childhood home during that infamous dinner, and knowing about this European 'vacation' Josh is going to take later this year, I'm a little confused about your financial status. I always figured that you were living off student loans all this time. Isn't that the case...or am I totally wrong?"

"Well...for all my parents' faults, financial irresponsibility was not one of them. They both make good money, and they were wise about their investments, and they never overspent. We didn't go to the Ritz every summer or spring, and we didn't go to fancy private schools. Because of that, my parents were able to put away a college fund for all three of us. Now don't get me wrong, I'm not criticizing your family. From all I've seen, there's no better family unit than the Reid family. I love that I'm a small part of your family, and even if it's temporary, I love all that I've learned from you guys. It's a real encouragement to see such a fun-loving family."

The thought of us being temporary didn't sit well with me.

"Can I ask how much your parents put aside for you guys?" I regretted having said that immediately. "Forget it. You don't have to answer." I backtracked as soon as I could.

Max only laughed. "You after me for my money now? It isn't just my body that you were after?"

"I'll take your body over your money!" I added happily.

"Good, because after med school, I don't think I'll have a penny left. I do still need to live on a tight budget if I don't want to take out any loans. Josh and I both went to the California state schools, so we didn't spend much money on undergrad. Because of that, I'm able to go to med school and not have to get any financial help. Josh has a lot of money left because he chose not to further his education in any institution. Instead, his money is going to a life of leisure in Europe, drawing and enjoying life."

"...with Laney..."

"Possibly with Laney..."

"What about Garret?"

"Garret really did not want to stay home any longer than he had to, so he chose to go far. He landed himself in Rhode Island, and used up a chunk of his money on tuition. But, he worked and paid for his own living expenses, so he's still able to go to grad school. He's quite careful with his money as well, and he still works, so he at least has an income. When all this schooling is said and done, I think I'll come out with a zero balance. Does that satisfy your curiosity?"

"Excellent. Thank you for that. I really was curious, but didn't know how to ask."

"Babe, don't keep it in. Ask whatever you need to ask."

I nodded an affirmative.

"Gem, after last night, I need a little shut-eye. Your prowess kept me up the entire night," he smiled a beautiful smile and kissed me.

"Take a nap," I said after a few more kisses. "I'm going to go up and sit with Emily."

I was thrilled that Max so openly talked to me about his life. It was as if we had finally formed a deeper layer to this relationship. *Comfortable.* Yeah...that's what we were...comfortable!

Walking up to First Class, I noticed that almost the entire section was empty. As soon as I came into the cabin, Donovan and Jake completely went silent on me. It was as though they were talking about me, and got caught with their pants down. Eew! I didn't need that visual of my brother, but Donovan...? Nope! Not going there...!

"What brings you up here, Commoner?" Donovan said as he and Jake laughed at the stupid comment.

"Ha ha ha," I muttered.

"What's with the covert conversation in the corner, here? You even separated yourself from your wife, Jake. Shocking!" I was doing my best to pry.

"That would be none of your business, and we only moved to the corner because Emily is sleeping."

"Bummer... I wanted to have a chat with Emily."

"Well," Jake said, "chat with her later, because this'll be her last peaceful rest."

"All right, I won't bother her. But I do have a question for you, o' brother o' mine."

Both guys looked at me expectantly.

"What do you think about Laney and Josh?" Neither man made a move. Both faces were frozen and it was dead silence for longer than it was comfortable. "Well?" I broke the silence.

"Negative, little sister. I don't think the two suit."

"What do you mean? They're darling together," I protested to further my case.

"Laney is darling with anyone. She's a grand prize no matter who the guy is, but Josh is not it."

I gave my brother a *what do you know* look and he returned it with *a helluva lot more than you do* look.

"Well, what do you think?" I turned it over to Donovan, hoping to get him on my side.

"What the hell do I know about relationships? I can barely get my own going. I'm not a Reid. I don't have a say."

Cryptic, much? I was fed up with the Donovan Downers in this corner of the plane, and Emily was stirring from her sleep, so I went to chat with my sister. As soon as I was settled, I noticed those two guys get back into their serious conversation, again.

"Hey. Have a nice nap?" I asked while handing her a glass of water. *You see how nice I can be???*

"I did. I tell you, lazy begets lazy. All I've done this whole trip is read and sleep."

"Perfect. That's why Jake brought you on this trip. You excited to see the little imps, again?"

"Oh yeah! I missed them so much. But the weird thing was, once I got used to the luxury of the hotel and the luxury of having me to myself, I didn't miss them as much as I thought I would. Does that make me a bad mom?"

"The worst kind," I kidded, and we both laughed. "I've wanted to talk to you about something for a while now, and haven't had the guts to bring it up till now."

Emily looked a bit scared and lost with my statement. She was so genuinely beautiful. If I were a man, I'd fall head over heels in love with this woman, in a heartbeat...just like my big bro'.

"Have I done something to upset you?" Classic Emily—she placed the blame on herself, first.

"Oh, geez, Emily!" That came off more exasperated-sounding than intended, "You did nothing wrong. It's me who's been in the wrong for a while." Now she looked thoroughly confused. "I'm sorry I've been such a brat to you all this time."

There. It was said. I've gotten it off my chest and I've confessed my sins.

"Jane." Emily hugged me. "You're so silly sometimes. Would you think I was a nut if I told you it thrills me to know that you feel comfortable enough to be a brat to me? I'm still learning about all the different dynamics within a large family. All of this is so new and so much fun." I saw Jake walk over, probably to make sure his wife was not being terrorized by the little sister. "I love you! And I love you and Max together, and I hope only good things for the both of you in the future. Let's always be open and honest with one another, okay?"

"All right..." A fitting word for all that was going on in my life... All Right!

April 18, 2013

Ferreting

"So...can I ask what happened between you and Laney in the hotel room back on the Big Island?"

"No...you may not ask what happened between me and Delaney in the hotel room back on the Big Island," he said with the same intonation as mine.

"Why not," I asked Donovan, "what's there to hide? What's going on between you two?"

"Why the 20 questions? It's not like I ask what happened between you and Max in the hotel room on the Big Island."

"Like that isn't obvious, already. Like you don't know the answer to that one." We both laughed.

"What happened between me and Delaney is no big deal, but I don't think she wants it known. And there's *nothing* going on between me and Delaney."

"But why did you guys argue so much in Hawaii? You two were behaving like brothers and sisters with all the fighting, or you were like an old married couple."

He just looked at me, but said nothing.

"So which is it? Are you the brother and sister or the old married couple?"

"We are neither, my little vixen. We are...I don't know what the hell we are. She sees me as an overbearing older man, and I see her as a pain in my ass."

Maybe it was because Laney and Donovan have known each other all their lives that they had this weird tug and pull going on these days. I was sure it wasn't that they were attracted to each other. They were so different and they were at such different stages in their lives. He was also so much older than she was. Why, there was like a decade difference between the two of them. I got the feeling that Laney did not want another older brother in Donovan. And Donovan felt the need to protect her when he was with her and our clients. And from there, she probably got upset with him meddling in her life. Oddly she was a lot more of a free spirit than I ever thought she would be.

Speaking of clients, we were having dinner tonight with our Taiwanese clients as a celebratory meal. They followed us back to Los Angeles, we accomplished a few more items that were not on the agenda, and before they left, they wanted to buy us dinner as a thank you for the great time in Hawaii. In all honesty, we should've been the ones thanking them. We hardly worked in Hawaii. I think we worked maybe eight hours, and even for me as the peon of the group, I didn't work that much. We should be buying them dinner, but instead, they insisted on buying us dinner. Another odd thing, Kate decided to go out of town, then go back to London for a little while. She said she needed to help the London office settle with the new clients she brought into the firm. I think that was just her excuse to step away from Donovan and their troubles. Whatever!

"So if you're not going to answer me about Laney, you gonna answer some questions about Kate?"

"Boy, you're really nosy tonight! I don't know if I'll answer any questions, but you can try asking..." he smirked.

"What's the story there? Why was she so upset and aloof with you in Hawaii and why is she in London now?"

He gave me that famous Donovan smile, but didn't say a word, again.

"Kate and I are at an impasse right now."

"Impasse? What does that mean?"

"Let's just say that she and I agree to disagree for now."

"So it's not over?" I sounded a little too eager asking that question. Donovan arched his eyebrow in response to my eager beaver question.

"I don't know if it's ever over between us. We just continue and are always at an impasse at some point in our relationship."

"How are you ever going to have a real relationship with a girl when Kate is always in the background hovering? What is she, iCloud? She's always ready and available for download?"

Donovan busted up. "When did you become my IT girl?"

"Isn't that a bit unfair to your next girlfriend?"

"Why, you want to audition for the role?" He asked as though it were a challenge.

"Are you offering?" I dared him back.

"For you my vixen, that offer still stands."

This time I busted up at his comment. "You're such a liar! You could've beaten Usain Bolt's 100-meter dash record with the way you sprinted to Kate as soon as she arrived. You dropped me like a hot potato."

"There was nothing to drop since I never held you to begin with." Once again, another dare.... Was I going to pick up the gauntlet and answer this dare?

"Things are really good with me and Max right now. I'm good. Max is good. We are good! I don't want to ruin it. We worked through a lot of stuff, and I think this is the best we have ever been. I like where we are, so don't dangle your apple." I left him with that ultimatum.

"If everything is so good, why are you even tempted? How can I possibly be the snake in the Garden of Eden, my beautiful Eve?" This serpent had such a way with words.

"Shut up," I said, and slapped him on the arm. "Just drive the car and let's drop this whole conversation." That was a cowardly way out, but hey, it was a way out. There was something about Donovan that was always tempting, no matter what stage of life I was in. Maybe it was his good looks, or maybe it was his cocky self-assured attitude. I don't know what it was, but he was definitely the fruit of temptation, waiting to be eaten (in the Biblical figurative-sense, of course).

We pulled up to the quintessential LA restaurant, Spago, the same time Laney and Josh pulled up.

"You're a bit out of your comfort zone, aren't you?" I posed a question that had a myriad of possible meanings and answers.

"Why whatever do you mean, Sis?"

His last word brought a huge smile to my face. Though, the last thing I needed was two more brothers.

"You want me to pick you up later?" Josh's voice changed whenever he spoke to Laney. Normally he sounded like a rascal, but with her, he sounded like a love-sick puppy.

"That's okay, Josh. You go hang out with your buddies. I'll catch a ride home with Jane. No need for you to make that extra trip."

"It's no trouble if you want me to come and pick you up."

"Thank you for the offer, but it's silly to have you bother when Jane and I live on the same street."

"You know it's no bother, right?"

Laney looked a bit uncomfortable, and Donovan and I looked like voyeurs.

"See you later," she said with a perky smile.

"I'll see you at the birthday party?" Josh added one more question in an attempt to stop Laney from departing.

"Absolutely." Laney answered with a dazzling smile that left Josh practically drooling, me smiling at the cute young love-in-blossom, and Donovan...I didn't know how to explain the look on his face— odd? Unreadable? Idk, Idc, whatever...

Laney gave us a tentative wave hello, and Donovan walked over and gave her a semi hug. It looked like she was about to refuse his hug, but quickly decided against it, so they looked very awkward.

"Thank you for joining us for dinner, Delaney." Donovan, too, was extra sweet to her. Did someone designate today as be-kind-to-Laney day and forget to send me the memo? "It was cool of you to agree to have dinner with all of us. Both Weston and Brad wanted to see you one last time."

"You're welcome. I'm glad I can help you and Jane."

Donovan held the door for both of us, and our clients were already waiting for us in the patio. They insisted on ordering the ten-course Chef's tasting meal, so there was no escaping this long night!

"Delaney, have you ever been to Hong Kong?" Weston asked, while sipping his champagne.

"No I haven't. But I would love to go. I've only seen Japan in Asia."

"You should come visit. Hong Kong is an amazing place to be."

"Aren't you both from Taiwan?"

"Yes, but Brad and I live in Hong Kong. When do you graduate?"

"May."

"If I sent you my plane, would you come visit me?" *Yikes!* Weston was coming on strong. And I'd say by the looks of that scowl on his face, big brother Donovan was emerging. Laney noticed as well, and quickly cut Weston off.

"Thank you for the invitation, but I'm going to London as soon as I graduate."

"Why London? What's in London?"

"Nothing is in London except my grandmother's flat. I've just decided that's what I want to do for a year."

"Then, can I come see you in London?" This guy was coming on even stronger, and wouldn't take a hint. I thought about helping Laney out, but a curious side of me wanted to see how she'd handle this situation. *And*, an even more curious side of me wanted to see how Donovan would handle this situation.

Laney looked really uncomfortable. She shifted in her seat just as five servers came with our next course and she knocked over the bowl of agnolotti pasta right out of the server's hands and into her dress. To me, that dish was the best thing on this menu, and it spilled all over her pretty dress. The server was horrified and mortified. The rest of us didn't quite know how to help her. As smooth as ever, Donovan got up from his seat, went over to her with his napkin, and carefully transferred the pasta from her dress to his napkin.

"You okay?" He asked her gently.

She looked like a Madame Alexander doll with beet red cheeks, embarrassed by the ruckus she caused, and nodded that she was all right. At this point, the general manager came over, the sommelier was over, and even Wolfgang Puck came over to our table. As soon as people started making an even greater fuss of her situation, she calmly excused herself and hied off to the ladies' room. Donovan actually looked more upset for her than she was for herself.

In the madness of it all, I got a call from Josh and stepped outside to talk to him, and to get away from the awkward scene waiting to develop when Laney arrived.

"Hey, what's up?"

"My bro' wants me to pick you up and bring you to the hospital. Can you let me know when you might be done?"

"Why does he want you to pick me up?"

"Dunno. I'm doing his bidding. Can you also have Laney with you when I come by?"

"A-ha! So that's your ploy? Use me and your brother as a decoy so you can spend more time with my cousin?"

"I wish I were clever enough to have come up with that." He cracked up. "It was entirely Max, but it benefits us all."

"Sounds good. Will be in touch."

Everything was back to normal, and everyone was politely conversing. Gratefully, the talk was all about business, so Laney was able to hide in the background.

When the meal was over, both our clients offered to drive Laney home, to which she politely but firmly said no. Good for her. I explained to her and Donovan about my ride situation, and she surprisingly declined my invitation as well. And even before Donovan uttered a sound, she told him she'd call a cab to come pick her up.

"Delaney...don't be silly. I live right by your parents' home. I can drop you off."

She sighed. "I'd really like some time to myself, and to be myself. I don't like it when I have to pretend to be happy." Now that the clients were gone, her lips formed into an impressive pout. I swear, she could make money modeling for doll makers. "Sorry. I've said too much. Ok...I'll go with you if we can leave now, and if you promise not to talk to me in the car."

Donovan looked like he was about to disagree, but saw how unhappy Laney was, so he acquiesced.

"Jane, I'm sorry but would you be angry with me if we left you here by yourself? I don't want to have to turn down another ride home. I'm mentally exhausted."

Um...well...angry would be a strong word, but I was irritated she'd suggested it. But...whatever! "No. Don't worry about it. Josh should be here soon."

"Thanks, Jane. I owe you one," she practically shouted her words while racing to catch the door the valet was holding for her.

Ok...ho-hum...

"Hey Sis, get in!" A cheerful voice called out.

I sat in the front seat, but Josh wouldn't leave. "What's up?" I queried. "Why aren't we leaving?"

"What about Laney? Where's she?"

"I thought it was me you wanted to see!" Of course I knew it wasn't.

"Would it piss you off if I said it wasn't? I was hoping to spend some more time with your cousin."

"Does my cousin know you're *this* interested in her?"

"I tried to tell her, but she wasn't willing to listen. She cut me off, and told me that she would like to get to know me solely as a friend." He sounded disappointed. "Is she seeing somebody right now? Is she interested in anyone?"

"I'm not sure what her status is, Josh." I felt a little embarrassed that I didn't really know my own cousin who lives across the street from me. "I know she dates, but I don't think she's dating anyone in particular. Guys ask her out all the time, and she doesn't say yes to everybody, but if she thinks he's a nice guy, she'll give him a chance."

"I wish she would give me a little more than a chance. And by the way, you never told me where she went tonight."

"Donovan and I put her in an uncomfortable situation tonight—and she had a rough time of it. After turning down everyone's offer to drive her home..."

"Yeah..."

"She decided, or better yet, Donovan convinced her to go home with him."

"Why him?" Josh sounded angry now. "Why is he always in the picture? Is he interested in Laney?"

"*Nooooo!* He has no interest in her. And she actually can't stand him. I think she has a hard enough time with one older brother, plus Jake looking after her, and she's irritated by the fact that Donovan is always looking out for her as well." I did feel sorry for Laney. Because of her age and her looks, every male, family or not, felt protective of her. She had it tough. She was going to have a hard time dating and getting to know anybody with so many interferences. "Donovan has four sisters and I think Laney's age just brings out the big brother side of him."

"Are you sure?" Josh was skeptical of my reasoning.

"Of course I'm sure! I'm her cousin and she lives across the street from me." Not that that had any bearing on my knowledge of her life. "Anyhow, she agreed to let him drive her home if he promised not to talk to her the whole ride home."

Josh started busting up. "She's so funny."

"Is that what you like about her? Her sense of humor?" I looked at him skeptically with one raised eyebrow. "It has nothing to do with her beautiful looks or the knockout body?"

"Hell yes! It has everything to do with her drop-dead gorgeous looks and her let's-get-horizontal body."

We both cracked up, hard.

The ride to the hospital was a quick one with such entertainment, and when Josh parked his car, I almost missed the two women mooning over my boyfriend in the parking lot.

"Shit! Why are Hannah and Psycho over there with your brother?"

"I think Hannah is working at the hospital now, and when you say Psycho, are you talking about Joyce?"

I stared at Josh, totally surprised. "What do you mean Hannah is working at the hospital, and how do you know about Psycho?"

"Max, with the help of your brother Jake, helped Hannah get an office job here. And as for Joyce, she calls Max all the time. I've met her a few times, too. By the pissed-off look on your face, I take it she's not in your Google+ circle of friends?"

"Your brother is in the doghouse right now. Let's go!"

I slammed the door and walked straight for those loser women hanging on a man who was already taken.

I was royally pissed until I saw the happiness on Max's face the moment he saw me. He looked like my nephew James when he saw his mother for the first time in almost a week after we'd come back from Hawaii. There was sheer bliss in his eyes. Damn. That felt good!

"Hello, Precious," he whispered while kissing me with both hands on my face. "I'm glad you're here." He kissed me a few more times in front of everyone, and I almost did a drunk, happy dance in the parking lot.

I kinda waved hello to both gals (and no, I didn't stick my tongue out at them and gloat) while Max put a helmet on me and told me to hop on. As soon as I got on, we went on a long ride before he headed for my house. Something about tonight's ride helped me to understand Max's love for riding on his motorcycle. I still wasn't crazy about all the wind and dirt and bugs, but I did dig being able to hold him tight around his waist and plastering my front side to his back side. I felt so close to him. Even after we got to my house, I couldn't peel myself off of him.

"Gem?"

"Hmm?"

"You gonna sleep on my back, on my bike, tonight?"

"I wish..." dreamily, I kissed his exposed neck. "If this position isn't possible, you wanna come sleep in my bed?"

He chuckled and helped me off the bike. "I'm not crazy about waking up and seeing your parents and grandparents at the breakfast table. Plus, you're such a moaner and screamer, I don't think I like the idea of waking up all the family members on this block," he said while nibbling on my ears. "Soon. We'll get an apartment together and we can sleep in any position you like."

"Dare I ask about the two drooling women at the hospital?" I got out a question mid-making out at the door.

"Hannah got a job in the accounting department, and Joyce was befriending Hannah."

"Scary...! Do I need to be worried?"

"Considering I asked Josh to bring you to me after your dinner because I didn't want to give Hannah a ride home—that should give you some indicator of whether or not you need to be worried."

"Really? That's why you wanted me there?"

"Hannah told me that she needed a ride home and when she asked, all that went through my mind was the fact that I didn't want anyone else clinging onto my back, but you. When I bought the Harley right before you came back to LA, I specifically asked for one with the most comfortable back seat because I envisioned you, and only you, on the back of my bike."

I was totally melting inside. A sweet Max was a sight to hear and behold.

"I love you, my precious gem."

Damn. I loved this man too!

April 22, 2013

The Big Top

This entire weekend had a three-ring circus theme starting with James and Ellie's 1st birthday party bonanza! My niece and nephew turned the big ONE on Friday, and we had a huge celebration. Gimpy and I stopped by their home early Friday, before work, and there were two huge balloon figures shaped into a giraffe for James, and a panda bear for Elizabeth. Both kids looked at them with horrified curiosity.

"Um...wow! These balloon figures are huge," I said to Emily.

"It's an 'Under the Big Top' themed party, and the balloons arrived early this morning. I hope they'll last all day."

Gimpy was enjoying holding James as James batted the giraffe's neck.

"Me!" Ellie yelled out to get her turn.

"She learned a new word," I commented.

"My little girl gets sassier by the day, and my little boy gets faster by the day." Emily looked haggard already, and it was only 7:30am. "Her favorite words are 'no!' and 'me!' and every time I blink my eye, I've lost James. The baby proofers came about a month ago and put a lock on every possible opening—doors, cabinets, toilets—and yet, I still can't find him."

"Maybe it's time to get a little help? Jake's always on you about accepting some help. What will you do about James *and* Ellie when both are mobile while you're stationary, nursing the newborn?"

All of a sudden, Emily's face looked like she was going to have a breakdown. She put her head in her hands and the white flag went up. "Maybe it is time to get some help...ugh!"

"Something to consider..." I said, as I saw Gimpy letting go of James. James ran towards me so I thought he might be coming over to hug my leg, but instead, the twerp ran right past me and greeted Laney who opened the door just in time to hug him lovingly.

"Hello, sweet boy! It's your birthday, today!" She cooed to him, while giving us a smile hello. "Are you having a fun day, already?" She walked him over to join his sister in the beat-up-the-balloon-animal game.

Soon, Uncle Henry walked in and joined in the conversation, while Aunt Babs pulled Emily out to inspect the tent that had arrived for our circus, petting zoo, clowns, dunk tanks...all around zoo party.

"How are my favorite grand nephew and niece on their special day?" Uncle Henry picked up James and threw him up in the air, and caught him in time to see James' face light up in giggles. He continued this till Ellie screamed, "Me," loudly enough for us not to be able to ignore her. When she wasn't frightened out of her mind, Ellie, too, loved being thrown up in the air.

"I see this is where the fun is at," Donovan walked in through the kitchen door, and joined the growing party.

"What brings you here at this early hour, Son?" Uncle Henry asked while still holding Elizabeth. The savvy little girl wanted nothing to do with her granduncle, and she hopped over to the younger, better-looking, eligible man. That Ellie—smart girl!

"Where else would I be on this festive day? Naturally, I came to wish my godchildren a happy birthday," he grinned. "And, I also thought I'd catch a ride to work with Roland and Jane since we'll be right back here for the party."

"Good thinking," Gimpy answered. "I'm going to say goodbye to my Estelle, and I'll meet you out front. The car will be here in ten minutes."

"Yes Sir," Donovan answered, while putting Ellie on top of his shoulders. She was loving the attention. "Where's Jake?" he asked Uncle Henry.

"Jake had an early surgery. He'll be home in a few hours to help Emily with the kids while Emily helps my crazy wife with her equally crazy parties."

"Got it," he answered. "Delaney," he called Laney over to him, "let's trade kids."

The two played with the kids for a bit longer and then it was off to work for us, and off to school for Laney. Gimpy had Laney ride with us since her school was only another five minutes south of our office. We'd drop her off, get to the office, then pick her up before going home.

"Laney, how is school going and when do you plan to leave for London?" Gimpy asked.

"School is wonderful, Grandfather," she answered so naturally and sweetly. That brought a smile to Gimpy *and* Donovan's faces. "I graduate in about a month, so I thought I'd leave soon after. Gosh, I'd better start getting ready. I don't have much time left."

"Why so soon, Delaney?"

"I don't know, Mr. Taylor." She thought about that question a bit longer. "I love my family, and will miss them while I'm gone," then she got a little teary, "especially the twins. But I don't really have anything keeping me here once I graduate. I'd like to go see what London has to offer me." She tried to cheer herself up, but still sounded bummed out.

"You won't even stay to see the new baby being born?" I asked, surprised. Laney loved those kids almost as much as Jake and Emily loved those kids.

Now, huge tears formed in Laney's eyes. As fragile doll looking as my cousin was, she was one tough cookie underneath the soft-looking exterior. This girl never cried in public. She used to fall off trees and hold back her tears till she was in the privacy of her own home.

"It kills me to know that I won't see the three kids for a whole year." Gimpy, our English gentleman, handed Laney a handkerchief before the tears fell. "But, this is something I've told myself I wanted to do, and I'll only be gone for a year..." Laney controlled her emotions and not surprisingly, didn't cry.

"What if you meet a special young man out there?" Gimpy posed a legitimate question.

She laughed softly. "Grandfather..." she said thoughtfully, "I haven't met a *special* young man in the US in the twenty-two years I've been here. I don't think I'll meet one in the UK in those twelve short months."

"Laney, have you never been in a serious relationship?" Donovan inquired.

She shook her head no.

"Why not?"

She shrugged her shoulders.

"No man has swept you off your feet and wooed you like a fairy princess from a Disney movie? No glass slipper at midnight...Prince kissing Sleeping Beauty awake from slumber...Beauty kissing the Beast into a prince...?" Donovan and I both laughed at his teasing comment. Anyone who knew our Laney, knew that she lived in la-la-land.

She kept quiet, which turned me into Maleficent again, and Donovan into Gaston right before he went to kill the Beast.

"Laney," Gimpy looked at her hurt eyes, "your time is coming soon, and you'll get all your sweet heart desires and more. Every time we see you loving James and Ellie, your Grandmother and I say that some man is going to be blessed beyond his wildest dreams to be loved by you."

"Thank you, Grandfather," she whispered weakly, and turned away from us to look out the window.

Damn! Now Donovan and I felt like morons and we scowled at each other for making fun of an innocent girl. Both of us felt guilty the whole ride to her school, and even during my short work day, I couldn't get rid of that look I saw on Laney's face. Fortunately, Laney called Gimpy to tell him that she'd ride back home with a friend, so we didn't have to face her again till we got to the party.

The party—it was OVER THE TOP! Aunt Babs went crazy!!! There were clowns, ringmasters, animals, petting zoos, carnival games, carnival "rides" in the shape of ponies, magicians and freaky contortionists. Though it was a kid theme, none of the little ones who were there enjoyed anything but the pony rides and the petting zoo. None were big enough to play any games Neither magicians nor contortionists made any sense to them, and the clowns just outright spooked every child under the age of two. Every time I saw Jake take one of the kids to visit the clown, neither wanted anything to do with him.

"Out of control!" was what Donovan said and I agreed. "Your aunt is something else!"

"That she is!"

"What'd you get the twins?" I asked.

"You see that tall giraffe and fat panda bear, over there?" He pointed to the still animals sitting on a low table.

"Yeah, what is it?"

"Two very costly cakes," he answered with a laugh. "Your aunt called me to tell me about some cake designer she found, and asked me if I wanted to buy these for the twins for their birthdays. What else could I say but yes?"

"Those look amazingly real. Freaky."

"I agree! Let's go join the party."

I searched the tent for my boyfriend, who was coming with his brothers. I found him sitting in front of the magician watching the show.

"Hi," I whispered and kissed Max on the lips.

"Hello," he whispered and kissed me back. "Good day at work?"

"Any day's a good day when I get a half-day to come hang out with you."

"Good answer," he smiled, and held my hand.

"Where's Josh and Garret? Did they come with you?"

"Garret is hanging out with Nick and Doug, and Josh is trailing Laney somewhere in this tent."

Aargh! Laney. Forgot about her. I'd have to apologize and make things right with her before the day was over.

We got up after the show was done, and explored the rest of the carnival.

"Sarah!" Max went over and hugged his college friend. We saw her while getting freshly made cotton candy. He looked really surprised to see her. "When did you, Charlie, and Audrey get back?"

"Like...yesterday," she answered and cracked up. "Literally, we got to LAX last night, came home to a clean, cozy and well-stocked fridge, thanks to Emily, and we must've woken up a few hours ago to make it to this glorious party."

"You guys back for good this time?"

"We better be! I'm done living outside of sunny California."

"Hi Sarah," I butted in where I could.

"Oh my gosh! Jane!!! Hi. Emily told me you two are officially dating." She punched Max in the arm. "Be good to her. I'm told you've met your match."

Max put his arms around me and answered, "Yeah. I think I've found my match made in heaven." He then smiled and kissed me lightly on the lips.

Sarah beamed. "Jane, you must be something really special to get Max waxing poetic like he just did. I'm happy for you both. Come say hi to Charlie and our baby girl who also just turned one." We followed Sarah, who headed in the direction of Emily, Jake and the twins.

Max and Charlie greeted each other with a handshake and a bear hug and he gave little Audrey a kiss on the cheek which brought out a beautiful smile from this girl. Taking after her mom and dad, Audrey was super tall for a one year old. She was at least half a head taller than our squirts. She had a mop of short curly brown hair and gorgeous brown eyes to match. She was going to be a heartbreaker one day as well with her good looks.

"Audrey, this is mommy and daddy's friend, Max and his girlfriend Jane," Sarah introduced us. "You want to let Max hold you?" She asked since Max had his hands out to Audrey as an invitation to rest in his arms.

Audrey was definitely shyer than the imp in Jake's arms because while Audrey was deciding whether or not she wanted to court Max's attention, Ellie adamantly called out, "No!" and she jumped into Max's arms instead. I had to shake my head at this attention-monger. It was always all about her, and she wanted no one displacing her.

"I love you, Elizabeth," Max whispered and kissed her on the forehead. She draped her arms around Max's neck and flirted with him. Totally smitten, Max put both arms around her and embraced her while kissing her a few more times on the side of her head. The sentimental picture these two made was so endearing, it brought a smile to everyone's face.

"Guess what?" Sarah said to Emily.

"You're pregnant, too?" I answered for Emily.

"Dear God! NO!!! I can barely handle Audrey." Sarah shook her head. "Charlie is interviewing with a firm right near here, and if he gets the job, we'll be neighbors."

Emily let out a slight yelp and hugged her best friend. "That would be so fantastic. We can see each other regularly, then."

"Yup! Even if it's a demotion, I told Charlie to take the job. We were so lonely out in Timbuktu by ourselves. I need to be near family and friends."

"Ellie," Josh called out. "You want to go to the dunk tank with us?" Laney and Josh joined us and greeted the Abner family.

My niece wasn't convinced that being with Josh was a more beneficial position until she saw James holding Laney's hand and walking to the other side of the tent. She jumped into Josh's arms and the happy foursome went to dunk their uncle Nick.

"Who are those beautiful people?"

Emily looked pleased to see the happy couple. "You know Josh, Max's brother, and the girl next to him is Jake's cousin, Laney."

"They make such an attractive couple." Sarah was still staring at them.

I was positively giddy for Josh! "They do, don't they?" I agreed.

"But," my brother butted in, "they are not a couple. Just friends."

"Shame." Sarah answered, clucking her tongue.

"That Audrey's darling, too," I said after leaving the two happy families, "and she's going to give our Ellie a little competition when they're a bit older."

"Babe, you've gotta get up awfully early to one up our Elizabeth. She's a force to reckon with right now. She's gonna give Jake hell when she turns about fourteen, I predict."

We both laughed.

"Kate, you're back," I announced mid-laugh, very surprised to see her at James and Ellie's birthday party of all places.

Donovan made a quick beeline over to us, and he greeted her with a semi hug and a cool kiss to her cheek. "You had a comfortable flight back?"

"Yes," she answered in her beautiful voice.

"What brings you back to LA so soon?" Maybe that wasn't the most sensitive thing to say.

"I told Emily and Jake that I would be back for their babies' birthday party, plus there's a bit of unfinished business here."

Weirdly, we all stared at Donovan. He looked a little self-conscious.

"I think they're about ready to cut the cake and sing happy birthday," I announced. "Why don't we all walk over towards that very real looking giraffe and panda bear."

We all sang happy birthday, clapped for the twins, and took paparazzi-like pictures. James and Ellie loved it. Unfortunately, the joie de vivre ended the moment the candles got extinguished. We were fast approaching 6 o'clock and the twins lost it at the same time. They both wailed uncontrollably, and Jake and Emily had to take them in the house to calm them down from party overload.

"I guess the party's over," I whispered to Max.

"Babe," Max said hesitantly, while we started walking towards his car. "I've decided to go on the summer trip."

"Okay..." I knew he was going, but it was still a bummer to know that he would not be with me for an entire month. I know I'm acting stupid by being bummed out, but no matter how I looked at it, it bummed me out!

"There are two groups going. The first group is leaving on your birthday in June, and the next group is leaving in July. I want to spend your birthday with you, and I want to see Emily and Jake's new baby before I leave. Then, I'll be back just in time to start my last year of med school."

"All right. Sounds like a plan."

"Since I'm not leaving till July, I thought maybe we could start looking for a place to live, and I'd get settled with you before the trip begins? What do ya think?"

"I'd love for us to start looking for a place together. When does your lease end?"

"In June, but if we find something we like, I'd like to start living together right away. I'll just pay rent at both places for a few months."

"All right!" I answered with a huge grin. I was doing my happy dance, again.

"Shall we go have dinner and plan for our future?"

"Let's!"

April 25, 2013

Everything's Shot

So the three-ring circus (three being the operative word) continued with us going apartment hunting while the rest of the
family attended a golf tournament. I was getting dressed, super excited that my man was coming to take me to look for our future
"home," when I got the freakin' spoiler for the entire month.

"Gem, I've got a bit of bad news."

Crap. Now what? I had no idea what this bad news was going to be,
and I really didn't want to hear about it, but I guess I had to ask.

"Okay. I'm ready to hear the bad news."

"Hannah is coming with us...apartment hunting."

What the freakin' hell! Why the hell was she coming apartment
hunting with us? It's not like she was going to live with us!

"I'm sorry, Gem. I know what's going through your mind right now,
but it's not what you're thinking."

"What's going through my mind right now?"

"You're wondering why the hell she's coming apartment hunting with us when she's not going to live with us. Am I right?" He started laughing.

"Yes, mind reader. So why will your ex-girlfriend be apartment hunting with your current girlfriend? This sounds like some sick reality TV show."

Max laughed even harder. "She wants to get a place of her own now that she has a job and she's not sure where to look. When I told her that I was apartment hunting with you, she asked if it would be possible to tag along. And since she doesn't have a car yet, she literally has to tag along."

Shit! This Hannah was reminding me of gum stuck to the bottom of your shoes. Unknowingly, it comes upon you, annoyingly, it follows you every step of the way, and unfortunately, you're never able to get rid of it completely.

"I'm on my way to pick up Hannah, and then I'll come pick you up."

"The three of us riding on your bike together? Who gets to spoon you?" I asked sarcastically.

"Ha ha ha. Very funny. If you don't lose the bad attitude, you may have to ride in the backseat while Hannah gets shotgun."

I was just about to tell him that he can go shove his comment up his ass, when he cut me off and told me he loved me. Loser that I am, those three words made it all better.

Sooner than expected, Max was at my door, showing me how much he loved me with a tongue-filled kiss. "Hello, Gem. You ready to find a home for us for the next year?"

"Yep!" I said with a huge grin. After I kissed him a bit longer with the door *WIDE* open—just in case any looky-loo was interested in looky-looing—we walked hand in hand towards Max's car. Every step we got closer to his car, I expected Hannah to get out of the front seat, say hello, and move back. But *nooooo!* She just stayed sitting, waved hello from the front seat, and had no thoughts of moving back. *BITCH! BITCH!! BITCH!!!* This was *NOT* going to be a fun morning.

"Babe." Max tried to appease me with a pleading voice. He knew I was pissed. "Don't make a big deal out of this. Please?"

I looked at him to say, *"Really?"* But he gave me such a desperate look that I sucked back what I was about to say, and sat in the back-seat like a good little girl.

"Hi Jane," Hannah said enthusiastically.

"Hey Hannah," I said unenthusiastically. I felt like a moron sitting back here while my boyfriend sat next to his ex-girlfriend.

Hannah kept asking Max questions that pertained to their past life, and I had no way of jumping into their conversation. The bitch was purposely leaving me out. Do I fight back and play the same stupid game, or do I act mature and keep my mouth shut?

Deciding to be the bigger person, I took out my phone and gave Max directions to some of the buildings I'd bookmarked. I wanted to look at apartments in the downtown area, and I possibly considered putting a down payment on one if we really liked it. I had so much money saved up since all I'd been doing till now was mooching off my parents' real estate investments. Every building I wanted to visit, party pooper up in the front seat lamented, "Oh that looks too expensive for me to rent." I knew she was purposely raining on my parade. I let it go the first few times, but now I was pissed.

"Pull over! I want to look at this building." I didn't care what the hell Hannah wanted or not wanted. She could stay in the car. This was the building I was going to look at.

The first unit we saw was a bit small. The sales guy said it was a one-bedroom loft, but it was small enough to be a studio. After living in New York City for so long, I preferred big open floor plans to matchbox-sized rooms. The second one was a two bedroom and it was nice, but I asked him to take us up to the top floor because I wanted to see what the penthouse looked like.

"Uh Jane," Max called. "I don't know if we can afford the penthouse." Of course we couldn't afford the penthouse, but could a girl not look and dream?

I didn't answer Max. Rather, I just followed the sales guy up to the top floor. The penthouse had a wonderful view of downtown LA, and on a clear day, I could possibly even see Catalina Island. It was more than spacious enough for the two of us. And there were enough rooms for each to have an office and go study or work without bothering one another. I also loved the open floor plan and modern kitchen that already came equipped with every appliance. I could see us living here, having a life here, possibly even having a family here during the early years.

But all those dreams shriveled up into thin air when Max dryly commented, "You want to discuss this before you fall in love with an apartment we can't afford?"

"What's there to discuss? We're just looking."

"You know this place is not for rent. I thought we talked about getting a place together."

"We are getting a place together. What does it matter whether we rent or buy?"

"Jane, I don't have the finances to buy a place, and even if I did have the money, I have no desire to buy anything right now."

I know he didn't exactly add the words "with you," in between "anything" and "right now," but with the snarky tone he gave me, he might as well have said those words. That really hurt my feelings. *Max* really hurt my feelings. It was bad enough that Hannah was right next to Max listening to this conversation, but it was worse knowing that Max only wanted something temporary with me. It really, really hurt to know that he was not looking into the future at all.

"Okay," I said, void of all emotions, "let's go."

The rest of the afternoon was spent basically looking for apartments for Max...and Hannah. It was almost as though *they* were moving in together, rather than *us* moving in together. They both seem to be in accord with what they wanted in an apartment. I kept my mouth shut, and stopped talking the rest of the afternoon. And, I purposely sat in the backseat every time we got in the car.

"Jane, you going to pick up your phone?" I had been in such deep thought, I didn't even hear my phone ring till Max called attention to it.

"Hello?"

"Jane, are you with Max?"

"Yes Dad, I am. Did you need to talk to him?"

"No, Sweetheart. I just wanted to invite you and Max over to dinner at the club. The golf tournament is over and we are all at the lounge right now, but will be having dinner in about an hour. Would you two like to join us? I'll reserve two more seats for our party if you'd like to join."

Having dinner with Max was not in my plans—as of about two hours ago. "I don't know, Dad. I'll think about it and call you back."

As soon as I got off the phone, I went back to silent mode. Max wasn't doing as much talking to the current girlfriend as he was to the former girlfriend, so I figured I was safe from inviting him to dinner. I was counting down the number of freeway exits till we got to my house. Obviously, he was planning on spending more time with his ex because he was dropping me off first. Whatever! At this point in the day, I didn't care.

"Hello Dr. Reid." Max's greeting caught my attention. "Yes, we're almost home. Um...no, Jane didn't mention dinner."

Shoot! Why did Dad have to call Max? I was almost home.

"Yes, Sir. We will be there soon," was all I heard, as he ended the call.

"Are you going somewhere?" Hannah, the *I-act-so-sweet-but-I'm-really-a-conniving-bitch*, asked.

"Jane's dad invited us to have dinner with everyone who was at the golf tournament."

"Isn't that where Josh and Garret went this morning? Can I join all of you for dinner, too?"

I didn't know how I held back all the four letter words that flipped through my head like a Rolodex out of control, but I did. Since I hadn't said a word both times my dad called, I continued to stay silent and let Max figure this one out. Next thing I saw, he redialed my dad's number.

"Dr. Reid, would it be all right if a friend joined for dinner as well?"

A friend? Seriously? Did he actually refer to this woman as a friend?

"Yes, Sir. Thank you." And just like that, I was not only having dinner with a man whom I didn't want to have dinner with, but also with his ex-girlfriend. Too soon, the two friendly exes carried their own conversation again. I didn't know whether to seethe inside or to cry.

"What's with the long face, Janey?" Nick was the first person I came across as soon as Max dropped me off. Actually, it was more like a Tom Cruise *Mission Impossible* stunt out of a moving car at the valet area, than a drop-off.

"Don't ask! I'm not good company right now."

"Are you ever?" He said and started laughing, till he saw the scowl on my face. He soon just ran away.

"I see your disposition is about as sunny as mine," Donovan said while plopping in the seat next to me. "What's the matter, my vixen?"

I looked over at Max and Hannah walking in.

"Trouble in the Garden of Eden?"

"I think I've decided to become a nun," I declared.

"Lead the way because I think I'm going to become a monk," he added and watched Kate walking in with a gaggle of men behind her.

"What's she doing here?" She was the second to the last person I expected to see. The last, of course, was Hannah.

"Perhaps she's here to stake a claim just like your friend over there." He pointed with his head towards Hannah.

"I think I need a drink. What do you want? First round on the Reid tab."

"A shot. We'll both start with a shot of tequila, then move on to the stronger stuff. Can you hold your liquor, Vixen?"

"I can..."

"All righty then...let's start!"

Donovan and I were feeling mighty buzzed by the time our families all assembled in the room. They had been at the awards ceremony, where apparently, Laney cleaned house.

"I thought she wasn't playing this year."

"She wasn't, but your Uncle Henry's team almost folded with two players coming down with food poisoning. On a side note, let me say, I think your uncle poisoned his teammates, himself. Of course, Delaney had to step in at the eleventh hour, and she brought a ringer with her."

"Who's the ringer?"

He did the head pointing again.

"What's he doing here? Doesn't Nolan live in Hawaii?"

"Part of his cush gig at the resort is to travel and experience other resort golf courses. What kind of lame-ass company offers those kinds of incentives?"

I cracked up. "You're just jealous you can't work for that kind of lame-ass company. Instead you work sixty+ hours a week making people like my grandfather, rich. You're the lame ass!"

"I am!" He lamented. "Oh, I didn't tell you who else is here."

"Who?"

He pointed the other way with his head again.

"No, freakin' way!!! Am I drunk already, or is that my old roommate Allison?"

"And Jake's old play thing, too, let's not forget. Jake almost had a heart attack when she called out his name and started running towards him at the golf course."

I died laughing! "Heart attack, good one. Was that supposed to be some play-on words with his profession? Or is that called a double entrendre?"

"No, dummy! It had no second meaning. He really almost had a heart attack and would've if Emily had been there." Donovan started slurring his words. I waited for the hiccups to start. "You're drunk, already."

"You're the drunk one!" I accused. "I'm perfectly coherent. In any case, what the hell is she doing here? This club is letting in anyone nowadays!" I sounded like such a snob, but I didn't care. I was buzzed, I was pissed, and I was letting out steam.

"Apparently, she was having an affair with one of the old geezers, and his wife left his ass as soon as she found out. And now, Allison is head of that household."

"Scary! Jake with his present and past, Max with his present and past, and you with your present and...that's right, Kate is present and past. This is one big scary family we've got going on here."

"So tell me, Vixen, who is that homey Midwest-looking girl that Max is with, and why are you so pissed off tonight?"

"She's his high school ex who's living in his parents' home, invading my apartment hunting time with my boyfriend, and trying to weasel her way into our lives every which way she can." I downed another shot after that explanation. Donovan and I never moved on, alcohol-wise. We were taking turns putting shots on our parents' tabs. "Why are you drinking with me, when you have Sea-foam goddess at your disposal?".

Unlike me, Donovan took his shot before the explanation. "I'm so damned confused with life. I don't know what I want, I don't know what I'm doing, and worst of all, I don't know why I keep thinking the way I do."

"That was the most convoluted way of not answering a question. Spill it, Donovan! What is it that you want?"

"You...Kate..." It sounded like there should've been a third name spoken, but no other name was mentioned.

"Don't be an idiot. You don't want either one of us. You're such a freakin' liar." Another round of shots came and we both downed them at the same time. "Okay, next...what are you doing?"

"I was told by a wise friend that I was physically with one woman, mentally thinking about another woman, but didn't have the guts to emotionally love the right woman. That's what I'm doing."

"Shit! Another damn mouthy answer. Next...what the hell are you thinking?"

"It's a matter of a thought I can't shut off, that's bothering the fuck out of me."

"Eengh!" I crossed my arms into an X and made the Family Feud buzzer noise. "Wrong, stupid-ass answer, again. Strike three, you're out!" I said, and we both laughed at one another.

"You done making a fool of yourself, here?"

I looked up at a pissed-off Max.

"You done playing boyfriend to your ex-girlfriend?" I challenged back.

Donovan laughed and congratulated me with a high-five. "Good one," he whispered.

"Dinner's over. I'm taking Hannah home. I'll take you home too, if you need a ride."

Something about this statement sobered me up real quick. He didn't offer to take me home. He didn't ask if he could make amends with me after such a horrible day. He extended a ride to me *only* if I needed one. My heart broke again, and I blinked back the tears.

"I don't think I drank enough to forget this day," I said and downed another one.

April 29, 2013

Take-out

$\mathcal{N}$INE days since our oh-so-successful apartment hunting and drink-fest have come and gone, and no word from my ever-faithful, loving boyfriend. Of course, I haven't made any effort to contact him either. Two weekends ago was painful. And it had nothing to do with the gnarly hangover I experienced the next morning. Every which way I looked at it, I did *not* do *one thing wrong*. It was Max who should come apologize, and it was Max who should beg me for forgiveness. Until he did, I wasn't budging. We, too, would stay at an impasse.

My heart wasn't feeling well, but I wasn't going to stay home and mope around. In fact, I purposely kept myself busy this past weekend so I wouldn't think too much about Max—not that I was very successful. Friday night, Donovan invited Jake and Emily to a Lakers' playoff game and once again, he got seats on the floor. I made such a stink about not being invited, that Donovan *had* to buy another ticket and "invite" me.

"You're the best!" I applauded his decision to buy a fourth, very expensive, ticket.

"You're a pain in the ass," he growled as he clicked the "purchase" button from the online ticket site.

Yes, I went to his office, stood by his side and made sure he bought me a ticket as well. Bratty, I know! "You buying dinner?" Donovan asked.

"No way! My brother can buy dinner. Where are we eating, by the way?"

"You're eating at home. The three of us are eating sushi."

"I'm sticking to you like glue today, so don't even think about getting on that shuttle without me," I smiled. "I'll buy you an egg salad sandwich for lunch today," I offered.

"Whatever. Go back to your cubicle, and let me bill some hours so I can pay for that ticket I just purchased," he shooed me away.

"Did I ever tell you that you're my favorite lawyer in this office?"

"GO TO WORK!" He commanded.

So that's how I got myself to a sushi dinner at a trendy hot spot at LA Live and to a floor seat, a few chairs down from Ryan Seacrest and the lesser Kardashian sisters, at a Lakers' game. Friday night was fun, but unfulfilling.

Saturday, I decided to hop in my car and drive down to San Diego to hang out with my cousin Sam and one of my best friends, Evie. I plopped my stuff down at Sam's apartment, and we had a late brunch, shopped and shopped some more. We then met Evie for dinner and went to a club after dinner. Though I had a good time, I felt empty.

Sunday morning, I drove back home, milled around the house, and even babysat for Jake and Emily so they could run some errands in the afternoon. The twins kept me crazy occupied, and eventually wore me out—but still, I couldn't stop thinking about Max and why he wasn't reaching out to me.

Today was Monday, and I was on the verge of thinking maybe we were done. Every time we got into a fight, Max and I usually went dark on each other, but it's never been this long, and it's never been this dark and silent. I didn't even want to contemplate what Max had been doing with a girl (or maybe even two girls, Bitch and Psycho) who I'm sure made certain Max came in contact with her daily.

Work was done early, and I thought about joining my co-workers for drinks, or calling out Nick or Laney or Doug for dinner, but decided against it. Instead, I went to a little hole in the wall take-out joint Max and I frequented. Crestfallen, but still mulish about not reaching out first, I went to a place where I could feel Max's presence.

I parked out front in the loading only zone, knowing I'd quickly pick up the order I'd called in, and stopped dead when I saw Max sitting at a two-top, laughing and enjoying dinner with Hannah. He didn't notice me right away so I made a split second decision and turned around. I fumbled with the keys, got in the car, and tried to contain the tears I was drowning in. I needed to leave before there was any chance of him seeing my car through the glass entryway, but I couldn't move. I'd never felt so betrayed and devastated. Now I knew what it meant to have my heart broken in a million pieces.

It was still early, and I contemplated calling Becky and crying my heart out to her. She'd understand and help me sift through the pain. As I reached for my phone, I remembered that she was in the early stages of pregnancy and quite ill, so I stopped myself from asking for help. I tried to call Evie, but she wasn't answering, and Ashley was in such a honeymoon stage about her wedding, I didn't want to spoil her happiness by bringing in my sadness. Emily was an option, but since I was always bemoaning my woes to her and Jake, I didn't want to be seen as an even bigger loser. Laney? After laughing at her in the car with Donovan and not making things right with her, she wasn't the right person to call, either.

If tonight taught me anything, I needed to be kinder to the people around me and make more friends. I was desperate to share my hurt with someone, but there were very few someones in my life, and even fewer someones available for me. Perhaps I should've been there first for my friends so that when my time came, they'd be there for me. Lesson learned!

After much introspection in a parked car near my home, I decided to go home and sleep this ugliness away. All the crying exhausted me, and a good night's rest was necessary to clear my head. I'd give Max a call tomorrow and decide together what needed to be done about our relationship. I didn't believe we were over, but a lot had to be said.

Walking into a silent home, I'd purposely stayed out later than I'd wished, so everyone would be asleep. I didn't relish having to explain myself. Last thing I needed was four elderly folks worrying about a sprightly twenty-seven-year-old.

"Hey," a raspy voice greeted me as I opened my door. "I thought you would come right home. Where've you been?"

Huh? Somehow, somewhere, someone heard my plea, and sent me a friend whose shoulder I hope, I could cry on.

May 2, 2013

Did I Miss Something?

"Where've you been?" Max sat up tall on my bed, back against the headboard, arms open for me. Pride be damned. I crawled perfectly into his arms and cried silently. My body showed all the signs of crying, but I didn't make a sound. Today I realized I'd have a very tough time living without this man. "Baby, don't cry. It breaks my heart to see you like this."

I didn't care that it broke his heart. My heart was broken too, and this is exactly what I needed—Max's shoulder to cry on.

"Hey," I heard Max whisper in my ear. "What time do you have to get to work this morning?"

I woke up dazed and feeling almost hung over, again. My head felt like it was splitting, and I was incredibly thirsty.

"I don't have much going on today," I croaked. "I can get in later. I just need to let someone know."

"Stay here. I'll take care of it for you."

Max left the room, and I reviewed what happened last night the best I could. I remembered coming home, finding Max in my bed, crying, then the reel cut off. I couldn't recall whether we talked, worked anything out, had sex??? From the looks of his wrinkled shirt, Max had stayed the night with me in my bed, but according to my memory, I couldn't conjure up any fun time had. I stopped thinking. My head hurt badly.

It took a while, but Max eventually came back with a tray of food, coffee, a tall glass of water, and some Advil. I guess he was close to knowing me pretty well by now.

He placed the tray on my lap and handed me the water and Advil first.

"Thanks," I said and did as the good doctor ordered.

"Let's eat first, then talk?" I agreed to his suggestion. "I take it you didn't have dinner last night?"

As soon as he mentioned last night, it all came back to me—dinner, Max, Hannah, laughter—and the tears fell again. I felt like a fool crying again, and I couldn't believe there were any tears left. So much for the tough girl persona I'd been putting on for the past twenty-seven years. It all got shot to hell in the last twelve hours.

"Sorry," I apologized and tried to put myself together.

Max took the tray away and sat in front of me looking serious. "I don't know where to begin with the apologies. There are so many things I've done wrong in the last week and a half, I'm embarrassed to count all my grievances." This wasn't the way I envisioned this conversation to go, but I wasn't going to stop it. "First, let's talk about last night."

"Ok," I croaked, again.

"What you saw at the restaurant wasn't what it looked like."

I said, "Ok," again, but not in any convincing manner.

"My initial intention was to pick up some dinner and come see you last night. But when I called to place my order, Tony told me that you had just placed the same order. I combined our orders and told him not to let you leave before I showed up. When I got there, Hannah was there eating by herself, so I stopped to chat with her till you came."

The explanation sounded feasible, but not enough to sooth my hurt. "How did you know I was there?"

"I didn't till I thought I spotted your car out front. When I went outside to greet you, you were going instead of coming. It didn't take me long to put two and two together and figure that you probably thought I was having dinner with Hannah."

I guess I didn't look convinced.

"I swear, Babe. The last time I saw Hannah was when I dropped her off at my parents' after our shitty Saturday. I've avoided her at the hospital, and I haven't returned any of her calls. I needed to talk to you, first."

The fight in me was slowly reappearing because I contemplated asking him why he didn't make me first the last time I saw him. But, for now, I liked being silent. It made Max more and more nervous.

"As soon as I saw you leave, I picked up our food, came straight here and waited for you. I didn't think you'd be out so late. Where were you all that time?"

"Nowhere in particular."

"You didn't go see Donovan?" Max treaded lightly.

"Unlike you, I know who I'm dating." Cheap shot, I know, considering I had wavered in the past with Donovan. "I sat in my car wondering how to put myself back together again after the damage you'd caused." Yes...another cheap shot. The snarky me was coming back, but something in Max's demeanor told me I should hold back a little. He looked kinda somber. Though he had NINE days to think about it, maybe he was trying to come up with plan Z on how to win me back. That was probably what his whole *I feel sad* look was about.

"Saturday. Let's talk about Saturday," Max sighed loudly. "I was angry when you took us up to an apartment I couldn't afford. I felt inadequate as a man, not being able to give you something you wanted, and I felt sorry for Hannah who could barely afford to live in the single we saw. Part of me was mad because I thought you were showing off to Hannah and trying to get back at her for the stupid games she was playing, and part of me was angry that I was such a moron for bringing Hannah with us. I was hoping to pull you aside at the club and apologize, but you went straight to Donovan and didn't leave his side the whole night."

Something about Max was really off, but I decided I didn't care. For NINE freakin' days, he left me alone to stew and worry about where we stood as a couple. What boyfriend did that? "First of all, I didn't go straight to Donovan. He was having a shitty day himself, and he sat next to me. We were just two friends commiserating! If you'd come to me, your girlfriend, rather than hanging with Hannah, your ex-girlfriend, I would have gladly done the shots with you instead. Second, I wasn't showing off, I wasn't asking you for anything, and I wasn't trying to make anyone feel bad! I wanted to see what a penthouse loft looked like. I can't afford one either, and I was..." I just stopped there. I didn't want to tell him how devastated I was when he told me he wasn't interested in buying anything with me.

He reached out and put his hand over my two hands. He looked so torn and devastated himself, I felt like I should comfort him instead of the other way around. *What the hell is the matter with you, Max? Why is my heart feeling your pain more than my own?* "I know how much I hurt you when I told you that I didn't want to buy anything right now. I saw your face and my heart broke when yours did. I'm sorry, Jane. After seeing how defeated you were, I felt stupid retracting my statement and telling you that the reason I couldn't buy anything was because I didn't know where I'd end up doing residency. I still have a long way to go before making any money as a doctor. I wasn't implying that I didn't want any future with you."

He wiped the tears that started falling down my face. This was the most fucked-up situation. He was apologizing, but my heart broke more for him, than for me. None of this was making sense to me. Maybe I needed to go back to sleep.

"When I asked your dad if Hannah could join us at the club, I was hoping that she'd hang with my brothers, so I could have a chance to make everything right between us. I had no idea Hannah would put us in such an awkward situation, and I felt like an asshole for hurting you. I still have a lot of guilt where Hannah is concerned. Because of me, she never went to college, she hasn't been in any other serious relationship...her life regressed while mine progressed. I see now how hard it is for her to see me so in love with you. It brings out all kinds of ugliness in her, but I try to be understanding. I was hoping you would, too, but I guess that was wrong of me to assume."

"What the hell was your problem at the club? You didn't once come and talk to me until you offered me a *ride*. Why didn't you make up with me then?" My voice got angrier than it should have, but Max deserved it. "And don't give me the lame-ass excuse about me hanging out with Donovan. You hung out with Hannah, too. If you don't want me to be upset about Hannah, then you can't be upset about Donovan, either." That's right. I told him! Fair is fair.

That's when the hovering clouds moved right above us and made everything seriously dark and gloomy. Max couldn't look at me anymore. He stood up from the bed and faced the door for *wayyyy* longer than it was comfortable. I was too scared to ask him if he was all right, and I sure as hell wasn't going to berate him any more—No siree, Bob! After thinking about it myself, maybe I was a bit hard on him. The whole NINE unanswered days are still a huge question mark in my head, but he did explain about Hannah. And of course, I do believe everything he told me. But...what was wrong with Max? Why was he so gloom-and-doom, today?

"There are so many things I thought I'd say to you when I finally got the chance." He speaks...! Now, if I could only figure out what the hell he was saying. "Whenever I think about you, about us, I know that you're the root that holds my bearing, the trunk that makes me stand tall, and the branches that help me bear fruit." *Whaaa?* When did this turn into a romantic botany lesson? I believe that was romantic..?

This was getting weird! I needed to lighten up the mood. There were still so many things I wanted to say to this man, but right now was not it. Plus, my head still hurt, my stomach growled, and I needed a cup of coffee.

"Can we go take a walk and grab a cup of coffee? I've a splitting headache."

"Sure." He said and said no more. Thank God. I was weirded out enough. Talk for now was done.

We walked hand in hand to the local coffee shop in total silence. I don't know what it was like for Max, but for me, it was a comfortable silence. Mentally, I was making a list of all the things I wanted to say to him. All the angry retorts, sarcastic remarks, witty quips waited in a nice long queue for their chance. After all the mental yelling and finger pointing, all I eventually said was, "Do you like seeing me with Donovan?"

"No, of course not," he almost yelled. I jumped back and wanted to yell as well, but held off since this Max was not my Max, today.

"Well, I don't like seeing you with Hannah, either. And just remember, I've never had any sort of a relationship with Donovan. The only time he's ever touched me was to give me an innocuous kiss on my head. You think about that, and let's talk again later."

I ended on that note and soon after our coffee run, I convinced Max to lay in bed with me. I seriously needed a nap at 10am. It had been an exhausting many days.

Max was half-sitting against the headboard, half-laying on the bed to accommodate my body that covered most of his. Sleep hovered and was oh so close when Max's phone gave me a slight jolt.

"Hello?" I heard my kind boyfriend whisper so I wouldn't be disturbed. "Hey Garret." Oh...it was Garret. It sounded like Garret was asking something similar to *"did you do it?"* Max kissed me on the head and whispered again, "No...I couldn't do it. I love her too much."

I tried to stay awake to listen in on this unusual conversation, but sleep was overpowering me. I'd try and remember to ask him later. Last I heard before going off into my own world was, "I love you, my precious Gem."

May 6, 2013

Honestly!

My honey was still walking on eggshells, trying to make up to me what he did a couple of weeks ago. Just between you and me, all was forgiven the night he came over and stayed with me, but he didn't have to know that yet. Secretly, I got great pleasure out of watching Max grovel. And boy, he was workin' the grovel.

"What's with the flower arrangement? Max?" Donovan popped by my cubicle to take me to lunch.

"Yep." I answered happily.

"You still holding a grudge from our tequila night?"

"Yep!" I answered happily, again.

"Damn, Woman! That was like a month ago. Remind me not to get on your bad side." He let out a hearty chuckle.

"Yep." I said a third time, still with a smile.

Since our bonding over tequila, Donovan and I had become even better friends. There was still a tiny bit of tension between us, but we were more buddies than anything else lately.

"Can we eat something other than egg salad?"

"Yep."

He gave me a funny look, which was still hot on this man, and told me to "cut out the monosyllabic answers."

"I'll stop saying 'yep' if you tell me what's going on with you and Kate."

"Holds a grudge for a month, stubborn, and nosy...and yet I still find her attractive. Why is that?" He asked a rhetorical question.

"Yep," I said again, laughing.

"Ok, stop with the yep. I've ended things for good with Kate."

Oohhhh! This was juicy info. "Why?"

"She wants marriage, kids, the Jake and Emily life..."

"And???"

"And I want the same...but not with her. I've decided to listen to my wise friend and try intimacy with my heart rather than just the body or mind." He said this while laughing to himself.

"Who?"

"Who what? And stop the damn one word Q&A."

I looked up from my tacos and gave him a questioning look.

"Please, stop with the damn one word Q&A?" He asked nicely, which made me crack up. "And by the way, that look you just gave me—you should do the whole librarian get-up and try it on Max. That should revive the relationship in no time."

I died laughing. "Ok, I don't need you visualizing me in a librarian get-up."

"Yeah, me neither. I don't need my body parts *getting-up* unnecessarily, and unfulfillingly."

"All righty! Let's change the subject 'cuz now you're giving me visuals I don't need. Back to Kate. Who told you to stop lusting and to start loving?"

"A friend."

"A friend, who?"

"That's none of your business."

"Why the secrecy? Why can't you tell me?" Now I was more than curious.

"I'll tell you if you tell me who Hannah really is. And don't give me the same bullshit you've been telling your family. I know she's more than a girl he dated in high school."

Did I want to do this trading of top secret info? Was it worth it to find out who's been giving Donovan love advice?

"Well...what's it gonna be? You gonna *put out*?"

"Damn it. Stop making everything sexual."

He laughed. "Do I need to *tie* you to the chair and *force* the info from you, *come* to my own conclusion, or will you *put out* willingly?" Now he was giving me the suggestive waggle of the eyebrow look.

Part of me died laughing, and part of me was seriously hot and bothered. But I *SWEAR*, I was thinking of my boyfriend Max! It wasn't Donovan who was on my mind sexually.

"You first. You *spill* your beans, then I *come* forth with my info, if I deem your info is worthy enough."

"Forget it. I'll *spill* only if you promise to *come...forth*."

This was a serious case of ROTFLMAO! "All right! Hannah and Max dated back in high school, he knocked her up, almost married her, then she lost the baby, he was relieved, she was depressed, her parents moved her to Michigan, and now she's back," I said all in one breath. "Beat that!" I challenged.

After being bug-eyed briefly (ok, he was still hot even with the bug-eyes), he said, "I kissed your cousin Delaney in her hotel room the night she went missing. That's where she told me that she had no designs on 'joining my harem', and that's also when she told me that I was 'with one woman physically, thinking about another woman mentally, but didn't have the guts to truly love a woman, emotionally.'" He smirked and continued, "By the look on your face and the hole in your mouth, I think I 'beat that!'"

"You what??? What the fuck???"

"Wow. My story was good enough for an f-bomb? I thought you never said *fuck*."

"Well...I do say it...it's just not in your ears."

Now he was ROTFLHAO. "We need to stop—unless you're willing to put out...with me."

"You are *not* turning this on me. I want to know about this kiss with Laney. What the hell happened? You kiss her? She kiss you? Is that what you were doing in there the whole time...kissing?"

"Let's talk about us first."

"There's no us, Donovan. I love Max."

"Let's be honest with one another."

"Shit, if we were any more honest with one another than we are now, we'd be Jake and Emily!"

"You ever wonder what it would be like with us?" *Hell yes!* "You ever want to know if we'd have as good a chemistry as lovers as we do as friends?" *OMG. I don't think I can answer this one even to myself.* "Well, I want to know. I want to know what it feels like to make out with you, to make love to you, to make you moan my name. I want to be with you in every physical way and see if that will lead to the emotions Delaney accuses me of not being capable of having. I know I'm being an asshole wondering this about another man's woman, but honestly, I can't stop wondering."

Honestly? I would've preferred a lie.

May 9, 2013

Oh...A Hunting He Will Go...

You'll all be happy to know, Donovan got called away the moment he finished his confession, and flew to London to help Kate with a client. PHEW! I haven't seen him, heard from him, nor really thought about him. *Honestly!* I haven't thought too much about us, but this whole idea of Donovan and Laney kissing, was bugging the crap out of me. He never finished telling me what had happened in that room and I couldn't possibly ask Laney. I asked Emily about it, and she immediately got on the phone with Donovan and chewed him out for "kissing and telling." After that, there was no way he was going to tell me anything. Emily also told me to mind my own business and to be more of a girlfriend to Max, than a girl friend to Donovan. Well, *excuse...me....!* Emily was pissed at me and Donovan, and I was pissed with her for being so pissy. Lucky for her, I got a text from Max, so I excused myself and went home.

You want to go out tonight?

Isn't it a school night?

Yeah...can we not go out on a school night?

No. We can. You gonna pick me up or shall I meet you somewhere?

I'll pick you up in 20. I have my bike. Wear pants...or not.

See you in 20 and I'll consider wearing (under) pants...or not.

That would give him something to think about. He he he!

"That was the quickest 20 minutes, ever. You on a different time zone?" I said to the man who hopped off his bike and ran up to me.

"Well, when your girlfriend considers not wearing any underwear, it is worth a speeding ticket to find out whether or not she made the right decision." He said with a luscious kiss. "Shall we find out?" I had to stop his roaming hands since we were on the sidewalk and any Reid could see our lusty ways.

"Where shall we go eat?"

"Before we eat, I want to show you something. Hop on."

We got on the bike and rode a few minutes to a more artsy neighborhood near my home.

"Where are we?"

"I've been doing a bit of research on my own, and I thought this might be the neighborhood you might want to move into..." He cut his statement short.

"Is there more?"

"...assuming you still wanted to move in with me...?"

Oh my gosh, the uncertainty in his voice and in that statement almost killed me. I'd given him such a hard time the last month— didn't return many of his calls, gave him the cold shoulder from time to time, purposely avoided him when he came over—that he was scared of me. I was just playing games with him, enjoying the upper hand I had in this relationship. What a total bitch I'd been.

"Max. I'm so sorry for my behavior the last few weeks. I was mad at first, but I shouldn't have dragged this out for so long. I didn't mean to make you wonder about my feelings for you. I love you, and I still want to live with you, assuming now that you still want to live with me after my confession."

"I love you too, Gem." His smile told me that it was *all* right in our world, again. "I want you to see how cool this place is, and if we wanted to, it's large enough for us to..." he stopped himself again. This time, I didn't ask why he stopped. I enthusiastically walked into the courtyard of the building and inspected the home he was so eager to show me.

"I talked to my financial advisor and..."

I cut off Max's sentence. "You have a financial advisor?"

"Kind of," he laughed. "Josh is actually all of our financial advisor. He's really good with investments. He day trades with his own money. That's partly how he's financing a year in Europe without having to get a job."

"Seriously?"

Max nodded in the affirmative. "He's been doing it the last six years or so. First he started secretly with his own money, back in high school. Once he successfully doubled his bank account, he showed us what he was doing and offered to do it for all three of us."

"Do I need to give him my money? It's just sitting in a savings account earning 1% interest." I learned something new every day.

"If you like. He's really good and he's very careful. I didn't quite understand how good he was till I went to him the other day and asked about my financial situation."

Fanfreakin'tastic! Now I had someone who would invest my money, without taking a huge cut.

"Why did you need to talk about your finances? Do you need money? I have money just sitting in the bank doing nothing if you need it. You're welcome to use whatever you need."

Whoa! Did I just say all those things? I hoped I didn't freak out Max, nor hurt his manly feelings. Men were so sensitive about the stupidest things.

"Thanks for the offer, Babe. I'm good." He answered with a very big smile.

"I mean it. You can use whatever you need."

"Thank you, Gem. It means a lot to me that you feel that close to me. But really, I'm doing okay. In fact, I'm doing better than okay."

"So...you're telling me all this because..."

"Come check out the place and I'll explain."

Max was right. The apartment was cooler than cool. They were individual, stand-alone units that had high ceilings, a wide-open floor plan, tons of built-ins and cabinet space and two bedrooms. The two bedrooms were both master suites with master baths and a massive walk-in closet. I knew this place was meant to be when I saw the mini shoe closet in addition to the master closet. I have a thing for shoes, if you haven't noticed already.

"This place is awesome! How'd you find it?"

"A med school buddy told me his brother just bought a unit, and because this is not the most desirable neighborhood, it's surprisingly affordable."

"All right. So what are you thinking?"

"Garret, Josh and I are each thinking of buying a unit. To cover mortgage, Josh will rent his place out before he leaves for Europe. Garret and I will live in our units. After a small down, mortgage won't be much more than our current rent."

And what of me? The question was on the tip of my tongue but I kept it there. It was all me who had put us in this precarious state again.

Max knew my worry and gave me a tender, reassuring kiss. "If you're okay with my plans, I'd love for you to come live with me."

Did I bring up the fact that I was hurt he didn't want to buy something with me?

"Whatcha thinking, Gem?"

"I'm thinking I love the place; it's close to my family, and it'll be great to live close to your brothers as well."

"But?"

I thought about it. Then I thought about it some more. In the end, I just shook my head no and followed Max to the lease/purchase office. Josh and Garret had joined us somewhere during negotiations.

The three Davises decided to hold off a bit longer before buying the units, thinking time may gain them more leverage. We all went to dinner and Josh called out Doug, Nick and Laney.

"So are you going to buy the place?" Laney asked. She seemed to know more about this housing situation than I did. I didn't realize those two had been talking without my knowledge. Not that Laney needed my permission to talk to Josh. In fact, I applauded her for getting to know him.

"I think we are going to buy it. We like how your whole family lives on a block together. We want to re-create it, on a smaller scale of course." Josh answered Laney.

"It's good to see any family having a good relationship. What do your parents think?"

"Well..." Josh stopped talking for a little bit. "My brothers and I have a great relationship, but my parents...whole other story for a whole other time."

"Okay." Laney said with a genuine smile. "You don't have to explain."

"I'd like to tell you, but I don't think we have enough time tonight," Josh chuckled. "One day Laney, you and I will have a long talk." What Josh just said held a lot of meaning I didn't think Laney fully understood. "You want to go watch a movie tomorrow night?"

"Um..." she hesitated. "I don't know if that's a good idea. I have so much to do before this month is over. I'm graduating soon, I have a lot of schoolwork that still needs to be done, and I need to get my belongings together to move."

"Why are you so set on moving as soon as possible?" Garret joined in the conversation. That was something I wanted to know as well.

"I…" She couldn't finish her thought. "I just want to…there's really nothing left here for me and I'd like a new start." There was sadness in Laney's eyes. I wondered if Donovan was in her heart and mind right now. I hoped she didn't have a crush on him. After what he said to me the other night, she would be crushed if she knew he had no interest in her.

"Laney, you have so many things here for you. Your family's here, your friends are here, and I'd like to be here for you as well." Boy! Josh was laying it all out on the table for her to take…or not. Brave man.

She gave him another genuine smile and answered, "I know. I'm a really lucky girl. I have the best family, wonderful friends, and you are kinder to me than I deserve."

"Is there a but in there?"

"Nope. It's getting late and I think I'll go home now. I need to study for my exams."

"Can I offer you a ride home?" Josh asked with a downtrodden look.

Laney looked like she was going to refuse him again, but thought better of it. *Smart girl.* I knew she was always the kindest one out of all of us. "Sure Josh, I'd love a ride home. Thank you."

The rest of us stayed a lot longer and hung out. I was glad to see my family getting along so well with Max's family.

"You ready to leave?" Max asked in-between kisses.

"Uh-huh," I answered in a breathy kind of way.

Max took a super long way home and I loved resting against his back. I tried not to think too much into why Max wouldn't want to buy a place together. I did my best to shoo away thoughts of him not wanting any permanency with me, or him not catching on to the fact that I was deeply bothered by his action.

"You gonna sleep on my back, again?" I heard his voice reverberating through his back.

"No," I answered slowly, but got off his bike swiftly.

"What's the matter?" He put his arms around my waist and pulled me close to him. "You've been unusually silent since the house hunt. You're either unhappy that I chose a place without you, or that I'm purchasing a place without you. Which is it?"

"Which do you think it is?"

"How about if I tell you the answer to both questions, and then you can see if you're still unhappy with my decision."

I nodded okay.

"After we got into our fight, I started thinking about us and our situation. And after Josh told me how much money I had left in my account, I agreed with your idea that it was better to purchase than to rent. You were right. This was much smarter, considering mortgage was really no different than my monthly rent. I had just never considered it before."

I tried to pull back a little, but he held on tight. It was almost as though he was whispering in my ears.

"I talked to Jake and Chief Reid, and asked what my chances were of staying at General Hospital for residency. They laughed and told me they'd only consider my application if I took you off their hands."

I gave him an appalled look; he gave me an adoring look, and expressed his adoration with a deep kiss.

"Once I got my ducks in a row, I started doing my research, and after we found this place I decided this is something I wanted to do on my own. How about if I say this is something I *need* to do on my own? As wonderful as your family is, I feel somewhat overwhelmed by your wealth and their generosity. I feel like I can never give you the privilege you are used to in life. Before we establish any permanency between us, I wanted to have my own place, to be my own man, and not to have to rely on you, or the generosity of your family to start us in the next chapter of life. Does that make any sense to you?"

"I guess..."

He gave me an unsatisfactory look, but continued. "And as for the place that I chose, I love the fact that it's so close to your family. I want you to always be near your family and I, too, want to always be near your family. Plus, I thought you'd dig the extra shoe closet. I knew this place was for us when I saw the home for all your shoes."

"So...am I to just move in and be a kept woman?"

Max couldn't stop laughing. "Can you actually be a kept woman? If so, please teach me how to turn you into a submissive girlfriend, and I will wave that magic wand immediately."

"But I feel like I'm just moving into your life, rather than starting something together."

"Gem," I loved the endearment in his voice, and the passion in his eyes, "save your money, till we decide that we'd like to be with one another till death do us part. At that time, you can use all your money to help us buy a larger home for that family we'll create. Until then, help me be the man I want to be, for me, as well as for you."

For now, I decided to let this man be the hunter, and I would submit to being the gatherer.

May 12, 2013

Happy Mother's Day!

$\mathcal{T}$he Reid family loves tradition as you can tell, and we have a lot of interesting as well as funny traditions in our family. I think Jake has told you guys about our Christmas tradition where we play a mean game of white elephant. We have no qualms about stealing from one another during this time to get the best present among the lot.

Then you most recently saw our wedding tradition that was started back in our grandfather's days, where the first man to get married in his generation picks from something old, something new, something borrowed, something blue, and buys a present to symbolize this adage. Gimpy's treasure chest will put new meaning to the word "wedding tradition."

For Mother's Day, we have a whole other tradition that hasn't been practiced in a while, but has been brought back from the grave. This tradition went on hiatus for several years when so many of us were off to college and couldn't make it back for Mother's Day. It really needed all of us to be at home in order to accomplish this gag gift.

Let me explain how this one works. Each family comes up with a gag gift for Mom. It could be as simple as a hand drawn portrait of Mom, or as complicated as a treasure hunt that leads nowhere.

Before the contest begins, we each put $100 into the pot. It used to be a lot cheaper, but ever since most of us graduated from school and got jobs, the buy-in grew to $100 per person. What, you ask, are we buying into?

The winning family gets to keep all the money. Correction, the winning Mom gets to keep the money. With five families plus Jake's family, and Gimpy, the pot's grown to *mucho dinero*!

We started the festivities on Saturday at Emily and Jake's home. Mother's Day was usually held at Uncle Dave and Aunt Deb's beach house, but with Emily being so big (and yes, overnight she popped and started looking like she was going to give birth today) and with the twins being so...mobile, active, unpredictable—you name it, they did it, Emliy asked to host the event in her backyard. Max and his brothers were invited (NO Hannah), and Donovan and his family were invited. The Taylors have never spent Mother's Day with us before, but considering it was at Jake's house, they decided to invite the Taylors as well. The Taylors, though, opted not to join in our competitive fun.

Brunch was a simple affair in Jake's backyard with your typical brunch food. Jake and the rest of the family made sure that Emily didn't lift a finger. The food was catered, we all helped set up and clean up, and then most of us dispersed to set up our mothers' gifts.

"Isn't this a bit morbid?" Max asked while carrying Mom's gift to our backyard.

"That's why it's a gag gift." I responded with an evil grin.

"You Reids have a sick sense of humor."

"Thank you," Jake, Nick and I answered simultaneously.

"Um...that wasn't a compliment," he said with a chuckle, "but whatever. Live in your delusional world."

"We will and we do!" Jake and I high-fived each other. We knew we had the winning gift.

"How much has the pot grown to, do you know?"

"Well let's see," Jake started doing the math. "We alone make $700 since you all insisted I pay double for Mom's entry and Emi's entry. Then there's another $1400 including Roland's entry."

"Geez. That's $2100! What's Mom going to do with all that cash?" I wondered aloud. "Maybe she'll share it with me. There's a pair of Prada shoes I've been eyeing!"

Jake laughed out, "Dream on."

"What did you do for Emily? It's not like the kids can do anything on their own."

"You shall see when the time comes." He could be so secretive at times.

"Does Emily's gift have a chance of winning?"

"Nope. I'm not looking to give a gag gift to my wife." *Of course not!* "But, it'll be humorous."

After reconvening back at Jake's, we did the grand reveal.

"You guys have no chance against Laney's brilliant idea." Josh decided to go help Doug and Laney set up their present.

"I don't know, little brother. Jane's idea's pretty brilliant as well."

"Why, thank you!" I answered with an appreciative kiss.

"For a response like that, I can kiss your ass some more," he added, for the enjoyment of no one else but us.

"Why you clever boy, you!"

"Okay!!! Let's move on from this love fest!" Garret broke us up by walking right in between us.

We started at my house, or better stated, my parents' house, and all walked up to Gram's bathroom, which had a huge yellow caution tape X'ing out the door. Gimpy opened the door and we all died laughing at what we saw. They (as in my father and his brothers) had created a throne for Gram to use on a daily basis.

Let me try and explain to you what the throne looked like. The chair looked like a 12th-century king's throne chair—think Games of Throne, Robb Stark, House Lannister, Stannis Baratheon, and dragon queen, Daenerys Targaryen, all vying, plotting, killing, to claim this chair that only a King or Queen may sit upon. Well Gram's chair looked identical to such chairs. It was built around the toilet already in existence, and only when you lifted the seat, could you tell that it was a potty. Perhaps a glorified port-a-potty was a more apt explanation.

"Whose idea was this?" I asked. "Uncle Henry's?"

"Believe it or not, it was Roland's. He wanted his bride to know that she was his queen. Watch this," my Uncle Dave explained. "Mom, please pull on the toilet paper roll."

Gram did as she was asked and a tune of *God Save the Queen* blared. This was one of the best Mother's Day gifts we'd seen in a long while!

"All right. To the next gift..." Uncle Henry declared.

I led everyone to the backyard, and the howling began again. Placed on our grassy land was a grandfather clock-shaped coffin for our dear old mom. You all remember that Mom's a nut for clocks and she collects them from all over the world? In honor of her clock-mania, we fashioned her coffin to look identical to a grandfather clock. It even had a beautiful Omega-like clock face with a working hour hand, minute hand, and even a second hand. On the grave, we had engraved, "Counting down your mortality, Sandra Jane Reid."

"You see. Mom loves it," I whispered to Max.

"I see." Max didn't know whether or not to believe Mom's sincere appreciation for the gift. "You Reids have an oddball sense of humor."

"That must be why I love you so much, Mr. Davis." That earned me a slap on the rear end. Of course, we were at the end of the Reid trail, who were off to Jake's house to view Emily's gift.

We arrived at Jake's hallway, and he presented to his wife a framed caricature of the twins. An artist had drawn our beautiful Ellie with exaggerated teeth and mouth, huge but gorgeous blue eyes and uncontrolled curls everywhere. She was shown to be yelling the words, "ME! and NO!" Truly, her two favorite words. Even as a caricature, she looked darling.

James was drawn to have a huge forehead, floppy ears and he looked like the road runner, wreaking havoc wherever he'd been. Furniture was turned over, toys were broken, and his sister was in the far background with food on her face from his tornado-like run. It personified him perfectly because that's all he liked to do these days. RUN!

Then, Jake took us to his office and unveiled an absolutely stunning montage of pictures of his wife. These pictures chronicled their relationship, starting from their second chance in Tokyo, to their wedding, to their honeymoon, her pregnancy, the birth of the twins, life with the twins, and even her pregnancy now. There were a few empty spots, for what I assume was their new addition in a couple of months.

And finally, we were led to Emily's favorite room in the house, her sitting room, off their bedroom. Here, Jake had carefully restored old black and whites of Emily's grandparents, her parents, and Emily, when she was younger and created a family tree with pictures rather than names. All our immediate family was on there, even Gimpy, and once again, there were several spots open for more babies in the future. Leave it to my brother to get all the women gushing about his wife's gift. Never in my wildest dreams, growing up right after an annoying, know-it-all, did I ever imagine Jake as the ideal husband. Laney was on the nose about wanting a husband like my brother.

Next, we moved to Uncle Henry's home where usually we found the most hilarious gift of them all. Uncle Henry was the jokester in the family, and his kids assumed his gregarious personality. When we got there, we were not disappointed.

"Oh, my gosh! Is that what I think it is?" Aunt Babs shouted. "That tub is my favorite place in the house. How am I to shower in there with that?!?"

Aunt Babs' bath curtain for her claw-foot bath tub was changed out to a clear curtain with Uncle Henry's naked image silkscreened on it. This image ran from the top of the shower curtain along the entire length of it and it was disgustingly hilarious. Praise God that he was holding a hanky just large enough to cover the parts that would've grossed us all out from here till the end of time!

"Who the hell came up with this idea? It's hysterical!" Donovan declared. "I don't know that I needed this visual of the Chief right after a meal, but it's a brilliant idea."

"You haven't seen brilliant, till you see the inside of the curtain." Doug opened the curtain and called out, "And now...for the pièce de résistance...the backside!"

When he proclaimed the backside, he wasn't kidding. The inside of the shower curtain had the same picture but of Uncle Henry's hairy backside. And this time, there was NO hanky covering the pertinent part. When it didn't gross us all out, we were dying—almost literally—of laughter. Aunt Babs would see her hubby's backside every time she stepped in her claw-foot bath.

"I will never, ever use that bath tub, ever again!" Aunt Babs said while flecking off the tears of laughter. "Who came up with this idea?"

"It was both our ideas, but Laney came up with the naked rear end idea."

"I declare Henry's ass the winning gift," Uncle Dave said, even before we went to the other three homes. Everyone agreed with his declaration.

"That was an ingenious idea, little girl. You're full of surprises, aren't you?"

"Why thank you, Mr. Taylor. There's a lot about me you'll find surprising, if you care to notice." Laney beamed.

"Did somebody call me?"

"No, Dad. This little girl insists on calling me Mr. Taylor for some reason. I've told her that I feel like my father, but she won't give it up."

"What's wrong with feeling like your father? He's a very handsome man."

"He's my stud, aren't you, Scottie?"

"Ma," Donovan pleaded. "Please! Don't start."

"Don't start what, Donny? I was just agreeing with this gorgeous young lady. Which Reid are you?"

I hadn't seen Mr. and Mrs. Taylor, better known as Scott and Jamie Lynn Taylor, since my dad's birthday party, where we didn't even get a chance to speak. We used to see them all the time when we were younger. Though they still lived near us, we hardly saw them because they traveled most of the y ear, visiting their children and grandchildren.

"I'm Laney, daughter of Henry and Barbara."

"My Gawwwd!" Mrs. Taylor practically hollered in her mix of New York / Italian accent. "Last time I saw you, you were in pigtails. When did you grow up to this?" She motioned her hand up and down Laney's body. "You're stunning."

We all laughed at Jamie Taylor's animated gestures.

"Ma. Calm down." Donovan turned to us and explained, "I'm sure you all remember that Mom's Long Island roots appear whenever she gets excited."

"Don't tell me to calm down, Donny. Why can't you get yourself a young lady like Laney and settle down? You're the last one, Donny," she whined to her son. "I want babies, grandchildren like Sandy and Bobby have. Those twins are beautiful. I want grandbabies who will live down the street from me. I'll move next door to you and babysit every day, Donny." Mrs. Taylor had both her hands on Donovan's face and she squeezed his cheeks in varying ways depending upon the degree of her plea. He was immobile to her begging.

"Donny. Listen to your Ma!" Mr. Taylor chimed in.

"Dear God. Not you, too. Both your accents are coming out."

"Kate's too old to bring sweet babies into this world. No more Kate, Son. I know she's sexy. Any man would be blind not to notice."

"Scottie! How can you talk about another woman being sexy when I'm right next to you?"

"I'm just trying to explain to our son that I understand his attraction towards her. But," Mr. Taylor turned to Donovan, again, "no more. You've had your fun. Now it's time to get serious. How about one of these Reid girls? There's plenty of them." Mr. Taylor looked at us as though he were searching for Captain Crunch cereal in the bread aisle of a grocery store. "What about Janey? I've always liked her."

"*Janey* is happily taken," Max answered, placing his arms around me from behind, possessively.

"Okay." Mr. Taylor just moved on to the next box of cereal. "What about Laney here. You married?"

"No, Sir."

"What do you think of my son? Isn't he handsome?"

"I guess he's all right." Laney answered nonchalantly. Was she nuts? She couldn't have been that blind to think Donovan was just all right.

"All right?" The three Taylors sounded like a harmonized chorus.

"My son is gorgeous!" Mrs. Taylor ardently preached to the choir, especially Laney.

"My son is even better looking than I am," Mr. Taylor said. "Didn't you say earlier that I was handsome?"

"I did, Sir."

Donovan also pushed his own cause. "I was told I was even better looking than Henry Cavill. You know...the new Superman?"

Laney giggled. "Mr. Taylor, I think you look like a mousy Harry Styles."

"Mousy Harry Styles??? Who, me, or my father?"

"You!" She pointed at Donovan.

"How can you call me mousy? And who the hell is Harry Styles?"

Donovan was getting all huffy-puffy with Laney's insult. He wouldn't let Laney off the hook. I took out my phone and pulled up an image of Harry Styles and showed it to Donovan. "Here you go, Monsieur Ratatouille." Everyone cracked up.

"So if my son's not good looking enough for you, Laney, then who is?" Mr. Scott Taylor asked with a rascally smile.

"Donovan Taylor is plenty good looking, but I prefer a bit more of a manly look."

I saw Donovan and his mother about to pass out while the rest of us choked on our laugh. Jake was loving this the most.

"Explain, Delaney Reid!"

"I like the weathered look," she mused. "You know, the Harley Davidson, beautiful tattoo, five o'clock shadow, mussed-up hair, look. You, Mr. Taylor, look a little too cleaned up. You're the James Bond when he's at the casino. I prefer the James Bond when he's firing his Walther PPK, all cut up, with dirt on his face. That's what I prefer."

Donovan's face gentled. "You truly are full of surprises. No Prince Charming from Cinderella?"

"Prince Charming from Cinderella with a few tats, riding a Harley."

"You should," Max whispered in my ear, "learn to embrace my bike, like Laney." Then he turned to Laney. "You want a ride on my bike? It's here. Maybe Josh can take you."

Laney all of a sudden turned shy. "Maybe next time, Max. It's a really cool bike. It's a Switchback, huh?"

"You speak Harley?" Max brightened up as though the manager at the Harley Davidson store offered him a 50% discount on a new bike.

"Some...I considered buying one last year, but Mom wouldn't let me. She said it was too unladylike. Don't tell anyone but I've saved up money to buy a Harley. You may see me on one when you visit me in London."

Who on earth was this girl? Wasn't she the Disney princess who forced all of us to play with dolls, have tea parties and dress up like Barbie princess fools? Where did the motorcycle, tattoo and five o'clock shadows come from, and when the hell did my cousin grow up?

"This is the girl for you, Donny my boy! You need to marry this girl and she can help you get rid of that metrosexual side. Real men don't take so long picking out their clothes and styling their hair every morning. Ever since he was a child..."

"OK! Pa. Enough, already..."

"What's all the fun, here? What's going on?" Mom and Aunt Babs joined our group.

"Babs," Mrs. Taylor called out in her thick accent, "Whatcha gonna do with all the money your kids earned you?"

"Jamie!" Aunt Babs hugged our guest. "You look phenomenal. How'd you lose so much weight?"

"Pole dancing."

Donovan spit up his drink and started choking. Laney pounded on his back and Jake positioned himself to give him the Heimlich, but Donovan waved him off.

After making sure her son wasn't going to die, she continued. "I got a pole in my bedroom and started getting private lessons. My Scottie loves it..."

"Maaaaa!" Donovan pleaded. "I give up. I'm going to the other side of Jake's yard. I'll see you before you or I leave."

"Bye Donnie." Mrs. Taylor called out. Max and I walked away soon after when the conversation turned a bit too risqué for our taste.

"I love your family." Max said sadly. I went from sitting on the bench next to him to sitting on his lap. "I hope I'll be able to recreate something this magical with my own family."

"What is your mom doing tomorrow for Mother's Day?"

He didn't answer me.

"Tell me you've at least offered to stop by the house or take her out for a meal."

"I'm afraid to see my mother, especially after that last dinner."

"Max. I know she's more mommy dearest than June Cleaver, but it's a day when we celebrate moms. You have to at least see her. Can I call her and invite her to dinner with us tomorrow night?"

"You really want to do that after what she did to you, to us, last time?" He doubted my sincerity and I, too, wondered what the hell I was doing offering to walk back into the lion's den.

"Yes. I think between you, me, and your brothers, we can have a peaceful meal with your parents."

"You're a glutton for punishment."

"I am...in so many ways..." I added suggestively.

We left the Mother's Day festivities to create some festivities of our own, across the street in my bedroom.

May 13, 2013

All That It's Cracked Up To Be...

*W*hat possessed me to invite Max's parents to dinner was beyond me. I thought since we were all on our own on Sunday,
I'd be the bigger person and suggest dinner with the three brothers,
me and the parents. I didn't exactly invite Hannah, but I supposed
she would be there as well. As a buffer, I begged Nick, Doug, and
Evie—who was in LA brunching with her parents—to join us.

An early dinner—reserved.
Gift—purchased.
Buffer companions—confirmed!

All that was left was to go have one dinner and get everyone on good
terms again.

"Are you sure about this? We can still back out, you know." Max,
Garret, and Josh all asked this question in some form during the
ride to the restaurant.

"I can't remember the last time we celebrated Mother's Day with
Mom." Josh added. "This'll be really interesting. You have any other
previously knocked-up girls showing up to this dinner, Max?"

My boyfriend actually laughed at his brother, even though he poked at a sore spot. "I have nothing else to hide from my girlfriend, anymore. She owns my heart, soul and body, now."

If Max's two brothers weren't in the car with us, I would've forced Max to pull over and the car would've done a jalopy on the side of the road. But since I couldn't do that, I just gave him a sinful smile, full of promises for later.

The two brothers rolled their eyes. "Jane," Garret addressed me, "I can promise you that not once was my brother this sickeningly in love with anyone—not even Emily."

"Garret," I addressed him just as seriously, "I don't think I've ever heard such beautiful words."

I was seriously going to give Max some lovin' tonight!

"Who are all coming?" Josh wondered.

"Did you invite Laney?" Garret wondered back.

"Hell no! Why would I scare her off even before she's decided she's in love with me?"

"In love with you?" Garret wondered even louder. "Bro', you can't even get a date with her."

Now this was a cute scene where the three brothers joined forces, aiding and abetting. Max began. "Have you used your Davis charm and asked her out? You know she's leaving soon."

"I've tried, but she's held me at an arm's distance. I wish she'd hold me with her long, sexy-ass legs, instead." The men chuckled. I didn't know whether to feel offended for Laney, or try aiding and abetting Josh along with my boyfriend.

"How about I set up a double-date as soon as Laney is out of school? I think she's been quite busy studying for finals, finishing up papers, and setting up home in London. I haven't seen much of her these days."

"You're the bomb, Sis! I knew you'd pull through for me." Josh kissed me on the cheek. "When Lancy gets to know me, she's bound to fall madly in love with me. Who the hell can resist the Davis charm?"

"Damn right!" Garret added.

"Damn straight!" Max agreed.

The sheer amount of machismo in this car made me laugh.

We revisited that little French bistro where I first met Mr. and Mrs. Davis. Are you all wondering why I still call them Mr. and Mrs.? I have no freakin' clue what their names are. And no one's clued me in, plus I suppose I never asked.

"What are your parents' names?"

The three men howled.

"What the hell's so funny?"

"Mavis and Davis," Max spoke between wiping off tears of hilarity.

"Seriously? Mavis Davis and Davis Davis???" I too started tearing from the joke. "Either you're all pulling my leg or someone above has a sense of humor."

"Our paternal grandparents had a great sense of humor and thought if Dad had the same first and last name, he'd have an easier time remembering and spelling. Then my grandfather told us that he knew Mom was the one, when her name was only a few spaces down the alphabet chart from Dad's." Josh continued the crazy explanation.

"What a hoot. Mavis and Davis...I guess I'll stick to Mr. and Mrs."

"Yeah. Good thinking, Babe. I don't know that they'll be happy if you brought up their names in the middle of dinner."

We arrived at the bistro and soon after, my brother, Nick and Evie came one after another. To Josh's delight—or chagrin?—Laney was with Doug. I couldn't gauge Josh's reaction since he beelined to my cousin.

"Josh filled me in somewhat on the Davis details. I thought the more ammo, the better," my sweet younger brother explained. "Jake and Emily were going to join us as well, but both kids have the sniffles and are cranky. They send good karma in their stead."

I love my family!

"Hello Jane," I heard Max's mom call out from behind.

I whipped around to a solemn face—a face that displayed penance over her past sins. Feeling sorry for her, and being in a brief state of insanity, I gave Mrs. Davis a hug and wished her a Happy Mother's Day. That hug stopped everyone in their tracks. They all looked over to us. That hug may possibly have been the reason why our evening turned out to be a surprisingly pleasurable one.

The dinner started awkward and everyone broke off into their own conversations, with Mr. and Mrs. Davis keeping quiet. It didn't go unnoticed in my eyes that they didn't bring Hannah with them. I don't know what happened there, but I wasn't one to complain.

"Have you seen the homes your sons purchased?" I asked both parents in hopes of getting them into the conversation.

They shook their heads no, and judging by the glance Max's mom gave her sons, it wouldn't have surprised me if she had no idea that her sons were now home owners.

"We all bought a very small home, not too far from Jane's parents' place and we'll be moving in soon." Max offered this info by way of apology.

"When do you move in?" Max's dad asked. "Do you boys need any help? Do you have enough money? Your mother and I are able to help financially if you need it." This generous offer sounded similar to an apology as well. It made me wonder if instead of emotional love and support, the only way the Davises knew how to support their sons was financially. Perhaps this was their way of showing love.

"We're all doing well, thanks to Josh and his expertise with the stock market. It's a very small, starter home and we got a good deal, so we thought it'd make a wise investment." This was about as loquacious as I'd seen Max get with his parents.

Mr. and Mrs. Davis looked over at Josh and cracked a proud smile. It was weird to see them smile since I had never seen one on their faces before.

"So, does that mean you are staying around for your residency? You're not moving far away?"

"Though there are no guarantees, I'm pretty sure I'm staying. I've been told by Jane's uncle and brother that if I keep Jane in line, they will consider keeping me at the hospital." Max actually cracked a joke at the Davis family dinner table, and his parents actually cracked a smile, again! Wonders never ceased.

"Can we come see your new place?" Mr. Davis asked, cautiously.

All three boys looked at one another, not only gauging each other's reactions but almost expecting Ashton Kutcher to pop out of the restaurant walls to tell them that they were being punked. It was sad on the one hand to see such doubt and vacillation about the sincerity of one's own parents, but what was happening tonight was progress.

The pause was longer than necessary so I jumped in. "Why don't we do a drive by tonight, then you can help us on moving day. I don't think we mentioned that I'm moving in with Max. Your son, in his machismo way, told me that I could bum off of his generosity. I'll be his 'little woman.'" I saw a smile bordering on laughter, again! I patted myself on the back.

"I'm glad you'll be close to Max," his mother patted my hand. "You're good for him."

I whispered, still loudly enough for everyone to hear, "Your eldest has no idea that I can't cook, I don't clean, and I also don't plan to be his 'little woman.'"

Max's mom cracked up—and cracked up loudly. "Max has always been quietly aggressive, turned obstinately aggressive, when he doesn't get what he wants."

"Oh my gosh!" I agreed, "You are dead-on in that assessment."

"And Garret has been the doer among the three boys. His dad and I always called him a man of action. He saw, he assessed, he conquered." There was, once again, that look of pride in both parents' eyes for all three boys. "And our youngest was the peacemaker. He always supported his brothers, never coveted any of their belongings or accomplishments, but equally matched their success in all ways. We are proud of and lucky to have three boys who practically raised themselves." I think I may have seen a slight reddening of Mavis Davis' eyes, but that left as quickly as it came.

Tonight's understated word—SHOCKING! We all kept quiet, eyeballs roving from person to person, wanting to see if anyone could explain what was going on. Were Max's parents drunk? Were they playing some sick game? Or were they now realizing that they'd missed out on having a relationship with three fantastic young men? I think and hope it's the latter.

"Thank you," were the last words I heard from Davis and Mavis before they got in their car after seeing their boys' new homes in the dark, from the outside.

"Thank you," were also the last words I heard from my boyfriend before he curled into me and fell asleep on my bed. Life was working out okay for us. If I had to look at the big picture, characters in the life of Max and Jane were taking shape, becoming clearer and sharper. Like opening night of a play, everybody knew their lines, clothes and makeup were done, and each stood in place, waiting for his or her cue to start. Was this the beginning of my standing ovation, or was I also waiting to be punked?!?

May 16, 2013

Diamonds Are a Girl's Best Friend

Since I promised Josh a double date with Laney, I needed to get one on our calendar, and fast. But with all our crazy schedules, it wasn't easy to pin down a date. Max had no real opinion on my plan, Josh was willing to go out on any night, and Laney...well Laney came along because I guilted her into coming along. I told her how uncool she was being, declining *ALL* of Josh's invitations. Plus, I had Max talk to her and tell her that we wanted to spend some time with her before she left for London. That did the trick. She could decline my invitation, but saying no to Max was another story.

"I bought us four tickets to see the opera, *Cinderella*, and we have a dinner reservation at the brasserie next door."

"That sounds utterly dreadful. Why don't we do something that'll allow those two to talk?"

"Shit! Why didn't you say something sooner? These tickets cost me a fortune."

"Have Josh reimburse you. We're doing this for his sake." My boyfriend was so not helpful in this matchmaking situation.

"I can't ask him to pay me back. That's so cheesy."

By this point, I'd lost Max to his textbook. I searched the internet for something fun to do and found nothing interesting.

"Hey Emily. I have a quandary." Against my boyfriend's will, I forced him off my bed and over to Emily's house, so we could see if she had any bright ideas.

"What's the quagmire?" She laughed at her own lame witticism.

I explained what I'd done and she didn't appear overjoyed with any of my choices. "I don't think Laney likes Josh in that way. Why encourage him? He'll be mightily disappointed when she leaves."

"But she hasn't gotten to know him. She may grow to like him if she gives him a chance." Max chuckled at Emily's doubtful look.

"How about if your brother and I take those tickets off your hands, or...you can invite *us* to go with you instead of Laney and Josh. You know how much I like opera." She gave me a wink, which I found utterly disturbing. Emily had more of a coquettish side than I imagined. I supposed she had many charms, not made aware to the likes of me.

"Just give Emily the tickets. I don't want to go see an opera. Emily would have to drag me to those things because I would protest so much. There were many promises made, which went unfulfilled, back when we were dating, Ms. Logan."

Emily only laughed at my boyfriend. "There were no promises made—only threats if you didn't go with me."

"I remember a time when you said we would..."

"All righty...!" I cut off the walk down the yellow brick road. "This isn't about you two in the past. It's about Laney and Josh in the future."

"A dead future," Emily tried to whisper, but we all heard loud and clear.

The door opened and in walked Jake. "Hello, Beloved. How was your day?" He gave her a sickeningly sweet kiss and somehow held her around her massive waist. "Kids down?"

"Oh yes. They were especially active today, so they were asleep even before Mr. Blue Fish appeared in the book."

"I'm going to go see the kids and change."

"Okay. I'll have dinner ready."

"What are you guys doing here?" He finally noticed us. "Stick around, I'll be back in a few minutes." After a pat on the back for Max and a squeeze on the shoulder for me, Jake went off to adore his sleeping kids.

"What got the kids so tired today?" Max asked.

"I took the kids to the park, and there was a little league t-ball game going on and the twins were mesmerized. After the game ended and the field cleared, James started running the bases and Ellie followed. I lost count of the number of time they ran around the field. Once we got home, they practically fell asleep during their bath, and they hardly ate dinner. They were knocked out by the time I reached the top of the steps."

"That must have been exhausting for you."

"Yeah, it wasn't easy giving sleepy children a bath."

As those two droned on about daily minutiae, I had the most brilliant idea! I took out my phone and started an email.

To: Jake Reid, Nick Reid, Doug Reid, Delaney Reid, Samantha Reid, Robert Reid, Henry Reid, Roland Ascot, Max Davis, Garret Davis, Josh Davis, Donovan Taylor, Becky Fritz, Al Fritz,
Cc: Emily Reid, Sandra Reid, Barbara Reid, Estelle Reid Ascot
From: Jane Reid
Subject: Reids vs. The Others, Baseball Game!

You all up for a baseball game this weekend? It'll be us Reids against the world! Dust off your old cleats, buy some new baseball pants and let's play ball. Reply all so we know how the team will be formed. The Others—you need a few more players.

Sent! What a fantastic idea this was. We'd use my parents' backyard as the baseball field and there was no chance The Others could beat us. We Reids all played baseball and softball.

Soon a flurry of email exchanges began.

To: Jane Reid, et al
Cc: Bee Taylor
From: Donovan Taylor
Subject: Baseball

You do know I'm an excellent baller? Game on! I've included my cousin Bee (yes, yes, Jane. I know she's technically my aunt—whatever...) in this email chain. She's in as well.

To: Jane Reid, et al
From: Roland Ascot
Subject: Who am I

Am I a Reid or am I an other?

To: Roland Ascot, et al
From: Jane Reid
Subject: Don't be silly

Of course you are a REID! You are with us, Gimpy!

To: Jane Reid, et al
From: Max Davis
Subject: Why are we emailing when we are sitting next to one another?

My beautiful Gem, what's the winning prize? Also, we are still 2 players short.

To: Max Davis, et al
From: Jane Reid
Subject: Prize

Loser buys dinner?

To: Jane Reid, et al
From: Josh Davis
Subject: Have you no imagination?

Seriously? Loser buys dinner? That's all you can come up with? How about loser is at the mercy of the winners' whim? We shall come up with some form of punishment for you losers. Ha ha ha! I say with an evil laugh.

To: Josh Davis, et al
From: Nick Reid
Subject: Talking trash

Get ready to eat shit. See you this weekend.

To: Jane Reid, et al
From: Delaney Reid
Subject: I am out of town this weekend

Sorry but I can't play. Have a great time.

To: Delaney Reid, et al
From: Donovan Taylor
Subject: What do you mean you are out of town?

Where are you going and with whom? You can't miss this event.

To: Donovan Taylor, et al
From: Delaney Reid
Subject: I can do whatever I please

None of your business. Really none of your business! You are not the boss of me.

To: Delaney Reid, et al
From: Roland Ascot
Subject: Stop with the emails

Your Gram is about to kick me out of this bed because my phone keeps pinging. I've had 60 years of sleeping without Estelle. Go argue at Jake's house. NO MORE MESSAGES!

That stopped the emails and one by one, the participants entered the kitchen. Doug and Nick were the first to appear. Then the Davis brothers came, then Donovan came with Becky, Al, and Bee.

"Hi Bee! It's so good to see you," I exclaimed with a huge hug. "It's been way too long."

"I agree! Becky tells me you're seeing someone?" She looked around and stopped in front of the Davis brothers. "Hmmm..." She did her browsing up and down. "You look too young," she said of Josh, "You're too serious," she swept over Garret. "But you look just right for our lovely Jane." She actually did a full circle around Max.

"I am just right for this woman," Max grabbed me and kissed me.

Bee whispered in my ear. "Sexy, hot, and domineering. I approve."

"Thanks," I chuckled at her purring in my ear.

"So how are we to form a team with seven players?" Josh asked. "You need to give us a player so we'll be even."

I didn't like that idea. "Can't you round up more players? Then it won't be The Reids vs. The Others if we lend you a Reid."

Josh had an evil glint in his eyes that made me think I didn't want to know what he was about to say. "All right. We'll just recruit Hannah and Joyce. They can play second and third base, flanking Max at shortstop."

I gave Josh a *damn you* look. "You are off my Christmas list." I whispered. "All right. Who do you want?"

"Hello, everyone." The door opened and in walked Laney in a sweet looking dress.

"How was your date?" Doug asked.

"A date?" Josh was bummed and kind of upset. "Why will you go out with everyone but me?"

"Why the hell do you date so much? I don't get why so many guys ask you out." It looked like Donovan said this without much thought, but Laney looked hurt initially, then got pissed.

"First of all," she addressed Doug, "it wasn't a date. A group of us stayed to finish our project, then went out for a bite to eat. Secondly," she addressed Josh, "I don't go out with everyone. And finally," her voice got louder and more pissed as she addressed each of her accusers, "maybe I date so I can one day have a meaningful relationship rather than just a meeting of the bodies. And what the hell do you care why guys ask me out. If you're that curious, why don't you do a Q&A with Josh and see how many times I've gone out with him." Boy, that last sentence slammed both men in one shot. *Damn.* She was tart when she wanted to be.

With that, Laney stormed out of the kitchen and slammed the door on her way out. Both Donovan and Josh looked like they wanted to go after her, but were in a state of shock and disbelief that our mild-mannered Laney pretty much told them to fuck-off. I loved it. The fiery Reid spirit was alive and well.

"You gonna go after her?" Jake asked his buddy. "It's only proper you bring her back since you pissed her off."

Donovan shook his head no. "She may chop off my balls and eat it for a late night snack if I go see her now. Damn! That girl has a temper."

"All women have tempers, and you tend to provoke Laney without cause." Emily warned. "Donovan, please bring Laney back. I don't like seeing her upset. You were both unkind to her."

"Oh, all right." Donovan huffed, and went to fetch Laney.

"How come you didn't ask me to go?" Josh pouted at Emily.

"You can apologize when she gets here."

While Donovan went to go get Laney, we decided on team names and colors for our uniforms. We only had tomorrow to practice so we each decided on a practice time and place.

"You're back!" Josh ran over to Laney who walked in pouting. "I'm sorry. You forgive me?" Josh went to hug her, but Laney did a cool duck and weave boxing move and Josh ended up hugging Donovan instead.

"Hello, again, Laney Reid. I see you took off my creation, and changed into sweats."

"And a beautiful creation it was, Bee! I get compliments on all your masterpieces." Laney hugged Bee. "How great to see you here. I was happy your nephew included you."

Bee cracked up. "Yes, my nephew has his good moments at times."

"Few and far in between," Laney didn't even try and disguise those disparaging words.

"How do you know each other?" Nick asked. "And where's my hello, Bee Taylor?"

"Your hello is still waiting for that phone call."

What the hell was going on with Bee and all the Reids. How did she know everyone?

"Seriously?" Laney asked Donovan of all people, and Donovan cryptically nodded yes.

Shit! When were these people going to clue me in on what's going on, and why was I not included in this chain of emails???

"You Taylors don't follow the norm, do you?" She said to him, again.

"We set the trend," he answered with a smile and a wink to my cousin.

Laney rolled her eyes. "Are we decided on everything? Can I go home now? I still have a few more things to do for school."

"We still have the issue of being 2 players short. Let us take a Reid." Donovan demanded.

"Which Reid? We can't give you Jake or Nick or even Doug."

"That depends on whether we're playing baseball or softball."

"I think softball would be easier." Jake made a unilateral decision.

"Then I want Delaney." He looked at Laney and they both kind of had this weird understanding—that, once again, none of us understood.

Jake spoke, "I thought you're going away this weekend."

"Your buddy here is forcing me to stay. I did have a room and a round of golf provided for me in Scottsdale, but a certain someone won't let me go." She stuck her tongue out at Donovan.

"I'll take you there myself." Donovan said and imitated her look. We all laughed at him.

"Promises, promises," she muttered and rolled her eyes.

Jake was our spokesperson again. "I guess we're decided. 9:00 am, Saturday at my parents' backyard?"

"We'll all be there." Donovan spoke for The Others.

Friday flew by and come Saturday morning, Mom and Aunt Babs had created a softball field for us. They brought out the old golf net to use as the backstop, and they also found the old bases we used to use. Dad bought a couple of t-ball sets for the twins to play with, and the two went crazy running around the "field." They also had no clue what to do with the bat and ball, so instead, Emily would place a plastic ball on the tee, they would bat it with their hands, then they'd run around the tee like they were running the bases. James was the leader and Elizabeth followed his every move. It was precious. Funny thing, by the time people were arriving for the game, the twins were so exhausted, they fell asleep in the EZ-up tent.

"What the hell are The Others wearing?" Nick pointed to everyone not a Reid, who walked into the yard, together.

"Becky." I called attention to my best friend. "What's with the outfit?"

"Bee made us all these baseball shirts."

We, Reids, all wore dark mismatched baseball pants, dark mismatched (again) socks and baseball shirts—you know those white ones with the colored sleeves and neckline, of course in all mismatched dark colors. The (freakin') Others came in matching grey pants, the same type of white baseball shirts with dark blue trims and each shirt was customized. That damn Bee Taylor (who's a clothes designer, by the way) sewed numbers, cut out from a cool gray-print fabric, and placed them on the left sleeve of the shirt. Then, the back of their shirts had their names sewn in with the same fabric. On the right sleeve of each shirt, there was a baseball diamond silkscreened on it and each person's position was colored in. For instance, Max was going to play first base, so she colored in that base for his shirt. And to top it all off, they all had matching visors with the name The Others embroidered on the front. They looked like professional players. Why didn't I think of doing something like that for my team?

"Shit, Bee. We look like some rag-tag Bad News Bears and you look like the freakin' New York Yankees."

"You know my motto. It's all about how you look."

"Tell me you don't all have matching cleats." I groaned when I saw the Davis brothers walking my way.

"Look at what Donovan got us." Josh pointed to his flashy blue baseball cleats.

"He bought that for all of you?" Now, I was getting pissed. I never liked being underdressed and today, I was feeling like the homeless.

"He said he had a big name client who offered these to him when he told him about our game."

"Damn Donovan Taylor! He couldn't ask his client for a pair for all of us?"

"Why would I do that for the enemy?" Donovan let out an evil laugh. "We have a couple more players now. My dad and Mr. Davis want to play."

I looked over at Max and he winked. "Really?" I whispered.

He nodded yes and smiled. This day was going to be awesome!

"Then what do we do about Laney?" I wondered since we, too, had gained Uncle Billy. "We all have nine players each. Now, Laney makes the tenth and she's outfitted as an Other."

After much discussion with Jake and Donovan, we decided to each have nine players on the field and use Laney as the tenth player. Without asking her, it was decided that she would pitch for both teams, since she was really the only one who's ever pitched as a soft-baller. When she was told, Laney looked neither happy nor upset. She took one for both teams and accepted her fate. Bee had made a special shirt for her, knowing she would pitch for them. It was a real (pink) baseball Jersey with her name on the back, number and baseball diamond on the sleeves, and a phrase that said, *don't mess with me* written in cursive, sewn across her chest. It was perfect for Laney!

Emily helped Jake into his catcher's gear as The Reids took position in the outfield. Nick played first base, I took second, Doug took third, Uncle Billy took shortstop, Dad was in left field, Uncle Henry in centerfield, and Sam was placed in right field. Gimpy was to be the impartial ump, Mrs. Davis was our scorekeeper, and the moms were the cheering crowd.

First up to bat, Donovan Taylor. Jake walked out to Laney and gave instructions she didn't like. She kept shaking her head in the negative and at one point laughed hysterically.

"Let's get the game going before the sun goes down," he yelled at Jake. Jake walked back to the catcher's position with a cocky look on his face. "Let's see what you've got, Delaney Reid. I plan to hit a home run off of you."

And damn, he almost hit a home run on the first pitch. Laney threw a perfect fastball to him and he got a triple off it. Next up was my honey, and shit, he also got a triple off of us. Perhaps Laney was purposely giving them good pitches to put us in the doghouse. I was getting suspicious, but Doug and Josh struck out, Mr. Taylor and Mr. Davis each hit a single, and Bee hit a pop fly and the inning was done with only two runs in.

It was our turn to hit and Donovan was catching for their team. He, too, had a long talk with Laney and she listened to all he droned on about during their time. I think he purposely held his meeting on the mound as long as possible to piss off Jake. For The Others, their outfield line-up consisted of Max, Josh, Garret on the three bases, Al as shortstop, Mr. Taylor in left field, Mr. Davis in centerfield, and Becky and Bee would take turns subbing into right field. We were just as successful at bat, and we were up 4-2 at the end of the first inning.

And so this game continued and at the end of the 6th and last inning, we were up 10-9. There were two out, the tying run on third base and Donovan was up. Jake called a meeting on the mound with his infielders, and I heard him whisper, "Laney, you need to spook Donovan with a fast pitch and try and hit him. The closer you can get to his manhood, without actually hitting him, the better."

"No way, Jake. I can't control my pitches to that degree and I will NOT be responsible for his posterity."

"You can do it. Just get close enough to scare him. He won't swing after that. I promise you. Just try."

"I don't know, Jake..."

"You can do it, Laney. It's all up to you," her dad came to the mound to encourage her. "Just remember who you are. You are a Reid!"

What a crack-up! She was told in so many words to scare the shit out of Donovan by almost hitting him where it will hurt—*badly*.

The first pitch Laney threw was a ball and nowhere near his manhood. The second pitch was perfect! It was fast, and Donovan's body formed an ending parentheses sign as he curved his body away from the ball. Laney quickly turned her body away from Donovan, put her mitt up to her face and giggled. Once she regained her composure, she turned back around and threw another strike, identical to the first one. This one too, was really close to his body. It was a 1-2 count on Donovan.

In a most unconventional move, Donovan called a timeout and walked out to the mound. Jake took off his mask to follow, but Donovan was done with his brief conversation before any of us could get to her. None of us knew what was said, but it rattled her enough to lob two balls. Now we were at full count and as soon as Donovan got himself back in the batter's box, she caught him unready, threw out another fast pitch, and struck him out.

Donovan was shocked, The Reids were elated and the game was over. We won 10-9!

By the time the game was over, lunch was set up in Jake's backyard, and the twins were already in their high chair noshing on fried chicken.

"James, Ellie, did you enjoy watching Daddy play?" Jake sat in between his kids and helped them eat. The kids had no clue what my brother was saying, but they smiled brilliantly at him and nodded yes. "Should we go swimming after lunch?" He asked the million-dollar question.

"Yawshhh," James answered with excitement as his sister yelled, "ME!" That one word was her answer to everything.

"Let's see which aunt or uncle might take you two in the pool. We have plenty of friends and family members to keep you occupied till dinner."

"Yawshhh," James repeated over and over.

"Janey, this was a fantastic idea. Let's do this every year," Mr. Taylor said from the other side of the long table.

"I agree," Uncle Henry raised his lemonade glass, "to my brilliant niece for a spectacular idea, my beautiful and athletic daughter for pitching for both teams, and to all the ladies for coordinating the entire day. Thank you and a job well done!"

"Here, here!" We all cheered.

"Laney," Mavis Davis surprisingly spoke up in the middle of our lunch, and to my cousin at that. "Why don't you come sit next to us, and join us for lunch."

This time Mrs. Taylor spoke up and loudly, "Laney, come join us instead. There's plenty of room over here."

There was an interesting tug-of-war going on with the two mothers and my cousin. I could see why Mavis was pushing Josh's cause, but I didn't understand why Mrs. Taylor was so interested Laney.

"Ne Ne," my darling nephew called out and saved Laney's butt.

"Thank you for the invitation," she said to both mothers, "but I'm going to sit next to James." As soon as Laney sat, both mothers went and pushed their way towards the other end of the table. Jamie Lynn was outright aggressive. Mavis had that passive-aggressive thing going on, pushing her younger son's cause.

"Go, Mom!" I whispered to my boyfriend. "I guess she's taken a liking to my cousin?"

"I think she's taken a liking to you, and figured Laney couldn't be half bad if she's related to you." He gave me a heartwarming smile and a body-tingling kiss. "You did good today. We all had a fantastic time and I'm glad my parents got a chance to hang out with your family. The Reids can be a role model for any family out there."

"I enjoyed today, too. And I especially enjoyed seeing your parents. It may take some time but I think they'll come around. How can they not with you three?"

"Who's ready to swim?" My brother asked.

The kids started jumping up and down in their high chairs. Laney quickly got up and took James and jumped in the pool before any mother could come in with her. Ellie started whining because she hadn't been picked up yet.

"Who do you want to go into the pool with, my princess?" Jake went fishing and Ellie took the bait. She pointed down the table, but that could've been anyone.

"I'll see you in a bit?" Max said with a quick kiss to my lips. "I'm going to be Ellie's knight in shining armor." He hopped over and swooped her out of the high chair. Ellie was in love! But in all honesty, she would've been in love with anyone who took her in the pool.

Looking around, I was beyond pleased with myself for getting everyone together. What started as an outing for the four of us, has now turned into possibly another family tradition. I guess the question that begs to be asked—will all the Davises continue to be a part of The Others? I sure hoped so.

May 20, 2013

Mother May I (Not Be)?

Me without you is like
shoes with no laces
a nerd with no braces
asentencewithnospaces

I thought of my brother and his wife when I read this corny saying this morning. Those two were like peanut butter and jelly,
bacon and eggs, SpongeBob and Patrick, two peas in a pod...well, you
get what I'm trying to say—one cannot exist in this world without
the other! Even their birthdays are positioned right next to one another on the calendar. Jake turned thrity-three yesterday and Emily
turned twenty-seven as of this morning and of course, neither my
brother nor his wife would let each other's birthday go quietly. As
a birthday surprise, Emily made reservations at Bazaar at the SLS
hotel for Sunday night (Jake's actual birthday) so they could dine on
a crazy twenty-two course dinner.

What Emily didn't know was that Jake planned an almost identical
birthday surprise that started a night earlier and included an overnight at the SLS hotel and a leisurely afternoon tea on Sunday. Even
their freakin' surprises for one another went hand in hand. Scary!
Tonight would be a family dinner to celebrate Emily's birthday, but
yesterday and the night before were anything but a party for me!

Before Jake whisked Emily off to their fun overnight, right after our softball lunch at their house, he charged the four of us—me, Max, Laney, and Donovan—with keeping the kids happy till their mother returned to them the next day.

Why Donovan was asked to help was beyond me. It's not as if he knew how to care for these kids. Being their godfather and sending expensive gifts, did not a caretaker make! This weekend was an eye-opener for me and right now, I was taking my time, enjoying my coffee, rejoicing that I didn't have to walk across the street and face those munchkins. I was not ready to have kids any time soon.

It all started Saturday after the game, and after work. Donovan and I had to go into work—yes, we lawyers work on Saturdays (and generally Sundays, too) after that fun game, lunch and a little pool time. We got called in for a few hours so we carpooled and decided to make it a productive two hours. When we arrived from work, Laney had the kids fed and was in the process of getting their baths ready in the farmhouse sink.

"Hey," she greeted the both of us with a calm smile.

"Hey, how's it going?" I asked.

Donovan just gave her a pat on the back hello and went to greet each kid.

"Hello big boy, beautiful girl! Did you enjoy your spaghetti dinner?" He asked, while wiping off their mouths with a baby wipe. "It sure looks like the ground enjoyed it." He proceeded to carefully pick up James and he held him far away from that YSL suit that looked oh so delicious on him. I think this man carried a secret closet in his car, since we never stopped by his house to get him changed. He went from baseball uniform, to bathing suit, to a dashing suit. I guess he believed Bee's motto—*It's all about how you look.* And he looked good—*always!*

Laney took James and proceeded to strip him of his Bolognese-laden clothes, and put him in his seat and quickly handed him a bath toy. Ellie got the exact same treatment. While Donovan went upstairs with his overnight bag and changed out of his work clothes, I didn't know whether I, too, should go home and change before getting my hands dirty. It didn't seem the right thing to do—leave Laney by herself with the two kids, but being this overdressed to take care of two kids didn't seem too smart either.

Laney read my thoughts. "You can go and change, Jane. Don't worry about us. We'll be all right."

Well, now that I got the boss' okay....

"Hello," I crooned over the phone to my boyfriend while walking to my home. "When are you coming back?"

"Hello my beauty! You missing me or my helpful hands?"

"I always miss you and your helpful hands." I flirted back. He was always so playful, when he wasn't upset with me. "But, I think I will really miss you and your hands if you don't get over to Jake's soon to help with the kids."

"I may not make it there at all now. I may have to join a study session tonight. I've been fooling around with you too much these days. I'm behind on all my studies."

"Max..." I whined. "You have to come over! How about if you come over tonight, I'll help you get rid of all your tension—and thus, you will be able to study even better come next week."

"Can I hold you to this promise?" I could tell he was smiling on the other end.

"You betcha! See you soon?"

"As soon as I can, my precious gem."

Donovan and I strolled back into the kitchen around the same time, and felt a pang of guilt when we saw that Laney had already washed both kids and was taking Ellie out of the bath chair and putting her Hello Kitty bathrobe on her little body. My gorgeous niece was walking around with a Hello Kitty-eared hoodie over a mop of curls as she tried, unsuccessfully, to put on her matching Hello Kitty bath slippers. I helped her put on the soft fleece slippers that were pink and blue with silver polka dots everywhere with a small Hello Kitty plush doll face planted between her two toes. She looked so adorable, I took a picture and sent it to her parents.

"You look so cute!" I exclaimed and kissed her face.

Freakishly, this girl replied, "Det tyu," which I think meant, "Thank you." She had quite a knack for the English language. I'm sure one day, I'll be wishing she didn't talk so much, but for now, Donovan and I looked like proud parents as he picked up his goddaughter and threw her up in the air. That made the Hello Kitty slippers fly to both corners of the kitchen. While we were making a fuss about how darling Ellie was in her outfit, Laney had put a matching Sanrio bathrobe on James. He was dressed as Kerokerokeroppi with matching slippers that fit over his feet nice and snug. He, too, looked gorgeous!

"I'll take James," I said and took him off Laney's hands. James started whimpering and called out "Ne Ne," which kinda pissed me off that he learned to say Laney's name before my name. Before she could take him back, I told Donovan to follow me, and we marched the kids upstairs so we could put them in their pajamas.

We laid them both down on their changing tables, and Ellie was as happy as a clam, but James started crying. I did my best to calm him down because I didn't want my nephew favoring a distant cousin to his aunt. I pulled out the toys that were next to the changing table and did a song and dance, but had absolutely no luck.

"I don't think he likes you much, Auntie Jane," Donovan teased. "Why don't you call Auntie Laney?"

"She's not his aunt. I'm his only aunt," I growled at Donovan while attempting to get a diaper under James' soft bottom.

I was doing okay with the diaper but the hollering got worse, and I heard Laney's footsteps along the hallway. *Shit! I can do this. I do not need anyone's help.* Just when I thought everything was in the clear, I felt a gush of water on my chin and neck, and I let out a louder than necessary yelp!

"What the hell?" I hollered, which in turn led to a chain of events I'm horrified to relive!

Before I closed James' diaper, he peed on me.
I yelled.
James got frightened.
He rolled himself off the changing table to get away from me.
James proceeded to fall, head first, onto the hardwood floor.

I don't know where Laney came from, but she caught him right as he was about to hit his head on the ground. She got to him literally centimeters before I would have been in deep shit with my brother.

At this point all hell broke loose. James hollered for dear life, Ellie hollered because her brother hollered, Donovan hollered at me for "dropping the baby," and I hollered back defending myself, trying to convince everyone that I did not "drop the baby!"

In the melee, Laney had quietly rounded up both kids, was sitting on the oversized rocking chair and had begun reading them a book. Both babies let out tearful hiccups here and there, but were soon calmed down.

"Ellie, you want me to read you a book?" Her godfather asked.

"NO!" She answered with conviction.

I was afraid to ask, but didn't want to lose out to my cousin so I started to say, "James..." and that's when both kids started crying again. *Hell!* I gave up and left the room.

"Don't think you'll be having kids anytime soon," Donovan cracked up and put his arm around me to console me.

"No, I guess not," I answered with anger. "I'm not the girl you want to marry if you need a mother for your kids. Go talk to Laney, instead."

"I think I prefer a woman to a little girl, when I decide I need to procreate." How does this man make everything look and sound so freakin' delicious?

"Shut up!" was my only lame answer to him as I elbowed him away from me.

In the course of reheating the Bolognese sauce for our dinner, Max came over and I recounted the entire saga to him. Rather than consoling me and making sure I wasn't in too much shock from the events of the night, Max scolded the both of us and said, "And you let Laney put both kids to bed by herself?"

He marched right up to the kids' room and we walked in on three angel-looking Reids sitting on the rocking chair, asleep. Laney had both kids protectively cradled in each arm.

"Laney," Max whispered, and gently put a hand on her shoulder. "Let me take James from you and I'll put him down."

When she looked up at my boyfriend with those big blue eyes, she really looked not much different than a child herself. She, too, had those cherub cheeks like the twins and that doe-eyed innocent look.

"Take Ellie. I'll hold on to James a bit longer. I don't think he'll part from me just yet."

Max did just that and gingerly transferred Ellie to her twin-size bed that my parents bought for each grandchild as a birthday gift. He then very slowly and carefully took a whimpering James from Laney's arms and rocked him a bit till he calmed down, and eventually put him in his own bed as well. Finally! The kids were down.

"Have you had dinner?" Seeing Max with Laney made me think that he would have made a great older brother—so opposite of my own!

"I haven't eaten yet, have you? Emily made spaghetti sauce before she left. If you want, I can heat it up for you." Laney answered.

"Why don't you sit and I'll heat it up for us. You're probably tired after taking care of both kids all afternoon. It's a good thing those kids go to bed so early."

"Today, I have to agree. I don't know how Emily does it every day. She's pretty incredible."

"That she is." My boyfriend agreed.

This love fest between Laney, Max and Emily was nauseating me. So, I cut into their conversation. "Who's staying here tonight?"

Before anyone could answer, Josh was at the back door.

"Hey, Bro'. What brings you by?"

"Laney brings me by. What other reason would I have for being here? It definitely isn't to babysit."

"Well, you should've come earlier if you really wanted to help your friend. She had a rough night."

"What were the rest of you doing, not helping Laney?"

"It's all fine Josh," Laney said. "How are you? You went and got your passport in order?"

"Yeah!" My cute little "brother" smiled wide. "We're gonna have so much fun together in Europe!"

"Why would you guys be in Europe together?" Big brother Donovan asked.

"Laney is moving there for a year and I'm going to go paint out there for a year."

"What's the matter with this graduating class? Don't you believe in getting a job after college, or going to graduate or professional school? You young people are too dependent upon your parents. You need work experience. You need to live in reality."

I nodded my head and concurred with every one of Donovan's words. "I agree!" I exclaimed.

Josh and Laney stopped talking for a brief moment, stared at us, checked each other out, shrugged their shoulders, then continued with their conversation as though neither Donovan nor I had said a peep.

Max laughed and joined in their conversation. "You need help with anything before you leave, Laney?"

She hesitated. "I think I'm okay, Max. Thank you for asking," was all she said before asking Josh, "When will you leave and where will you go first?"

"I'm leaving in June and I think I'll start in London and make that my base. You think your grandparents will let me live with you in the flat?"

Laney kept quiet. We could tell that wasn't her cup of tea.

But, Josh kept pushing. "Jane, can I ask your Gram for permission to room with Laney?"

Before big brother Donovan could bark at Josh, I answered, "You can ask Gram yourself." I was all for those two becoming roommates!

We all decided to make an early night of it, and I was up and ready to leave. I figured Max and I would come back in the morning, and it wouldn't matter whether or not Donovan chose to come back since Max was around.

"Can we leave?" I don't know why I had to ask Laney for permission, but I did. "Max and I'll be back early in the morning to help you?"

"Sure," Laney agreed.

"Babe, I don't feel comfortable leaving Laney here by herself with the babies. Maybe I should stay here with her."

Say what??? I don't think so!!! "We'll be right across the street. Jake never said which one of us had to stay here."

"Why don't I stay for a while, then I'll leave when Laney is ready to sleep." Max kept insisting. This big brother bit was going too far. Max could tell I wasn't happy.

"How about I stay with Laney?" Josh suggested with a squirrely smile. He was such a cutie!

"Out of the question," Donovan said.

Max concurred. "No. If something were to happen, I don't know that you'd be much help."

"Gee, thanks for the vote of confidence." Josh complained, Max chuckled.

"I don't need any of you here. Thank you, Max, but I have my stuff here already and I'm happy to stay with the kids by myself. I'll go to sleep as soon as you guys leave so you don't need to worry about me."

"I'd feel much better if you let me hang out a bit longer."

"Well, suit yourselves," I exclaimed and headed to the back door. "I'll see you bright and early in the morning." I waved goodbye to the three men and started out the door.

"I'll see you in a bit," Max whispered.

"Don't count on it," I whispered back.

Believe or not, that earned me a quick, but wet kiss. I was blushing by the time Max let go of me.

Fast forward to today, Monday, early evening, Jake's backyard for Emily's birthday dinner. I walked in with a beautiful gift in hand, ready to greet my sister.

"...next thing you know, James pees on Jane's face, she screams like a little girl, and he rolls off his changing table trying to get away from her..." Everyone gasped as they heard Donovan, *that rat*, tell an exaggerated version of what happened the other night. My brother is glaring at me even though he's told that nothing happened to his beloved one-year-old.

"That's the last time I put the care of my kids in your hands," was the thanks I got for playing tirelessly with both kids on Sunday to try and make up for the near accident. I lost count of how many times I stacked both sets of nesting blocks so Ellie and James could karate chop / karate kick them down. I even gave them their first lollipop, which did not make Laney happy, but those twins sure were happy.

"Ellie, you want to play with Auntie Jane?" I asked the little girl who was draped over my boyfriend.

"NO!" was the emphatic answer that greeted my question. If that wasn't enough, she said a few more times, "NO! NO! NO!"

Obviously, this motherhood stuff wasn't for the weak-hearted, and obviously it wasn't for me...at least not yet!

May 23, 2013

Introducing James

and Elizabeth Reid

*M*ax and his brothers decided to lowball the already low price on the house, and the builders accepted the bid. I think it had everything to do with the fact that they would have three sales at once. The Davis boys were psyched, and we all ended up celebrating at Emily's house, of all places.

"Emily, you're the greatest!" Josh brown-nosed my sister. "Thanks for inviting us to this impromptu barbeque."

"I'm glad you could make it. I want you and Garret to visit more often. I see Max because he comes over with Jane, but you guys haven't been here since the birthday party. Don't you miss me?" She smiled while Jake frowned.

"Of course we miss you," Josh said, while putting his arms around Emily's shoulder. "But," he then whispered, "that man you married doesn't look like he wants us to miss you."

Emily laughed so hard, the twins stopped what they were doing and laughed with her. Babies were the oddest creatures. They had no idea why their mother was laughing, but they decided that if it was funny enough for her, it was funny enough for them.

It may sound like I'm bragging, and I kinda am bragging, but I will swear on the Bible that my niece and nephew are the best looking one-year-olds on this planet. When they were first born, they looked almost identical to one another but as they grow older, not only are their appearances contrasting, but their personalities are like night and day.

They both started with a full head of black hair and beautiful blue eyes. I guess you could say they looked like a Reid since we three have the same coloring. Ellie's blue eyes remind me of a deep sapphire sometimes. They're almost as black as her hair, but when she's out in the sun like she is now, they look like a beautiful ocean. She shares the jet-black hair with her dad and her aunt and uncle, but she has something I'd give half my shoe closet for—curls! Think ringlets now, but soon will look like Victoria Beckham / Kate Beckinsale's loose waves with giant curls at the end. Because of her curls, her hair only appears to reach right below the ear, but once she grows and her hair relaxes, she'll have beautiful waves from head to halfway down her back. In the skin department, Ellie has beautiful baby skin with naturally rosy cheeks. No matter what she's doing, even while sleeping, her cheeks have a blushed glow.

James started with straight jet-black hair and sparkly blue eyes, but now his hair was turning a wavy dark brown, with curls at the end. His eyes have a cool blue-green hue to them and he is a sight to behold, especially when he smiles. Though his cheeks aren't naturally flushed like Ellie's, his are fuller and even more lovable than Ellie's. He has those great big cheeks you wanted to kiss and squeeze all day. I can see why Laney was always kissing his cheeks.

At age one, it was hard to tell what my niece's body would eventually look like since there were so many rolls of fat everywhere, but she had long legs (even for a one-year-old). And if she had her mother's genes, she'd have no issue with weight, no matter what and how much she ate.

James was already taller than his sister, and he was looking more like Emily as he got older. Ellie looked and acted like Jake as the days passed us by. It was amazing how their temperaments were so different from one another. Ellie was a "NO!" girl, and James was a "yawsh" boy (that's how he pronounces his yes—*yawshshshsh*—it is so damn cute). Just like my brother, Ellie wants everything NOW and she has to be FIRST in everything. It is like Jacob trying to usurp Esau's birthright. If James wasn't careful, his sister wouldn't surprise any of us if she tried to convince everyone that she was the firstborn.

Of course, with James' easy-going personality, he probably won't care whether Elizabeth acts like she's his elder. He'll wait his turn in playing with certain favored toys, in receiving his snack, in getting in his cuddle time with Mom. Emily does a great job of making sure he comes in first at least half the times, but with a vocal daughter, it isn't easy. But, I do notice that if there is something of importance to James, he doesn't lose out to his sister. Case in point, James loves the Dr. Seuss book, *One Fish, Two Fish, Red Fish, Blue Fish*, and he makes sure he is the first one to "read" that book and only when he is done, does his sister get to even touch the book. James is also very protective and possessive of his mother. She is the cat's meow for him. Of course Ellie loves Emily, too, but there is an extra special mother-son bond, for now. Ellie, being an attention monger, is an equal opportunity lover. My brother once stated that she'd "charm anyone within a smile of her" and he wasn't kidding. She spreads the love and men fall like flies already, and she's only one. Imagine her lure when she turns eighteen. SCARY!

"What are you smiling about, my muse?" Max whispered in my ear, and kissed it the same.

"I was thinking about my niece and nephew and how cute they are."

"They are as adorable as they come. You think if we had babies, they'd be that cute?"

Babies...us...??? Yowza, I'd never thought of making babies with this man!

"I think they might have a fighting chance...we definitely will have a good time trying..." I left it at that with a wink and a pat to his inner thigh.

"Wawa! Wawa!" Ellie called out, and pointed to the pool as soon as her meal was done.

"Again, Elizabeth?" My brother asked.

"Ellie and James love the water, and she's been badgering Jake to take her in every night since the weather's warmed up." Emily explained.

My brother got smart and picked up Ellie and started asking her, "Do you want Uncle Max to take you in the pool?"

In my brother's mind, he was trying to pass the buck, but in my mind, all I could think about was the moniker, *Uncle Max*. It had a great ring to it.

"NO!"

Okay...

"How about Uncle Nick?"

"NO!"

"What about Uncle Doug?"

"NO! NO! NO!"

It looked like Jake wasn't getting out of hopping in the pool with both kids.

"Anybody home?" Donovan walked in through the back yard gate. "Am I too late for dinner?" He asked while giving Emily a kiss on the cheek and dropping a huge bag of presents.

"I'm glad you could make it. What's in here?" Emily started rummaging through the bag.

"Just some stuff Kate and I picked up for the twins in London." *He and Kate???* "I'm afraid Ellie has a disproportionate number of gifts, compared to James." He confessed while picking up James, making double sure that the mashed potato all over James' face did not get on his suit. "Sorry, Bud! There's just more girl stuff in this world."

My gorgeous nephew gave Donovan a beautiful smile, and patted Donovan's cheeks with his gravy and mashed potato-stained hands. Donovan couldn't get away from him quickly enough to avoid being "mashed." We all had a good laugh.

"You want your godfather Donovan to take you in the pool?" Jake was still looking to replace himself.

I always knew this girl was going places, but was absolutely convinced when I saw her jump from Jake's arms into Donovan's body. She nodded her head yes—like a million times—smiled a brilliant gummy smile and kissed Donovan on the cheek. Then, she hung her chubby arms around Donovan's neck and cradled her body into his. Her godfather had no chance of resisting. He smiled wide, gave

Ellie a kiss on her head and took her toward the pool. Damn! That little girl was good. I needed to take lessons from her.

"Um, you need to change before going in the pool," Jake reminded him. "Bring Ellie and let's go upstairs. I'll lend you swim trunks."

"You know I just got in and haven't had dinner yet."

"I'm sure they fed you plenty on the plane. Plus, Emily has food put aside for you. But first, you can appease your goddaughter."

"The things I do for you Reids..." Donovan chuckled and carried Ellie with him, not that he had a choice.

"Where's Laney, Emily?" Of course, Josh was the one to wonder.

Emily whipped out her phone and called Laney, I assume. "Hey. You busy? I tried calling you earlier, but you didn't answer. You did?" Emily's voice went up an octave with those last two words. "Come over with your bathing suit and have dinner with us. There are some people who'd like to see you."

Emily gave Josh an affirmative wink and then proceeded to clean up James. "I'll be right back. I'm going to go change James so he can go swimming as well. Why don't you all go and put on your swimsuits? I'm sure the three of you can borrow from the three men here."

"I love watching you Reids," Max whispered after giving me a delicious kiss. "This is what a family should be like."

"If you keep kissing me like that, swimming's shot. We're going to have to go back to my room...like now!" I whispered back.

"Then stop caressing my inner thigh. I can't get up from this table without showing a lot more than I'd like to show."

That, to me, was a challenge, and I always rise to a challenge! As the four boys were getting up to get bathing suits, my hands went further up his inner thigh and fondled the parts that needed to be fondled, but only briefly, so he'd be frustrated. Then, my hands came right back to my lap.

"More?" I asked innocently.

"Anymore and I'll embarrass myself. Let's wait till we christen your new toy tonight. I hope the four seniors in the house sleep soundly 'cuz you're going to make some noise tonight."

My body shivered in anticipation. "You spending the night?"

"Yeah, but I won't be sleeping. Since we won't see each other all weekend, gonna have to get my fill tonight to tie us over till next week."

I shivered again. "New toy? What kind of new toy?"

"All I'm going to say is 3-speed."

"Can't wait," I kissed him a little more enthusiastically than necessary in front of an audience.

"You two not swimming?" Jake was back with James in his Superman swim trunks, while Donovan carried Ellie in her Wonder Woman two-piece. They were DARLING! James' swim trunks were red, almost speedo-like and his rash guard was blue with the red and yellow Superman logo. It even came with a cape that attached to the rash guard. He looked so darling, I just wanted to eat him up.

Ellie had on a blue bottom with white stars and her rash guard was a red top, with a golden eagle emblem drawn onto it. Attached to the rash guard was a little loop where she carried her lasso of truth. She also wore her floaties-cum-bulletproof bracelet, and she even had the red-starred golden tiara-cum-headband. All she needed were a pair of red and white go go boots and her invisible plane, and she was ready to star in a Marvel comic. Already, this sassy girl knew she looked adorable. As we ooh'ed and aah'ed over her swimsuit, she insisted on walking and practically pirouetted towards the pool. Of course, as she got to the gate, she demanded, "Up!" from her god-father and the two jumped in the pool together.

Ellie wasn't expecting the jump. She almost looked like she was going to cry, initially, then she giggled and loved it. She now demanded, "Morrrr!" Donovan obliged and got out of the pool and jumped in again. By their fourth jump, all the men, except Jake and Max were in the pool.

"Max, you want to borrow swim trunks?" Emily offered so kindly.

"Naw, Em. I think I'll stay here with Jane."

"Good choice," she said with a loving smile.

"Ne Ne!" We heard James greet Laney, and she immediately went to him and adored him. Those two had a bond that not even I could break.

"Hello, sweet boy. Are you my superhero, today?"

"Yawshshshsh!" He nodded his head furiously, then pointed to the pool.

"Can I take him in? Is he ready?"

"Be our guest, Laney. By all means, enjoy your nephew." Jake sent those two off then approached his wife. "Finally! Alone time, Love."

"Uh... you're not alone. We are watching." I warned. "Please don't make me want to throw up my dinner. And let me just reiterate that Laney is *NOT* James' aunt. I am his only aunt."

"Then start acting like an aunt and stop threatening my kids' lives with your baby-handling ways."

"Oh my gosh, did you just tell me that I baby-handled your kids? Do you know how much I love those kids? I..."

"Enough." Jake cut me off. "You want to clean up here while I take Emily upstairs? I think she's done enough work for a day." Though this might have sounded like a question, it was a command.

"Do I have a choice?" I dared, but Max interceded.

"Emily, you go in and rest. We can all clean up after ourselves. We'll even bathe the twins and bring them to you ready for bed when they're done in the pool."

Jake looked happy. "Great, Davis! I knew there was a reason why I liked you. Keep Jane in line and I think you'll do all right in this family."

Before I could say anything, Jake pulled Emily towards the house when all of a sudden, we heard a screeching sound from one of the guys.

"Jake! Emily!! What the hell is this in the pool?" Nick hollered.

We all ran over to the pool as quickly as possible, and died laughing when we saw what was in the pool. The guys on the shallow end with Ellie had no clue.

"Um...guys," Emily said while motioning for Nick to hand over Ellie. "It seems as though our princess has had a *little* accident. I'm sure the chlorine will kill the germs, but you're all swimming in a mass of diarrhea." Emily busted up as soon as she finished her sentence. I'd never seen five guys fly out of a pool so quickly.

Well, I'd gone through how beautiful these two were on the outside, but on the inside, their bodies functioned like a one-year-old. They ate whatever, slept whenever, and pooped wherever. What a life!

May 27, 2013

Truth or Dare

I took off a few days from work this holiday weekend and joined Becky and Evie in planning our bachelorette party before Ashley and Jared's Sunday wedding. Max was unusually busy with school and the hospital so he didn't make it to any part of this celebration. My parents arrived on Saturday to join in the fun, and Jake and Emily, who were considering joining since Austin wasn't too far from Emily's parents' grave, ended up making it as well. Since Emily was seven months prego and the twins were an absolute handful these days, theirs was a last minute decision. They also brought Laney as their babysitter. We all grew up together, and Ash's parents were still buddy-buddy with my parents, so Ash had no issues with Jake's family + Laney being a last minute add-on.

All of the Taylor sisters came in to Austin between Friday and early Sunday morning, and Becky was my date since Al was out of the country on a business trip. Donovan came without a date, so the three of us kind of hung out the whole weekend. It was a fun time of catching up with all our childhood friends.

"What's up with you and Max these days?" Evie started a long round of conversation between the four of us. We were sitting at the bar of a posh restaurant because Ashley decided she only wanted the four of us at her "bachelorette party" and she wanted a mild one. She was exhausted with wedding prep and her three other bridesmaids who lived in town were driving her nuts.

"Let's table Max for a few minutes. What in God's name is going on between you and my brother?"

Evie and Ashley choked on their drinks, and Becky just stared at me expectantly and demandingly.

"There's nothing going on between me and your brother. Why do you ask that question?" Unfortunately, I wasn't very convincing.

"Donovan said something to Al, and Al mentioned something to me, and...spill the beans Jane, what's up with you and Donovan?"

"Donovan and I are friends, we are coworkers, and..."

"Shit Jane," Ash was getting impatient. "Just say it. Did you cheat on Max and do the nasty with our favorite older brother? Was Donovan good in bed? He's so tall and long everywhere, is he as anatomically perfect as we all believe he is?"

"Eew! That's gross, Ash. I don't need to hear that about my brother."

"Well we do. I want to know everything about Mr. Donovan Taylor." Ashley downed her first drink before the rest of us even got started.

"I can't believe you girls would think that I would cheat on my boyfriend. Of course I did not cheat on Max, and of course I did not do the nasty with Donovan. He and I just have this unnecessary tension between us from time to time."

"What the hell? Details!" Becky demanded.

"You know I've always crushed on your brother. A man doesn't get much hotter than Donovan Taylor. Geez, he could audition for the role of Christian Grey with his brooding looks and charming charisma."

Ash and Evie both shouted, "Amen!"

"Well, around the same time Max came back to me, or better stated I came back from New York, your brother started showing interest. We went to a Laker game at the onset of my 'dating' period with Max and that was it. We went out once, enjoyed ourselves and...what else is there to say...we've always gotten along really well."

"You haven't done anything with my brother, have you?" Becky asked, sounding disgusted.

"No!" I told all the ladies. "We've had a few meals together, and most of those are innocuous lunches during work time. Your brother has confessed that he is attracted to me, and I confess to no such thing. We are...we are nothing to one another."

Becky wanted to know, "What does Max think? Does Max even know?"

"I made Max plenty angry and insecure thanks to your brother, Becky! Once Donovan and I worked the entire night, separately, but your brother gave me a ride home, and of course Max was there in the morning waiting for me and totally jumped to the wrong conclusion. That was not a happy morning."

"Now that you know that the hot Donovan Taylor is attracted to you, you going to act on it?" Ash asked suggestively.

"How can I act on it? I am dating Max. I'm also in love with Max. I don't want to ruin anything. Things are *so* good between us right now."

"But..." Ash kept at it.

"Donovan asked me not too long ago if I thought that we would be as good in bed as we are out of bed."

"No!" All three girls spoke aloud.

"And in all honesty, there are times when I can't help but wonder what it would be like to be with him. I know that's not the thing to say, or the right thing to think when I'm with such a wonderful man, but I can't help what's looming between me and Donovan."

Ashley suggested, "I think you two should just do the nasty, get it over with and see if that'll go anywhere. Then you need to come back and give us every detail of what a fine specimen Becky's brother is."

"Ash," Becky chided. "That's disgusting. I don't care to know about my brother's sexual escapades." Then she turned to me, "But I think if you are that curious, and since my brother is in agreement, you should give it a go with Donovan. I feel bad for Max because I know he's a great guy, but there's a part of me that knows you would be great for my brother! I'm so sorry to Max but I'm rooting for my brother, and hoping you'll become my sister—though there is the slight complication with your cousin."

"What???" Ashley, Evie, and I gasped.

Becky took a sip of her drink, a bite of her food, and an inordinate amount of time explaining herself.

"Shit, Becky. You can't just drop a bomb like that and eat and drink like nothing's pressing! Which cousin are we talking about? Which cousin is within age range for our favorite big brother?" Ashley started mentally going through her Reid contacts.

"When I was out in LA for the week of Mother's Day, I saw my brother and Laney together—A LOT!"

"Laney?" Ashley choked on her drink. "Is she even out of high school?"

"Where have you been? She graduates this week from college." Becky seemed to know more about my cousin than necessary.

When had this Donovan-Laney connection happened and where the hell was I when this memo was disseminated? "Explain." I demanded.

"Well, there was...oh never mind. Al asked about Laney, and Donovan flat out told him that he thinks of her as another Rachel. You remember how overbearing he was with me and my sister, Rachel? Al and I thought there was something going on with the two of them but if Donovan says there isn't, I believe him. So back to you and Donovan..." Becky turned the attention back to me.

"Ladies!" Evie brought us all back to reality. "Let's not forget that Jane is dating Max! She is going to move in with Max! She is in love with Max! Jane," she now started scolding me, "I think what you are thinking and feeling is terrible. I'm sorry but you are being a total bitch for even contemplating another man, when you are with the perfect guy whom you consider marrying." Great, now she made me feel guilty. The preaching continued. "Just because you find Donovan attractive...shoot, who doesn't find Donovan attractive...does not mean you need to act upon every attraction that's out there. I know you've crushed on Donovan since you were little. All of us have had a crush on him at some point in our lives, but we were little. And that's just it; he was our obsession as little girls. Just because he's shown some interest in you, it does not mean you are still attracted to him. Curious maybe, but not attracted."

"I certainly would be tempted if Becky's big brother wanted to do the nasty with me."

Evie rolled her eyes. "You would really give up Jared for one night with Donovan?"

"Today, no. A couple years ago...maybe?"

"No you wouldn't and you know it, Ash. You know you were in love with Jared from day one and there was no way you would cheat on him, no matter how gorgeous the man."

"I suppose you're right, Evie, but Jane just started dating Max again, and it's not like they're getting married tomorrow. I don't see anything wrong with Jane and Max taking a hiatus and Jane exploring other options."

"I agree," Becky nodded her head yes. "I think you should check out life with my brother and see what happens. You've known him your entire life. There are no secrets with him, at least not that we are aware of."

Our saint Evie put in her two cents again. "Well I think it's wrong. And I think this entire conversation is wrong. I just wonder Jane, what you would be thinking and feeling if you knew that Max was having this same conversation with his buddies about his ex-girlfriend, Hannah. If you knew that he still found her attractive, I think it would kill you inside. You know you're in love with Max. I know you're curious about Donovan, but that's just curiosity, Jane.

It's not love. Don't throw away love for a roll in the hay. Because in the end, you're going to regret it!"

"Evie makes all the sense in the world, but I still say go for it." By this point Ash was a little drunk and I think she was getting sloppy with her words. "In fact, I dare you to have a one night stand with Donovan. He's going to be here this weekend. Sleep with him."

"I don't know Ash. I think she should get together with my brother, but I don't want her to cheat on Max. I want her to break up with him, then have a relationship with my brother. So no sleeping with my brother this weekend, unless you're going to break up with Max via phone. Or you can do it Taylor Swift/Joe Jonas style and do it via text."

At this point Evie was furious. "Jane Reid, if you cheat on your boyfriend, I will never speak to you again. That is just not something any decent woman would do. I have a good mind to call Max right now and tell him about this entire conversation."

"You wouldn't dare," Ash and Becky said at the same time.

"Why not? You dared Jane to have a one-night stand with Donovan. Why don't you dare me and see if I'll go running to Max." Now she was taunting us with her threat, though I knew she wouldn't go through with it in the end. Even if I did something so wrong as cheating on Max, Evie would stay true to me.

"Okay, Ladies!" I called out. "Let me clear up this fight. I am not cheating on Max. I love him, I'm going to move in with him, I'm going forward with him. Becky, as much as I'd like to be your sister, I don't know that you truly want me as a sister, especially when you already have three very bossy ones."

"She's got a good point there," Ash slurred her words and Becky giggled.

"And I admit, there is some attraction between me and Donovan Taylor, but I think Evie is right. It's just an attraction and more of a curiosity than anything else. But that ship has sailed. Evie, no need to say anything to Max, I will not cheat on him. I really do love him," I confessed.

"Hello pretty ladies." Donovan, in his 3-piece pin-striped suit and black Ferragamo dress shoes looking smokin' hot, just walked up to the bar. He was our ride tonight. Every woman eyed him as he stood at the bar. Did I mention he looks like Henry Cavill? Shoot, Mr. Cavill had nothing on this man.

"You ready for me to take you all back to the hotel?"

"Yep. We're all bachelorette partied-out. Where are you staying?" I asked innocently.

"Same hotel, right next door to you."

Oh dare—I mean, dear!

May 30, 2013

Which "Gap" Do I "Mind"?

*L*et me open with...NOTHING happened! Literally! Donovan, Becky, Evie and I had a fanfreakin'tastic time at Ash's wedding, and I did not touch Ash's dare with a ten-foot pole. Even Al, Becky's husband, made a surprise appearance which thrilled my best friend. You see! I can be a good girl when not with Max, and show everyone that I am totally committed to making this relationship work. It's no joke when I tell you that I am *SOOOO* in love with Max right now. Why, you ask? Because we are getting along, there's no more petty jealousy, no more misunderstandings, and we *LOVE* each other despite our flaws. Is that reason enough?

Having said that, my cousin Laney became a bona fide unemployed college graduate today. With there being so many graduates and so few jobs, it was no wonder people her age were seeking alternative "jobs." Laney's "job," will come in the form of living off our grandmother's generosity and discovering life on a new continent. Josh, who also graduates this year, will find his "job," in the form of gallivanting from town to town, making beautiful art and enjoying life.

What the hell was wrong with these young people? Didn't they believe in getting a 9 to 5 job and putting money away in the bank, like the rest of us? This devil-may-care attitude only postponed the inevitable entry into daily society. It didn't seem fair that some of us worked hard, and worked hard some more, while others of us went off to live in Japan and England just to satisfy their fancy.

If I'm honest with myself, much of what I've said comes from jealousy. Being in the lawyer rat race, I wish I could've stopped and taken some time for myself, rather than having been so driven to succeed, and succeed young. It wouldn't have killed me to go away for a year or two and just live, before starting law school. I know I've done a lot of traveling in the past, but it was always within the comforts of a family member. I was never brave enough to go out and explore life without having life mapped out first.

And also, in fairness to both Laney and Josh, they're not just postponing life with no thoughts of ever jumping back on the human tram. Laney started her own little business of editing student papers, and I'm sure she put aside a nice slush fund for herself. Josh does well day trading and has built up enough capital to spend it on his artistic side. Who was I to critique how they should spend their money?

"Hi Jane." The woman I was just begrudging and admiring in my head popped into my office.

"Laney." I knew I sounded surprised. I hoped I didn't look too guilty. "What brings you here?"

"I came to say goodbye to you and Grandfather."

"Goodbye?"

"I'm leaving today for London. My plane leaves in a few hours and I'm making the rounds. You and Grandfather are the last people on my list."

I stared for a bit. "Didn't you just graduate? Isn't there a barbeque at your house tonight, in your honor?"

Laney laughed softly. "Yeah. There is a barbeque, but I won't be there."

"Does your mom know this?"

"She knows..." Laney laughed again. "I let my parents know about a month ago that I was leaving the day I graduated, but I think Mom believed that if she planned this party, I'd postpone my trip."

I didn't know what to say.

"Can we go up to Grandfather's office and I'll explain it to the both of you? I don't have too much time."

I followed her up to Gimpy's office and was at a loss for words. I suppose I'd miss her, but in reality, we hadn't been too close in years past. Laney was never my cup of tea. It's not that we had a bad relationship...we just had no relationship. Somewhere along the way, life got busy, we ran in different circles, and her "stop and smell the roses" style of living wasn't the way I looked at life. Perhaps in my narrow-mindedness, Laney wasn't goal-oriented enough, empowered as a woman enough, or life-experienced enough. Who the hell dated, but never relationshipped??? She was like an endangered species to me where everyone made such a big deal about her, she never had to do any of the work herself. Was I wrong in this assessment? After knowing her for 22 years, I didn't think so!

"Hi Grandfather," Laney beamed. "Gram called you, already?"

"Delaney Reid," Gimpy said with much disapproval. "You did this purposely, didn't you? I told you I'd get the plane ready to take you to London."

She went over and held Gimpy's hands in her hands. "I know, Grandfather. You and Gram are too generous to me. I'm grateful that I have a place to live in London."

"That place belongs to your grandmother, and it'll eventually belong to your family. You're not staying anywhere you shouldn't be staying." Gimpy took a few steps back and sat on the edge of his desk with Laney's hands still in his. Neither person noticed that I was still in the room. *Hello?!?* "Your father was damn proud of your accomplishments today. He said no one knew about it till the ceremony. How can this be?"

What accomplishments?

"It wasn't a big deal, Grandfather."

"Not a big deal? Your gram tells me that you're the only one in the family to graduate summa cum laude. None of your cousins, nor your aunts and uncles have reached this honor."

Summa cum laude??? How the hell did she do that?

"I thought you were an English major, but your dad tells me that you graduated with a double major in chemistry and English?"

Laney laughed. "A chem major who struggled in statistics, Grandfather. My parents hoped that one of us would become a doctor, but neither fulfilled this dream. I thought maybe being a science major might be close enough."

"So are you really going to film school after taking this year off, or..."

...Or what???

"I don't know, Grandfather. I have a year to decide. For now, I'd like to go to film school, but I'll explore my options when I have time to think."

Damn it! Stop being so cryptic!

"Let me walk you out, Laney. I know you've a plane to catch."

"Thank you."

Still, no one acknowledged me, so I trailed behind the two who walked hand in hand towards the elevator. Gimpy slowed his steps as we got near the all glass conference room. I peeked in and saw Donovan with his M&A team working on their latest merger or acquisition. Laney slowed her steps to the same beat as Gimpy's and turned her head to look in the room. Donovan stared at the three of us wondering, but didn't move from his chair. Like an old-fashioned movie reel, Laney delicately and beautifully waved goodbye. Bemusedly, Donovan waved back, and then gave me a *what the hell is going on* look. I could not tell you why, but this scene broke my heart and made me want to take out my nonexistent hanky. Her goodbye was straight from a scene where the heroine leaves her lover for reasons unknown to him, never to come back and reunite their love.

"You sure you want to leave?" Gimpy asked with a knowing look that had me wondering what the hell everyone but me knew.

"Yes, Grandfather. I wish you and Gram good health. I'll miss you, but I'll keep in touch." She kissed his cheek. "I promise." She then hugged him one last time.

At this point, I saw movement from Donovan's side of the conference room and Laney sensed the same. She barely blurted out a goodbye to me and left.

"What just happened?" I asked Gimpy.

"Hey." Donovan greeted me. "Where'd Delaney go?"

"She left."

"I can see she left, Jane." Snarkiness didn't suit this man in the sharp Don Draper Mad Men-esque two-buttoned suit. "Where did she go?"

"To London."

Donovan gave me a *do I look stupid to you* look and I gave him back a *yeah, you look like an idiot right now* look.

"Lunch?" Gimpy broke up our stare down.

Donovan was pissed at me throughout lunch because Laney didn't say her farewells to him. "Like it was my fault that Laney didn't find you important enough for much more than a wave," was not the right thing to say to him. He left lunch all gruff and boorish. I stayed the hell away from him the rest of the day.

Unfortunately, Gimpy invited Donovan to catch a ride with us to the BBQ, so my respite from the Grump didn't last long. While Donovan went straight to Laney's, I stopped by home, changed and took my time walking to Aunt Babs'. The atmosphere I discovered at the BBQ was more of a funeral than a celebration. Both Uncle Henry and Aunt Babs didn't break a smile, and everyone ate without making a sound. The only noisy ones were the twins who were slurping, chomping, and dropping their food without a care.

"Hello James! Hi Ellie!" I went over and patted their heads. They were way too messy to kiss anywhere on the face.

They waved their barbeque sauce-laden hands and smiled.

"Hey, Babe." Max came from nowhere and kissed me right where I like to be kissed—behind the ear, top of the neck. But then again, there aren't too many places I don't like, when his lips choose to meander.

"Where'd you come from?"

"I got here a while ago. I went back in the house to bring out more salad for the picnic table. Your aunt is not quite in the entertaining mood."

"Can you blame her? I can't believe Laney left so suddenly. That girl can be so flippant."

"I think she's been planning this for a while. She didn't want her family making a big deal out of her leaving so she thought it best to go quietly."

"But what about her parents?"

"Her parents would have been just as sad no matter when she left."

"But her mom threw her a party and she's not even here. What kind of person does that?" I was trying to prove my point that Laney was an irresponsible brat, but my boyfriend wasn't helping my cause.

"Your aunt knew Laney was planning on leaving today, but chose to throw this party in order to thwart her plans. The tickets were purchased; the arrangements were made. There was no changing her plans without penalties."

"Uncle Henry would've gladly paid the penalties to have her here another day."

"Jane," Max admonished in that warning tone I disliked. "That's not the point. Laney's a grown adult. It wasn't like she didn't give everyone plenty of notice about her plans. Apparently, Roland was going to give her his Net Jet time, Gram and your aunt were going with her to help her get settled in the flat, and she didn't want to put anyone through the trouble, nor did she want the fuss. What makes you so pissy whenever Laney's name is mentioned? I don't get that about you."

"And why are you always her #1 cheerleader?"

"Seriously? Cheerleader?" He grinned and kissed me on the neck again, though this time it was a little more of an Edward Cullen-type of kiss. You know, the wet and sucking kind???

I giggled, but tried to stay upset with him. "I didn't appreciate you spending the night with her the other weekend when we babysat."

"*Whaaaat?* I did not spend the night with Laney!" Max protested. "I stayed like an extra fifteen minutes until Donovan showed up, then I *came* and spent the night with *you*." Normally, the sexual double entendre would've done something for me, but I couldn't believe what I'd just heard.

"*Whaaat?* You mean *Donovan* spent the night with her?"

"I don't think they spent the night *together*. They were just in the same house." Max gave me the answer I wanted to hear. "But then again, who knows? Why don't you ask him?"

"Hey, Donovan," I got up from the table and was going to confront him about sleeping with my cousin. But Max wouldn't let me, and Donovan wasn't paying any attention to me, so I assumed all was innocent and copacetic that night.

"So explain! Why do you like her so much?"

"What's there not to like? She's sweet, she's your cousin, and Josh is crazy about her. She's the little sister I would have loved to have and protect. Growing up with two younger brothers, I always wished we had a girl in the house. Mom wasn't exactly girly."

All right. I think that answer was good enough. "You pass." I answered with the same kinda kiss on his neck. I would be the Bella to his Edward.

"Uncle Henry," Nick called out in the middle of dinner. "I heard a strange rumor at school today. Care to confirm or deny?"

Finally, both Uncle Henry and Aunt Babs broke into the hugest smile.

"If you are referring to my daughter graduating summa cum laude—an accomplishment no other Reid can claim—*PLUS* the fact that she deferred her med school acceptance, yes I can confirm that rumor as fact."

There was a shocked silence reverberating from table to table.

"I thought she was going to film school." Nick voiced the same thought in all our heads.

"She still may…" Emily added to this conversation.

"What does that mean? How can she go to both schools? And both schools are so different." I commented.

"Just goes to show you what a genius my daughter is." My uncle's peacock feathers waved at all of us as he strutted over to the bar.

Doug laughed at his dad. "Yeah. She was such a genius that none of us knew any of this till today."

"Can you believe," Aunt Babs started a small tirade, "that she even fooled her own mother and father? We had no idea she was a double chem and English major, we had no idea she was doing so well in school, and we had absolutely no idea that she applied to med school! What kind of child did we raise? She told us nothing!" Laney's mother was upset, but proud.

"We raised a summa cum laude genius is who we raised." Uncle Henry took a swig of beer and continued the story. "The dean of med school told me today that she begged him not to let me know that she'd applied!" He then turned to Jake and accused, "Did you know? You and Emily knew, huh?"

"I did know, but only recently." Jake declared. "I'd heard rumors all year, but didn't bother confirming them since I believed Laney was looking only at film schools. Apparently, she applied to several med schools and got into..." Jake abruptly stopped his train of thought and turned to his wife. "You knew, didn't you? Did you actually keep a secret from me?"

Emily smiled beautifully. "Wasn't my secret to tell." She squeezed her husband's hand as a gesture of affection and apology. "Uncle Henry and Aunt Babs," she addressed them only, "not only is your daughter bright, but she also is just headstrong enough, and has enough common sense to live life the way she wants to live. Nobody is going to push your daughter around. I hope I can do just as good of a job with my little girl as you have with yours. She's a phenomenal young lady."

Now we had Aunt Babs bawling. "But why does she like to leave me all the time? This is the second year in the last four where she's away from her mother..."

"Laney will always come back to you, Aunt Babs. She's just spreading her wings and looking at life from a different angle," Emily reassured.

From where I was sitting, it was ridiculous that my cousin did all this and didn't want anyone to know. I think in secret, she knew that if it all came out at once, there'd be an even bigger deal made about her accomplishments. I know I sound spiteful, but her actions make absolutely NO sense to me!

"Why didn't Laney want anyone to know she got into med school?" Josh, who sat with Emily and Jake, spoke. I'd forgotten he was here.

"She wanted to figure a few things out for herself before letting everyone know."

"What does that mean?" Aunt Babs stopped crying just enough to be curious.

Emily thought through her answer before speaking. "In some ways, she wants to go to med school and follow in her father's footsteps." That brought out the peacock in Uncle Henry again. "But in many ways, she wants to get married, have kids and live the housewife life like her mom."

This is what I mean when I say I have no idea what is wrong with my cousin. If she's so damn smart, why would she want to stay at home and veg out with kids all day? No offense to stay-at-home moms like mine, Emily, and all my aunts, but we live in the 21st century. What woman wants to just stay home all day???

"Laney always said she couldn't be a part-time doctor or a part-time mother, and therein lies the dichotomy in the life of Delaney Reid," Emily continued.

"In short, she wants to be a housewife? She'll give up med school for a chance to be barefoot and pregnant?" I blurted out those words and immediately regretted it. That's exactly what every married woman in this backyard was or had been at one point in their lives. *Uh-oh...!*

Emily wasn't even fazed at what I'd just said. "I think our Laney has a way of looking further into the future than most of us. She doesn't want to start something now, or maybe *not* start something now, that she will regret later in life. She believes whatever she chooses to do, she'd like to do her absolute best and not have any regrets."

"Then why film school?" I had to know.

"She also likes writing and she wants to try her hand at script writing. She figures she could do this at home while she's 'barefoot and pregnant.'" Emily mimicked me and caused a riot among all the Reids under thrity-five. "If you get to know her, Laney is insightful and deep. Very few things are left to chance with her, and whatever she does or feels, her whole heart goes into that very action. Why, you only need to see her with my kids to know that some man out there will be loved profoundly."

With that sycophantic speech, Emily went back to caring for her kids, the mood got a lot livelier, but I didn't understand my cousin any better. If I were her, I'd stay here, enroll in the best med school, become a doctor as quickly as possible, and work under her dad. How much easier could life get if your dad is the Chief at a major hospital? There'd be plenty of time to get married and have kids in her thirties. Not everyone was an Emily, who got married practically straight out of college, and popped out three kids in under two years. I shook my head in disapproval. No wonder we never got along. She so did not understand life!

June 3, 2013

Playing House

We started furniture gathering for our new home! Though the Davis boys weren't closing on this property for another few weeks, we decided to make a checklist of what we already had, what we needed to purchase, and what we needed to fleece from Emily's basement.

If you'll all remember, Jake and Emily moved into my grand-parents' (that's Jerry and Estelle Reid, not Roland and Estelle Ascot) home. This massive home came with tons of furniture. Our money-conscious Emily recycled a lot of furniture, but there are still a large number of pieces sitting in the gigantic basement. We decided to make an afternoon of rummaging through all this fur-niture, rather than spending unnecessary money.

"How you feeling, Emily?" Max went and gave her a generous hug and kiss on the cheek.

"Too close to her lips, Davis. Stick to the head, or hand," Jake warned while carrying a sleeping Ellie.

Just to annoy him, Max gave Emily a quick peck on her lips, which surprised us all. Emily giggled, Max gave a rascally chuckle, but Jake and I didn't know how to react to this school-boy prank.

"If scowls could talk," Max said while pulling my hand in his. "You've got a sleeping baby in your arms. You don't want to wake her with your scowl."

Jake's scowl became even more pronounced. I think I followed suit as Max laughed and took me downstairs.

"What was that?" I know I mentioned earlier that I didn't have bouts of petty jealousy anymore but kissing another woman on the lips??? Nuh-uh! Stuff like that is not all right in my book.

"GEM..." he crooned and started making out with me in the corner of the basement. "You can't possibly be upset with that millisecond of a kiss to a mother of three. Why it's no different than me kissing your Gram on the lips. Consider it familial," he chuckled again, and proceeded to feel me up under my dress.

I considered arguing with him. I considered telling him that he did *NOT* date my grandmother for four years. I considered telling him he may not kiss any female Reids on the lips, ever! But once his finger started gliding in places it shouldn't be gliding in and out of, when my brother could walk in on us at any moment, all considerations were forgotten. The rhythm of his thumb brushing over, in combination with his middle finger gliding in and out of, and his mouth grazing me up and down my neck, I literally bit my lips to keep from moaning the house down.

"Shh," he whispered, "you'll wake the baby."

"Damn you," I uttered somehow. "Why here? Why now?"

"You still upset about that little kiss? You want me to stop so we can talk about it?" The jerk did stop and briefly shot a deadpan look, then smiled wickedly. "I didn't think so," he added and continued his torment.

The nearing sounds of Emily and Jake, and the fear of being caught forced the both of us into a frenzy and I dug my nails into the antique chair as he dug his middle *AND* his index fingers inside...and out. It was so close...I was so close...I moaned into his mouth and literally saw shooting stars, a full moon, an entire freakin' galaxy when my eyeballs rolled over. There was a point where I'd thought I'd stopped breathing.

"HUH!" I let out a loud breath.

"Enough? Or shall I continue?" He asked in an almost lazy drawl.

I realized our position had not changed and his fingers stayed right where they were five seconds ago, only it was gentler.

"I think that's enough for now. We can continue later, in the privacy of a bedroom....unless *you* need finishing up?"

"Let's do what we came here to do, then retire for the night."

"Mmmm...let's..." I was still basking in the afterglow.

Furniture "shopping" was successful but took longer to finish than expected. We picked out all the pieces we liked and needed, measured some of the questionably big pieces to check against the rooms in the house, and wrote up the pieces we still needed to purchase.

"Let's sneak out before anyone catches us. I believe I need to pay someone back for a good deed performed earlier?"

"How about paying it back right here on this bed?"

"Are you insane? Let's go before we get caught."

We were almost to the kitchen door when the entire crew walked in.

"I'm glad you're still here."

"What's up, Garret?"

"Escrow closed early, we got the keys and the go ahead to move in. If you've picked out your pieces, we'll help you move right now."

"Now?" I asked. *But we have things to do!*

"Josh is bringing a U-Haul over and Emily said we could use any of the furniture in the basement that we'd like. So, mark your pieces and let me and Josh go through the left-overs."

Oh, all right! We can have sex later.

Everyone pitched in and we practically cleaned out Emily and Jake's basement. Emily was salivating at the empty space and dreaming up plans for a craft / gift-wrapping room. What a life. Our entire home could fit into her basement, and she was portioning out a part of the basement for the crap that she keeps all over the house.

Since we hadn't turned on the electricity, we called it a night after the sun went down, and Max refused our brothers' invitation to have dinner with them. I saw him texting someone, then calling in for our favorite takeout. We stopped by Emily's one more time, for reasons unknown to me, picked up dinner and surprisingly went back to the house.

"What are we doing back here?"

"We're having our first meal and spending our first night here as a couple," he said with excitement in his voice.

He brought in a huge duffel bag while I brought in the dinner, and we carefully went to our small four person dining table.

"Sit, while I get things together," he suggested. Once Max got to unpacking, there were more candles than there was space on the table. All were lit throughout the dining room, a bottle of wine was opened, and dinner was out on table. This was insanely romantic! Max, me, candles everywhere, and feelings of contentment and love. It didn't get much better than this. "To our new home, our new adventures, and our future," he toasted.

To our future...

June 6, 2013

Life Uninterrupted

$\mathcal{G}$ uess whose birthday is coming up? Yours truly, if I may share that personal info. I'll be turning twenty-eight years old in a few days, and I have to say that for the first time ever, I feel old. I feel like my life's always been on a straight and narrow course, and I've walked that course without any hiccups. Once I got to college, I towed the line, never veering far from success. Good grades, law school, passed the bar on the first try, clerked for a big time judge, become a young partner in a big law firm...I wasn't too far from my end goal.

Feeling older and a bit introspective today, I thought about what I wanted in life on a personal level. I'd achieved or was on my way to achieving my work goals, and personally, I guess I was quite successful relationship-wise as well. My parents and I were close, I adored my brothers, sister, niece and nephew—and of course they adored me back, and I had a phenomenal boyfriend. We were days away from completely setting up house and I couldn't be happier with the way we were communicating.

In fact, life was so good with Max, I didn't freak out when he told me that Hannah was also going on this "mission" to Mexico. I figured it was her right to do whatever she wanted to do. It was her life, her money...whatever! Of course it helped that she was going with the

June group and not the July one that Max was going on. He he he! You knew there had to be a catch, didn't you? I'm not *that* understanding. It's not that I don't trust Max; I just don't want him spending any unnecessary amount of time with *her*. After that apartment hunting stunt she pulled on me, I have every reason to use caution.

"Jane, can I throw you a party for your birthday?" Even eight months pregnant, my dear sister cared enough to offer.

"Absolutely not!" Jake answered for me. "You are about to burst. You have active one-year-olds. You are giving birth in four weeks! You do not need to be throwing any more parties."

"Oh Jake." she poo poo'ed his edict. "I'm not an invalid. I can throw a small—or big—dinner party if Jane wants one. I think it'd be fun. We can invite..."

"No!" Like father like daughter, my brother sounded just like Ellie. "Mom can throw Jane a party if she wants one."

"Um, hello??? Do I have a say here?"

"No!" was his retort.

No different than usual, I ignored my brother. "Thank you, Emily, but I don't want a party. We might actually start living in the house on my birthday and celebrate it there."

"How about a little dinner?" Emily then quickly added, "I'll get everything catered and hire help to set up and clean up," to appease her husband. "Once the baby comes, I won't be able to do anything for months. All I'll do is nurse and change three diapers," she walked over to my brother and put her arms around him. This was the first time I'd seen Emily in action and she was quite the charmer. "Please, Honey? I love you and the kids and the home we've created, and I love sharing it with our friends and family. I hate the thought of not having friends and family over after the baby arrives.. Please, Jake? I'll be really careful and get lots of help." She had both arms around his waist and she formed her body into his, the best she could with that mountain of a belly. Of course my brother was a goner from the moment she touched him and asked to throw "a little dinner."

"You promise to get help?" He asked so sweetly and so full of love.

"I promise!" She answered back in the same manner. "I love you," she whispered and kissed him on the lips. When he tried to return her kiss, he was a step too late as she was already over by me demanding a guest list.

Jake only shook his head and said, "I'll get the door," when it was obvious that both Emily and I were oblivious to the fact that anyone had even rung the front door.

"Josh, what brings you by today?"

"Hi Emily," he sounded a bit down. "I came to ask you for some advice."

A downcast Josh was a really cute Josh. "No hello for me?"

"Hey Sis. What's up?"

LOVED that moniker! "Emily and I are planning my birthday dinner. You wanna come?"

"Will Laney be there?"

"Um...no...she's in London. I highly doubt that she's going to make the ten-hour flight back just for my birthday. Maybe for Emily's birthday, but not for mine."

"I'll consider it..." he moaned. He was in such the dumps that I didn't even bother feeling offended by his *"I'll consider it."*

The kitchen door opened and in walked Donovan with two big bags again.

"Ellie! James!" Emily called. "Uncle Donovan is here. Time to go."

"Where, might I ask, is *Uncle* Donovan taking the twins?" I could *not* believe Donovan was spending quality time with the twins.

"Since James likes Toy Story so much, I got the firm seats to the Arena for the *Toy Story on Ice* show." James ran into the kitchen with his dad and my gorgeous nephew came dressed as Sheriff Woody with the yellow shirt, blue pants, cow-print vest, red neckerchief and all. Donovan pulled out of his bag, a cowboy hat, a brown plastic belt and holster, matching brown cowboy boots, and a sheriff's badge.

"No g-u-n?" I spelled out.

"Negative, ma'am" Donovan answered in his lame wanna-be Buzz accent. "Where's my Ellie?"

It was actually cute the way he was "fathering" these kids.

"Meeee!" Our adorable life-size Jessie came running into the kitchen in her Jessie replica button-down shirt, denim and "cow" pants and a brown belt with a huge plastic buckle. Emily had even tied back Ellie's hair in a thin braid and held it together with a yellow tie, just like Jessie in the movie. Uncle Donovan completed this outfit with a red hat and brown boots. My niece made the most beautiful Jessie! I took lots of pictures of our life-sized toy story doll and sent them over to Max who was at the hospital.

"You're taking these kids on your own?" I asked surprised.

"You want to come? We have two extra seats." Donovan offered. "Ellie, James?" He called out to them and they looked over. "Should we take Auntie Jane to go see Woody and Buzz?"

James incessantly shook his head no and went from elation to fright and Ellie just yelled, "NO!" Damn these kids had a long memory. I thought kids forgot everything.

Donovan and Jake laughed. "I guess they don't want you." Donovan said and Jake agreed.

"Can Uncle Josh come with you?" Josh was brave to ask. This was a tough audience.

Both kids ignored Josh as though he didn't exist and Ellie kept yelling, "Yund...yund...yund...," while James kept point his finger up in the air.

"What the hell are they doing?" I quietly asked Emily.

"That's Elizabeth's way of mimicking Buzz when he says, *'To infinity and beyond,'* and James is mimicking Buzz's hand motion."

What a crack-up. Watching kids all day wasn't as boring as I thought.

"You going, too?"

"As a matter of fact, I'm not. You and Josh want to stay for dinner? Donovan and Jake are taking the kids."

"Perfect. They'll make a good-looking gay couple with two beautiful children." I busted up as soon as I saw Donovan and Jake make that connection. "You know that's what everyone will think. I suppose they'll know that it was Jake's sperm that created the babies. Then, does that make you the effeminate one, Mr. Pink Penguin polo-shirt man?"

Donovan looked at his pink metro shirt, casual white Tommy Bahama pants, and brown suede slip-on loafers and looked horrified. "Oh, hell no. Jane, you want to trade places with Jake?"

"Nope. I'm taking my sister and little Joshie here to dinner."

Emily giggled. "You two will look adorable with my kids. Please take good care of them and bring them home at a decent hour."

"Will do, my beloved." He kissed his wife goodbye.

Josh lamented, "I need to learn to talk and act like your brother, Jane. Then maybe Laney will return my calls."

"She hasn't called you back at all?" I was surprised since I thought those two were getting along well.

"She called once when I wasn't able to pick up and left me a brief, 'all is good' kind of message. I need some advice, Emily."

"How can I help?"

"What can I do to catch Laney's interest?"

"I don't know, Josh. I think you might be better off letting Laney go," she said in between nuzzling her kids and giving them their goodbyes.

"Why?" Josh asked, disgruntled.

"I talked to her this morning and it sounded like she was seeing someone."

"What?" Donovan said loudly enough to make Ellie jump in his arms. "Sorry, Sweetie. I didn't mean to scare you."

"I don't get how she could have met someone already. She just got to London. Her bags are probably still unpacked." Josh was now just plain pissed.

"They met at the airport. In fact, he saw her on the plane and waited for her at the airport when they landed, to introduce himself. I talked to him as well this morning and he sounded very sweet and very, very sweet on Laney. From the sounds of it, they're both smitten with one another."

"So that's why she's been avoiding all my calls."

"*All* your calls, Donovan? How many times have you tried reaching her?" I asked.

He ignored me and said, "I'll check him out for you, Emily. I'm due in London on Tuesday for a meeting. I'm sure she'll have a hard time avoiding me if we're in the same city."

"You do that, Donovan. And give her a hug and a kiss for me as well." Emily's eyes twinkled as she said this to him before shooing them off to the show.

"Were you serious when you said Laney was seeing someone?"

"They're not dating yet, Josh, but he's very much pursuing her."

Dinner turned into a cheer-up Josh time. As gently as possible, Emily did her best to discourage this would-be suitor. Before we got to dessert, Max joined us, and I happily told him about my birthday party.

"Max, you want to invite your parents on this special day?" Emily gave him an expectant look. "Don't you think it'll be nice if they are there?"

Max thought about it for a while. "I guess so...yeah. Thanks for the suggestion, Emily. You think of everything." He flashed her his good-looking smile and squeezed her hand.

There was some weird message/talk going on between the two of them that I did not understand.

"What was that all about?" I asked Max when we got to my door.

"All of what?"

"You and Emily...you guys were talking in code."

"No we weren't. We didn't say anything you didn't understand."

"It's what you didn't say that makes me wonder...!"

"Gem, you are too smart for your own good. I have a sweet surprise for you on your birthday."

"Yeah?" I asked bringing our pelvises together. "What kind of surprise and why does Emily know about it?"

"Let's just say what I have planned may catch you by surprise, but I hope you're as ready for this as I am."

Will he really catch me by surprise, or will it be me who catches him by surprise?

June 10, 2013

A Birthday Co-prise

$\mathcal{T}$oday was going to be a fabulous day. The sun was shining, June gloom hadn't made an appearance yet, and I was twenty-eight, going on conquering the world. I woke up before my alarm went off, showered, and put on my best lawyer suit. Research last night taught me how to add that extra touch to my makeup, place that curl just so, and I even pulled out my Louboutin heels that had been sitting in the shoe bag while I contemplated taking them back to Neiman's, because of the house mortgage-like price tag.

Andrea was actually allowing me to lead in the trial of a very important case. Very rarely do any of our cases go to trial, but this one did and I was given a chance to prove that I was a trusted name in this firm. I definitely looked the part.

"Don't you look like a sexpot! Damn, you look hot this morning."

Shocked! What on earth was he doing here at this hour? "How'd you get in?"

"Are you worried at your ripe old age of twenty-eight, that your parents will catch you with a boy in your room? Your parents still do bed checks?"

"Um...not since high school."

"Well good because I dropped by to give you your birthday present before I left for London."

"How'd you know it was my birthday, Donovan?"

"Jane, Jane, Jane...I know a lot about you," he said while coming closer to me. I didn't want to seem rude but I had to step back. Donovan had a predatory look about him that scared me, and if I was honest with myself, excited me as well.

"Okay, give me the present and get going. I have to get ready for court." I put my hand out to speed up this process. Though I used court as an excuse, I needed this alone time with Donovan as much as I needed a girls' night out with Andrea.

He handed me a thin legal-sized envelope. And without losing a beat I opened it up to find two plane tickets.

"Explain..."

"Go away with me for a weekend. Let me show you how good we can be together."

"Donovan..." I let out a weak complaint.

He put up his hands to shush me. "I don't care what you tell Max. You can lie to him, break up with him, tell him the truth...don't care! Just give me one weekend, Jane. I want to know! I need to know! And I know that you feel the same way."

"Don..." He wouldn't let me continue.

"Just think about it. It's an open-ended offer. You can use the ticket at any time."

At least ten different thoughts ran through my head. But the first and most horrible thought was, *how do I go on this trip without letting Max know?* I shook my head like an etch-a-sketch board, hoping to dissolve that ugly thought.

"Donovan. I'm practically all moved in with Max..."

"I don't need reruns of your life." He came right up to me and looked me dead in the eye, but didn't touch me. "Just give me a chance..."

With that, he left my room and I was left reeling. Do I go? Do I stay? Do I tell Donovan to stay the hell away from me? Do I indulge in a weekend and put this curiosity to bed? (Yes...I didn't mean to do it, but I still kinda laughed at my unintended pun—stupidly grotesque, I know.)

What about Max? Do I tell him and ask for a bye? Do I offer him a bye? Do I do it when he's out of town so I don't even have to explain anything? *Shit!* What the fuck was I thinking? I must be losing my fucking mind!!! I am in love with Max. We will be living like a married couple and I was contemplating cheating on him.

"NO!" That's what I'd say to Donovan when he got back from his business trip. I'd also tell him to stop all advances. Then I'd move in with Max, be a good girl while he's away, and all would be copacetic in this world.

I felt great after making those wise decisions and went to have breakfast with my family.

"Happy Birthday, Jane!" My mother, father, and grandparents voiced one after another.

"Thank you. And thank you, Mom, for my favorite breakfast every year."

Mom would make these sickeningly sweet cinnamon rolls from scratch every birthday that we all adored. But the amount of calories in one roll was scary enough to keep anyone from consuming lunch and possibly dinner.

"Open our present, Dear." My sweet Gram and Gimpy have me a brilliant circular diamond pendant on a white gold chain.

"Gram! Gimpy! This is stunning. Thank you." I hugged both of them separately.

"Ours will be boring after that gift," Mom kidded.

Mom and Dad had gotten me a gift certificate to Pottery Barn, with the thought that Max and I would need to pick up a lot of everyday household items for the new house. "We really like Max. We are hoping everything will work out well with you two." Mom beamed.

"Me too, Mom," I said with a guilty conscience after all the terrible thoughts that ran their ugly course this morning.

"What did Donovan want so early in the morning?" Gimpy asked. "Wasn't he leaving for London today?"

"Yeah. He just came by to drop off a gift and to wish me a happy birthday."

"That was nice."

I waited. Then I breathed a sigh of relief when no one asked me what Donovan had given me.

"Did Max come by for the same reason?" Mom asked.

My head popped up from the cinnamon roll at the mention of Max's name. "What do you mean? I'll see Max later at the dinner."

"Didn't you see Max this morning? He came by but left before I could offer him any breakfast."

My chest pounded and I ran out of breath simultaneously. "What do you mean Max came by this morning? I didn't see him at all, Mom. Please explain when this was and when he left."

Panic shot through my heart. There was no explanation needed. Shit! Shit!! Shit!!! The only answer I couldn't get straight was whether Max showed up before or after Donovan.

My head burst into pain, I wanted to throw up everything I just ate, and I hated myself for ever wavering between the two men.

"Excuse me," I said to everyone at the table, "I have to find Max."

June 13, 2013

Like Alice Falling Down That Little Hole...

No surprise. I couldn't get a hold of Max all morning before I went into court. But to my surprise, I kept my composure and presented my case well enough to earn me a small praise from Andrea. Lunchtime came and left with no return calls. I desperately wanted to drive to the hospital and plead my case to Max, but I was stuck in the courtroom till 5:00p.m..

By the time court ended and my phone showed no records of having received any calls today, I started getting desperate.

"Nick, have you seen Max today?" I called my brother in full panic mode.

"Yeah. We had lunch."

"You did?" My stomach relaxed a little and I prayed this was a good sign.

"Did he say anything?"

"Like what? We talked about this and that, but we were with a bunch of people in the cafeteria. It was kind of a send off lunch for the first Mexico group, so there wasn't much time to talk to him. Are you trying to get a hold of him? Won't he be at your dinner tonight?"

"Yeah..." I answered, deflated. "I'll see you tonight."

Jake and/or Emily would have been the two I should call, but I was afraid. Nick was right, I'd talk to Max tonight. And sure he'd be upset with me, but I'd plead and beg and swear up and down that my wavering would never happen again. This morning was the last time. I was done with Donovan Taylor. Really! I was done with him.

"Hey, Auntie Jane," my sister greeted me when I walked through her door. "Don't you look pretty today. Happy Birthday!" She hugged and kissed me on the cheek. The twins saw what their mother was doing and each came up and grabbed a leg to hug. I loved my family. Even the twins were unwittingly comforting me. "You all right?"

"Yeah, I'm good," I lied. "You need any help or can I go home and change?"

"Go home and freshen up. Everything is under control."

Since the twins still had a hold of each leg, I swapped my leg for two fingers and walked them to my house where they were greeted like royalty from the elderly folks.

I dialed Max's number again for the 20th time today and this time got a message that his service had been temporarily halted. Did he not pay his bill on time? Was he doing this to punish me? What was going on?

"Josh? Do you know why Max's phone is not going through?" I prayed that there was a simple solution to this gigantic mess.

"No clue. I just called him myself and noticed that his phone wasn't working."

"Do you think maybe he didn't pay his bill on time and the phone got temporarily disconnected?"

"I doubt it. Max is pretty meticulous about his affairs. I've never known him to be late on any payments."

"Do you think you can find out for me what's going on? I'm a little worried."

"Will do. But I wouldn't worry. I'm sure there's an explanation for what's going on. You'll see him in less than an hour."

I hoped I'd see him in less than an hour. As time sped by, I could feel Max slipping by and I had absolutely no control over this precarious grip.

"Happy Birthday," was the greeting I got from everyone who came through Jake and Emily's door. I did my duty and participated in all small talk, ceaseless chatter, and answered numerous questions. The one question I couldn't answer, *"Where's Max?"*

I didn't know where Max was, an hour and a half into my birthday dinner.

"Jake." Emily was worried as well. "Please find Max for Jane."

"I'm trying, Love, but his phone is disconnected and there really aren't too many people to call since his entire family is here."

"Jane," Max's mom spoke, "Max unexpectedly stopped by my work today."

"He did?" That was news to me, and happy news. Max was still around and taking care of whatever he needed to take care of. "Why did he stop by?"

"I'm not quite sure. It almost seemed as though he was trying to say goodbye. Part of the conversation was about him feeling bad that he was not a good son to us, and part of the conversation was him going around in circles about how unclear his future was, except for his summer plans. Did you two have a fight today? He seemed uncharacteristically down."

"I haven't seen him at all today, but I think he misunderstood something that happened this morning. I've been trying to get a hold of him all day, but he's avoiding my calls and now his phone is disconnected."

"Maybe something happened to his line. I see no reason why he'd disconnect his phone." Mrs. Davis tried to comfort me with her words, and she actually briefly touched my hands. I would have been thrilled with this progress, if I weren't so worried about my status with Max.

"Will you excuse us a moment?" Jake smiled politely and pulled me to the corner.

"Did you find him?"

"Maybe. I've got a few calls in, but I need you to fess up and tell me what happened between you two."

"I'm not sure what exactly happened." I *so* did not need to tell my brother about me and his best friend.

"Cut the crap and tell me what happened. I can't help you if you're going to lie to me."

"You need my help?" Now the entire Reid siblings were here.

"Yeah, Nick. Hang out and let me hear about your lunch with Max after I hear about what our dear sister did wrong this time."

That statement pissed me off enough to keep my mouth shut, but today wasn't the day to pout. So, I started the explanation. "Donovan came over this morning..."

"Shit!" Jake exclaimed. "I thought things were over between you two!"

"What the fuck, Jane! You two-timing on Max with Donovan?"

"Will you both shut the hell up and let me explain my story?"

Both my brothers looked furious. Jake, because he'd told me a million times Donovan wasn't the guy for me, and Nick, because Max and he were tight. In fact, Nick was tight with all three Davis brothers. And praise the Lord the Davis brothers didn't choose to join in this conversation.

"Go on," Jake demanded.

"Donovan stopped by with a birthday present this morning."

"That sounds innocuous."

"That depends on what the gift was, Nick. Knowing my best friend, he didn't bring her just a birthday card."

"He brought me carte-blanche plane tickets and asked me to go away with him."

"Fuck!" Both Reid brothers exclaimed simultaneously and with the same tone.

"Does Max know about Donovan's gift? How would he know? Were you idiotic enough to tell him?"

"You're getting on my last nerve, Nick. Stop interrupting!" I yelled.

"Sorry." He put up both hands in surrender.

"Mom asked me at the breakfast table why Max had stopped by this morning and between that information and Max not picking up any of my calls, I'm assuming he showed up when Donovan was in my room."

"You and Donovan are both idiots. Max has every right to be pissed." Jake was not happy with me! He pulled out his phone, undoubtedly to call his best friend to give him a piece of his mind when the phone rang. "It's the hospital. Don't go anywhere!" He warned me.

The call took no longer than ten seconds. "Shit! Get your ass over to the airport, NOW! Max is leaving tonight for Mexico with the first group."

When will this nightmare end?

June 17, 2013

In a Deep, Dark Pit

"Breathe Jane, breathe. We're almost there and you have plenty of time. The plane leaves at midnight and it's not even 9 o'clock yet." Jake thought it would be a good idea for Nick to drive me to the airport since I was in no condition to drive a car. Originally, Jake was my driver, but considering Emily was due to give birth soon, he didn't want her to be concerned about what was going on. So we all decided to keep this story from Emily, and Nick drove me to the airport to help me win over Max.

"Can't you drive any faster?" I was in such a state of anxiety. I had never felt so distraught in my life.

"Look, Jane. We're getting off the freeway. You'll get your chance with Max. Don't worry. Everything will be okay." My brother Nick was sweet to try and reassure me that everything would be all right. But I knew better. I knew this was the last straw for Max. I had done this too many times. I had one too many toes leaning towards Donovan for Max to forgive me easily this time.

"Will you just drop me off out front and come meet me later? If I can't find Max in the baggage area, I'll need to buy a ticket so I can get over to the proper gate."

"No problem, Jane. You do whatever you need to do."

At this point, my nerves gave out and I just started bawling in the car. "What if he doesn't want to see me? I fucked up so badly. What if he tells me he never wants to see me again? What am I going to do if he breaks up with me?"

"Once he hears your side of the story, I think everything will be okay, Jane. He's not going to break up with you. He's sick in love with you. I know for a fact that he was thinking you were his forever. That's what Josh and Garett kept telling me."

Nick was babbling on and on to try and comfort me. He was beyond freaked out watching me go ballistic on him.

"But you don't know about all the things that I've done to him. I've been such a bitch, and you were right—I am a two timer!"

"Did you actually do anything with Donovan?"

"No, but I've been tempted so many times and Max knows about all these times."

"I saw Max right after he found the house and he was pumped to start the next chapter of his life with you. He couldn't wait to show you the house and get your approval. A guy like that isn't going to leave you over a misunderstanding."

"I hope you're right, but I think it's too late, Nick. I've done this to him too many times. He's not going to forgive me."

"Here we are. Go in. Grovel, beg, grab him by the leg and don't let him leave...do what you must! Jake is right when he preaches that Max is the right guy for you. And plus, I really like the whole Davis clan, so don't mess this up for me!" Nick said with a smile.

When this nightmare was over, I'd take the time to think about the kindness both brothers have shown me throughout my seven-month relationship with Max, but for this immediate moment, I needed to 'beg, plead, grovel' like my little brother instructed me to do.

Looking around the Delta counter, I didn't see anyone who looked like Max. I looked for groups that were traveling together, but only found families and couples. Jake had told me this was where they were going to be, so I got in line thinking I'd have to buy a ticket in order to pass security and get my chance with my boyfriend at the departure gate.

The sick feeling inside the pit of my stomach was not a feeling I'd wish upon anyone—even Psycho or Hannah the Bitch. This was so many times worse than those out of control butterflies that showed up in the middle of a bombed speech in front of your entire class, or when your parents caught you in a serious lie and were about to ream you till dawn. This dread spread through my entire body. It was that sense you got when you knew something was horribly wrong, and there was absolutely no recourse and no hope.

No hope—this was what made me sick, frantic, manic, and angry all at the same time. I was insanely angry with myself for letting the situation get to this point. When we got into the last argument after apartment hunting, I knew I couldn't live without this man anymore, and yet when Donovan dangled his apple, I couldn't say no. I was tempted again.

"Jane," Nick called me back to reality. "I see Max over there." He pointed to the international line rather than the domestic line I was standing in.

I saw my boyfriend, but was deathly afraid to go to him. I didn't want to face him, be rejected by him, and lose him.

"Go." Nick encouraged. "It'll be fine. He doesn't look like an angry man."

He may not look angry, but I knew better.

"Will you walk over there with me?" I sounded like a little girl, so unsure of where she was going.

"Let's go." Nick practically held my hand and led me to my end.

"Hey, everyone!" With a cheerful voice, Nick called attention to us. It was then that I saw the blank look on Max. His eyes didn't light up to see me, he didn't smile, he didn't even bother to say hello. Every cell in my body shut down like a huge factory losing power. The big question was, did the circuit breaker trip—something easily fixed with the flip of a switch, or did the power lines go down—to be discarded and never repaired.

"Hi," I whispered. As soon as I spoke, the entire group gave us a wide berth and walked far away from us. "Will you please let me explain?" Perhaps the way I started was an admission of guilt, but I didn't care. I just needed my boyfriend back.

"Go ahead, but make it quick. I don't want to keep my teammates waiting."

The way he said those two sentences cut me like a dagger, ripping through my heart. They were void of any emotion.

"I don't know what you heard when you came over, but it's not what you think."

"Really, Jane? Tell me, what am I thinking?" He almost laughed at me in disbelief while asking me these questions. They were filled with doubt and distrust, but I preferred this to apathy.

"Donovan came over to drop off a gift—a couple of plane tickets as a birthday present—and he asked me to go away with him. He told me I could tell you whatever I wanted, but he wanted a weekend away

496

so we could see if it would lead to anything. He didn't let me answer, but I'm going to return the tickets. I don't want to go away with him. I only want to be with you. I don't know what you heard and saw, but I promise, that's all that happened. *NOTHING* happened between us, I promise, Max. I promise!" I rushed all these words out in hopes that the quicker I pleaded my case, the sooner Max would believe me, and the sooner this nightmare would be resolved.

Max kinda laughed in disbelief again. "You don't even know what you did wrong, do you?"

"I didn't do anything wrong! I'm telling you the truth when I say, *nothing* happened. The explanation I gave you was it."

"Yeah? Well, I came by in the morning to be the first one to wish my girlfriend a happy birthday and what do I find?" He asks, cynically and rhetorically. "I find her complacently listening to another man telling her that she could lie to her boyfriend and go away with him. She waited patiently and listened to all that was offered in front of her so she could make an informed decision. She never once stopped him, she never once told him that she didn't want to go away with this man. She just listened. And from where I was standing, it almost seemed as though she was wondering if she should take this man up on his offer."

"But I didn't take him up on the offer and Donovan never gave me a chance to say no. He's out of town but as soon as he's back, I'm going to tell him to stop bothering me. I'll tell him all about us, all about our love, and how much I love you." I was desperate. It felt like Max was using all his strength to loosen our tie with each and every accusation. His once strong fingers that held tight our love, were relaxing, and the hold was quickly coming loose. Our bond was unraveling and I had no idea how to latch myself back onto him.

Then he went in for the kill. "What hurt me most was your contemplation. I might have even preferred you being your spitfire self saying, 'What the hell. I'll go!' over your silent vacillation. You don't have faith in our relationship. You doubt us."

"I don't, Max. I really, really don't!"

"Go with Donovan. I'll give you your freedom," he said sadly. It was at this point, I wrapped my arms around him and glued myself to him.

"I don't want to go," I said, tears finally falling.

He pushed me away slightly and gave me a sad smile. "I'm letting you go. Do what you want to do, be with whomever you want to be. Figure out what you want, and with whom you want it."

This statement almost gave me hope that maybe we were taking a respite from one another for the month that he was away. It was almost too good to be true. He was giving me my freedom for a month to get Donovan out of my system, and all would be back to normal when Max returned in July.

"Max," I whispered with some hope.

My boyfriend's next statement destroyed this hope. "As I don't expect you to come back to me when I get into town, don't expect me to come back to you, either. Take care, Jane..."

"Max. It's time to go in," a girl called out to him.

Max gently unwrapped my arms that were glued to his waist, and looked at me one last time. He gave me a weak smile and walked toward the girl who called his name.

Max left—without a glance back, without a word—with Hannah, onto the next chapter of his life.

June 20, 2013

Twenty-Four Hours, Give and Take

I slowly backed into one of those plastic chairs after Max left me, and thought through what Max accused me of, what I had done wrong, and where I would go without Max. All day long, I dreaded this scene between us, and I knew everything was going to be different. I knew he was angry, I knew he wouldn't forgive me, and I knew I blew it.

At this moment, I felt so numb. It didn't seem real. This couldn't be happening to me, to us, when less than twenty-four hours ago, we were moving the last of our furniture into our new home. Less than twenty-four hours ago, we had made love on the rug of our new living room, ordered pizza, and messed around some more till we absolutely had to leave, because I had to prepare for my trial today. Less than twenty-four hours ago, Max told me how much he loved me, how much he wanted us to be together forever, and how much he wanted to see what an offspring would look like between the two of us. How could things go so wrong in less than twenty-four hours?

"Jane."

"MAX!" He was back. He came back to see me, to make up with me, to love me.

I stood up from the seat and practically mowed him down with my enthusiasm. I shouldn't have been so quick to judge him, nor our situation. He gave it some time, he understood that what had happened this morning was nothing serious, and we'd move on with our lives.

"I couldn't decide what to do with your birthday present, so I held onto it, but I decided I don't want to hold onto this gift like I did the last time. I want a clean break." He reached into his coat pocket and pulled out a sky blue Tiffany box. "Happy Birthday. Do what you like with this. I already have one too many of these in my possession." He plopped it in my hand and walked away.

Max's action just now was the meanest thing he's ever done to me. If Max's break-up speech was a knife to my heart, then him raising my hope by making me think that possibly he had forgiven me, and given me another chance, was stabbing me repeatedly with the knife just to insure that I was dead.

Whatever this gift was that I held, I didn't want to know. I almost threw it in the trashcan, but I wanted the satisfaction of throwing it back in his face. I was pissed. I was royally pissed that he came back only to rub it into my face that he dumped me, and was giving me my gift so there would be no more reminders of me. After seven months of building a relationship, if he was going to throw me away for a misunderstanding (okay, I know it was a bit more than a misunderstanding), I wasn't going to mourn him.

"You want to go home?" Nick appeared out of nowhere.

I ignored him, went to the departure screen next to me, made a phone call, and made plans of my own to move on!

"Can you make my excuses to everyone for me and tell them I needed to leave for a few days? I'll call Gimpy and let him know I'm taking a few days off from work."

"Where are you going?"

Instead of answering my brother, I took out my cell phone and purchased a very expensive last minute plane ticket. What the hell, I decided to go for the gusto and booked myself a first class seat (in all cash—no free upgrade, no points used) to be on a red-eye flight in comfort.

"What the hell are you doing? You don't even have a change of clothes. Where are you going last minute?"

"I need a few days away and there's something I need to do and it can only be done on the other side of this airport. Thanks for the ride. I'll text when I land." I gave my brother a quick hug and ran to catch my flight that was leaving in forty minutes.

Why were there so many freakin' people flying on a Thursday at midnight? Didn't these people have to work the next day? I was so annoyed with how slowly the check-in process was going. We moved like cattle in this Autopia-at-Disneyland line, when I realized my check-in line was separate from this one. Once I switched, I breezed through the line and went straight for Gate 48A. My gate was 58B, but I had a bit of unfinished business with one Max Davis!

I ran to 48A, scanned the room and found the large group of volunteers all in high spirits, even Max. That pissed me off even more. I walked straight up to the group who saw me coming. They all stared and wondered what the hell I was doing on this side of the airport. They probably thought I was here to beg Max to come back to me. Hannah, the bitch, sat right next to Max—*I do not care anymore, I do not care anymore*—and her mouth was wide open from the shock of seeing me. Max actually had a chuckle in his eyes as soon as the surprise wore off. He, too, probably thought I was coming over to plead my case one more time. *Well, buddy, you're in for the shock of your life if you think I'm groveling to you.*

Max didn't even show the courtesy of standing up to greet me. He stayed seated, with that bitch next to him, so I decided that if he wanted a public showdown, I'd give him one. I threw the Tiffany box at him and it bounced off his chest and into his hands.

"Keep it for your collection!" I said firmly, but calmly, and walked away.

Even though curiosity was killing this cat, I didn't turn around to see Max's reaction to what I'd just done. I kept walking down the airport looking for my gate, hoping that Max would run over and stop me. I didn't feel that tap on my shoulder as I'd hoped, and no one grabbed me from behind to tell me he loved me. All I was left with were uncontrollable tears. That split second of anger towards Max made me feel even worse. I now knew for sure that we were over, and that Max was done with me.

With my (very expensive) ticket in hand, I sat in my seat headed for Chicago to see my best friend, Becky. She was the one I called earlier, and though timing-wise everything worked out so I could throw the gift back at Max and get on a plane right before take-off, life-wise, nothing worked out. A few days with Becky would hopefully put my perspective back in order, so I could move on to the next phase of *my* life.

June 24, 2013

7 Stages of a Break-up

$\mathcal{M}$urphy's law states that anything that can go wrong, will go wrong. Case in point, an ugly break-up leads to a hideously expensive plane ticket, which leads to insomnia and thus, no need for this flat bed. This case of insomnia led me to read every magazine available in the front cabin of the plane, and I came across some woman's magazine that had an article written just for me. The author described the 7 stages of a break-up and just to push myself into an even deeper depression, I had to read it.

Stage 1—Deep Shock: "What the hell just happened?"
Um...yeah...! What the hell did just happen? I lost the man I considered to be my happily ever after. I threw back a Tiffany box which probably contained some form of jewelry, in his face, in front of a gaggle of people, which probably pissed him off even more. Plus, he went off with his ex who was just waiting for us to break-up so she could take my place. Was I really the star of my own life? If someone was scripting this for me, could she go back to her Word document and rewrite this scene, or just delete the last few altogether?

"You look like hell!" Becky was waiting for me with a sign that read—"The girl who just broke up with Max Davis!" as I got off the plane.

"What the hell, Beck? Is this sign necessary?"

She laughed. I laughed. We both started howling in the middle of the airport.

"Yeah, it was necessary. Look at how it made you laugh." Becky was the ultimate best friend. "You do understand that I had to get up awfully early to make this sign and get my ass over here to pick you up. O'Hare is not an easy place to get to, nor to navigate. So be grateful I'm here!"

"I am grateful you're here, but it's all your brother's fault that I'm in this mess, so you need to clean it up for him."

"It's always his fault. Growing up, we used to blame everything on Donovan, because my parents never got mad at him. Just like your brother Jake, Donovan was the golden child."

"Well that *golden child* put me in an awful mess and when I see him, I'm gonna kick his ass back to Nepal."

"What did my brother do? Or better yet, what are you blaming on Donovan?"

It was at times like these where I knew blood was thicker than water. I gave my best friend my meanest school-girl look.

"Don't give me that Rachel McAdams' *Mean Girl* look. We are adults now! I am going to have a baby in seven months." She reprimanded with a lame giggle. Talk about stupid-ass! "Let's go home. Al is making breakfast for us, and you can tell us all about what happened with your love triangle."

"Jane!" I got a nice big welcome from Al, Becky's undergrad love and husband of five years. "Beck and I are taking the day off and taking care of you. Come have breakfast and tell us all about your worries."

Somehow I got the feeling that these two were laughing not only behind my back, but straight at me. "What's going on here? Why are you treating me like an invalid?"

"When you called, you sounded like a pissed-off invalid." Becky said with a mouth full of eggs and sausages.

"Do you need to shove so much food in your mouth, and at the same time?"

"Hey. I skipped breakfast this morning to go pick you up, Girlfriend. Al offered to go, but I didn't think you wanted to see him—so I got up, made a sign, skipped breakfast, and drove in crazy traffic to make life a bit easier for you."

"Um...lovely wife?" Al approached cautiously. "I think that plate of sausage belongs to you. I'll cook some new ones for me and Jane."

"Why?" She answered with her mouth stuffed with food.

"Because you spit all over that plate. You need to stop talking and just eat."

"All right, Miss Jane Reid. I'll stop, if you start."

I went through the last twenty-four hours, event by event, with these two who were hanging on my every word. Becky even stopped eating for a while when I told her what Max said to me at the airport when he broke up with me. Then, she almost choked on her food when I told her what he said to me at the airport when he gave me my birthday present. By the time I got to the story of me throwing the Tiffany box back at Max, she was almost hyperventilating.

"But what if there was an engagement ring in there?" Between her food OD and my story, she was short of breath. Was this the kind of stuff that really happened when a woman got pregnant, or was my best friend just being overly dramatic? "How could you just throw it back at him without looking to see what was inside? What if it was a cute locket or your favorite pendant, or even a pair of earrings?"

"Who the hell cares what was inside that box?" I was angry that Becky cared more about the gift than what Max did to me the second time. "He pissed me off. He raised my hope, then he crushed it. He didn't just crush it, he demolished it, stomped on it for good measure, then spit on it for fun. That's what he did."

"Tell me one more time what he said to you when he gave you the box."

I had to think about that for a while. Once I realized he hadn't come back to be with me, I was in such a state of shock, his words were like adults talking in muffled-trombone voices in a CBS Charlie Brown Special. All I heard was *"wa, wa, wa, wa, wawawa."*

"Well???"

"Shit, Beck. I don't know! He said something about having too many of these in his possession."

Her eyes lit up like the Christmas lighting festival on the Magnificent Mile. "You see!!!"

"No I don't see!!!"

"He still has that ring he gave Emily, and with your ring...that makes for 'too many of these in his possession.'"

The possibility that Becky opened up, hit me like a freight train. FUCK!

Stage 2—Denial: "This was so not happening to me!"
"Shit, Becky. I have to call him. I need to see if he was really going to propose. Where's my cell phone? I gotta find out." I kind of lost it.

Becky got up and hugged me. I wanted to push her away, but since she was pregnant, I just sat back in my seat and cried. I was such a stupid, selfish, moronic bitch. I actually made a mockery of our love and I threw the ring back in his face. Why the hell did I do that? What would make me want a stupid fling with Donovan when I had the best man I could have ever asked for, in Max?

"What am I going to do, Becky?"

"You are either going to pull yourself together and move on from this, or you are going to catch the next flight out to Mexico and make amends with Max."

"But he doesn't want me anymore," I bawled. I cried loudly and pathetically enough to force Al into the other room. "He left me. He's left me for good."

Becky kind of shook me and told me like it was. "A man who was going to propose to you doesn't just walk away and end things because of what might have happened between his girlfriend and another man. It's not like you slept with my brother, or even kissed him...right?" She doubted me, too.

Stage 3—Desolation: "Just leave me alone. I wanna be by myself!"
"Forget it, Beck. I'm going to get a hotel room, sit in the dark and cry all day. I can't believe I threw back my engagement ring." I howled some more. "What if I never get married?"

"Will you get a hold of yourself? I might have to do what they do in the movies and slap you if you don't stop crying."

"My life is over!"

I just lost it. I'd never been so pathetic as I was this morning. Al came out, whispered something to Becky, nodded yes, and went back in the room.

"Here. Eat this." Becky brought out two tubs of Ben & Jerry's ice cream. I thought both were for me, but she took Cherry Garcia and left me with Coffee, Coffee, Buzz Buzz Buzz. Who was the freakin' genius who came up with these names? Someone actually got paid to do this kind of stuff?

We were both silent until the last bite of ice cream was in our stomach and were satisfied.

"Everything good?" Al peeked out the bedroom door finding it weird that I went from loud to silent. He probably found it weirder that Becky and I were drunk off of ice cream.

It took me a while to answer back. "Sorry, Al. I'm good now. I think I'm done crying. I'll try and put everything into perspective, and get out of your way, soon."

"Stay as long as you like, Jane. You're always welcome here."

I wailed again. "I'll never find a guy as nice as your husband, Beck!" Al made like a tortoise and put his head and limbs back into his shell.

Stage 4—Detestation: "I hate you for breaking my heart!"
"I'm going to fly over to Mexico and give Max a piece of my mind, that freakin' heartbreaker. Who does he think he is? It wasn't like I was going to cheat on him. So I wondered for a split second about

a possibility with Donovan Taylor. His ex is living with his parents! He's still in contact with her, and he's going to be alone with her for an entire fucking month!"

I wanted to scream, but didn't want to freak out Al anymore than he was already freaked out.

"Just get it all out, Jane. Once you do, there's no more crying over spilt milk. You move on with your life, you got that, Jane Sydney Reid?"

"Damn right, I got it!" And here's where the ice cream really kicked in and I went a little Taylor Swift, karaoke-loopy. "Max Davis—'*we are never, ever, ever getting back together*! *WeeeeE are never, ever, ever, getting back together!*'"

"Uh-oh!" Becky lamented. "How the hell can a pint of ice cream make you deranged enough to sing a teeny-bopper song?"

It was downright embarrassing, but I couldn't help myself. It was total diarrhea of the mouth. "'*I used to think, that we, were forever ever ever, And I used to say never say never...But we are never ever ever ever getting back together!*'"

"Shit! Where is your brother?" Al joined in the lamentation.

"I'm such a mess. Sorry, Al. Sorry, Becky. Let me get out of your way. You are both so happy with your marriage and your new baby. Sorry to cast a shadow on your rainbow of happiness." I was a blubbering mess. How was I going to ever live this down?

Stage 5—Dealing: "What can I do to get him back?"
"Jane. You'll get married, soon. You'll have kids soon after, and you'll create your own happy family." Becky put her arms around me and hugged me. This made me cry even harder.

"Do you think I should go and apologize to Max for thinking about cheating on him?"

"Do you want to? Did you really think about cheating on him?"

"To be honest with you, your brother has been a damn thorn in my side since I got back, and I did wonder what it would be like to be with him."

"I think this time away will do you both some good. Since you and Max are broken up now, why don't you hang out with Donovan for a while and see if this is what you really want. If it is, then you'll know it was a good thing you and Max broke up. If it isn't, then go to Mexico and charm Max back into your life."

Stage 6—Depression: "It's over. I'll never get over him"
"Max won't take me back, even if I beg. He'll always be the one who got away. Or maybe, it's more like, he'll always be the one I sent away."

"There are many more fish in the sea." Becky answered.

"But none as understanding and loving as Max. You don't know him like I do. He loved me so much and I couldn't just accept it and be happy. I had to be a greedy bitch and want more."

"How do you know there's not another one better than Max, out in the ocean?"

"You think your brother would have patiently waited for me while I flirted danger with another man?"

"You've got a point there."

Stage 7—Defeated Acceptance: "I'll be all right."
"I'll get through this, Becky. Life will be okay. It'll take some time getting used to the fact that we are no longer together, but I'll be fine. You're such a good friend."

"That's the spirit! You're a tough cookie. A breakup isn't going to bring you down. Be strong. You'll be better than fine!"

"Thanks, Becky. What shall I do first as a woman on the loose?"

"Hello, my vixen. Don't you look like hell," Donovan stated, walking into the guest bedroom.

Shit! Did I just call myself a loose woman?

June 27, 2013

5 + 2 Stages of a Hook-up

Stage 1—Confrontation: "Look at what you've done to me!"
"What the hell are you doing here?"

"My sister called me right as I was about to board my plane and told me to come fix the mess I created, then hung up on me. I had no idea what the hell she was talking about, so I rearranged my flight plans and stopped by Chicago to visit my favorite sister and brother-in-law."

"You're such a kiss-ass." Al laughed.

"And you can kiss my ass, dear brother," Donovan retorted. "Who died here?" He asked all of us, then pointed his attention to me. "And why do your eyes look like Antonio Margarito's after Manny Pacquiao beat the shit out of him a few years ago?"

"Smooth, big brother. Really, smooth!" Becky was holding me back because she knew that right about now, I was about to beat the shit out of Donovan for putting me in this situation.

"Was that when Kate bought you those ringside tickets at Cowboy's Stadium? That was an awesome fight. You get all the cool chicks." Al took this conversation somewhere I didn't want it to go.

"That knock down fight was the best..." Donovan joined in the conversation completely non-sequitur to the situation at hand.

"YOU!" Donovan jumped back a few steps when I yelled at him. "It's all your fault. If you hadn't brought those damn 'let's have sex' tickets yesterday morning, I wouldn't be in this mess. I'd be settling into my new home with Max."

Donovan turned to Al and whispered, "You know what's going on?"

"Yep, and it's not pretty. You're in deep shit, my man."

"How deep?"

"Asphyxia, deep!"

Donovan touched his neck and got uncomfortable. "Lunch, anyone? My treat." He smiled.

Stage 2—Conciliation: "Can we all just get along?"
"Yeah. Why don't we go to our favorite brunch place, get some food into our stomach, and figure out where we should go from here." Becky spoke and Al wholeheartedly agreed.

"You'll feel so much better after you've eaten, Jane. You said you didn't even have dinner last night. Once you get food in your system, you and Donovan can go somewhere quiet, or stay here while Becky and I go somewhere quiet, and talk this all out." Al kept us as far apart as possible in the cramped elevator.

I gave Donovan the evil eye all the way to the restaurant, at the restaurant, and our ride to the Magnificent Mile for some unwanted shopping. Damn, you know it's a bad day when I use the most sinful oxymoron—unwanted shopping.

Somehow, in the middle of perusing the racks at Nordstrom, Donovan snuck up next to me. "You want to tell me what happened, so I can try and fix it for you?" He did look apologetic. "I assume something went wrong with Max, and I'm sure I'm not your favorite person right now, but I'd like to make things better for you. You know you're very special to me, my vixen. I don't like seeing you sad."

I decided his openness and genuineness won him a bye.

"See you tonight...or not," Becky winked at us and walked off into the sunset with her husband.

"Where shall we talk? At a restaurant? A walk in the park? Right here while shopping? Go for a drive? Somewhere private like my hotel room?"

"You have a hotel room, already? You're not staying at Becky's?"

"I don't invade my siblings' privacy, unlike my siblings." He flashed a comforting smile that made me think perhaps everything was going to be okay...for now. "I'm right here at the Peninsula. Let's go."

I decided to walk in silence and think through what I wanted to say to Donovan, what I wanted from Donovan—whether I wanted anything from this man at all, and where the two of us would go from here.

Stage 3—Candor: "Let's get it ALL out."
"What happened?" We sat in two very comfortable chairs with a glass of brandy or whatever this shit was that I was drinking, and I started the long-winded explanation.

"What Max was not happy with yesterday morning, was my wavering."

"I don't recall you wavering."

"I didn't tell you to go to hell, but instead I listened to all you had to offer. And if I were to be honest with myself, I did wonder for a brief second whether or not I could go away with you without Max finding out." I took a large gulp of this nasty drink. "So, I did more than waver. To Max, I cheated on him."

"Al mentioned an engagement ring?"

"We don't know what it was. Becky brought up the possibility that the Tiffany box might have been an engagement ring. It doesn't matter since I threw it back in his face."

Donovan busted up laughing. "I love that about you. You can't hide your feelings...unlike someone I know," he whispered those last few words.

"I'm going to be completely honest with you."

"All right."

"I know I'm being unfaithful to Max again by saying this, but I *am* attracted to you, or so I believe."

He laughed. "Thanks. I ditto the sentiment, especially the 'or so I believe' part."

"Since you've shown interest, I have wondered if a relationship would be possible with you, easier with you. But, I've never ever thought that a relationship would be better with you."

He didn't look offended with that remark. "Ditto!"

"What do you mean, 'ditto?' You're not even in a relationship right now so how could you think a relationship would not be better with me?"

He raised his eyebrows and told me I was being stupid with just one glare. "Next..."

"I'm hurt right now. My heart is broken and I don't know when it'll mend." I paused to hear him utter, *"Ditto,"* but he didn't make a sound. "I don't know what to do, or if I should do anything at all, other than shut myself in a room and cry."

"I'll be honest with you." I welcomed his honesty. "I regretted what I did yesterday morning. I shouldn't have tempted you, I shouldn't have encouraged you to cheat on your boyfriend, and I'll be the first to admit that I was an asshole for doing what I did."

"My brother get a hold of you?"

"Yeah, but as soon as I left your room, I thought this and wanted to kick my own ass for being such a prick."

"If you are having such regrets, why'd you do it?" Now I was pissed that he made me even think about getting together with him, when he regretted his indecent proposal, immediately.

"Your brother told me I was an immature, selfish, dickhead. And, I think he's right. I believe I'm attracted to you..."

"You *believe*???" What the hell happened that made him have this big change of heart?

"You're hurting. I'm confused. You need time to get over Max. I need time to clear out my head. I see only one solution."

"And what would that be?"

"I'm not going to be stupid and let go of this opportunity. We both need to satiate this curiosity and be done with."

Now I was just a curiosity to satiate? Truly, what the hell happened to me being his '*VIXEN*'? "So what do you propose?"

"Let's date. I'd like for us to go out, have a good time, and see where this may lead."

"But you and I are both not of sound mind—though I have no idea why you wouldn't be of sound mind, but whatever..."

"No pressure, Jane. If anything, we'll have our easy-going friendship to fall back on during this date. What do you say?"

Was it a good idea to break up with one guy at midnight, and date a new guy by noon? If Max and I were to get back together, would I be able to justify dating Donovan? There were so many complicated thoughts going through my head. *Aargh!*

Stage 4—Consent: "What the hell do I have to lose?"
"Let's try it." I agreed. "Where do we go from here?"

"How about a matinee production of *The Book of Mormons*? Have you seen it before?"

"No."

"Let's go watch that. Then we can have a nice dinner, and I can drive you back to Becky's, get you a room here, or you can stay with me. Your choice. Absolutely no pressure. I'm good with any of your choices."

I was also good with all that he proposed. There really was no unspoken pressure, no false promises, only the trust of our friendship.

"I need to pick up some clothes in between the show and dinner. I wasn't intending to leave LA, but after Max pissed me off and went into the terminal, I needed to have an excuse to get to the other side. *Sooooo,* I rashly bought a first class red-eye ticket to Chicago in order to throw the stupid, possible engagement ring back at his face."

Donovan smiled, kissed my forehead and led me out to our first real date.

Stage 5—Comfortable: "This is how easy a relationship should be!" We fell into step and reverted to our effortless friendship, rather than trying to pretend we were a couple. It was too early for that and I wasn't ready. Though broken, my heart still belonged to Max. Neither of us was into the show. I kept wondering where Max was at this point in the day—whether he got to his location safely, whether he was with Hannah, whether he had thought about me at all. Donovan, too, was in a world of his own. I glanced over at him a few times, and he was a million miles away. He had no idea I was watching him, and he didn't care. I'd have to ask during dinner what was going on with him.

"You liked the show?" I asked as soon as we got seated outdoors at a trendy restaurant on Michigan Ave.

"Yeah..." he answered noncommittally. "And you?"

Staring into his eyes, I realized something had shifted between us. I could be wrong, but we weren't the flirtatious, I-gotta-get-in-your-pants, excited about one another. We were the I've-known-you-all-my-life, friends sharing a meal and talking about life. Was I wrong about this? Were we not attracted to one another anymore? Had we not been flirting with this idea the last half a year?

I didn't give him an answer and he wasn't bothered. Instead, he refilled our wine glasses and put a slice of pizza on my plate and went back to drinking and brooding.

"Okay. I give up. What's wrong? Are you regretting this decision to 'date' me?"

He had to think about the answer, which was not a good sign. Shit! Was I getting dumped twice in a twenty-four-hour period?

"It's nothing like that. London didn't go as well as I'd hoped, and I just have a lot on my mind."

Shit, again! Now I was feeling insecure for some moronic reason. "Kate?" I treaded lightly.

He shook his head no. "Kate's no more. We have a prudent work relationship now."

"A prudent work relationship? Is that your way of saying no sex on the expensive office desk, relationship?"

He laughed. It was good to see him laugh. But seriously, why the hell was I trying to cheer him up? Who was the one here with the heartache?

"I don't think Kate and I've had sex since...God! I don't even know when the last time was when I had sex—with or without Kate."

"So you're in a funk because of this dry spell?" I expected some sexual quip or an extended banter but all I got was, "I guess so."

"How long are you staying?" I tried to make more conversation.

"I don't know. How long are you staying? I'll go home with you. We can stay for the weekend or we can take a few days off and stay a bit longer. You want to fly up to Canada?"

"Canada?" That wasn't even on my radar.

"Toronto, Montreal, Quebec, Ontario are all on this side of the US. You a foodie like your sister-in-law? There's great food at all these places."

"I'm not that into food. Emily is the foodie, I'm the shoe-whore, Laney is the clothes-horse, and if I have my niece pegged right, she'll be everything combined. I love that little girl!" I gushed.

"My goddaughter is something else." Donovan all of a sudden was in a rush to pay the bill. "Let's go shop for the twins. I saw a cute Chloe dress in a magazine on the airplane. Let's see if Neiman's carries it."

"Only you would know a Chloe from an Oililly," I said with a smirk. "Lead the way, Mr. Fashionista."

Shopping for the kids eased our tension, and we were back to the friendly Donovan and Jane "relationship." Donovan went out of control and bought out the children's department at Neiman's. Our lucky little squirt was getting the gamut from Juicy rompers, to a RL pink seersucker retro bathing suit, to Splendid summer dresses, to an insanely cute but obnoxiously expensive Gucci monogrammed, pink-strapped Mary Janes with a tiny pink bow off to the side. Where was my godfather when I was growing up? I would've eaten all my spinach for those little girl shoes. Not to be outdone, James got his share of RL polo shirts, Splendid tees, a ghetto looking but hideously expensive Moncler tracksuit, and a bowtie and fedora hat to go with the tweed jacket and Armani jeans. I didn't even have a pair of Armani jeans. Oh my gosh! My nephew was going to be a lady-killer when he walked the neighborhood!

Donovan was in a really good mood once the shopping was done. "I've never seen any man enjoy shopping as much as you do. You and Laney would get along famously. This girl was the original internet shopper, using her mom's credit card, pretending to be Barbara Reid."

Donovan looked like he was about to laugh, but turned grim instead and said, "Let's go get you a pair of shoes."

Hot Damn! Lead the way!

Our bags got to Donovan's hotel room even before we got there. Being the recipient of a pink Prada satin bow, T-strap high-heeled sandals, I decided to wear the dainty shoes all the way back to Donovan's room—all 1/2 block of it.

"These shoes are beautiful. Thank you."

He finally smiled that electric Donovan smile. "You're welcome. What do you want to do about tonight? I can take you back to Becky's if you like."

"Well...I kinda wore out my welcome this morning."

Donovan laughed loudly this time. "Al mentioned something about someone going a little apeshit in his apartment." I was so embarrassed about my behavior this morning. "It's all good. I'm sure he'll love to have you back."

"Please tell me he didn't use the word 'apeshit.'"

"All right. I won't tell you." There was that dumb-ass grin on his face that made me go red again. "You want me to get you a room here?"

I hesitated, but decided to express my true feelings regardless of a possible rejection. "Any chance I can stay here with you?" I was so freakin' nervous. "I don't want to be alone tonight and I'm scared."

He closed our gap and put both his arms around me. Donovan's first touch did *NOT* come close to how I thought it might feel. Before I could analyze every butterfly, nerve, tension, or friction between us, Donovan pulled away slightly and looked me dead in the eye. "I need to know," was all he said as his hand curved around my neck and he put his lips on mine. It started slow and tentative, but soon he dug deeper and pressured the both of us to open up and experience a full kiss.

"Fuck!" He said, breaking off immediately.

"Shit!" I said, stepping back.

"Did you feel that?"

"Yes, dammit! What are we going to do?"

"Fuck if I know..."

July 1, 2013

The +2 Part of 5+2 Stages of a Hook-up

Stage 6—Confession: "Let's *REALLY* get it all out."
"Well?"

"Well what?" I asked.

"On a scale of 1-10, how incestuous was that kiss?"

"Off the chart at about one million!"

"Fucking hell!" Donovan exclaimed and fell on his back, on his bed.

"Fucking hell is right," I followed suit in word and action.

We stayed staring at the ceiling for a long—and I mean a *LONG*—time. Who could've seen this one coming? All this time, I thought if we got together, there'd be off the chart chemistry. With all the flirting and sexual banters, Donovan and I were made for one another in every physical way. He thought I was his vixen, I thought he was the hottest man—ever! Hey, I know Max is good-looking, but Donovan is on another level of good-looking. Even Jake doesn't come close.

"What do we do now? I've fucked it up for all of us. How do I make this up to you, Jane?"

"I think I did a pretty good job of being a fuck-up on my own. What the hell was that when we kissed? As soon as you deepened the kiss, I swear, I almost threw up because your face morphed into Jake's face."

Donovan let out a disconsolate laugh. "No woman's ever told me that before, but I agree with you. I, too, saw a pregnant Becky instead of you. What a mess!"

"What do you think happened to us? All those months of flirting. How'd we go so wrong? I was so attracted to you, and I thought you were attracted to me, too."

Donovan sighed and rubbed his face a few times. "I think I know where it went wrong for both of us. But, let me start with me, first."

"Be my guest, Dr. Freud."

"Though it's not for certain, I think it all started for me before Delaney left for London. The night before she left, she came by my house with the intent of telling me something."

"Why would she stop by your house? Have you been seeing her without any of our knowledge?"

He shook his head no...and then yes.... "Of course there were days when I saw her, one on one, but it was nothing, or so I thought."

That statement of *it was nothing* didn't sound like it was really nothing. "So what happened? What was so important that she drove to your home to talk with you? I was under the impression that she didn't like you much."

"Delaney and I..." he trailed and thought about her. NEVER in my most asinine of dreams would I have pictured those two in any form of a relationship, outside of a brother-sister relationship. Where the hell was I when all this was going down? Was I that much in my own world not to notice a *tendre* developing between those two? "I think she came by to tell me she was leaving the next day. Perhaps she wanted to say goodbye, but..."

There he went again, leaving off in the middle of a sentence and then brooding. "You're seriously acting like a chick right now. I feel like I'm reading one of those Emily Griffin novels, listening to you talk."

He chuckled, got up, and pulled me off the bed. "Let's go take a walk. Chicago is beautiful at this time of the year. Maybe we'll go find a bar and have a drink. I'll tell you all that's going on in this fucked-up head of mine."

With all the idiotic wanna-be angst between us, being alone with Donovan would've been stressful, but now, we were feeling mighty free and fine with one another. This is how it had always been in the past and this is definitely how it should've stayed.

Situated in a cool bar where Donovan says whiskey is the winner here, he ordered what sounded like an insane amount of hard alcohol.

"Dare I ask what a ten-flights of whiskey is?"

"It's ten different varieties. Your capacity for alcohol is about as good as any of my buddies. Let's try them all. I think I need to be a bit drunk before I can sort out my head."

"All righty, then!"

The drink fest began. I'm not a hard liquor kind of girl, unless it comes in a swanky glass or has a cute umbrella in it with lots of foo-foo syrup. But tonight, after what happened with Max, then Donovan...what the hell?!? I'll drink all ten flights to forget this mess.

"Talk, Donovan Taylor. What happened after Laney stopped by? And stop pussyfooting around the answer."

"Kate, who was with me to finish up a case, greeted her at the door."

"Shit!"

"You can say that again."

And so I did. "Shit!"

Donovan didn't even crack a smile at the joke. He gulped down four of ten, so I had to do the same.

"I convinced Delaney to wait for me at her house because I had a gift for her, and sent her off smiling. Then, it all went to hell. Kate and I got into an all out brawl about Delaney. Kate accused me of cheating on her, back in Hawaii, with Delaney, and it took hours to get Kate calm and off to her hotel. After Kate left, I laid down to clear my head and next thing I knew, my alarm was going off at 6:00 a.m."

"Shit!!"

"There was a part of me that wanted to go see Delaney that morning, but I knew she had an 8:00 a.m. graduation to attend, so I figured I'd see her at the barbeque and give her the graduation present then. I didn't think she'd be upset I didn't show. Hell...she probably didn't even wait up for me."

"But what if she did?" This time, it was my turn to gulp down number five. "I have to tell you, that day when she came to the office to say goodbye, I was filled with the oddest, saddest emotion when I saw her wave goodbye to you. It was totally reminiscent of an old movie where the heroine leaves her lover and the lover has no idea what's going on."

"That's not the worst part of this story."

"There's more?" The bartender poured number six. "How long is this story?"

"This stubborn girl has not returned any of my calls, texts, emails, or visits. I dropped off her graduation gift at Gram's home and either she was there and avoiding me, or she's been out every fucking time I've visited."

"Is that why you've been to London so many times these days? It wasn't for work, but to see my cousin?"

"Work was the primary reason, but it wasn't something I had to do in the London office. For some reason, Roland suggested I go and take care of it in person, so I did. But the kicker of it all..." he stopped to throw back number six, "I finally saw her yesterday."

"Yeah?" I said happily after doing the same with my drink. "So what happened when you two met?"

This unfolding story was like reading about Mr. Darcy revealing to Elizabeth when he began to fall in love with her in *Pride and Prejudice*. I'd never seen Donovan so enamored and befuddled by any one person or event.

"I didn't get a chance to talk to her. The cab driver was pulling up to Gram's home and I saw her waiting out front. She flashed a blinding smile and I thought she was smiling because of me. I asked the driver to stop and just as I was about to get out, some guy ran over to her and spun her around in his arms. She looked...happy..."

Damn! My friend Donovan looked miserable. Number seven went down without another word. At this point, neither of us could taste anything. We were borderline drunk. Before it got any worse, I paid the tab and we walked out into the cool air, back to the hotel.

"For the first time in my life, I feel this shitty feeling in my chest. What is this feeling, Jane?"

"Rejection, heartbreak, betrayal...all girly feelings I believed guys were immune to?" He laughed and kissed me on the forehead, like old times.

"I'm sorry, Jane. I think I've had feelings for this little girl for a very long time but couldn't admit it till I saw Delaney with this guy. Jake kept preaching Delaney as my perfect girl, but I didn't believe him. I really didn't. I thought my feelings for her were no different than my feelings for my sister, Rachel. I honestly believed it was you I was attracted to—otherwise, I wouldn't have trifled with your feelings and hurt you and Max."

I kept quiet. I'd actually forgotten about the mess I was in with Max.

"I was attracted to you for years, but I think some time ago, this attraction turned into a curiosity and a thrill of the chase. You and I have always been good, lifelong friends, and that's the best place for us to be, past, present and future."

I agreed without having said a word.

Stage 7—Course of Action: "Will there continue to be a Max & Jane?"
"What can I do to help you, Jane? I'll make a visit to Mexico if I must to help you two get back together."

"I think it's me who needs to get my ass over to Mexico, and soon! There goes my track for partnership. No partner is going to vote for me with all these days I'm taking off."

Donovan laughed. "Really? That's your worry when you're in deep shit with your boyfriend?"

"I think I've lost him for good this time. There's no recourse for this one." Donovan hugged me as the tears fell heavily. My drunken state wasn't helping.

"I'm sorry, Jane. This was all my fault. Jake and I will fix this for you. I'll rely on your brother's resourcefulness to come up with a plan. And I'll do everything in my power to get you and Max back together."

"There's nothing you or Jake can do. And I'm just as much at fault. I'll ask Jake where Max is staying and make a visit. I'll give it one last try and if that doesn't work, I don't know..."

"You let me know if you want me to go with you to help explain the situation."

"Are you an idiot? If Max saw us walking together, he may hire the Mexican mafia to take you out."

"Me? Why just me?"

"Because Max at least loved me at one point in his life. There's no love for you, Buddy!"

We laughed because if we didn't, we'd both be in tears.

"Hell, who's trying to reach me at this hour?" I answered the phone. "Hello?"

"Where are you? Emily's water broke, come to the hospital."

That brought me out of my drunken stupor. "All right. I'll see if we can book a red-eye home."

"Who's *we*?"

Shit. Shouldn't have told my brother. I spit out the next long sentence in one breath before Jake started verbally tanning my hide. "Donovan-is-here-with-me-and-we-talked-everything-out-and-are-no-longer-playing-any-more-games-and-I-will-go-to-Mexico-and-beg-Max-to-forgive-me-because-I-love-Max-and-can't-live-without-him!"

"I have never had to deal with two more idiotic adults than you and Donovan. Come home safely." Jake said those last three words with much affection.

"I love you, Jake. And thank you."

"I love you too, little sis. Come meet your newest niece or nephew."

July 4, 2013

The British Are Coming, The British Are Coming!

*I*t's a BOY! We didn't get to the hospital in time before the birth of my newest nephew, but when we got there, he was a gorgeous bundle of joy. But, before I give you details of what this little one looks like, Donovan and I got into another HUGE mess! And this time—yes, I am laughing—it's Donovan who's in deep shit, not me.

"Why are you pulling me into this room? Emily's room is next door."

"I know. But, I need to try one more thing."

"No...!" I whined. "I don't want to do this again. I thought we agreed that this was gross." Donovan had his arms around me and was attempting to put his lips on mine. "Why the hell are you doing this again?"

"Look, I'm sorry. Just humor me, one last time. I need to be 100% sure that this isn't it for us before I decide what I'm about to decide."

"You are so convoluted with your words." I tried to pull away, but he lightly tickled me and pulled me even closer to him during my moment of weakness.

"We were drunk on emotion when we first kissed. It was like we were on the rebound. Let me try this when we are both of a clear mind and decide this is definitely not it."

"NO!!!" I pleaded. This situation made me laugh at this point. "I don't want to make out with my brother, please...!"

"This will be the last favor I ask of you, Jane."

"Oh, all right!" I acquiesced, but soon started giggling when his face got real close to mine.

Donovan, too, started laughing. "This is a shit of an idea, huh?" He said when our lips were separated only by an invisible sheet of paper. He couldn't go any further than this. Donovan, too, knew this was unnecessary. We were NOT attracted to one another. Instead, Donovan lifted his head and was about to talk when we were distracted by someone.

"*...Miss, that's not the right room. It's the one next door...*"

"*Okay...sorry...*" a voice cried then disappeared.

Donovan dropped me—literally, he cursed everything and everyone to hell, then he did another Usain and *bolted* out of the room. I followed so I could see this hilarious situation. (Okay, this situation was hilarious only in my mind. And it's payback time for all the grief Donovan has caused me)

"Where is she?" Donovan ran into Emily's room, with me following suit.

"Emily is where you expect her to be." My brother answered. "She's in bed with our latest addition to the family."

"Hi Emily," he kissed her on the cheek and only glanced at the newborn. "Delaney hasn't come here, yet?"

"Laney?" They all called out. "What do you mean by that, Donovan?" Jake asked.

Before he could answer, there was a knock at the door and a stranger walked in with a flower arrangement the size of this room. "Are you Emily?" He asked with the sexiest English accent I'd ever heard. I suppose all English accents were sexy, especially on a good looking man.

"Yes," my brother, of course, answered—looking none the happier. "And you are?" He did his damnedest to sound intimidating.

"You Michael Bennington, grandson of Harry, the old geezer?" Gimpy interrupted Jake's stare down.

"Yes, Sir." This Michael answered. We all wondered, first—who is this man, and second—how does Gimpy know him?

"Harry, that impatient bastard, has called me all morning. What have you done to court his ire? He can be an arsehole when you deviate from His Dukeness." Gimpy and The English Stranger laughed heartily. "Well...what have you done and what's my granddaughter have to do with this? It puts me in a shite of a mood that the bastard is upset with my granddaughter for no reason." Wow, the English Gimpy was coming out. "There he is again," Gimpy sounded annoyed as he pulled out his phone.

"What is it now, Your Grace?" The sarcasm was dripping, so I was unsure whether the words, "Your Grace" were for real, or just

Gimpy mocking these English people. "Hold on, let me put you on speaker and you can talk to your grandson. I'll warn you not to upset my granddaughter who just gave birth, and her three babes sitting on the bed with her."

"Michael, what is the meaning of this? Who the hell is this girl that's got your head up your arse?"

"Language!" Gimpy warned.

"Grandfather, she's the shine to my sun and the light to my moon. I would give up my future dukedom, if she would agree to spend the rest of her life with me." The English Stranger declared.

Shit! If those weren't the most romantic words ever uttered, and with a beautiful English accent at that! Damn. That was swoon-worthy. Plus, I now felt like I was transported back to my Regency romance novels. What the hell was all of that about his dukedom? Was Gimpy not joking about Your Gracing the grandfather? And hell...where was Laney? I finally came out of my daze to look at Donovan's face and he looked upset...very upset. I don't think I mentioned, with all this English craziness, that it was Laney who opened the door when we were about to "kiss." Right now, Mr. Donovan Taylor would kick his own arse, if he could. Maybe for what he's done to me, I'd offer to kick it for him in these beautiful shoes purchased back in Chicago.

"Hi," Laney whispered to The English Stranger.

This was a total romance movie in the filming. Our sexy English man rejoices at finding his love and they go off into a conversation of their own that has no meaning to any of us. I saw Donovan turn away and Jake whispering something to him. Emily had a sad smile on her face, Gimpy was balking at The Duke on the phone, Doug and Nick were confused, and the twins kept trying to get Laney's attention. Laney only looked up when everyone started clearing their throats.

Laney made all the introductions, but wouldn't look at me or Donovan when she introduced us. Shit! I realized she was probably upset with me. But then again, why would she be upset with me? It's not as though our almost kiss had anything to do with her. Maybe she was just embarrassed. And where had she been all this time? The bathroom? The wrong floor? Did she have feelings for Donovan? My life was crazy enough without adding one Laney Reid to the equation. I had more important worries on my mind.

There was an entire conversation going on that I wasn't interested in. My hope was to get Jake's attention and have him help me get over to Mexico so I could salvage this mess. I sorted through all the work that needed immediate attention, and what I could take care of after my trip to Mexico. Most likely, this weekend would be the first chance I'd get to go there and grovel.

I was minding my own business when everyone called out, "Now?" This woke me up to Laney kissing Emily and the twins goodbye, and giving Gimpy a hug right before stepping out of the room with Michael. What had happened while I was daydreaming about fixing my nightmare? Immediately, Donovan went after her and my head was spinning.

"He finally opened his eyes," I heard Jake mutter.

"I think I'll leave you to get some rest, Emily. Your Gram and I will be back later with some dinner."

"Thank you, Grandfather. We'll see you soon." Emily touched both twins and encouraged them to "say goodbye." And obediently, the two waved at Gimpy.

Donovan came in with his shoulders sagging, much sooner than I expected. The conversation with Laney must not have gone well. I'd never seen this kind of a look on him before—sullen, torn, depressed, almost a bleeding-on-the-inside look.

"Nick would you and Doug take the twins outside and maybe walk around the hospital with them? They've been here the entire time and I think they would like some fresh air." Emily waited patiently till the four of them went out and shut the door. "What the hell is the matter with the both of you?" Emily's eleven words formed into a question made all of us jump back three spaces and seriously quiver in our boots.

"SHITE!" as the English would say.

July 8, 2013

Brothers

I never did get to tell you what JR looks like, did I? Before I get sidetracked again, JR is gorgeous! I'd say he looks more like Emily than Jake. He has her coloring, her face, and her long, lean physique. His face still looks like one of those squishy stress balls you form in your hand, with tiny eyes (which are closed most of the time), puffy cheeks, and red lips—but he's my nephew, and he's beautiful! This little one has light brown, bordering on blond hair (apparently, Emily's mom was blonde), and deep brown eyes. I was happy that JR had a look of his own, though he did still look much like his siblings. With a set of twins above you, he needed to stand out and make his own mark in this world. Especially if you have Elizabeth Logan Reid as your sister. She'll be the boss of both brothers, that's for sure.

JR stands for Jonathan Robert Reid. Jonathan is Jake's full name— dunno why he was called Jake instead of John or Johnnie—and Robert is in honor of my dad. Emily is doing well but she's still royally pissed with me and Donovan. We are both scared to go over to her home, though Jake says she's fine with what's happened. Donovan and I did our confessional in her hospital room and my brother filled in any blanks. I think Emily is more concerned with Max's feelings than my own. She hasn't asked how I was doing after

Max dumped me before leaving for his trip. Should I be mad at her for not considering my feelings?

If Emily was interested, I'd tell her I was not doing well—physically, mentally, or emotionally. I've been spending my nights in our bed at the new empty house and my days wondering how Max was faring. Was I acting like Alex Forrest, myself, by staying over at a home where I wasn't welcomed anymore? Max and I had finished moving in but had not "lived" at the house, yet. We thought we'd start after my big trial.

Prophetic word—TRIAL. That's exactly what this was!

"Anybody home?" Garret and Josh walked into Max's house as I sat on the chair doing what I've become an expert at—zoning. "If you're going to stay here by yourself, you need to *CLOSE* and *LOCK* the door, Sis."

"Hey," was all I could say.

"We just talked to Max."

"You did?" Nobody had been able to get a hold of Max since he'd left. This was the sign I'd been looking for, from above. "What'd he say?"

"Well..." Garret elbowed Josh for telling me about their conversation. "We can tell you what Max said, if you'll tell us what the hell is going on. Josh and I are in the dark. Max won't say much."

We changed locations and went out for a burger and a beer. Here, I told the Davis brothers about my infidelity.

"Shit, Jane!"

"Do you hate me, too?" I put my head down. I'd have nothing to say if Garret and Josh hated me for the rest of their lives. "I know I hate myself for what I did."

"Jane...we still love you. You just caught us by surprise." Josh answered and hugged me and Garret joined in. "We'll help you."

"Please help me by telling me what Max said to you today. Is he doing all right? I've sent him a few emails asking if I could call him, but he hasn't responded. Do you have a number where I can reach him?"

"Max is...Max. He didn't say much except he told me to..." Garret stopped but I encouraged him to continue. "He told me to get the house ready to...rent..."

"Which house?" Surely, Max was NOT kicking me out of our home!

"Well..." Garret couldn't answer. "Would it piss you off if I said, the house you are living in?"

That's when I lost it and started to cry in a public restaurant.

"Jane..." Both brothers hugged me. "Don't cry. When Max told us to clear out his place, he didn't know you were living there. He stopped talking once I told him you had been there since right after he left. I think he was dumbfounded."

"You have his number? Can I call him?"

"He called from someone else's line just to say he was okay. Max didn't take a phone. Are you just going to wait for him to come home and try to fix everything, then?"

"No...I'm going to go see him. Jake is working everything out for me, but it's taking longer than usual because Jake's been so busy with the new baby."

"What can we do to help you?" Josh asked.

"Did Max ask about me at all?"

Garret and Josh looked at each other before answering. "He didn't in so many words but we know he misses you. When he was here, he talked about you incessantly. You were his life, his every breath. I swear, there were times when we told him to shut up because we were so tired of hearing about you," Garret acknowledged.

"Janey..." Josh put his arms around me and kissed me on the cheek. "Max still loves you. Most likely he feels betrayed, but it's not like you did anything with Donovan—that asshole! I knew I never liked him. Where the hell is he now? I'm gonna go kick his ass."

"I think he's planning on flying to London to see..." I stopped mid-sentence wondering why Josh was still here. "Why haven't you left yet? Weren't you supposed to be in London by now?"

"Everything is not quite settled with my house. I had a few things that needed fixing. I hope to leave by next week."

Would it be a good idea to tell Josh about The English Stranger as well as Donovan? It didn't seem like a good idea now, but maybe he'd be better off knowing that odds were stacked against him.

"Why are you staring at me like that?"

"It's nothing Josh. I was just thinking."

Talking with Josh and Garret depressed me enough to go visit Jake, regardless of Emily's feelings for me.

"What brings you here at this hour?"

"Hello, big brother. I need help."

Jake took me into his office and closed the door. "Everyone's asleep. Keep your voice down."

Sure! In this freakin' desperate situation, all he could think about was making sure his family slept. Well, *this* part of the family hasn't slept well in days. *This* family member cries to sleep every freakin' night because of the mess she's in.

"Stop yelling at me in your mind. I can see your eyeballs twitching which means you're cursing me to hell and back. Emily gets up every three hours with JR, and since two nights ago, the twins have been taking turns getting up every few hours, looking for attention."

"Why don't you get up and give them the extra attention they need?"

"First, because they don't want me. Second, because my wife won't wake me up. You know I'm a deep sleeper."

"So Emily is up all day, all night?"

"Practically."

"What about getting some help?"

"For now, I've got everyone scheduled to come in each day of the week, starting with Mom and Dad. This will allow Emily to nap when the baby naps during the day."

These two lovebirds were depressing to be around. Their life was too perfect. Their love was unattainable. Who could compete?

"Jake, I know you're really busy with the new baby and all, but were you able to find out about Mexico for me?"

"I'm trying to get you clearance to go into this area. But it isn't that easy. This isn't Cabo San Lucas or Cancun-type of Mexico."

"I understand Jake and I really appreciate all that you're doing for me. I really messed up this time and I want to try and make this right even if it's for the last time."

"Are you sure this is what you want?"

"Why would you ask me that? I thought you always said Max was the guy for me. Are you doubting your own words now?"

"I'm not doubting what Emily and I believe, but if this isn't what you really want, then cut it off now before you both get any deeper. You wavered from day one and I think it's time you really sit down and ask yourself if this is what you truly want. Emily and I are not going to live your life for you. We want you to be happy whether it's with Max or with Donovan or with another man. That is what is most important to us."

"I don't want Donovan and he doesn't want me either. I think he has finally realized that the woman he wants is Laney not me."

"I don't know when this clearance is going to happen. I'm going to be honest with you, you may never be allowed to go down there. Just sit tight and I will do what I can."

I was thoroughly depressed when I got home after talking to Garrett and Josh, and then to Jake. It seemed as though I may have to wait out the entire month before I could talk to Max and try and reconcile.

"Hey there sis. How you doing?" Nick always had a bright smile on his face for me. It was nice to see somebody smiling.

"I'm miserable and at the last depths of despair." And I wasn't exaggerating when I said that.

"I got an email from Max today. You want to read it?" Well why didn't he tell me sooner? I grabbed his phone from him and opened up Max's email immediately.

The email asked Nick to bring much needed supplies from the hospital. Apparently, they'd underestimated how many children would show up for care. "You going to go?"

"I thought I might go and have my big sister tagalong with me for a few days. You up for a trip to Mexico?"

"You'd be able to get me cleared to go?"

"I would let everyone know that was a prerequisite before I agreed to go."

"You're the best brother, Nick. Thank you so much. Let me know when you're leaving and I'll be ready to go."

The four men I came across this evening are truly wonderful men. The first two are not my brothers by blood, but they love me no less than the two brothers who are blood related to me. Finally I feel a little hopeful that maybe Max and I might have our day of reckoning.

July 11, 2013

Misery Loves Company

"When do you leave Jane?"

"In a couple of days. When do you leave?"

"I don't think I'm going back to London anytime soon." Donovan sounded thoroughly discouraged.

"Why not? You didn't get to see her when you went this last time?"

"She dodged my every attempt to see her. The housekeeper swore up and down that she wasn't home, but I still waited around and you know, she never came home that night. I think I lost her for good." Donovan was down in the dumps.

We were having drinks after work commiserating about our pathetic situation. All of this was entirely both our faults and we really had nobody else to talk to, but each other.

"How about we go see Jake and Emily right now and see if we can get some answers out of them. I had no idea what was going on in Laney's mind and heart, but I was sure Emily was privy to all of that information."

"That's the best idea you've had in a long while Jane." Finally, a smile on that handsome face.

We picked up some dessert and coffee and let Jake know ahead of time that we were coming over. Surprisingly Jake was not hostile about us coming over at nighttime, disturbing his wife's rest.

"Hey, what's up?" Donovan said in a gloomy way.

Jake only laughed at us, and he laughed heartily.

"Emily is nursing right now, but make yourselves at home." Jake led us into the family room.

"Hey guys," Emily said cheerfully. She came in sooner than we all expected.

I felt terrible that I hadn't seen her or the kids since she gave birth. "How are you doing and how's JR?"

"I feel good and JR is beautiful," she said without pause. "You have to see him. He looks so much like James and Ellie when they were first born, and yet he has his own distinct look about him, too. And he's such a good baby. He never fusses, rarely cries, and I can confidently say I love this child as much as my first two."

I looked at her confused. "Why wouldn't you love this child as much?"

"You'll understand when you have kids. The first one, or ones in my case, occupy all the real estate in your heart and you think there's no more land. Surprisingly, your heart gets bigger and there's just as much love for the next one. Even at 3:00 in the morning, JR is the apple of my eye." It was crazy how much love she had for her family.

"How are the twins handling the birth of the baby?" I continued to ask since I hadn't been around for a while.

"Every day has been different. One day they love their new brother. The next day I need to make sure Ellie is not trying to stuff something up JR's nose. They find fascinating the concept of another human who is smaller than they are, but they don't like how much attention I give the new baby. The twins both want to nurse again and they keep climbing on top of me." she said with a chuckle.

"I can stay here with Jane and Donovan if you want to go up and sleep, my love. And I don't have class till late tomorrow so I want you to sleep-in, okay. I'll give JR a bottle in the morning."

"I'll take care of JR in the morning, if you'll take the twins out to breakfast. I think they'll love the extra attention."

"How about if I take care of JR and you go out with the twins. That might work better for them, seeing as how they want more attention from you."

"That's a great idea Jake, I'll do that."

My brother and Emily had such an easy rapport; it really was beautiful watching them as a couple. They always try to put each other's needs first and work to love each other more. Donovan was thinking what I was thinking because he had a sweet smile on his face, watching his buddy and Emily.

Emily was the first to speak to us. "I want to apologize to the both of you for being so upset that day at the hospital. Laney and Max are both very special to me, not that you two aren't. It's just that Max, Laney, and I are similar in temperament and thought, so I know their pain...I can almost feel their pain."

"You were right in being upset with us, Emily. We trifled with every-one's feelings just to satisfy our own curiosity." Donovan confessed. "I've ruined several relationships with my action. I'm deeply sorry and embarrassed."

"What will both of you do now?" Emily asked.

"Emily has no idea. I didn't think she needed to know every goings-on. She has enough to deal with." Jake explained.

"I'm leaving tomorrow with Nick to Mexico and I'm going to try and reconcile with Max, assuming that's what he wants."

Emily looked so happy; she came over and hugged me. "Of course that's what he wants. Did Max give you your birthday present?"

"Well...yeah...but I kinda threw it back at him."

"*Wha???* Why would you do that?" Jake and Donovan both laughed. I explained the entire story of what happened when Max came back out to the airport and Emily half-laughed and half-frowned. Overall, she didn't look very happy with me. "Do you know what was in that box?"

I shook my head, no.

"You didn't even open it?"

"No. I literally threw it back at him." I did regret having done that since now curiosity was killing the cat. "Do you know? Can you tell me?"

"It's probably best I don't tell you what it was. I'm sure there will be another chance where Max can give you the present again."

"Please, Emily! Can you please tell me what was in there?"

Emily shook her head no. "It's not my gift to give, Jane. I'm not try-ing to punish you for what happened between you and Max. This is truly something Max should give you." Emily looked really sad—probably more for Max than for me. Damn! What have I done?

"Emily, if you can't help Jane out, can you help me?"

"What did you need help with Donovan? I'll help you if I can."

"I've come to the realization, a little late, that maybe my feelings for Laney are not what I thought they were."

"What did you think they were?"

"I just thought they were..." He had a hard time coming up with an answer. "I thought they were just feelings of an older brother caring for a younger sister, or a younger cousin, or...I don't know what the hell I thought, Emily!"

"And now?"

"Honestly Emily I don't know what it is that I feel for your cousin. I have feelings for her, but do I like her? Do I still think about her in a younger sister kind of way? Am I in love with her? I don't know, but I'd like to know and I can't figure anything out till I see Delaney. But she won't see me. Can you please tell me what is going through her mind? Why won't she see me? How does she feel about me?"

"After all those weekly softball games, and the fiasco at Ashley's wedding, you still don't understand your feelings for her?" *What softball games? What fiasco at Ashley's wedding? I was at the wedding. How could I not have known that something had happened there?* "Donovan, I'm sorry, but I cannot tell you anything you really want to hear. Once again that's not my story to tell, either. This is something that the two of you need to work out on your own."

"I would like to work it out with her but she won't see me. I've been over at Gram's flat copious times, and either she's in and not opening the door, or she's out all the time."

"All I can tell you is that she is seeing somebody now. He's a really nice guy, who is very much in love with our Laney, and she is trying for a relationship with him."

"What do you mean she's trying? When did this all happen?"

"This guy wants to marry her and ironically, you pushed her into his arms. Laney does like him, and he is a really good guy from what I can tell, but I don't think she's in love with him."

"Why won't she talk to me?"

"You really don't get it do you?" Donovan gave a little-boy confused look. "You don't understand why she left?" Once again he shook his head no. Emily only sighed. "I don't want to betray Laney's confidence so I can't tell you much, but all I can say is, initially she left because she wanted to live a life separate from the comforts of this Reid life. She thought it would be her last chance to have this kind of freedom before she went back to school and eventually joined the workforce. But in the end, she was desperate to get away. A part of me was really sad for her that she left the way she did, and I was angry for her when she came back to find you and Jane in an embrace. She was absolutely ripped to shreds when she left the hospital." My sister started tearing a little bit as she brought up our past sins. "I don't know where this whole relationship with Michael is going to end up, but I do know that he genuinely loves her. And if this is the guy she wants, I support them."

"Why was she so desperate to get away?" Donovan slowly asked, still trying to figure things out.

"You're such a moron," my brother added to this conversation.

"She always made it sound like she wanted something new, something different, like she wanted to experience a new life. Even as a young girl, Delaney always had an independent streak to her."

"She did want something new," Jake said in an exasperated tone. "And she also wanted to be free of the old—namely YOU. Now, I think you're too late buddy. This Michael guy seems to be determined to win her hand."

I think Donovan left Jake and Emily's place even more confused and dejected than when he arrived. I was really shocked to hear about Laney's feelings for Donovan. This was really the first time I'd even considered it. I guess that's how much I was wrapped up in my own world and never thought about anybody else around me. I admit I was a very selfish person.

Nick and I are leaving tomorrow for Mexico and possibly by tomorrow night, Max and I could either be completely broken up, or we would be back together. I was scared to see Max again, but relieved to be able to say I'm sorry. As for hope for our future...the jury is still deliberating on that one.

July 15, 2013

Day of Rec(k)on(cil)ing

"We're here." Nick woke me up from the long drive from the airport to middle-of-nowhere Mexico. I'd been so wound up the last few days about seeing Max that I couldn't sleep. Even with a couple glasses of wine to relax the nerves, the plane ride was ugly. So when we got into our car that Jake had arranged for us, something kicked in and I fell into a deep sleep. Even now, knowing Max was just up the road, I couldn't fully wake myself up.

"Will the driver wait here?" I asked. Nick gave me a confused look. "You know...just in case I'm not welcomed here?" I answered insecurely.

Nick only laughed at me. "You'll be welcomed with open arms. But we can ask the driver to wait a little while if that'll make you feel better."

"Let's do that. I have no idea what to expect. For all I know, Max may have gotten himself married to a Latina here in Mexico and they could be expecting their first child, already. Sounds ridiculous but then again, who thought a teeny tiny slip of paper, that would take me anywhere in the world, would get me into this much trouble?"

"Don't fret." Nick said grabbing our suitcases, the medical equipment they asked for, and my hand—not necessarily all at once, or in that order.

Ahead of me was flat desert land with lanterns everywhere outlining the pop-up tents. These were sturdy tents—the kind I'd imagine the army would use during a war. Though it wasn't that late, it was dark enough where no one was out and about. Nick and I put all our stuff down and we went in search of a human being who could lead us to Max's tent.

"Jane," Nick called over and pointed towards a guy who could help me.

I spoke slowly and gave Max's name and described his build, hoping this guy could point me in the right direction. And that's what he did. He literally pointed to the tent to the right of me. *Finally!* After too many weeks of no communication, I'd get a chance to put everything back in place.

How would I react when Max and I finally got together? Would we immediately kiss and make-up? Would it be awkward? Would he look at me in disdain? Would I have to grovel, or would he greet me with open arms?

I stood right outside the tent for longer than necessary, and time for composure was done. I needed to face the music.

"Max?" I called out weakly. "Max?"

My first glimpse into the tent showed a super tidy one. There was very little in it. There was paperwork on a pop-up desk, a plastic chair, a thick rope that crossed from one end of the tent to another—similar to a zip line—that held newly washed clothes, a cheap mirror hanging off that same clothesline, and finally, there was a cot in the corner.

The cot was one of those army green looking ones that appeared super uncomfortable. There was a foot wrapped in a blanket at the bottom of the cot and as I perused the sleeping body, something was seriously wrong. This body wasn't long enough, big enough, or manly enough to be my boyfriend—or ex-boyfriend, depending upon whom you ask. Just to be real clear, I got right behind this body and undid the blanket just enough to see red— not dark brown hair—under the blanket. SHE, as in HANNAH, was sleeping underneath that blanket.

I fell back a few steps and before I could think about anything else, I ran out of the tent. All I could do was run as fast as I could to the car waiting on the other side of the tents. My heart was crushed. No, it was more than crushed. It was blown to bits and there was no way I'd ever find it again.

I figured Max would be pissed. I knew I'd have to grovel because this time, it was solely my doing. Never in my wildest of dreams, did I imagine finding Hannah in Max's bed. We'd only been apart a few weeks! Maybe they, too, were trying things out the way Donovan and I tried back in Chicago? Did I need to give him a bye, since I pulled the same stunt? I was so hurt and confused.

"Jane!" I ran out of there as though my life depended upon it, thanking God that there was a car waiting for me.

"Jane!" I didn't bother turning around. Nick would figure out that I was going back home. He didn't need to know the particulars and I wasn't going to be the one to explain it to him.

"Dammit, Jane. Slow down." That didn't sound like Nick so I slowed my steps but still didn't turn around.

I stopped running and waited for this person to catch up with me. Did I want this person to be Max?

Did I need this confrontation right now? I sure as hell wasn't going to apologize anymore, not after what I saw in that tent.

"Gem," a gentle voice turned me around.

I lost it as soon as I saw Max's face. Why did he need to look so desperately happy to see me? He'd lost weight, and he was sunburned, but he looked perfect to me. He pulled me into his body, I pushed myself into his body. I don't know what happened, but I was crying my eyes out, holding onto him.

"I've missed you," he whispered without letting go of me. "I'm so glad you're here. I've thought a million times about blowing out of here to go talk to you and make things right with you."

"You have?" I asked with tears pouring down my face. "Then why haven't you responded to any of my emails?"

Max tried to answer my question several times but couldn't quite form his words. "An email couldn't do justice to all the thoughts I had in my mind. I have so many things I want to say to you and so many things I still need answered from you. Would you mind staying here tonight? We need to talk and decide one way or the other how we want our relationship to go."

"Where would I stay?" I got angry all of a sudden as I remembered who was sleeping in his cot. "I can't believe you! We've been apart for a few weeks. How can you?"

"Um...you want to explain why you're going batshit crazy on me, again? You were just in tears because you were happy to see me."

"That was because I forgot about Hannah!"

Max closed his eyes and shook his head in disbelief. "We have so much crap to talk about and you're upset because Hannah is here? You knew she was here. You saw her at the airport."

"Yeah, but I didn't know you were sleeping with her!" I accused.

"Shit!" He yelled. "You drive me fucking insane!" He yelled even louder. "You were the one who had thoughts of cheating on me, and you come down here and accuse me of having cheated on you? What the hell is the matter with you?"

Max was so angry, I thought maybe I shouldn't have brought up this minor detail? Or, could I have seen a mirage of Hannah?

"Um…" I answered meekly and quietly. "I saw Hannah sleeping in your cot when I went into your tent?" I squeaked out a question-answer.

"Which tent did you visit?"

I walked over and pointed towards the tent in question. Max just stayed where he was and put both his hands on his head and groaned aloud. He then marched over to me, grabbed my hand, pulled me into a different tent, put both hands on my face and kissed me like we have never, ever, ever kissed before. It was seriously the kiss to end all kisses. At first, the way we kissed was all wrong. It had been so long, we were out of practice. And if we were making music, it would have been a disastrous cacophony. Our teeth clashed into one another (and yes, that hurt) and I felt like Max's tongue was down my throat (and yes, I thought I may barf at times), but we couldn't stop kissing. We kissed till I was lightheaded and couldn't breathe anymore, but damn did that kiss feel good.

"Stop." I pulled away. "I need to breathe. You're making me dizzy."

Max let me go and sat on the cot. He still had his head in his hands. "This is my tent. Do you see Hannah in here?"

I looked around and noticed a different room. "Well..." I backpedaled. "I went into the tent that the Hispanic guy pointed to..."

"Did the Hispanic guy speak English, or did he just point?" He started grinning.

"Well..." I started laughing. "I don't know. I wasn't listening. I just did as I was told."

"Good God! You actually did as you were told?" He said in a snarky way.

"All right, already. Let's drop it. I went to the wrong tent. BFD!" I was starting to get a bit defensive, which wasn't going to be good for either of us.

"Come here," he commanded.

I thought for a second before following the command. As much as it killed me to be the soldier to this commanding officer, I knew this wasn't the time to go AWOL.

I sat right next to him on the cot.

"You want to start?"

The jerk was putting the ball in my court, first. FINE! Grudgingly, I started this round. "I'm sorry."

He waited for me to continue but that's all I could say for now. "Is there more?"

"No. I said all I needed to say at the airport, but you didn't believe me. You told me to do what I want to do, be with who I want to be with, and to figure out what I want out of life. I did what you told me to do, and I'd like to be with you. I'm sorry I hurt you, and I..." I slowed my speech, "love you still very much, and if you don't feel the same, just let me know now and I'll get out of your way." There. I put myself out there for Max to take or to throw away.

"What did you actually do that you wanted to do, and who were you actually with, that you wanted to be with—in order to figure out what you wanted in life?"

SHIT! Perhaps, I shouldn't have said so much when trying to reconcile with my boyfriend. Do I tell him about the incestuous kiss with Donovan? I knew Donovan would never tell. Jake and Emily would keep this secret for us as well, especially since they knew it resulted in us coming to the conclusion that we'd never work. But, if Max and I were starting new, was this the healthiest way to restart a relationship—with a BIG FAT LIE?

This was one hell of a dilemma! Perhaps we needed to reconsider reconciling, after this time of reckoning.

July 18, 2013

Rec(k)on(cil)ing Res(v)is(i)ted

"**W**ell?" He needed a damn answer and I had to give him one.

"You remember the day I threw my birthday present back at you and I went into another departure gate?"

"Yeah." He let out a snort. "This entire Mexico team remembers the day you threw my gift back at me and laughed at my face."

"I didn't laugh at you!"

"Go on...!" He demanded in an exasperated tone.

"I went to go see Becky in Chicago and after crying all over her the entire morning, I kinda ran into Donovan."

"Fucking hell. Maybe you should stop here and just go home." He let out another ugly snort and got off the cot and walked around the tiny tent. He was making me dizzy and I wanted to tell him to sit the hell down, but I couldn't exactly raise my voice since I knew the rest of this story wasn't going to sit pretty with him. I needed to pick my battles. It was a while before he stopped moving around in circles.

"You want me to continue or shall I really go home? The driver is still waiting for me if you want me to leave."

"Am I going to regret asking you to stay and continue your story?"

How was I to answer this one? On the one hand, the one kiss might be a sore spot for Max, but on the other hand, Donovan and I are finally done. We've figured out what we both wanted and it's not each other.

"Before I got to Chicago, Becky asked her brother to come by and help me. Donovan and I...after...well, after all was said and done, we decided we didn't suit. In fact, we thought it was kind of incestuous. I mean, it was like a million on the scale of 1 to 10."

"What is *it* that was a million on a scale of 1 to 10? And what is *it* that was done that brought you to this conclusion?"

"Donovan and I kind of..." My palms were sweaty, my body was shaking, I didn't think I could explain this little kiss.

"Did you fuck him?"

I went bug-eyed and slack-jawed on Max. "Did you just ask me if I *fucked* Donovan?" I couldn't believe Max asked me this question and in such a crass way. Did he really think I'd go as far as sleeping with Donovan? "What do you take me for—some slut, sleeping with any available guy?"

Max quickly apologized. "I'm sorry. I shouldn't have jumped to conclusions and I definitely shouldn't have said that. Anytime you mention his name, you put me on edge. I don't know what to expect."

Fair enough. I decided to let that one go. "Well, Donovan and I had a long talk and we finally understood that our 'attraction' was not really an 'attraction,' but more of a curiosity. At some point in our lives, we were attracted to each other, but that got replaced with the easy-going friendship that we have. We just needed to test it out and confirm that what we felt for each other was neither like nor love." There! That was a great explanation.

"You're evading the question. What is *it* that was done to test out these feelings?"

"We had brunch with Becky and Al, then we did a little shopping, and then we decided to go back to his hotel room," I could see Max getting red, so I emphasized the last two words, "AND TALK." The beet redness came down and he was back to his usual coloring.

"Go on."

"Donovan wanted to know what had happened between you and me and I told him that you were correct when you accused me of contemplating going away with Donovan."

"Fuck." Max whispered in pain.

"I also explained to him that my wavering was no different to you than cheating, and on that, I agreed with you."

I looked at Max, but he didn't look back. He was in so much pain. I felt like a complete bitch for hurting this good man, *AGAIN*!

"Then, I told Donovan how I felt about him—or at least what I thought I felt about him. I explained that I believed I was attracted to him, and he, too, thought he was attracted to me. I also told him that I did think at times that a relationship with him would be easier, but never did I think a relationship with him would be better."

Max just put his head in his hands.

"Donovan confessed that he regretted giving me the carte blanche tickets and that he was an asshole for telling me to cheat on you. He really regrets what he did."

Max now looked at me and shook his head. I translated that to, *you both are unbelievably fucking stupid.* "So that's it? You have this confession time and you're both cured of your attraction to one another? How do I know you two won't start up again?"

The way he said that was a little mean-spirited and calloused, but I let it go for the sake of our relationship.

"No." I sighed. "There's a bit more."

"Of course there is. That would have been too damn easy."

"We decided at that point to go out on a date."

"Shit!"

"We went to see a matinee of *The Book of Mormons*, we had an early dinner, then we went shopping for the twins. Then..." Shit, here it was...the big confession.... "Then, we went back to Donovan's room and we...kissed..."

"Dammit, Jane." Max sounded like he was about to cry. "Why do you do this to me? Why the fuck did you need to kiss him, and why the fuck did you need to tell me this? Do you get some sick satisfaction in knowing that you're the only one who can hurt me this badly? For the last month, I was tormented that we'd broken up, that I'd ended our relationship in such a shitty way, that I'd hurt you. During this time, I wondered how I could make things up to you, whether or not you'd want to get back together with me, how sad you must have been because I was such an asshole to you. Never did I think you were out dating another guy..."

Damn and double damn! "I'm not done with my story. And it's not what you're thinking," I tried to do damage control. "We kissed once—and not even for that long. We broke it off immediately because we both came to the realization that it felt more like a brother and sister kissing, than a man and a woman kissing. It was actually the most disgusting kiss for the both of us."

"So, because it didn't work out for the both of you makes it all right to have kissed one another? All is good in this world since Jane and Donovan have figured out what they want?"

"Now wait a damn minute." This man was starting to piss me off. I had a difficult enough time explaining myself, and in my mind, it all ended with everyone understanding each other. *All's well that ends well, no?* "I'm trying to tell you that Donovan and I don't like each other. We are friends—good friends. We probably haven't liked each other in a very long time. It was probably a stupid curiosity we needed to get out of our system. It's out. It's done. You and I have no more issues."

"Jane. If you believe that because you were able to satiate your curiosity, that everything turned out for the better, we have some *serious* fundamental differences that I don't know if we can overcome. You kissed another man."

I did my best to keep my voice even-tempered. "Yes, but you told me to go figure myself out. I did just that. And let me remind you, *WE* were broken up when I went on a measly date with Donovan. *WE* were no more because *YOU* decided *WE* didn't suit. *WE* were no longer together so *YOU* can't be upset with me. I only did what *YOU* told me to do."

"If that's your philosophy, then why the hell did you go batshit crazy on me when you thought Hannah was sleeping in my tent? So, it's no big deal for *YOU* to go out on a date and kiss another man, but I can't have someone sleeping in my tent?"

Damn freakin' Max! "I thought you were fucking her, *excuse* my language." I said in a most sarcastic way.

"You are so damn hypocritical. Why is it okay for you, but not for me?"

"Did you or did you not break up with me before you left for this trip?" He wouldn't answer me. "We were *NOT* together, which means, we were free to do as we pleased. It pleased me to go out with Donovan—once—and it pleased me to kiss him—once. After that, I finally understood myself and what I wanted."

"You still don't get it, do you?"

What the hell didn't I get? "Maybe it's you who doesn't get it!" I yelled. "I came here to make up with you. I came all the way here to say I'm sorry and that the Donovan issue was all cleared up. I want to have a relationship with you and no one else. I still love you. If you can't understand that, then maybe we do have *fundamental* differences we can't resolve."

The asshole didn't stop me from leaving his tent. I was never so grateful to see the driver still waiting. I'd go back to my hotel, catch a flight back home, and contemplate later if this was really it. This was supposed to be a time of reckoning and reconciling revisited—not reckoning and reconciling resisted! Damn. Why is life so complicated?

July 22, 2013

Movin' On

"Well?" Donovan asked me at lunch. "What happened?"

I explained the entire story of what happened in Mexico, and how Max was back in LA, but living at his parents' home *with* Hannah still there. "Josh says that Hannah is moving out this weekend, but I don't know what the hell to think."

"You know there's nothing going on with Hannah. Max is hurting, and I don't blame the guy. I tried to visit him at the hospital but he wanted nothing to do with me."

"When did you do that?" Though we were at lunch, I had no appetite to eat anything. "Two days ago, I went to go see Jake and the Chief at the hospital and I asked Jake to page Max for me. Max came into Jake's office for all of half a second, till he saw me, then he blew out of there. I tried to go apologize, but Jake stopped me."

I sighed, heavily. "I get why he's mad, but it pisses me off that he's that mad. I mean, he and I weren't together when you and I hooked up." Donovan gave me a look that claimed innocence from any hooking up. "I know we didn't really hook up. I mean..." Now, it was Donovan who was pissing me off. "You know what the hell I mean. Max was the one who told me to figure things out with you."

"Jane. No man wants to hear that his girlfriend figured anything out with any other man."

"But that's just the thing—we were *not* boyfriend-girlfriend at the time."

"Semantics, Ms. Reid."

"Speaking of Ms. Reid, what are you going to do about Laney?"

"I was in London when you were in Mexico and no luck, again. I don't know where she goes all the time. She's never home."

"Are you sure she's just not answering the door?"

Donovan sighed, heavily. "It could be. But, I don't think she could avoid me that many times. I've sat on the steps waiting for her for hours."

"Tell me something—you seriously contemplating dating her?"

"Jane, I don't know heads from tails right now. Kissing you in Chicago is up there as one of the biggest fucking wake-up calls of my life. Never was I so wrong about my feelings about anything and anyone."

"If I'm not your biggest and worst wake-up call, what is?"

"Watching Delaney and Brent walking into Ashley's wedding reception, together."

"Is that why you went all mute, deaf, and angry on us at the table? Becky and I thought it was weird how moody you became, out of nowhere. What happened that night?"

"Too long of a story to tell over lunch. I've got a conference call to jump into in about ten minutes. Let's wrap it up and go back upstairs."

The rest of the day went slowly. I dreaded going "home" as it wasn't my home. I'd see Max this weekend at JR's christening. Of course, Jake and Emily—with their sadistic sense of humor—named us the godparents of their newest little one. I hadn't seen Max since he got into town and neither of us made any effort to reach out to one another. Feeling pretty low, I went to "our" new place and started packing up my stuff. It seemed as though our relationship was over. There was no need to pretend that things were going to go back to normal.

"Knock, knock." Josh and Garret said and walked in. "What do you think you're doing?" Garret asked.

"Packing. It's ridiculous that your brother is living at home because I've taken up residence in his place. He did buy the place and he is still paying the mortgage."

"Just give him a little more time. He misses you a lot, Jane. He's a mess right now." Josh revealed.

I stopped packing, briefly, then went right back to what I was doing. I tried hard not to believe half the stuff the Davis brothers were telling me. "Your brother knows where I stand. I went to reconcile, and he's the one who kicked me out of his tent."

"Jane..." Garret called out and dragged my name and my arm. "You two have to stop this."

"Guys, I'm tired. I can't keep hoping. I did wrong, I tried to make amends, but your brother isn't willing to forgive and forget."

I took out my phone and texted Max.

I will have my stuff moved out tonight.

There was no answer back, so I figured that's what he wanted. Was it so wrong of me to hope Max would text back and tell me to stay? Was it so impossible for us to work this out? I was still willing to try for a relationship. I still loved Max. Did he still love me? I couldn't answer.

Friday morning, Gimpy called me into his office and surprised me with a proposition I had never considered. This could change just about everything I thought was stable in my life.

"What's going on in your life, Janey? Have you and Max called it quits?"

"I'm unsure, Gimpy. I don't want to think that we're over, but it may be the best way to describe our situation..." I really didn't know how else to explain our status.

"How would you like to move back to the New York office and be in training to be a partner, and eventually move to our London office?"

Say what??? "Gimpy, This is only my third year as an associate. How can I be a partner, already?"

"Well, you knew you'd end up being a partner at this firm, someday. I need you on a faster track since I'd like to retire soon."

"I don't follow..."

"Estelle wants me to retire. I agree with her, but this firm is what's stopping me. After my two partners died, I bought their shares of this firm from their families."

"So you own this firm, outright?"

"Almost. There are a few senior partners who own a small percentage of the firm, but the majority of it is mine. And since I don't have kids, when I pass away, this firm will eventually belong to you Reids—you and hopefully another male partner here, if he can get his head out of his arse and do the right thing, will share the majority of the firm."

Whoa!!! What the hell??? "Back up, Gimpy." I had to sit down. This was big news! "First of all, this male with his head up his arse—are you referring to Donovan?"

Gimpy nodded yes.

"How'd you know? And how long have you known?"

"It's only obvious that Donovan and Laney are in love. Laney knows her true feelings. It's up to Donovan to open his eyes and realize it. And he better wake up soon. Michael is a formidable rival, and a good chap all around."

"So, you and Gram are assuming that Donovan and Laney will get married? And somewhere down the road, you will hand down this firm to us???"

"That's the simplified version of it. Yes." *Hot Damn!* "The way your Gram and I have it set up, each of the five sons will get a share of the company as well as sit on the Board of Directors, along with you, Donovan, if he marries Laney, and Jake. Since you and Donovan are the only two practicing lawyers right now, you both will get larger shares—since most of the work will fall upon you two."

"And what happens if Donovan and Laney don't get married?"

"Donovan will get a chance to buy into the firm. But David will step in if Donovan chooses not to exercise this option, since David is still technically a lawyer. He'll start practicing, again."

"That's huge, Gimpy."

"It is. But even if I were to retire today, you wouldn't be made partner right away. You still need to work towards it. But, your road to equity partnership is cut by several years, out of necessity. That's why I'd like for you to go back to New York, and eventually work in the London office, in my stead."

"How long do I have to think about this?"

"Take your time. It's not something you have to decide right away, but I wanted you to know what's in store so you'll start preparing for the inevitable." I nodded my understanding and started to head back to my cubicle. "And Jane?"

"Yes?"

"I'm sure I don't need to tell you that you are not to say any of this to anyone in the firm? Especially not a certain male partner with his head up his arse?"

I nodded my understanding once again.

Last night I moved from Max's home back to my parents' home. Soon, it looks like I'll be moving back to my New York home, then off to Gram's London home? That's an awful lot of moving for someone who thought she'd live in that tiny little home with the extra shoe closet for years to come.

July 25, 2013

Paging Jerry McGuire

I was told that a christening was an act or an instance of naming
something new. This happy occasion fell upon my newest nephew, Jonathan Robert Reid. Emily put Jake's old christening gown
on him and their home and backyard were set for the ceremony and
lunch.

After my conversation with Gimpy the other day, I had so much on
my mind, I bumped into Max without realizing what was happening.

"Jane." He called me with more emotion than I cared to admit.

It killed me to see him. Max looked like hell. His suit was way big on
him because he'd lost so much weight in Mexico, and he honestly
looked worse than when I saw him a week ago. At least another five-
ten pounds came off this man. His face was gaunt, his eyes too big,
and his once beautifully chiseled face was now angular and sharp.
Good to know this breakup was hard on him as well. Or, it could've
just been the hardships of Mexico and the whole team looked as
hellish as he did.

"Hi." I stood there and waited for him to say something, anything,
but he didn't, so I walked away.

Donovan walked in looking sharp as usual and gunned straight for Max. Jake also headed that way and so did Nick, Josh, and Garret when they saw what was happening. Too nervous to watch, I went upstairs to help Emily bring down JR for his big day.

The ceremony was quick and sweet and seeing as how Max and Donovan were still standing in the same room, I assumed their talk was also quick—though maybe not as sweet. Lunch was a crazy affair with so many people in and out of Jake's house. During this time, I also saw Emily on her iPad and James in front of her happily kissing the iPad. I walked over to see what the excitement was all about and he was "talking" to Laney. She had called to be a part of the celebration. Uncle Henry and Aunt Babs talked to her, and she even said a brief hello to me, before I ran off to get Donovan.

"Hey." I rushed over to him. I could see Max's eyes on me as they were sitting at the same lunch table. "Get your ass in the kitchen. James is skyping with Laney." That's all it took for this man to practically mow me down and run into the kitchen. Josh, too, made a mad dash into the kitchen.

Gimpy walked over and talked to me further about New York and Max feigned an interest in our conversation, but in all honesty, I didn't think he cared anymore. After seeing his apathy and feeling his detachment, I thought perhaps moving to New York wasn't a bad idea.

"There's a partners' meeting on Monday." Gimpy said. "Donovan and I are headed to New York, tonight. Why don't you come with us? You can see what happens at these meetings."

"Maybe, Gimpy. I'll think about it."

Emily came out with JR and told Max and me that we needed to go see the photographer. She handed JR to Max and pointed in the direction we were to go.

"How are you?" Max asked while we walked with the baby.

"Busy. Work is keeping me busy. How are you? Do you get a break at all?"

"I've got a break till late August."

"What have you been doing? And what will you do till then?"

"This whole week was just time to get my life back in order here—answering mail, catching up on sleep, getting better acquainted with my parents—and I'm considering going to Europe with Josh for a couple of weeks to help him get settled out there."

I didn't know what to say to that. I kept my lips pursed and just nodded my head.

"You didn't have to move out." He added after a few minutes of silence. "That's not what I wanted...that's not what I thought...you would do..." The confession caught me off guard and made my heart break for the both of us. How had we gone so wrong and so far off track?

"I didn't know what else to do. I told you how I felt about you, and about us. And you pretty much told me how you felt about us when you let me leave Mexico. You didn't give me too many choices."

"What happens now?" Was he seriously asking me this question?

I was a bit pissed. "The last words I said to you were 'I love you' and you had no response to that except to kick me out of your tent. I don't think you have any right to wonder what happens next. You are in the driver's seat." Why the hell had I given him so much power to this relationship, or non-relationship? "If you're going to throw this whole Donovan incident back in my face every time we get into an argument, then I don't want to get back together. Think about that while you're wondering *what happens now.*"

JR's christening pictures probably looked like two pissed off people holding a baby. As soon as pictures were done, I told Gimpy I wasn't ready to leave with them today, but I'd leave on Sunday and join them for their Monday meeting in New York.

"If you haven't hired a driver yet, I'll take you to the airport, Gimpy."

My grandfather was one wise man. He knew I was desperate to get out of this backyard and away from Max. "All right. We'll leave in fifteen minutes?"

Jake and Emily also understood why I didn't want to be here any longer and they, too, were fine with me leaving the party early.

"Your Max wasn't too pissed with me anymore," Donovan said while driving the car. "Did you two make up?"

"He's still pissed with me. I don't know what to think. I moved out of his place the other day and I'm trying to figure out what to do with myself."

"Roland mentioned you might want to move back to New York?"

I nodded yes.

"Don't do that, Jane. You're in love with Max and you hated life in the New York office. You'll only work yourself to death. You'll end up an old spinster with cats, next time I visit you." Donovan and Gimpy both laughed.

"What about you?" I turned the tables on him.

"Hell if I know. I'll end up an aging playboy with young women all around me, while you're with your cats." Donovan and Gimpy laughed even harder.

"You get to skype with Laney earlier today?"

"Nope! She conveniently had to go, according to Emily."

"Bummer. Maybe I'll hop over to London after the Monday meeting. I think I have a bit of apologizing to do to my cousin. You think she'll be in when I decide to visit?"

"Who the hell knows with her!"

The phone rang as we exited the freeway and Jake told Donovan he needed to speak with him privately. After a bunch of "got its," he hung up.

"What was that all about?"

"Nothing."

"Then why'd you have to speak to him in private?"

"Damn, woman. Don't be so nosy." He chuckled. "Jake just gave me a grocery list of things to buy for Emily while out in New York." That was enough to satisfy my curiosity.

"Gawd! He's become such a family man. It's beautiful to see and yet sickening all the same. I never ever thought I'd want a man just like my brother—someone whose entire focus is only his family."

"Jake always had it in him to be a good husband and father. He was always good to Kelley when they dated."

"He was never this devoted to anyone. Emily and the kids are the fuel to his fire. He'd never survive without his family."

"I agree. But, he's good to the entire family, and not just Emily and the kids. Your brother always has your best interest at heart as well, Jane."

"Whatever," I answered. "Hey, why are you parking? I thought I was dropping you off?"

"I need someone to carry my bags in for me," Donovan said with a chuckle. "Walk in with us. You've got nothing better to do."

That was true. I walked a few steps behind the two men and wondered what my life would be like to be married to a man who thought I walked on water, and to be a mother to three children. Then, I thought about how I'd do all that and still be an equity partner of the firm. Too many conflicting thoughts ran through my mind, so I decided to drop those thoughts for now and join the two men ahead of me.

"Why are we hanging out in front of check-in? Is the plane not ready?" Then I thought about how stupid I was for going tomorrow when there was a private plane available for me, today. "Shoot! I'm such a moron. I should've just left with you today. Why the hell am I flying with the masses? Are there just two of you on the plane, today?"

"Yep." Donovan grinned. "You can still come with us. You have nothing left in your New York apartment?"

"I do have some clothes and supplies left to last me a few days..." I started weighing my options.

"This is New York we are talking about. You have everything at your disposal."

Donovan was right. The only reason I was going to fly out tomorrow was because I hadn't packed. How stupid was I? "All right. Let's go. I'll buy whatever I need tomorrow."

Gimpy and Donovan looked at each other, looked outside, stalled for a bit, then had no choice but to get on the plane. Whatever was going on, they weren't about to share it with me. The three of us walked out of the waiting room to the short walkway that led to the steps of the plane when I thought I heard my name. Deciding there was no way anyone here knew me, I kept pace with the men.

"Jane!" I heard again. This time I knew I wasn't wrong. My name was being called. All three of us stopped when we heard, "*Jane*" again. "Hello!" We all heard the voice trying to stop us from getting on the plane, and turned around. I turned to see a frantic Max waving his arms, stopping us from getting on the plane. Donovan and Gimpy were at the top of the steps, I was a few steps short of the top, and Max caught up with us at the bottom.

We met halfway and there was this weird sense of movie-scene déjà vu, but I couldn't figure out which one.

"Don't go." Max pleaded. "Don't move. Don't leave me again. I'm sorry, Gem. I know I took my time licking my wounds. I love you and can't live without you." He was now begging me. *Where the hell did he think I was moving to?* "We belong together. You are my other half. I am completely lost without you."

Then the light bulb went off and I had no choice but to say, "Shut up. Just shut up. You had me at hello."

July 29, 2013

Contents of a Certain Black Box

Max ended up on the plane with us, and as much as we needed to talk, it was impossible with Donovan—the man who
caused much of our grief, and Gimpy—my grandfather who didn't
need to know about our stupid-ass ménage à trois, on the plane with
us. They did their best to sit as far away from us as possible, but
there's only so much privacy you can have when there are only four
passengers, and three flight crew on board.

"Max, tell us about your trip." We ended up joining Gimpy and
Donovan in the four seats facing one another, for dinner.

"To say that it was an eye-opener would be an understatement.
There's so much poverty, and ignorance, and crime down there—
and those poor kids are stuck in the middle."

"Do you think you'd want to go and stay there indefinitely to help?"
Seeing as how it looked like we were on our way to reconciling,
Gimpy sounded like he was scoping out Max's thoughts.

Max looked over to me before answering my grandfather. "Definitely,
I'll go back from time to time for short periods, but it all depends
upon on Jane and our future together." He gave a 10+ answer on a
scale from 1-10.

"So if Jane were to move to another city, then you'd move with her?" I tried to give Gimpy a warning but he didn't care to look my way. Max and I had so much to work through at this moment. The last thing I needed was to add my work to our list of unresolved problems.

"If she were to move before I decided on a hospital for residency, then yes. I'd be willing to relocate. Once I start residency, that'll be hard to do. But, we could do it after those four years."

"Gimpy..." I pleaded.

"If you want to move back to New York, I'll ask the Chief to help me get a residency out there. I'm okay with that. What I don't want is for us to have a long distance relationship." Max voiced quietly. I saw Donovan purposely engage Gimpy in a separate conversation. "I don't want to be apart anymore."

"Let's talk when we get to the apartment." I squeezed his hand and stopped this conversation before it got any heavier with two spectators.

Once we landed in New York, we took a cab into Soho, while Donovan and Gimpy went off to their hotel. Between the five and a half hour flight plus the addition of three hours, it was quite late. Or better stated, it was very early in the morning Sunday morning.

"You want to sleep or do you want to talk?" Max asked.

Truth be told, I'm embarrassed to say I wanted to have sex with him. We were alone, it looked like we were back together, and we had a bed at our disposal. It had been an awful long time since we did anything of a naughty nature. Was I being a total slut for wanting to get it on with Max before any conversation happened? Probably.

At this point the wisest thing to do would be to talk it out, get back together, then have sex the rest of Sunday.

"Why don't we talk first."

"When Roland ask me about New York..."

"Before we get into that," I interrupted his thoughts, "what did you mean when you said back at the airport for me not to move?"

"Jake told me that you were moving to New York."

"What? Why would he tell you that?"

"Jake told me that you were moving to New York today, and if I didn't stop you from going, I would lose you forever. He said he had no idea when you might come back."

My wheels started turning, and I thought back to what Donovan said to me on the ride to the airport and the cryptic conversation he and Jake had. I picked up the phone and called Donovan right away.

"What was said between you and Jake during the conversation when we were driving to the airport?"

"Jane, it's almost 1 o'clock in the morning. Can a guy get some sleep?"

"No! I need some answers from you."

"Don't you and Max have better things to do right now than call me?"

"You spill the beans right now and I'll tell you about Emily's conversation with Laney earlier this morning."

"Did I ever tell you you're scary when you want something? Damn, Max better watch out," Donovan chuckled. "Jake called to tell me that he told Max that you were moving to New York forever."

"I knew it! What did he need to do that for?"

"To quote your brother, he said, you were both 'being dumbasses' and you both 'needed a wake-up call.' Now you spill the beans Jane Sydney Reid. What's going on with Delaney?"

"I wasn't going to tell you this because I didn't want you to be upset, but I overheard Emily and Laney talking this morning, and Emily was cautioning her against going away with Michael to his grandfather's summer home for a month."

"What the fuck? Who the hell is Michael and why is she going away with another guy?"

"Don't you remember that British guy...? Remember from the hospital?"

I heard Max clearing his throat, getting a bit annoyed with me. "Hey Donovan, let's meet up and talk about this a little later. I need to finish my conversation with Max."

"Sure, now that you have your information, hang up on me why don't you."

All I said before hanging up was, "You're a great friend Donovan." Then I hung up before he could rebut.

"So Jake kind of told you a little lie. To his knowledge I am not moving. What he doesn't know is... Before I tell you this complicated story, let me just ask you point blank. Are we reconciling? Are we actually getting back together or are we just clearing the air and going our separate ways?"

"Gem, didn't you hear me before we got on the plane? I love you and I don't want to separate from you ever again. You are what makes my heart beat and my soul have life. Our time away gave me a clearer perspective on my life without you—and I didn't like what I foresaw."

"So tell me all that's on your mind concerning me, Donovan, us— don't hold anything back. Let's get everything out. Let's be completely honest with one another and if possible, let's start again."

"The morning of your birthday, I came to give you this." He pulled out the wrapped box I threw at him. "Open it." He urged.

This box, I did not expect to see again. I'd actually forgotten about my birthday present. Slowly, the ribbon and wrap came off and in my hand was a dainty black velvet box. Not one to be shy about birthday presents, I opened the box and found a diamond ring...of the ENGAGEMENT-kind!

"Imagine my surprise and disappointment when I saw you listening to another man enticing you to go away with him. The forever I imagined in my head was shot to hell."

Shit! This was not what I was expecting.

"That's why I couldn't listen to, or accept any of your reasons at the airport. But, as soon as you came to me in the terminal and threw this box back at me, I knew I couldn't live without you. You actually made me laugh so hard my teammates thought I was nuts. They pretty much saw us breaking up out front, then I was brooding the whole time inside, then I completely changed my demeanor and was laughing like a lunatic. After killing my heart, only *you* would be pissed at me and throw my gift back in my face. *What* may I ask, did I do to piss you off enough to come after me?"

My face was red from embarrassment. "You gave me hope. That's what you did."

"And how did I give you hope?"

"When you left with *HANNAH*, I thought I'd lost you forever. Then you came back out and I thought you'd changed your mind and were going to tell me I was forgiven. What a shocker—you handed me a gift only because you didn't want to hold onto it any longer. *That* pissed me off!"

"Gem..." Max decided to carry me over to the bed at this point and we lay there laughing with one another. "What am I to do with you?"

"I don't know...what do you want to do with me?" I asked as seductively as possibly. That made him laugh even harder.

What the hell? Had I lost my magic touch on this man?

"Babe. It's been a long and shitty month. Let's get some shut-eye and talk more tomorrow. As much as I'd like to make love to you from now till the end of August, we still have a lot to talk over and a shit load of decisions to make."

Still in his travel clothes, Max fell asleep immediately. His worn-out spirit broke me in a way I couldn't explain. I didn't fully understand what I'd done to this man. I still don't fully understand what I've done to him. We had so many issues, and one major unresolved absolution. While he was resting tonight, I'd think through what Max professed and what else might have made him so weary and wary.

August 1, 2013

Proposals

ax and I made plans to meet Donovan and Gimpy for an early dinner. After getting a decent night of sleep, we decided to walk down the street to the local brunch hangout. New Yorkers love to brunch. They live for the weekends so they can drink mimosas and Bloody Marys, and eat a meal large enough to give you sustenance for the rest of the day. When we arrived without a reservation, the wait was an hour long so we decided to take a walk and talk out more of our problems.

I started the conversation this time and told him about Gimpy's proposal. "So, I'm not sure if you want to change your life to that degree since you just bought a house, and life would probably be simpler for you if you stayed at General Hospital." This was not what I wanted, but it would be best for Max.

He didn't even think twice about his answer. "I am willing to move with you if that's what you want. As long as you pick a location and stay there for four years, I'm good with that. Here's what I don't want." Did I want to hear his list? "I don't want a long distance relationship."

"Is that because you don't trust me?"

It was uncomfortably silent for too long. "I trust you, but maybe I don't trust us to be apart."

"Isn't that the same thing? That just means you can't trust me to stay faithful. I told you this at the christening—I don't want to be with you if you are going to throw Donovan in my face every time you're unhappy with me."

"I can't say I'm comfortable with you and Donovan, but I know whatever was between you two is over. It really should never have been since neither of your hearts were in it. I won't throw him back at you. In fact, I probably won't ever refer to you and him in any conjunctive way."

"If you knew our hearts weren't into one another, then why'd it take you so long to reconcile with me? And how do you know what Donovan is feeling?"

"You'd have to have been blind not to see the attraction between Laney and Donovan." Max answered with a bite and a sting. *Ouch!* "Seeing the five-ringed circus between me, you, Donovan, Laney, and Josh was more comedy than I can take for a lifetime." This time, he oozed dark and heavy sarcasm. Obviously, he was still upset with me. "Because I thought Donovan was as into Laney as she was into him, I didn't see his indecent proposal coming. I thought he'd go to London and bring Laney home."

"You knew all this? Why didn't you mention anything to me?"

"What was there to say?"

"Maybe if you had mentioned that Laney and Donovan liked each other, we wouldn't have gotten to this point in our relationship."

What I'd just said was stupid, and the sarcasm I put into this statement was even stupider. I wasn't looking forward to Max's rebuttal.

"You, Jane Sydney Reid, needed a wakeup call. Perhaps we all needed one."

I thought about this statement while we sat and perused the menu. Max stopped talking and took some time to order his meal. What could I say next to make this all better? We were still nowhere near finished in our break-up/make-up session.

"Can you explain your last statement concerning us all needing a wakeup call?" I asked carefully and defensively.

"You needed to decide who you wanted in your life, once and for all. Donovan needed to understand that he couldn't trifle with everyone's feelings without consequences. He may be letting out a sigh of relief that you and I will eventually be okay, but he's going to soon be in hell and he may never come back from hell when he realizes how much he hurt Laney. He may have lost her forever. Me," Max finished his Bloody Mary in like three gulps and ordered another one, "I need to exercise my right to keep what's mine, mine, and not let life be so predestined for me."

"Huh???"

"For a lack of a better phrase, you will be on a short leash with me, Gem."

"Whaaat?"

He cracked-up. "What I mean is, I am not going to take you for granted anymore. I've decided I am going to be clear on what I want, what I don't want, and you, too, will be clear with me on what you like and do not like. We will be open, honest, and share all that's in our hearts. We are going to live in each other's pockets for the time being."

"And we haven't been doing this already?"

"If we had, I don't think we would've had problems with Donovan. I should have let you and Donovan know whenever I was uncomfortable with your friendship, rather than bringing it up only when we got into a mess. And as for you, I hope you can be honest with me even if it's a difficult subject. We can never grow as a couple if we can't share everything—no matter how uncomfortable the topic."

"So...you've forgiven me for what happened on my birthday?"

"Yes."

"And you've forgiven and will forget what happened in Chicago?"

"I believe so." Still it wasn't a 100% affirmative. "That's what's kept me from coming to you right after Mexico. I was in agreement with you on the fact that I didn't want us to get back together if I couldn't let go of your..." *Kiss? Infidelity?* I didn't know which word he was about to say, but the pain on his face expressed both. "I can't say that I've forgiven or forgotten completely, but I'm working on it. Without a doubt, I know myself well enough to believe I won't throw Donovan back at you, ever. There's no part of me that's crazy about him, but if we are to be close to one another—whether by mutual friendships, or as a family, I don't think I have much of a choice but to forget."

"Tell me what you're thinking in terms of Laney. What makes you sure that she likes Donovan? I always thought she found him annoying."

"Gem," he said in a what-am-I-to-do-with-you tone, "you like to see only what you want to see. You close yourself off to any possibility that doesn't suit your plan. As far as I can tell, Donovan and Laney are in love with one another. Donovan either never understood what he wanted or he fooled himself to believe he wanted the wrong Reid. Laney understood her own feelings, and didn't want to continually watch the man she fell in love with, look at every woman but her."

"When the hell did you become Oprah Winfrey?"

Max finally laughed freely and comfortably. "All anyone had to do was open his or her eyes. I think this was a secret only to you, Josh, and Donovan."

"You know for a fact Laney is in love with Donovan? If so, I need to let him know. She's not talking to him at all."

"I am not Laney's keeper. As you can see, I haven't done a good job being a keeper of one certain dark-haired, stunning blue-eyed Reid. You may not repeat my words to Donovan."

We started walking back to the apartment and I thought we were finally headed in the right direction with one another. Our conversation flowed as usual, we were able to joke with one another and the chemistry appeared to be back.

"Are we good, now? Is this all we need to talk about? You have anything else on your mind?"

Max stood pensive. "For now, I think we're good. I will support your decision to move to New York, but I need to know soon. I don't know what we will do if you have to move this school year, but we'll work something out. As long as I know we're moving forward..."

Max never brought up the issue of the my birthday present—the engagement ring, again. And I let it go as well. As we headed into the bedroom to consummate our reconciliation, I knew for sure that we were headed in the right direction.

Fast forward many hours and an orgasm—or two, or three—later, we headed towards Columbus Circle to have dinner with Donovan and Gimpy at Milos.

"Dinner with Donovan going to be a quiet affair? Or shall I call and tell them we won't make it?"

"Nothing is quiet when your Uncle Henry is around."

"What?"

No question was necessary as we were the last to make it to the dinner for six. Everyone was already seated at a round table and they were having a serious conversation.

"You're late...as usual..." Jake made his commentary. "I take it all is right in the world of Max and Jane, again?" He gave a smug grin.

Max shook my brother's hand. "Yes. Thank you for the lie. Ellie's done a good job teaching her dad the finer points of drama. You were right. I didn't want to lose Jane."

I didn't know what to say. Maybe it should be stated now, and in front of everyone, that my brother will forever be throwing me lifelines to get me out of the mess I create, created, and will create. Thank God for families and thank God for my older brother who understands what it means to love someone.

"Emily and the kids here?"

"They are not."

"Oh my gosh!!! You left Emily alone with three kids?" I couldn't believe my brother would do this without a dire reason. "You're actually going to sleep apart from her?"

"I know. It kills me, but I had to be here. I'm going home tomorrow."

"Why are you here?"

"Sit down," he pulled me into a chair next to him. I didn't know why the hell I was standing the entire time. "Uncle Henry and I are attending a medical conference and I agreed to speak at one of the seminars, long before Emily got pregnant with JR."

"I'm shocked you didn't bring the whole family."

"Well, I was going to at first, but we've got a major change happening in the Reid household."

"Which Reid household?"

"It'll start with us, but will have a ripple effect with everyone else."

"What's going on?"

"We're moving."

Whaaaat???

August 5, 2013

The European Invasion

"Where are you going with the kids? How can you take the kids away from all of us?"

Max and Jake both laughed at me. "I didn't realize you liked the kids so much—seeing as how you almost caused brain damage to one of them." Now the whole table was laughing.

One freakin' near-accident and I'd have to live this one down the rest of my life. "Whatever! Explain yourself."

"There are a lot of exciting heart procedures and experiments happening all over the world and our hospital is doing an 'exchange' program with other hospitals. I've been asked to teach and work at the college hospitals in Europe—mainly in the London area. In return, they will send one of their heart surgeons to our hospital and this makes for a great way to learn other hospital's innovations."

"Where will you be teaching and working?"

"A day at Cambridge, a day at Oxford, and two days at the University College London and their corresponding hospitals. And then there will be occasional trips to medical schools and hospitals in the neighboring countries."

"With three kids, you're going to uproot your family to do this? And for how long?"

"Technically it's only for the winter term, going from September to December. We'll be home by Christmas, unless we decide to stay another term."

"Where will you stay?"

"At Gram's. Her house is big enough to house all of us, plus a few more." He said this and looked only at Donovan. "And Roland has homes all around the major cities in Europe, so we'll stay there when we're away from London."

I kind of shook my head at this huge change. What kind of nut would move three kids under the age of eighteen-months to another country?

"Emily's okay with this?"

"She's the one that's forcing me to go. I didn't want to go because of the upheaval in her life, but she didn't want me to miss out on this opportunity. It was only yesterday I made this decision. *AND,*" my brother stressed that last word and faced my boyfriend, "I've told UCL med school that I have a lovesick, soon-to-be-brother-in-law who needs to finish off his fourth year of med school apart from my equally lovesick sister who might be based in London, and they've offered you a spot in the school. Of course, that's if you want to take it, and if you," he was now facing me, "choose to transfer to the London office."

How did my brother know all this about me and how in God's creation did he pull off a medical school transfer for Max? Did I ever tell you that I LOVE my big brother?

"You know?" I asked Jake.

"I know everything little sister."

"Let me remind you, Janey, that you will be in the New York office part time as well. There will be quite a bit of traversing the Atlantic Ocean."

Donovan jumped into this conversation. "Why is Jane moving offices? I thought you hated the New York office." He turned to me and I had no answer for him. I wasn't allowed to tell him what Gimpy had proposed to me, but I also didn't want to lie to my friend.

"Now that you've got your head out of your arse and have made a wise decision to go after my granddaughter, I'll fill you in on my plans."

No one could ever say that my grandfather ever minced words.

"I'm not getting any younger and now that I'm married to Estelle, I'd like to retire. And I can't retire unless I know this firm is in good hands. Of course I have no issues with any of the partners, especially the senior partners, but I do need to make sure somebody will eventually fill my shoes."

"And you've handpicked your granddaughter, a third-year associate to fill your shoes? You know none of the partners will go for that, Roland. Even if you do own majority of the firm, the partners will not be happy." Donovan wasn't trying to belittle me in any way, or be mean. He was only speaking as a voice of the partners, and in a large way, he was trying to protect me and Gimpy from an all out revolt. It was true. No one would be happy with me at the helm. And even Gimpy would not flippantly offer me a partnership without the approval of all the other voting partners.

"When I die, this firm will be turned over in equal shares to all five sons and Jake. They will sit on the governing board and David will be the spokesperson for the six of them since he's also a lawyer. But," Gimpy emphasized, "a larger share will be given to Jane and..," while the rest of us knew this story and knew who belonged after the "and," Donovan had no clue. I could tell Gimpy was wondering whether or not to enlighten Donovan. I wasn't even sure why he was telling him this info now. Obviously something had changed in the last few days that made Donovan "go after" Laney, whatever that meant.

"And who?" Donovan asked. "Doug? Is he switching over to law school? Or Laney? Did Ms. Mensa get into law school as well?" Our entire table chuckled.

"You know she's smart enough to have gotten in," Uncle Henry butted in. "But no, Laney's not going to law school. You still have no idea?"

Donovan shook his head and answered, "No freakin' clue."

"It's you, you dumbass," my brother answered and I cracked up. "How long have I been telling you to pursue my cousin? She's beautiful, brilliant, and the bearer of shares to your law firm."

"Good one, big bro'." I high-fived him.

"What the hell is Jake talking about?"

Gimpy answered the question posed to him. "I'd like for you, and eventually Jane, to be the face of the firm when I retire. Of course I'll still be around even after I retire, but when I die, my hope is that you and Jane will lead Ascot, Ascot, and Pemberly." Donovan looked shocked. "If Laney accepts you as you think she will, and if you become a part of the family, you will get equal shares as Jane.

But, if the relationship doesn't work out, then you get first choice to buy into those shares."

"Shit. Seriously?"

"Yeah." Jake added, "And if it doesn't work out with Laney and you choose to buy into the company, I'll make sure you make monthly person-to-person payments to Laney's future husband."

We all laughed at Donovan again.

"You sure you can win my baby's heart?" Uncle Henry slapped Donovan's back.

"No," Donovan became glum. "I need to unglue her from this Michael, first."

"So you get why I'm making the move?" I asked.

"Yeah." Donovan was now deep in thought.

"And when are you making your moves on my cousin? When did all this come about?"

"The other day—I went and got everyone's blessings to court Delaney, and I'll be learning the ropes from Roland out of the London office."

"That job requires you to travel all over Europe. You won't be staying put in London the whole time. Come up with a new game plan of wooing my granddaughter while you're separated from her."

"I'll just take her everywhere with me," he said, looking only for Uncle Henry's approval.

"You can do whatever it takes, as long as you can look me in the eye and tell me exactly what you've been up to, every time I call and ask."

"Damn," Donovan muttered. "I guess I'll have to pull a Jake and Emily in Paris and get double rooms everywhere."

"Damn, RIGHT!" My uncle called out a bit too loudly.

"Roland has homes everywhere," I heard Jake whisper to his best friend. "Take advantage of that."

We all separated and I hadn't failed to notice that Max didn't say anything during dinner and even now, he was silently getting ready for bed.

"What's going on in that mind of yours?" I approached cautiously. This was one aspect of our relationship that irked me. I now thought through everything before bringing it up with Max. We'd lost that spontaneity and sense of ease where I could just blurt out what was on my mind without worrying about what he'd think. In short, I still felt guilty—whether by my doing or by Max's.

"Just processing all that was said during dinner."

"And what have you processed? Or maybe I should ask, what did you conclude?"

"First, honest thought...? How we'd have kids with your busy schedule."

Shit! How does he always do this to me? His comments are out from left field. Whenever I feel like we've resolved one problem, there's another larger one facing us.

"And your answer to this thought?"

"No answer," was his answer as he led me to bed.

When will we ever have an answer to all our issues?

August 8, 2013

Another Birthday...This Time No Co-prise

So much has happened since Sunday's dinner, I don't know where to begin. I guess the best place to begin would be from Monday.

The partner meeting was a lunch meeting, so I had all morning to hang out with Max, or so I thought. We started the morning with a nice little wake up call for Max. "Happy birthday," I said as soon as I finished him off. I didn't leave him hanging like that one time at the hospital student lounge. This time, I finished him off nice and clean.

"Thank you." Max said with a very satisfied grin. "How did you know?"

"How did I know it was your birthday???" I asked surprised. "Ummm...you're my boyfriend, I'm your dutiful girlfriend. I should know these things."

He smiled and pulled me back to bed as soon as I finished grabbing the large bag in the corner of the room. "Have we ever talked about my birthday? If we have, you know I don't celebrate it."

"Just because I wasn't with you for your last birthday, doesn't mean that I don't know when it is. In fact I have a bunch of presents for you."

I dumped all the presents on the bed.

"You bought me all this stuff?" He sounded somewhat horrified now. What kind of person didn't celebrate birthdays? "Sorry," Max said. "I don't mean to be such a party pooper. My mom never made much of a big deal out of our birthdays when we were younger, so I guess that kind of stuck with me."

"Well, as you know, we Reids make a big deal out of everything. And birthdays are a big deal."

"Where did all these gifts come from?" I handed him the first gift, from his parents.

"Emily gave them to Jake, who gave them to me. Your *ex-girlfriend*, and *my sister-in-law*, collected these gifts from everyone and sent them across the country with her *husband*."

Max found my sarcasm cute because we ended up making out on the bed and of course, you can't just make-out on a bed and have it not lead to other, more exciting activities—of the copulating-kind.

"I don't have to be in till noon today. I'll make you breakfast, but won't see you again till your birthday dinner."

"I have to leave in thirty minutes," Max countered after looking at his watch. "Shit. I'm late."

Whaaa? "What, pray tell, are you late to?"

"Your brother's picking me up and I'm going to listen to him speak." I gave him a *why the hell would you want to go to a medical seminar when you're in Manhattan,* look. "Because, my precious gem, it's your brother. I'm sure there will be many attendees, but it doesn't hurt to have as many people fill the conference room. I'm hoping I'll have to stand because the illustrious Dr. Jake Reid is in the building."

I picked a winner! This man had goodness written all over him, inside and out. "Did I ever tell you I love you?"

"Not lately." He frowned.

"Well I do. I don't know why my eyes would ever stray when I had you with me the entire time." Now I got a bit sad and weepy. "I'm sorry. I'm sorry that I thought anything less of you than almost-perfect. I'm sorry I was so greedy, self-centered, and selfish. I don't deserve you." I started bawling, and bawling hard. It truly was a wonder why this man would love me so much when I've given him nothing but hell. Sure we've had many good days, but the bad ones were generally instigated by me.

"Gem, stop." He said gently and lovingly as he wiped my tears away. "You are no more flawed than I am. My theory is that if there are things about you that bother me, I assume there are lots of things about me that bother you. Those negate each other."

"I feel like I messed up so badly. You don't treat me the same anymore."

"What do you mean?"

"There's a distance between us, an awkwardness that wasn't there in the past. You don't laugh as much with me, you're uncomfortable with me, and I feel like I have to be so cautious whenever I'm with you now. I can't spurt out my thoughts like I used to because I think you might dislike me even more." I don't know how I got that all out since I was crying so hard, I was doing all the crazy hiccupping, nose-running, face-a-mess business.

Max took off his night shirt and cleaned my face the best he could. "I'm sorry if you felt all that. I won't lie to you and tell you that our relationship hasn't shifted. But I still love you the same, and I'm working on being comfortable with myself."

"I don't understand. Do you mean you're working on being comfortable with me?"

"No, I mean exactly what I said. All last month, I've been trying to figure out where I went wrong. What did I lack? Why would my girlfriend want the attention of another man?"

I made all kinds of crazy noises as I cried even harder.

"Gem, I'm not trying to make you feel worse. I'm only being honest. I don't blame you for my shortcomings. Maybe I didn't pay enough attention to you. Perhaps I didn't do a good job of telling you how much I love you...I don't know. But after much thinking, I don't have any better answer as to how I'll hold onto you. If I seem moodier than usual, that's what's on my mind. It's my own insecurities. I'm *not* uncomfortable with you, I don't want there to be any awkwardness or distance between us, and you are always free to speak your mind with me. That's one of the complexities of Jane Reid I love most. Just give me a little time. We'll be better than before."

How, when I was the one who cheated on him, he found something to blame himself for, I couldn't tell you. The undisputed fact that reared its ugly head—I was the reason this near-perfect man felt insecure.

"You did nothing wrong. I take all the blame. I know if our roles were reversed, I wouldn't take you back. And there'd be a hell of a lot of bitterness and anger in my heart. I love you and I'm so very sorry for having stepped away from the security you built for us.

I've learned my lesson. Please don't put any blame on yourself. Let's work on making us stronger than the start."

"Agreed." Max's demeanor relaxed with his growing smile.

"Can I bring out the last elephant that's hiding on my nightstand?" I pointed to the birthday present that hadn't been addressed yet.

"That..." I had no idea what was coming next. "I seem to have a repulsion mechanism whenever I have a ring in my possession." He laughed on his own. "The first girl I attempted to give a ring to, turned it flat down. The second girl threw it back in my face. I possess more diamonds than any man my age." Now he was laughing even more. "Let's table this until we are both better prepared." I had no idea what that meant, and I was super disappointed, but I let it go.

"When will you be back? I have reservations for us for dinner."

"I don't think it'll go later than 3-4:00." He kissed me one last time and asked, "Are we good? Can I get in the shower and be ready before your brother kicks my ass for making him late to his own seminar?"

"We are good." And we really were. All this time of reconciling, and this was the first time I felt like the air was completely clear, the chalkboard was blank, the slate was clean!

The partners' meeting was an eye-opener for me and the partners. They all stared at me when I came into the meeting flanking Gimpy to the left, while Donovan flanked him to the right. There was no stupid man in that room. They all knew Gimpy was married to my grandmother and the cryptic writing was on the wall for everyone to surmise. I sat, listened, and kept my mouth shut the entire time.

"What'd'ya think?" Donovan whispered. While the meeting was done, there were still partners in the conference room speaking with the man who signed their checks.

"You partners get better lunches than we associates." He laughed and tousled my perfectly coiffed hair. "Hey. I worked hard to look like Alicia Florrick today." Donovan gave me his trademark *what the hell* look. "Good Wife?" After a brief while, he dismissed my entire statement.

"You look better than Alicia, whoever the hell she is. All is good with Max now?"

"All is freakin' good, now."

"What will you do concerning the firm?"

"Unsure...still need to talk with Gimpy."

Birthday dinner ended up a surprisingly larger affair than I originally planned. The two of us had a romantic dinner planned at my favorite, Le Bern, but something happened between the time Max left with Jake, and my lunch meeting with Donovan. This was the text I got right before the start of the meeting.

Can you add two more to our reservation?

Yes, I suppose. I'll call and ask. Who are the other two?

Your brother and the man sitting next to you right now.

Gimpy?

No. Maybe he's next to Roland.

DONOVAN???

BINGO. CUL8R. <3 U!

What the hell??? I died laughing from the last line of the text, and I looked over at Donovan and he gave me a *what the hell* look as well. I suppose I'd figure this out later.

"So I've kind of made a decision in my mind about what to do concerning this move. I'd love all your opinions," I addressed the three men at the table. "Max, I should probably talk to you about this first, but since Jake is here, I thought I'd bring it up and see where this leads. But, just know that your opinion weighs the most and I'm not demanding anything. I'm just throwing out what I've come up with after talking with Gimpy."

Before I go on with the rest of the dinner conversation, I should note that Jake didn't go back home tonight. His seminar was a standing-room only kind of success and the Q&A went so long, Emily convinced him to stay another night and come home the next day. Gimpy had a dinner meeting with the senior, senior partners so he didn't join us in this celebratory meal.

"Speak. We are all ears." My brother encouraged.

"I'd like to stay put in LA until you," I turned to Max so he'd know I was talking about him, "finish your last year of med school. It's not fair for me to uproot you during your last year."

"Babe, I don't mind." Max put his hand over mine and squeezed it at the dinner table.

"I know you don't. I love how selfless you are. Laney was right when she said you upped Jake in that category."

"What???" Jake brought down his glass of wine to address me. "I thought I was Laney's ideal man."

"Why the hell is Laney speaking so highly of either of you?" Donovan was even more irked than Jake.

My boyfriend's next statement was his payback to Donovan. "She only said that when I offered her my bike after she was devastated upon hearing you tell Kate to use her keys to your place. Do you remember that morning when you spent the night at Jake's house with Laney?"
"Yeah, I remember."

"You remember your conversation with Kate?"

"I think so..."

"You never saw Laney's beautiful face completely crestfallen during your conversation? But then again, I don't know anyone who could school his or her emotions as well as Laney. I'm not surprised you didn't see the hurt in her eyes."

"Fuck." Donovan sighed.

"I spoke with her, today."

"She called you?" Donovan and I simultaneously asked.

"She called to say hello, to wish me a happy birthday, and she sounded good. She sounded much better than the last time I spoke with her."

"When was that?" Donovan and I had the same question again.

Max kind of did a bit of backtracking in his mind and answered, "She emailed sometime right after her visit to LA to see JR and the email read like a river of tears so I called her to make sure she was all right."

*Damn, Shit, Fuck...*what other words can I use right now? *Freakin' hell!* I forgot about that almost kiss. *Damn it all to hell.* Do I tell Max about this one and go back to square negative 100? Or has Laney already squealed to Max and he's been waiting for me to confess? *Shit!* Were there any more sins committed by little ole me that needed confessing? I couldn't look Donovan's way and I was sure he felt just as guilty.

"What did Laney say when you talked to her after her LA visit?" I gingerly approached this subject.

"Not much. When I asked her what was wrong, she told me she was homesick and she also told me about Michael and her decision to date him."

My sigh of relief was internally deafening. Laney was a good person not to take revenge upon me for all my ill-will and for toying with Donovan.

"What did she say about Michael?" The normally confident Donovan Taylor was shrinking by the second. "What did she say to you today?"

"She was with Michael today when she called and I got a chance to converse with him. He told me he was taking her away to his grandfather's country home for a month. He was as psyched as any man would be, taking his girlfriend away for a month. He sounded like a good guy. In fact, I liked him immediately."

"I am so screwed." Donovan finished off his drink.

"You better get over there fast. He's taking her away on Wednesday."

"What's Wednesday?" Donovan asked.

"Her birthday." Now how my boyfriend knew this when I even forgot...he was truly a good man.

"Ahem," trying to break up the glum mood, I brought the attention back to my decision. "I'm staying in LA during the next year, but I'll be working in New York, a lot. But, Gimpy promised that the firm would send me back home every weekend to spend with you."

Max smiled and nodded, which made me think he approved.

"Sometime during the year, I'll know whether I am to go live in New York, or move to London. So, can you apply to residencies in both places?"

"Of course I can. For you, anything, my precious gem."

With dinner done, I figured it was time to go home and have another round of birthday fun, but that wasn't the case.

"Davis, can you stay away from my sister for an hour and come have a drink with us?"

Max looked to me for approval, of all things. I suggested, "By all means. It's your birthday. Go enjoy yourself."

And that's how I ended up alone, in bed, waiting for my boyfriend to come home from his men's night out. I still didn't get to ask him what had changed between him and Donovan, but I was just happy that all was perfect in my world right now.

August 12, 2013

Where is Platform Nine and Three-quaters?

My life has been absolutely crazy! I am writing to you from London as this very moment, enjoying my time with the Davis brothers, Jake, Emily and the three kids. Laney and Donovan have been all over this part of Europe and will be here any day now. I have so much to tell you. Let me try and go back to my few days in New York.

If you'll remember, we all got to New York very early Sunday morning and ended the trip with a nice dinner for my boyfriend's birthday in midtown on Monday. Donovan left for London on Tuesday and somehow, hijacked Laney to Amsterdam before she could go away with her boyfriend for a month. I don't know any of the details as they've been pretty much gone the entire time. We will see them here, very soon.

Max chose to use our birthday present from Donovan and booked us on a flight to London the day after Donovan left. He figured I could get a taste of the London office, he could help his brother get settled, and we could have a little vacation before our insane school and work schedule started up later this month.

Jake and Gimpy went home Tuesday morning, and by the end of the week, a plane full of Reids and Davises invaded Belgravia. Jake and Emily + three, Gimpy and Gram, Mom, Dad, Nick and Doug, and the two Davis brothers hopped on Gimpy's plane and are now here making life absolutely crazy in the flat.

Let me explain a few things about the plane and the flat. Gimpy does not own his own plane, not really. Think of it as a timeshare. He owns a fraction of the plane and shares it with a lot of other people. He gets so many hours, miles, days (not quite sure how it's settled) and he uses his allotment whenever he travels. This time, he transported so many people, he got his money's worth! And Gram's flat, which has been in her family forever, is no ordinary flat. It's massive! It has FOUR levels, and let me tell you—the twins are going nuts over the staircases. All day long, they go up and down the stairs and wear themselves out. What great exercise. Maybe I should join them. In any case, the house has six bedrooms, a couple of kitchens, and some big entertaining rooms on every floor.

Gram and Gimpy are in the master bedroom on the first floor. As Gram got older, she and my grandfather turned the ballroom on the main floor into a master bedroom. Jake's family take up the entire fourth floor. They created a new bedroom in the large ballroom as their own (which technically makes this a 7-bedroom flat), the twins are staying in one of the bedrooms, Jake has an office / study in the other bedroom, and the baby stays with Jake and Emily for now. Jake and Emily quickly added a bathroom and a closet to their room. Actually, once they decided to move, Gram called her peeps and had them take care of that before the family got there. Mom and Dad are right below them on the third floor. Uncle Henry and Aunt Babs live in the bedroom next to theirs, though Uncle Henry had to go right back home and back to the hospital. With so many of us here, Uncle Henry would be back here in no time.

Nick, Doug, Josh, Garret and Max all share the second floor ballroom as their bedroom. Basically, they all got air mattresses and a rolling rack and are calling this big room a bedroom. Laney was already on the second floor, so I just moved myself into her life for the short time I'd be here. I didn't think she'd mind. Luckily, there are two bathrooms up on the second floor. What will be comical is where Donovan planned to stay. Technically, his qwaters (I know, I know...my English accent is bad) are near the Square Mile, in the financial district. This isn't that far from Belgravia, but it's not exactly walking distance. We are all wondering whether he will stay in the comforts of a high-end company apartment, or slum it with the other five single guys and buy himself an air mattress. He'll probably need three rolling racks for all the clothes he has. We turned the ballroom on the third floor into an entertainment room and put a tele, some random couches gathered from around the house, along with the billiard table and grand piano that already existed in the room.

Though the house was crazy, within a month's time, most of us would be gone, and I figured it may seem almost empty once we leave. Before Laney left for Amsterdam, she was here to see construction on the fourth floor begin, but when she gets home, she will be in for the shock of her life. Laughter spilled out of my mouth.

"Whatcha laughing about, Gem?"

"The fact that Laney left LA to get away from all of us and voila... here we all are!"

"I don't think she left to get away from everyone...just one."

"She really liked him that much?" Now I felt bad. When Laney got back, it was time for a heart-to-heart.

Max shrugged his shoulders. "Ask her."

Fast forward a few days, we all settled into our space and Max stayed in my room and would go back to the frat house next door when Laney returned. Our gang of six went sightseeing and pubbing (is that a word?) every day. Of course, I went into the office, but since I wasn't full time at this office, yet, there wasn't much for me to do.

"Babe," Max said while we were lounging around after I came back from work. "How about we give Em a break and take the twins out? She looks exhausted from the move, from trying to settle down in the new home, and Jake hasn't been around as much as usual because he's trying to get settled with the new hospitals and schools."

"Sure!" I agreed. "Where should we go and what should we do with the little buggers?"

"I saw a great toy store the other day not too far from here. I believe both carseats have been installed, so why don't we take the kids out for a ride in the car?"

"Ellie, James?" They were once again going up and down four flights of steps. It was a wonder that neither had broken any bones nor bruised themselves yet. "You want to go out with Auntie Jane and Uncle Max?"

They thought about it for a little bit, they looked at each other, and then they nodded yes. These two were a laugh-and-a-half. It's not as though they fully understood what I said. I didn't know why they looked at each other, and what silent communication happened in the split second before looking at one another and nodding yes. Who understood this world of twins?

Max got permission from Emily for us to take them out and we strapped them into their carseats and proceed a couple miles to the world of Hamleys. The kids were in awe from the moment we stepped into this marvelous store. James and Ellie were both pointing at every toy that caught their fancy, and each sound that made their heads turn.

James wanted to get down to a magnetic board that held these spinning cogs. They were called Clever Cogs and five different-sized cogs moved in various ways and made unique sounds without breaking apart. At first, James and Ellie stood behind the older children and watched in wonder. Soon, I saw both kids inching closer to the board to touch the cogs and to move them around in different formations as they saw the other kids doing. Quite a few kids bumped one another to get closer. The twins were the youngest ones there so I was about to jump in and pull them out of the fray when Max stopped me.

"Let's see what happens. I don't think James and Ellie are in any danger."

As soon as Max finished his words, the twins methodically pushed their way to the front of the board, with James leading, holding his sister's hand, and soon they were front and center. I cringed when I saw them touching the cogs that had been touched by so many little booger hands. As soon as they were done looking, I'd have to take them to the restroom, wash their hands, then sanitize them again! They were having a fantastic time playing with the cogs but I just couldn't stand the possibility of them getting hurt by the older kids, and also the possibility of them contracting the staph disease with so many germs in this toy store.

Using my own bit of cleverness, I picked up two boxes of cogs and a magnetic white board and lured the twins with the promise of their own set. After thoroughly cleaning their hands, Max and I bought them a few other items and put them back in their car seats.

"That was fun!" I exclaimed looking back at my beautiful niece and nephew. They were itching to tear open the box that contained the cogs.

"That was fun." He agreed.

"Today I think I kind of understood the joy Emily gets from being with her kids, everyday. I won't experience that kind of joy if I work all the time, huh? If I'm on this track to partnership and I become part owner of the firm, when will I have babies, let alone get a chance to play with them and watch them at a toy store?"

It was unfair that being a woman, I had to choose between staying home and watching my kids grow up, and working. And if I married Max, it wouldn't be kosher to ask a medically trained man to stay home. But, then why was it kosher to ask the woman to stay home? Why couldn't the man sacrifice?

"It was beautiful watching you with the babies, Gem." That made me feel so good! If the twins weren't in the car, I'd make Max pull over and give him a kiss or two. "You're an accomplished woman and a clever one as well. When we get to that stage in our life, we will figure something out."

"But what choices are there for a woman? Either I stay home, the kids get a nanny, or go to daycare all day while we work."

"There are tons of options if you're willing to be flexible."

"Such as...?"

"Maybe while the kids are young, you can do a four-day week and I can do a four-day week. Then there's your mom and dad who'd be willing to help out a day, and my parents who would love to do the same, and that last day...a babysitter? Until they are of school age, we can both work a little less and stay home more with the kids, if that's what you want. We don't need the money. Between the both of us, we will live fine."

I guess there were options out there I'd never thought about, since kids were never on my radar.

"You think we'll be able to handle you as a doctor, me as a lawyer, and still have a few beautiful children?"

"If they look like you, they will be beyond beautiful, Gem!"

We took two sleeping kids up to their beds and decided to have a little bed time of our own. Max and Jane were definitely back and stronger than before.

August 15, 2013

Rolling Hills of Tuscany

"Gem," a sexy someone whispered in my ears while it was still dark outside. "Get up. We have to go."

"Where are we going at this hour?"

"Surprise, my beauty. Now get up," he slapped my ass and got me up at the crack of dawn.

We got to Gatwick Airport with a small overnight bag Max had packed without my knowledge, and flew into Florence. He kept mum about today's plans and all I heard was that we were staying at Gimpy's villa in Florence.

"It's so great to have family members who have homes everywhere."

"It sure is, Gem. As soon as we drop off our stuff, we're headed to the Uffizi Museum, the Accademia Gallery, lunch somewhere in between, then to a surprise in the evening."

"What's the surprise?"

"I can't tell you, my precious Gem. If I did, it wouldn't be a surprise."

We did all Max promised and stayed a bit longer at the Accademia, staring at the statue of David.

"David is almost as anatomically perfect as my own man," I said while goosing him.

"Keep that up naughty girl and you will not be receiving your surprise tonight."

"Is it still considered a surprise if I know what's happening?" This time I grabbed him full-on rather than a childish goosing. "There's no element of surprise when something happens in the dark between you and me."

"Keep talking like that, young lady. You're going to have to get a spanking after I give you your surprise."

I turned around and faced him, put both my hands on his butt cheeks and brought him right close to me. "We're never going to finish this museum if *you* keep talking like that."

"We have to finish. We are meeting some friends for an early dinner."

"But we just had lunch."

"Are you done staring at David's penis?"

"Oh, I suppose..." I pretended to be exasperated with Max as he held out his hand for me to follow along.

"Random question..."

"Hopefully not a random answer..." he said and gave me a kiss.

"Do you think I'll run into Laney sometime soon? We're headed back in a few days and I'd really like to talk to her."

"Yeah? About what?"

"About Donovan." Max didn't flinch when I brought up the D word. In fact, he was perfectly fine with me talking about him. "I need to apologize to Laney and set things right with her."

Max didn't ask but I knew he was curious as to what our conversation would entail. I wanted to tell him everything. I had nothing to hide, and I was comfortable with him knowing what was in my mind and heart.

"I don't think Laney is expecting anything from you."

"Even if she isn't, I've a lot to say." We exited the museum and Max led me to what I assumed was our dinner location. "Laney and I've never really gotten along and most of that was because of me. Being almost five years older, Laney was always at an age where she bugged me. She was not quite old enough to be my friend, and not quite young enough for me to find her a 'cute little girl.' And the fact that she didn't adore me and look up to me like my other girl cousins, bugged me as well. Something about her blonde hair, blue-eyed look made her look like a follower, but she was always a leader in her own right. I think what irritated me the most was that she marched to the beat of her own drums, rather than mine."

"Were you a mean cousin to her?" He asked in a kidding-way and kissed the hand that he was holding. "Did you lock her up in a dark closet somewhere when no one was looking?"

"Nothing like that, but I don't think I've ever really said a kind word to her whether verbally or mentally. In many ways, I envied her individuality, and the fact that she was brave enough to march to the beat of her own drums and not care what others thought. I also never liked the attention Donovan bestowed upon her."

"Aha! Now, we get to the crux of the matter." He was still kidding. If I still had doubts about Max, me and Donovan (which I didn't), it was completely obliterated with this conversation!

"Donovan always liked Laney."

"He perved on her...as a child?"

"No, silly!" We both laughed. "Being Jake's best friend and Kelley's younger brother, Donovan came over all the time. I think he met Laney for the first time when she was in fourth or fifth grade and I can still remember how sweet he was to her. Laney was beautiful as a young girl..."

"...and as a grown woman..." Max added to my (slight) irritation.

"And between her looks and her precocious nature, Donovan was taken by her—of course not in any weird, child predator-like way."

"Uh-huh..." Max wasn't convinced.

"I can still remember getting pissed every time he spoke to her or played with her in the pool, rather than showering me with attention."

"Gem, I've no doubt you forced his attention back to you. I can see where our little Ellie gets it from—it's definitely a Reid trait." He laughed.

"Anyway...that's all old news, but I do need to make sure we're okay, and I'd like for us to be friends. If she's good friends with Emily, and I'm good friends with Emily, there's no reason why she and I can't be good friends."

"I like the attitude, Gem."

"Plus, I need to help Donovan. He's done everything he could to help me. I'd like to return the favor."

"Well, here's your chance."

Max walked us into a restaurant where Jake, Emily, JR, Laney and Donovan were holding court in the middle of the room.

"What are you all doing here?" I was so happy to see my family!

"Well, hello to you too, little sis."

I went around the table and hugged Jake and Emily, kissed my newest nephew, gave Laney a warm, longer than usual hug, then slapped Donovan on the back as a greeting. Most likely no one (not even Max) would object if I hugged Donovan like the rest of the family, but I wasn't sure what his status was with Laney, and I wanted to err on the cautious side.

"What are we all doing in Florence in the middle of the week, and where are James and Ellie?"

My brother spoke. "It's a surprise what we are doing tonight. And our older babies are still in London having the time of their lives with Uncle Nick and Uncle Doug. I just spoke to Gram and I could hear their cackles over the English Channel. We are only here for the night. The three of us will be heading back in the morning."

"Excuse me," I heard Laney say when her phone rang. She walked outside to answer the call.

"How goes it?" I asked.

"Damn, you Reid women are a difficult lot! It goes well on some days, and not well at all on other days."

"You're so damn cryptic all the time. Details, Donovan."

"You don't want to know. I've never worked so hard for anything. Law school, the Bar exam, life—all a breeze compared to winning over one woman." Donovan rolled his eyes, but he looked happy.

Laney walked back in looking unhappy, and rattled.

"You all right?" Donovan was the first to address all our concern.

Laney just shook her head no and took an extra large gulp of her water. "May I hold JR? I haven't seen him since he was born. He's grown so much." The baby exchange was done and Laney ignored the rest of us while she played with the baby. "When I first met him, I thought he looked like James. Now I think he looks more like Ellie. He's so beautiful, Emily." She spoke to Emily, but cooed to the baby. With a baby in her arms, Laney was in her element and none of us missed the look of adoration on Donovan's face.

Dinner was a lively affair with all of us talking about our time in Europe. Donovan and Laney had done the most so far, but they'd also been here a bit longer than the rest of us.

"Are you really working for the firm in all these exotic places, or is this just an extended vacation, compliments of the firm?"

Donovan put his finger on his lips signaling me to keep my mouth shut. "Don't tell anyone, especially not Roland." He said it in such a serious tone, but we all laughed at his joke.

"Laney," an unfamiliar voice called. "Duchess!" *Uh-oh!* I knew who this English accent belonged to and by the frozen look on Laney's face, this was not going to be a fun evening. Though...it was just a slight bit-o-fun for those of us who were spectating. Hey, I may have turned a new leaf, but I was still human. Drama is fun, entertaining, addictive—as long as it ain't my drama!

Laney got up with JR in her arms and Donovan got up with her. *Oooh!* He was making his stand, marking his territory, not letting anyone take away his woman. This was better than any drama I'd ever watched.

"I need to talk to Michael. This has gone on too far. Let me go, Donovan."

Damn! My cousin could bark when called for, though it didn't make Donovan happy.

"You'll come right back here after you talk to him?"

"Yes. I won't let Michael drag me away to some foreign country like some people I know," she let out a weak smile. This was just enough for Donovan to feel reassured and to sit back down while Laney walked over to Michael.

Michael met her half way and grabbed her in his arms and hugged the breath out of her. Max, who was sitting at the end of the table got up and held Donovan back before he beat the shit out of Michael.

"Give her time to work it out. She'll come back to you if you're meant to have her." Can you believe this was MAX giving relationship advice to DONOVAN? Hell must have frozen over because now I'd seen everything! Max was counseling Donovan in matters of love.

"Can you guarantee me that she'll be back?"

"No, but I can tell you karma is a bitch and what goes around comes around." Our entire table busted up laughing with Max as its leader. That actually brought out a disgruntled smile from Donovan as well.

The four of us continued our conversation on what we wanted to do while we were still in Europe, while Donovan kept his eye peered to the door.

"Delaney," he stood up and walked over to a very unhappy girl. She actually looked like she had been crying. I wish I could console her and tell her everything would be okay like it was with me and Max, but I couldn't because I had no assurance everything would be okay for her.

Donovan brought her back to our table with his hand somewhere on her the whole time and she didn't say much to any of us.

Emily asked, "Are you all right? How can I help you, Laney?"

"I'll be okay," she said wiping off the last of the tears that were dripping from her eyes.

"And Michael?" Emily left that question wide-open.

"He left."

"How did he know where you were?" I think my brother asked that purposely to alleviate his best friend's curiosity more than anything else.

"I had let Michael know daily where I would be and he called me earlier today asking exactly where I was. So I told him, not realizing that he was really coming here for me."

Poor Michael. Or was it poor Donovan?

We could all tell Donovan was unhappy, but he tried hard not to let it show. He was actually being sensitive towards Laney's feelings.

"If we are all done eating, I think we have a bus to catch," Jake said and got us out of the restaurant. Laney and Donovan trailed behind us whispering to one another. I was curious to know what was going on over there, but my knowing boyfriend pulled me along so I wouldn't eavesdrop.

"Leave them be, nosy Jane." Max warned.

"I'm not being nosy." I defended myself. "I'm just trying to help. I have both their best interests at heart."

Max abruptly put both his hands on my cheek and kissed me. In the middle of a laugh he said, "I love you, Gem."

Well, I loved him too! I was all smiles after that kiss.

The bus was filled with a horde of very excited Italian people ranging from my age, all the way up to Gram's age. They all spoke in a flurry of Italian so we had no idea what was going on. Emily and I tried to figure out where we were going, but Laney sat against the window staring out looking like she had lost her best friend. I saw Donovan put his hand on her hand and he held it the best he could with her not being compliant.

We were all dropped off near the city of Pisa, and in the middle of nowhere. There was a large stage, thousands of chairs—well maybe not thousands, but hundreds of chairs set up and obviously, we were watching a concert.

Emily gasped, turned to her husband and said, "Is this what I think it's going to be?"

"It is, Love. Happy anniversary. I'm a little late, but I thought this would make up for my tardiness."

"What's going on, Emily?" I asked in eagerness.

"I believe your wonderful brother is crossing off another item on my bucket list and we are about to watch an Andrea Bocelli concert in the middle of Tuscany!"

Hot Damn! I loved my brother!

"This is so romantic!" I squeezed my boyfriend's hand in excitement.

"Yeah," Max chuckled. "I think your brother invented the word *romantic.*"

"What a fantastic surprise! Isn't this great, Laney?" I turned to my cousin and attempted to infuse some of my enthusiasm into her.

"It is," she answered back with a little more eagerness than I saw on the bus. Donovan once again tried to hold her hand, but I saw her ball up her right hand and continually twist it out of Donovan's hand. He had no reservations about showing his disappointment at his dismal result of wooing Laney. To add salt to the wound, Laney walked over to Emily and offered to hold JR for an indefinite amount of time.

"She's not giving you an inch is she?" Max asked with an evil smirk on his face.

"Shit. She's not even giving me a millimeter." Donovan shook his head in disbelief.

"Karma I tell you..." Max announced loudly, and walked ahead and started chatting it up with Laney.

"What are you going to do now?" I asked Donovan

"Who the hell knows? Are relationships normally supposed to be this difficult?"

"I think good, long-lasting ones are."

The concert started and even Laney, who was originally in a glum mood, was mesmerized as soon as Andrea Bocelli started singing. The world's favorite tenor crooned love song after love song after love song and in Italian, to boot. Emily's body leaned into Jake's with their baby in the center, I was tempted to sit on Max's lap because I was in such the mood, and even Laney softened and slightly turned her body into Donovan when he put his arm around her chair.

"Andrea Bocelli is putting me in a really good mood right now," I whispered to my boyfriend suggestively.

"Are there any other moods for you, but good ones?"

"If it wasn't for the fact that there were hundreds of people here I might've pulled you behind a tree and had my way with you." I said and quickly sucked on his earlobe.

"Hold that thought my precious gem. We still have another half a show to go before we can see any action."

During intermission we left JR with Jake and the three of us went to the restroom while Donovan and Max went and picked up some refreshments.

Before the show began, an American emcee, or at least a gentleman who spoke perfect English, started talking to us about the origins of the songs and he got into a whole discussion on romance and relationships. He walked around the audience and asked questions about people's relationships—such as how long they'd been married, whether or not this was a date, and what they thought about romance in general. We weren't far from the stage so I was getting a bit freaked out when this guy kept coming closer and closer to us. I did not need the world to know what my thoughts were on relationship and romance.

"Buonasera, Sir," the emcee spoke to Jake. I was so glad Jake would be our spokesperson.

"Buonasera," Jake replied.

"I see you are here with a beautiful woman whom I assume is your wife, and your baby."

"Yes this gorgeous woman is my wife, and yes we are here as a family."

"Tell us what brings you here, and tell us a little bit about your relationship and any romantic stories you might have had during your courtship."

Man, did this guy hit the jackpot. My brother could spend the rest of the evening telling the audience about his courtship.

"When my wife and I were dating, I asked her to make a bucket list of all the things she wanted to do, and hearing Andrea Bocelli in Italy was one of them. It was our anniversary about six weeks ago, and she had just had a baby, so with this concert I am able to give her an anniversary present and cross off one of her bucket list items."

The crowd loved it. They all clapped for my brother.

"That's a beautiful story. Did you date very long?"

"No. I think we dated maybe seven months, and five out of the seven months she was in another part of the world from me."

"Why were you separated?" Now the man turned towards Emily and put the mic in front of her for an answer.

"Um...well..." Emily stuttered for an answer. "We kind of had a disagreement and I thought it best I leave."

"What happened?" I could see that the emcee would not leave Emily alone. I was all good with the story until now, since Max could be dragged into this scenario. I could see where this was headed and it wasn't headed in the right direction.

Jake covered Emily's bumbling explanation with, "her ex-boyfriend proposed marriage to my wife, my girlfriend at the time, and that's what caused our break-up." Jake not only chuckled at Emily's, Max's, and my discomfort, but he also threw my boyfriend a *karma's a bitch* look.

"That's quite a story." This damn emcee wouldn't leave. "But what I really want to know is why you looked over to this gentleman over here when you said those words. What does this gentleman have to do with your separation?" Now the emcee was just playing coy knowing he was about to go for a kill. "If I were a betting man, and trust me I'm a betting man, I'd say this guy," he pointed over to Max, "is the infamous ex-boyfriend who proposed to a girl who already had a boyfriend."

The audience gasped with Jake's comment, then roared with the emcee's comment.

"Did I win the bet?"

With full admission of his guilt, Max held up both hands, as charged.

"So obviously everything worked out well for you two, seeing as how you have a baby together and I assume this is *your* baby?" He look piercingly at my brother, while the audience roared again.

"He sure is mine, and we have a set of twins as well."

"How old are the twins? And where are they tonight?"

"The twins are sixteen months old," all the women in the state stadium gasped in horror. "And they are with my family right now."

"You don't waste time do you?" All the gentlemen around gave my brother a round of applause.

What I forgot to mention was that some time ago, this conversation became so interesting a female interpreter started following the emcee and relaying my brother's story in Italian to those people who did not speak English. We could tell it was time for the concert to begin, but the emcee would not let go of our story.

"Let's get back to this love triangle. Who are you?" He pointed at me.

"I'm Jane," was all I was going to answer. Shoot, I wasn't a lawyer for nothing.

"What are you doing here, why are you holding this man's hand, and how are you related to everybody here? Or are you related to anybody here?"

Damn. I forgot that we were holding hands. I guess I had to give the audience an answer. "My name is Jane. I am his sister," I pointed to my brother, "and his girlfriend," I pointed to Max.

"Oh! Mio! Dio! Ava Maria! Madonna!" He called anybody and everybody in the spiritual realm. That needed no Italian or English translation. The audience loved it. And they wanted more.

Comically, Andrea Bocelli actually had to cough to get everyone's attention back to him. "Gino," he said in his beautiful Italian accent. "I'm ready to continue. You going to let me sing?"

"Andrea, uno minuti. Let's finish sharing this story, because I think there's more to uncover."

Mr. Bocelli put up his hand and nodded his consent. The audience clapped in appreciation.

"So you," he pointed at Max, "tried to steal his," he pointed at Jake, "girlfriend, and now you're dating his," he pointed at Jake again, "sister? Did I get the story straight?"

Max and Jake both chuckled. "Yes, you got the story right." Max agreed.

"And you are okay with this?"

Jake spoke again. "Emily and I are more than okay with the two of them dating. In fact, we would welcome Max into the family if they chose to go that route." Jake once again got a round of applause.

The emcee wasn't done. "Now for you," he pointed back and forth between Donovan and Laney. "Now if I was a betting man, and trust me I'm a betting man," he said again, "I am going to bet that you two have an interesting story as well, and it's somehow related to the four of them." He pointed his fingers back and forth to us.

Jake and Max busted up laughing again. Neither Donovan nor Laney would say a word.

The emcee and the audience alike got impatient. "Okay if you don't want to talk then I'm gonna talk to somebody who will talk. Who are they?" he asked the four of us.

Jake spoke. "That's our cousin Laney, and the man next to her is my best friend, Donovan."

"Hmmmm..." He made a most nefarious *hmmm* and tried to figure out their relationship.

"Laney?"

She looked at him and the camera panned in on my cousin. Seeing her larger than life on the jumbo screen, I could see why so many men were attracted to her. She was one beautiful woman.

"At some point in your life, did you date him?" He pointed to Max and the audience roared at our expense.

She shook her head no.

"There's got to be some connection here. Did you," he asked Emily "date your husband's best friend?"
Emily broke into laughter, and shook her head no.

"Then the only other possibility is..." Shit! By the glint in his eyes, I'd say he figured us out. "You and you dated at some point." His finger waggled between me and Donovan.

Both of us kept mum.

"Aha!!! I knew it." Mr. Emcee jumped up and down in glee. "You all have quite an incestuous relationship going on. Did you know or did we just out these two?" He asked Max.

"I knew," Max said in an exasperated tone.

"Now did you date Jane while you were with Laney?"

"No." Donovan denied. "And we didn't really date. It was one date while both of us were technically single."

"Technically single..." He dragged out those two words. "Is that correct, Laney? Was he not a part of your life when he dated your cousin? You know, the camera zoomed in on your face when it was mentioned that the man you're standing next to dated your cousin..."

Donovan pulled the mic and clearly stated, "only one date!"

The emcee took the mic back. "...as I was saying, you looked shocked and hurt when you heard about these two. We all want to know what you're thinking. You're the only one who hasn't weighed in on this soap opera."

With hundreds of people expecting an answer and the camera zeroed in on her every move, she didn't have much of a choice.

"I just broke up with a good man who told me once that he started living the moment we met, for a man I've been in love with since I was ten, only to find out that he recently dated my cousin while pursuing me. Yeah...I'd say I'm shocked and hurt." Her voice broke and the heart of every woman in the rolling hills of Tuscany cracked in pieces.

Talk about shocked. She shocked the hell out of all of us with that revelation and she walked off, away from us and away from the limelight. Donovan of course chased after her. He was in for a hell of a night.

"Oh my gosh. Did you know all this?" I asked Max, Emily and Jake. "She's crushed on Donovan since she was ten?"

No one answered me as the lights dimmed and the musicians began lightly playing.

"Gino, do I have your permission to sing, again?" Mr. Bocelli asked and the audience chuckled.

"That all depends upon this one big happy family. You have anything else to add?"

"If I may, Mr. Bocelli?" Surprisingly, it was my boyfriend and not my brother who spoke up.

"Please..." He gestured. "Be my guest. I'm only here to put on a concert. Who am I to interrupt your family saga?" The audience laughed, again.

"What never got mentioned during this big reveal is how much we three men love our women."

"Well, please, enlighten us. How much do you love your woman?" Andrea Bocelli asked. The spotlight was on just us as Max began to elaborate.

"Jane and I have always had a passionate relationship. We are mad with love one day, mad with anger another day, but I've always known that I couldn't live without this woman. I think you and Elvis were singing what was in my heart when you said, '*Like a river flows surely to the sea, darling so it goes, some things are meant to be, take my hand, take my whole life too, for I can't help falling in love with you.*'" Max turned and addressed me and only me with the spotlight, the camera, and thousands of eyes solely on us. I began shaking when I saw him get on one knee. "My precious Gem. I love you and I can't live without you. Will you do me the honor of becoming one with me? Will you marry me?"

"Yes," I whispered without hesitation.

I couldn't exactly tell you what was going on with the audience because Max and I were lost in each other once the ring was placed on my fourth finger. We were both in a daze the rest of the concert. Only later when Emily recounted the congratulations from Andrea Bocelli and the rest of the audience did I remember bits and pieces of the rest of the night.

"Congratulations!" Donovan and Laney, who had come back after they saw Max's proposal on the big screen greeted us with sincerity and love. "I'm very happy for you," Laney said to the both of us.

Max walked over and gave her a hug and spoke a few words with her. I hoped he was comforting her as well as encouraging her to fall in love again with Donovan.

"Congrats, my vixen. You and Max are perfect together and I'm sorry I didn't realize that from the start."

"Thanks, Donovan. I wish the same happiness for you and Laney. No matter how long it takes, you'll get there."

"I hope so." He didn't sound as deflated as I thought he might. "We had a good talk. I'm hoping to see the light at the end of this very long and dark tunnel, soon."

"You will."

The rest of the night was a blur. I was sure we got on the bus, we got back to the villa, and Max and I celebrated very quietly since Jake and Emily were in the very next room to us. I wasn't quite sure what happened to Donovan and Laney but I knew they, too, were somewhere here in the villa.

Mr. and Mrs. Max Davis. Jane Sydney Davis. Mrs. Davis. It all sounded good!

August 19, 2013

We Are Family

I woke up in the middle of the night psyched from last night's excitement. Even in the dark, I stared at the diamond on my ring finger and smiled endlessly like a moron. I was in such bliss while my boyfriend, no...fiancé, was knocked out. We'd made love, talked, made love again, then fell asleep. Rather than nudging Max awake to an extra early morning romp, I put on my robe and went downstairs for a glass of water.

"Hey." I had interrupted Donovan and Laney as they were having a drink at the kitchen table. "You guys haven't gone to bed yet?"

"Not yet. We've been talking." Donovan confessed with a wide smile. All must have gone well during the talk because he was only smiles now. "Though it is late. You want to head up to bed?" I assumed he meant to separate beds since I didn't think these two were together, yet.

"Any chance I could talk to Laney for a bit?"

"She's tired, Jane."

"I know, Donovan," I answered in the same pedantic voice. "I won't keep her long. But I'd like for you to leave."

He looked over at Laney and got up slowly from his seat. "Come see me before you go to bed?" He walked over and kissed her on her temple and squeezed her arm. She just nodded an agreement.

"Everything copacetic between you two?"

"Not wholly yet, but we're getting there. We both have a lot to work through and Donovan has a past that keeps creeping up on him."

"About Donovan's past...I've been waiting for you to come back to London so we could talk. I'm glad we got to meet up before I went back home. I've got a lot of apologizing to do."

"You don't have to apologize to me. As long as you and Max have worked out your relationship, I'm happy for you. Max is up there with Jake in my eyes. He's perfect for you."

"And Donovan is perfect for you." I could tell Laney didn't fully believe this statement. "I've always been jealous of you, ever since we were young."

Laney's eyes almost popped out of their sockets. "Why would you be jealous of *me*? You're the smart one, the beautiful one, everyone's favorite—well, after Jake of course..."

"Of course! No one could beat my brother in that category."

"I've never harbored any ill will against you—well, maybe I did a little when I saw you and Donovan kissing—but I've always believed you had everything going for you. Your personality commanded attention, while people thought mine was 'unique.' Your looks are exotic, while mine are everyday Americana. You oozed intelligence, while I always got the dumb blonde looks. What on earth would make you jealous of me?"

Laney really had no clue all that she had going for her. And I guess that's what people loved about her. She was an understated overachiever. "Laney, you graduated summa cum laude, got into med school and film school, men adore you at every turn, and I don't know anyone who didn't think you had an adorable personality. Aside from all that, what I always admired and envied about you was your independent spirit. Whatever you want to do, learn, experience—you go for it. Students generally don't leave the comforts of a very comfortable home just because they want to experience a new culture. Students also don't take classes in both spectrums of the major, just because they like it. You're unconventional and that makes you unique."

"I think odd is a more fitting term." We both giggled. "It's not like you couldn't have done all that."

"But I didn't. I found safety in the conventional." I put my hand over hers and held it, hoping to convey my sincerity. "What makes you truly special is your unconditional love for everyone around you. Even in a difficult situation, you find the good in everybody. And I'm sure that's one of the reasons why Donovan is head over heels in love with you. When I think back, he's always given you more attention than the rest of us—and that was another source of envy for me."

"Donovan..." Laney chuckled. "Perhaps he's the root of all evil." She laughed some more.

"He's not and he loves you. I'm sorry I was selfish all this time. It bothered me whenever I thought he had feelings for you and that selfishness almost cost me my relationship with Max." I sighed heavily. "I was stupid—beyond stupid. I wanted to be the center of everyone's world, rather than enjoying my relationship with Max. You believe me when I say Donovan and I were really never anything more than friends?"

"I believe I do. Donovan explained it all to me and I'm not upset with you. I still have some unresolved issues with Donovan's selfishness, but I meant it when I said I wish you and Max only the best."

Laney looked over at my ring and I held out my hand to give her a better look. "Thank you for understanding, and I wish you and Donovan this kind of happiness as well."

She gave me a true hug and got up to go to bed. "I appreciate the talk and let me know if I can help you in any way when you prepare for your wedding. I'm sure my mom and yours will be thrilled with the news."

"Can we try and be close friends, starting today?" I asked cautiously.

"Of course. I'm going to go up and sleep a bit. I'll see you in a few hours."

"Goodnight."

Walking back up to my room, I thought that went well. Finally, I was on the right track with Laney. And knowing my cousin, we'd be good friends in no time because I didn't think she held grudges—though Donovan may differ in opinion.

"Good morning," I woke up my fiancé with my mouth.

"If this is my wake-up call every morning," he said while pulling me up to him in bed, "I think I'm going to like being married to you."

"Are we really getting married? We're almost at the Jake and Emily stage?"

Max laughed. "Babe. We're there already. No more unnecessary battles, lest I tie you to a bed until we resolve everything."

"With a promise like that, you're asking for unnecessary battles."

"What are you doing up so early? I could've sworn we just got to bed."

"I couldn't sleep with this heavy rock on my finger."

Max grinned his beautiful grin. "You approve? It's a third of a diamond to what your sister-in-law has. That doesn't bring out the gem in you?"

"No, silly. I'm not a jewelry person."

"Neither is Em. I had to purposely get a diamond twice the size as Em's because I knew you wouldn't be happy unless you upped my ex-girlfriend."

By the look on his face, he wasn't kidding. I started busting up. "Damn. You know me so well. There's no hiding anything from you. You have my number." I got up and started getting dressed.

"Why are you getting dressed at this hour?"

"I saw this little bakery around the corner from us. I'm going to go and get us all some fresh baked goods for breakfast." I threw his shirt and pants and said, "You could join me in this early morning walk."

"Do I have a choice?"

"Fiancé, you always have choices."

"Shit. I know that tone. I'll get up." He slapped my ass on the way to the restroom and we quietly went out for an earlier than necessary walk.

"Can I ask you something?"

"Anything, Fiancée."

"What happened to the engagement ring you gave Emily?"

Max answered, "I gave it to our godson on the day of his christening."

Whoa! I didn't expect that answer. This man found more and more ways to surprise me every day.

"What made you give it to JR?"

"Well, I couldn't exactly recycle it, lest you cut off my balls and mash them up for good measure."

That earned him a punch in the arm. Of course that earned me a make-out session in the middle of an empty street in Florence. I loved this man!

"So okay...I admit. I wouldn't have been too happy had you given me Emily's ring..."

"You wouldn't have been too happy??? That would have been cause for a divorce even before we got married!" He held onto my hands before I punched him again. "I had no damn clue what to do with Emily's diamond. She had no need for it and Jake would have seriously maimed me had I given his woman any piece of jewelry. I couldn't turn it into anything else since I knew you'd do worse and castrate me if I gave it to you as a gift. I thought about giving it to our gorgeous niece, Ellie, but somehow I knew she'd end up with more diamonds than her mother one day. So, after much thought, I realized that diamond would be the perfect gift for JR. He can do whatever he likes with it, so this six-week old is now the proud owner of an engagement ring."

"That was brilliant. I'm glad you thought of that and I feel like that diamond has come full circle now. I assume Jake had no objection to you giving it to JR?"

"As long as it doesn't get on Emily's finger, he could care less."

"We're going to have to outdo Donovan and Laney as godparents. We only have one whereas they have two. I'm going to show them."

"My sweet Jane." Max kissed me some more on the empty street. "I don't think you or I will be able to do anything for JR that we don't do for the twins. I love those three equally. I just need to be careful that I don't favor that little girl who reminds me so much of my gorgeous fiancée. She's a hard one to ignore, ever."

"You're right. You think we'll love our kids even more than those kids? I can't imagine."

"Knowing our kids are a product of love between you and me, I may love them even more than I love you," he answered with a cute smile.

"I think I'd be okay with that." I smiled back. "So when shall we get married and when do we produce kids?"

"That's up to you, Gem."

"How about we get married as soon as you're done with school, and as for kids..." I had to think about that for a bit. "As much as I'd like to pop them out right now, I don't want to have them if we're away from family. We're both young. Can we have them after you finish residency and I find stability in the firm?"

"We can do it whichever way you like. We'll just have to do a lot of practice so we can produce the perfect child from our union."

"Sounds perfect to me."

"Let's hurry with breakfast and get home. We have many phone calls to make."

"Yes. We need to spread the good news!"

August 22, 2013

A Ducati Man!

ax and I are stateside now and Max started his last year of med school, today. After our engagement in Florence, Jake, Emily, and JR went back to London, Laney, who was originally going to go back to London with them had a change of heart and decided to stay with Donovan while he was "working." The four of us traveled to Rome and while Donovan was "working," Max, Laney and I helped Josh settle into his new home.

Josh leased out a teeny, tiny apartment in the posh district of Via Condotti. His apartment was so small, there was just enough space for a twin size bed, and his art supply. Good thing he didn't have Donovan's wardrobe. He'd never make it in this matchbox-sized place. It was great to see Josh settled and it was even better to see the friendship between Josh and Laney. I know I was once their champion, but Laney convinced Josh that they'd be better off as good friends, and somewhere along the way, Josh accepted it. I liked that he had Laney nearby for support. Nick, Doug and Garret left for home as soon as Jake and Emily got back to the twins.

Max and I'd miss the babies while they were in London. I may have chances to pop into London from time to time, but Max was grounded in LA until his studies were done this year. Lucky for us, Uncle Henry, Jake, and my father all offered to help Max find a residency program wherever I would be stationed after this year. Secretly, I hoped I'd be in New York. That was midpoint to home and to my brother's family in London. Max won't give an opinion, but I know he feels the same way.

"There's a package here for you," my cubicle mate said to me, handing me a DHL envelope.

The contents of the package made me crack-up as I picked up my phone.

"I see my engagement present arrived."

"It sure did, along with the note you sent."

"You calling to thank me?"

"You seriously think I'm going to thank you after all you've done to me? Your freakin' note said, *'This is the game that started us on our path to misery.'* Never is a date with me miserable, Donovan Taylor!"

"It wasn't the Laker game that was miserable. It was all the shit that came after that." We had a good chuckle over what happened that morning of our Laker game "date." "I never got to properly congratulate you and Max on your engagement."

"So you're throwing floor seats our way to their first game this season?"

"And don't forget the gift certificate to The Palm. You two can recreate *our* first date." We busted up again. "Thank you and I'm sorry. You've been a great friend all these years, and I'm glad our friendship is still intact after all you and I have been through."

"I am too, Donovan. You be good to my cousin."

"I'm a damn dream to your cousin. She's the only one who hasn't opened her eyes to it."

"She still giving you a hard time?"

"No." He affirmed. "She's a dream as well. She's my dream come true."

"Damn. I can't believe Donovan Taylor is waxing poetic. You're a goner. Take care of my cousin," I warned, "and thank you for our gift. Max and I will enjoy the dinner as well as the game."

"You're welcome. Just remember to return the favor when Laney and I are engaged."

"You anywhere near that stage?"

"Who the hell knows? I've told her time and time again she's marrying me, but her answer is always, 'No I'm not.' Sometimes I think I'm talking to Ellie."

"How about if you ask her to marry you rather than commanding and demanding it?"

"You may have a point there, my vixen. Enjoy your day and let's talk again soon."

"Bye."

That was sweet and comical of Donovan to send us an engagement gift that replicated our first date. Max would find the comedy in this gift as well.

"Hello Gem." I called my boyfriend before putting my head back into the pile of work.

"Can you meet me at home tonight? I have a little something for you."

"Of course. I'll meet you around 8:00p.m.? I've got a little surprise for you too."

"Fab! See you then."

With Donovan and Gimpy away from this office, it was lonely here. But, the mound of work kept me busier than busy. Even though I was nowhere close to being finished with work, I rushed home to make sure Max's gift had arrived.

"Hello." I called out to this empty house.

"Yeah. I'm here." Nick walked out of the kitchen. "Weird now that everyone's gone, huh?"

"This entire cul-de-sac feels so empty. I miss those little buggers."

"I do too. It's not like I saw them that often, but their absence is huge."

"Whatcha up to tonight?"

"I've got a date."

"A date??? With whom??? Was I that much in my own world that I had no idea you were seeing anybody?"

"Naw. No one but Laney knew."

"And how did Laney know?"

"Bee told her."

I stopped dead in my tracks. "You're dating Bee Taylor? As in Becky and Donovan's aunt, Bee Taylor?"

"Well..." my brother was being evasive, "we're not exactly dating... yet. We've been out a few times in the past year and we're taking it slow. We aren't sure we want to date one another."

"You've been seeing her for a year?"

"Damn, Jane. Listen carefully. We are not seeing each other. We went on a date about a year ago, but got a bit freaked out when we made the Reid / Taylor connection. And now, we're even more freaked out because this feels like serious incest. We do our own things, and date from time to time."

"I'm so excited you're seeing Bee. I think she's fantastic! Plus, she makes the most beautiful clothes."

Nick laughed at me. "Max's present arrived. I think that's the coolest present I've seen a girl give a guy, especially the pink bow part." He chuckled some more. "It's in the garage."

"Thanks for being here to accept it. You think Max will like it?"

"Are you stupid or something? Of course he'll like it. Hell, if he doesn't want it, I'll take it."

I went over and hugged my brother. "Be nice to Bee. Don't make the same mistakes we all made with our significant others."

"Yeah, well, you and Jake have not been role models for dating, that's for sure. Don't push me, Jane. I'm still young. I don't want to be tied down. We're taking this slowly."

"What are you taking slowly, Nick?"

"Hi." I whispered and kissed my fiancé, who walked in without either of our knowledge.

"Hello, my precious gem."

"Nick and Bee are dating." I rushed out an answer but added, "They're kinda dating, testing the waters, not wanting to make the same mistakes we, Jake and Emily, and Donovan and Laney have made."

"Happy for you, Bro'. She seems like a great woman." Max patted my little brother on the back. "If anything, she'll keep you on your toes." He had a knowing chuckle I'd have to ask him about later.

"Uh...thanks...but this is all premature. We're just having dinner." He started walking away from us. "See ya later."

"Bye," we both called out.

"So you want your surprise, first, or you want to give me my surprise, first?"

"I've moved your stuff back into the house and we will be living there starting tonight."

"When did you have time to do that?"

"Early this morning, Nick, Doug, and I moved most everything back. It was easy since you hadn't even unpacked what you'd taken from the house. We can come back and pick up the rest of your stuff when you're ready."

"Well, I guess your gift is an extension of mine. Let's go see your gift." I held his hand and led him towards the garage. When I opened up the garage door, Max was pretty freakin' speechless.

"This is for me?"

"All yours...it even has your name engraved on the chrome part, under the name Ducati."

Max toured his new motorcycle from top to bottom, side to side, back to front, then back over again. "I can't believe you bought me a new bike." He was so busy fawning over his new bike, he didn't notice me trying to throw the key to him.

"I figured it was only fair I buy you something since you bought me this." I held up my shiny diamond ring. "It's your engagement present and I'm sure I don't have to tell you to be extra careful when riding these scary machines."

"Babe...I'll think of you every time I ride this thing."

"Ooh...sounds sexual...I like...!"

He slapped my ass and told me to get on the bike behind him. "How'd you know what to buy and when did you buy this?"

"I saw you drooling over the bike parked in front of Gimpy's villa, and that night when Laney and I had our talk, I asked her to help me order one for you. Since you proposed in Italy, I thought it only apt to buy you an Italian motorcycle. Maybe we'll have a small ceremony in Gimpy's villa in Florence next year for our wedding. What do you think?"

"I thank you for the wonderful gift and you can do whatever your heart pleases with this wedding. Just tell me when and where and I will be there."

"Shall we?" I got my helmet on (and yes, I got us matching helmets with the name Davis on the back) and cuddled against his back.

"Hold on tight!" He called out these same three words that started our first date back in December, with a knowing grin.

And this time, there was no way I was letting go, ever again.

Extra, Extra

I believe I've told my Reiders in the past that I hear fictional voices. When a story doesn't get told, I see specific characters (minus a face) recounting their side of the story. That's how most of the blogs and novels begin for me.

While writing from Jane's point of view, many times my characters would jump in and tell me their side of the story. The following blogs are just that—everyone else's point of views. Rather than confusing the reader and adding these blogs to the storyline, I put them in the end as extras.

Hope you enjoyed Max and Jane's world. They, along with the rest of the Reids will of course make guest appearances in the next novel, *Unlikely Attraction*. See you soon in Donovan and Laney's world.

(Max) April 20, 2013

Between a Rock and a Hard Place

Shit! How was I going to explain this one to Jane? As it is, she's not crazy about Hannah. How do I tell her what just transpired with this phone call? And damn Hannah! Why did she need to ask today of all days? I would've taken her some other time, of course with Jane's approval. *Hell.* This was either going to be one ugly day, or it'll work out better than I hope, with Jane accepting Hannah as a friend who needs some help.

"Why can't she just ride the bus and find a place of her own?" My girlfriend whined in a cute way.

"Gem, you know there's really no such thing as public transportation in Los Angeles. She wouldn't know what buses to take; she'd have to switch buses at least ten times. I know this isn't ideal, but think of her as a friend who needs help. We'd be willing to take any other friend along, if s/he needed help."

"Well, no other friend has the special moniker that Hannah holds."

Would I always have to live this down with Jane as well? Since I got Hannah pregnant, my parents have constantly reminded me of what a screw-up I've been to "knock-up a girl in high school." Once I got away from my parents, I thought my days of reliving that nightmare were over. I hated being reminded of my carelessness in high school.

"Never mind, Jane. I'll take Hannah another time. You're right. This is our day, we are starting our future together and we shouldn't have anyone interrupting this special day." What was I thinking, asking my girlfriend if Hannah could come along? Why would I want this headache? And after Jane's reminder about my mistake with Hannah, seeing the two of them together would only perpetuate Jane's negative view of me. I could be such a damn idiot at times.

"There's no way in Satan's lair that I'd allow you to spend *ANY* alone time with Hannah. You did enough of that in high school. Just bring her along," Jane said reluctantly.

"I'm on my way to pick up Hannah, and then I'll come pick you up."

"The three of us riding on your bike together? Who gets to spoon you?" Always ready with a witty retort.

"Ha ha ha. Very funny. If you don't lose the bad attitude, you may have to ride in the backseat while Hannah gets shotgun." I answered with my own sarcasm. This was going to be a shitty day!

"Hi Max." Hannah came out with my mom.

"Hey, Hannah. Hi Mom," I answered uncomfortably.

"Hello, Max. How are you?"

"Okay." I hated being so formal with my own mother. You'd think that by now, at age twenty-six, I'd have gotten used to the coldness. I guess being around the Reids only accentuated my mother's sterile attitude towards me. "And you and Dad are well?"

I hadn't seen my parents since that last disastrous dinner with Jane, and I was embarrassed and scared to have any contact with them. It was one thing to have your parents disappointed in you, but it was wholly another crazy world to have your own parents try and sabotage your future. I didn't need Jane seeing any more of the ugly Davis drama.

"We are doing well. Your father and I were hoping you'd stop by. Did you get my messages?"

"Yeah, I did. I'm sorry. I've been busy with school."

"We understand." Mom's usual harsh tone cracked a bit. "Your dad and I would like to talk to you one day soon? Could you give us a few minutes of your time?"

"Um, sure. I'll check my schedule and get back to you."

I was scared shitless to meet with my parents, alone, without my brothers as a buffer. But there was that small part of me that hoped maybe Mom and Dad would finally want to be...my Mom and Dad. *Damn!* It was too early for this kind of shit. I sounded like a maudlin teenage girl. Has this day only just begun?

"Thanks for allowing me to tag along. I tried to find a place through the internet, but it was so difficult to check any of them out without a car."

"No worries, Hannah. I know it's been difficult for you to readjust back to life in Southern California. Is everything going well?"

"I think so. The accounting job at the hospital is great. All the other employees are friendly, and it's a bonus to see you and your brothers from time to time. You remember in high school when we used to..."

I decided to cut this kind of conversation off before it started. "Hannah. I know we had some great times in high school, and I'm sorry I was an asshole to you in the end, but that's not a time I like to revisit." *Aw, shit! Why do women cry so readily?* "I'm sorry, Hannah. Those days are a distant memory for me, and I hope you'll be understanding enough not to bring it up again, especially in front of Jane. I hate the reminder of what a screw-up I was."

"So that's what I was to you? A 'screw-up'?" I seriously felt like Job from the Bible and wanted to rip my clothes off and run in the middle of the street and ask God, *"Why me???"* "I can't believe after loving each other that much, you'd think of me as a 'screw-up'."

"Hannah." Pause. Pause. Pause. I needed to take a chill-pill and stop all this fucking drama at nine A.M.! "We were in high school. *We...* no, let me say, *I* should have known better than to start something I couldn't finish. Getting you pregnant was stupid."

The tears. The fucking tears! I need to rewind this day and start all over with Hannah *NOT* in the picture.

"Look. I'm sorry if that was harsh, but we were too young to get so seriously involved. Think about your own kids. Would you like them being sexually active and having your daughter pregnant at such a young age?" The tears only got worse. "I've been doing a lot of thinking lately, and what we did was just wrong. I don't want my kids making the same mistake."

"Sure, now that you have Jane in your life, you can think about a future and having kids. I don't have that same luxury. I've never gotten over what I went through in high school. You were the love of my life, and I thought you would take me away from my parents and we'd create a life together with our baby. But instead, I lost the baby, you turned on me, and I've been miserable ever since."

Fuck. There was no reason for this, but I guess we needed to hash this out once and for all. It did seem a little odd that Hannah was so reasonable and reassuring after the dinner fiasco. It was almost a dream that she was so forgiving of what I did to her back in high school. It was time to get it all out in the open and to let her know that there was no more us.

I pulled the car over. "I have no excuses for the way I treated you after you lost the baby—absolutely none. You can call me every name in the book and I couldn't, wouldn't fight back. But Hannah... it's over. This has been over for ten years. You need to move on."

"You killed a part of me when you turned away from me. Then you killed the rest of me when you dated Emily." *How the hell did she know about Em?* "And now, I feel my heart being beaten to death all over again when I see the love in your eyes for Jane. You've never looked at me like that. You have so much love for her...I just can't stand it."

Hannah started bawling, but I couldn't do much more than pat her on the back and repeatedly tell her how sorry I was for everything. No matter how hard she cried, there was no woman I wanted in my arms, other than my girlfriend.

"I love Jane, and she's who I see in my future." I started the car again. "I hope you'll find someone who'll bring you that same kind of happiness, as Jane brings me. I think when you find that person, you'll understand that what we had wasn't it."

With that, I sped to Gem's house and greeted my love with a heavier kiss than I should have, considering Hannah was probably watching. I wasn't trying to gloat. It was just me realizing how special Jane was to me and how lucky I was to be in her life. I had one too many shortcomings for Jane to be content with me, and yet we loved each other and were starting a future together. Life was good with this Gem.

We walked hand in hand, and I could feel Jane's grip getting tighter and tenser, the closer we got to the car. I didn't understand it at first, but soon realized my asinine comment about Jane sitting in the back of the car coming to fruition. This was like a self-fulfilled prophecy. Truly, I was a fucking moron for allowing Hannah to join us.

I thought about asking Hannah to move back. But after what I'd truthfully and somewhat callously said to her not five minutes ago, I thought I'd let things be and pleaded with Jane to be the bigger person. I knew I was not wrong in thinking that Jane would stick by me and always be on my side.

Being the bigger person didn't last long for my girlfriend. Hannah pulled all kinds of crap out of her very short sleeves, and it was actually cute watching Jane hold back. I kept staring at her from the rear-view mirror and at first, she was amused with my flirting eyes. Soon, I saw her button nose wrinkle a few times when Hannah nixed Jane's apartment choices, then I saw the forehead crease, and I knew we were in trouble. What the hell would possess a Mormon man to have more than one wife? I could hardly handle the one girl-friend I had.

"Remind me to be extra nice to you for being so patient during this time of discomfort." I kidded.

"How will you relieve my discomfort?"

"I have my ways. An ace never reveals his secrets."

"You better be an ace tonight in bed, because you're ex is giving me a serious headache."

"I have a definite cure for that headache." With a quick kiss to her lips, we went in.

This apartment hunting was a mixed-up (Jane) version of *Goldilocks and the Three Bears.* The first apartment was too small. The next one was too cold. But the last one—the penthouse apartment—was just right. The penthouse wasn't for rent, and there was no way I could ever afford anything this extravagant. Jane's eyes perused every inch of this place, and I could tell this was where she wanted to live.

"Jane, you know this place is not for rent. I thought we talked about getting a place together." I reminded her. That didn't faze her. She looked with the intent to buy and that's when it all went to hell.

"I don't have the finances to buy a place, and even if I did have the money, I have no desire to buy anything right now." Jane looked at me like I'd slapped her in the face. What I meant as a statement of fact, since my life and future as a medical student were so unstable, turned me into the biggest asshat on the face of this universe. She had no idea how desperately I wanted to live with her and show her that we were meant to be together, always. It bugged me that her eyes still wandered.

Well, when I said earlier that it all went to "Satan's lair," that was an understatement for what happened at the club. We shouldn't have gone to the club. I should've dropped off Hannah, then explained myself to Jane, but I needed a break from all the shit going on in my head. I needed people around us, I needed time away from both girls, and I thought being with the Reid family would help.

"What's the matter?" Nick asked.

"Don't ever get into a relationship," I answered.

"Dude. You're preaching to the choir. I know! Women are trouble." He answered back with an evil grin.

"You okay?" Josh and Garret sat next to me and after a quick perusal of my demeanor, they understood enough to occupy Hannah at another table.

"How'd the apartment search go, Davis? You and Jane find anything?" I had nothing to say to Jake but stared at Jane and Donovan's friendship / relationship. "Don't let that bother you, Davis. They're two people who have been friends a long time and will continue to be good friends in the future."

"Would I sound like a chick if I told you how insecure I get whenever I see those good *friends*, together?"

Jake laughed at me and laughed hard. "Yeah, you sound like a complete woman. But," Jake got serious, "I understand your pain, because you did the same damn thing to me when I was dating my wife. I was very close to locking her up in that house of hers so she'd see no one but me. The hair on my back stood straight every time your name was mentioned."

"Jane and I went apartment hunting with Hannah tagging along."

Jake practically fell out of his chair, laughing. "Are you a fucking idiot?"

"I'd say allowing Hannah to join us today was about as 'fucking idiotic' as leaving my girlfriend behind in Arizona." I shot back.

"Low blow, Davis. You know I still haven't recovered from that mistake. God, when I think about what Emily must have…"

"Also...!" I cut him off before he recanted that whole damn story again. "I didn't mean to, but I think Jane believes I told her I didn't see a future for us."

"You are a fucking moron." Jake laughed again. "What are you going to do to make this all up to my sister? She can hold a mean grudge."

"Tell me about it. I've no idea what I'm going to do." I sighed. "I truly don't know how this day went from hope to complete despair." I stared at the two laughing carefree and making all kinds of hand gestures at one another. "Whenever I see her with him, I lose courage and hope."

"Max." Jake got really serious now. "I tell you the truth when I say that they are only friends. Go to Jane. She wants you, not Donovan."

Even with Jake's pep talk, I suddenly felt hopeless. As soon as I saw Jane and Donovan when I walked into the club—something ugly happened to me. Recognizing the seamless yin and yang of their relationship, I wondered if I was holding on to a woman who really shouldn't be with me. Was a relationship this hard for everyone? Did everyone have this many misunderstandings and difficulties? What was wrong with me that I had so many insecurities about myself? Why couldn't it be enough that two people loved each other?

Sunday wasn't any better.

"Max! What a nice surprise." Emily answered the door with a warm greeting and a sweet hug. This was a woman who always oozed tranquility. "You here looking for Jane?"

"Yeah."

"Jake tells me you and she got into another misunderstanding?" I nodded yes. "You want to have a slice of cake with me? I have your favorite." I nodded again.

"Do you think I'm not the right guy for Jane?"

Emily looked at me mid-bite. "Why would you ask that crazy question? Of course you two are right for each other."

"I don't know, Em. The closer Jane and I get, the further apart our misunderstandings become. It shouldn't be that way, should it? If two people love each other, shouldn't life get easier with one another? I don't think Jane and I have that same fluency that she has with Donovan."

"Don't, Max. You're always too hard on yourself. You've always worked so hard to create the ideal relationship and when it's not perfect in your eyes, you blame yourself. Nobody's relationship is perfect and you really have to stop looking at your life through your parents' eyes. You've done well for yourself. You're a wonderful boyfriend to Jane, and you were just as wonderful to me. I always hated seeing you so troubled. Your parents aren't judging you anymore. They're proud of all you've accomplished."

"Thanks, Em. Something got turned on in my head yesterday when I saw Jane with Donovan. I wondered if I should let her go..." I couldn't continue as those same doubts I once had about me and Emily swirled in my head again. "You know...just like I let you go. It worked out well for you...maybe I'm being selfish holding on to her..."

"No, Max! You and I weren't meant to be, but you and Jane are. I know it's hard. Look at me and Jake. We misunderstood each other for half a year before we got back together. No one has it easy. Don't think such thoughts."

Abruptly, I decided to get up and go. I needed time to think. "Em, I need to go."

"You want me to tell Jane you stopped by?"

"No. I'll stop by her office tomorrow."

Monday was even uglier.

I decided to take to heart what Emily said yesterday, and she was right. Even strong couples like she and Jake had their difficulties. Complications in a relationship were a part of the package resulting in a stronger love and personal growth. Emily was dead-on when she told me that I looked at my life through my parents' eyes. *Damn!* I'd definitely stepped way too far into the get-in-touch-with-my-feminine-side. Not good!

Picking up some flowers, I took my bike for a long ride, then I parked near Jane's office, hoping to have lunch with her and get *her* in touch with my "feminine" side. I parked the bike and was fumbling with my helmet when I saw Jane walk out with Donovan, her arms casually around his arm, cackling their way to lunch. If that wasn't bad enough, she walked right by me and was so engrossed in a conversation with Donovan, she never noticed me. That knocked the wind and sail and the whole damn ocean out of me. I watched in the rear-view mirror till they turned the corner and were out of my sight.

Friday...

"What's the matter?" Garret and Josh finally pulled me out of my stupor and out of the apartment. "Nick tells me you haven't been to class and you've been missing from the hospital. Are you sick?"

"Mom and Dad really did a number on us, huh?"

"Hell yes!" Josh answered immediately. "But why do you bring this up and why are you so depressed?"

"I think I'm going to let Jane go."

"What the hell?" Both my brothers answered simultaneously.

"I thought you wanted to marry this girl." Josh spoke.

"I do."

"Then why are you breaking up with her?"

"Did I ever explain to you why I broke up with Emily?"

"Max...you're a different person now. You're not lost, you're not angry, you're not the Max that Mom and Dad accused you of being. You weren't 'a screw-up' then, and you're definitely not one now."

"I don't think I'm good enough for Jane. She deserves better than the likes of me. There's already a someone waiting for her, and they may suit better."

"Isn't this something that you should talk to Jane about rather than deciding by yourself? What you did to Emily back in undergrad wasn't fair, and it's not fair to Jane to say you're letting her go." Josh was wise beyond his years, sometimes.

"Look at how well it worked out for Emily."

"Shit!" Garret said, "Come on. Don't do this to yourself. I know Mom and Dad were always riding you harder than the rest of us, but you're a good guy. You love Jane. She loves you. Don't hurt by yourself. I don't know what happened, but talk to Jane. I'm sure she's miserable, too."

My last vision of Jane—walking with her hand on Donovan's arm, making jokes, laughing effortlessly—convinced me that I had made the right decision.

(Max) May 30, 2013

Making the Rounds

"What's with the formal get-together, and where's Jane?" Garret questioned as soon as we all sat down to a meal at home. I was grateful Hannah had gone out tonight, because I wanted this time to be a special one with just the family.

"Before we start dinner, I wanted to let you all know...and I was also hoping to get your blessing on....Jane." Garret and Josh, of course, loved Jane but I wasn't sure what was going on in my parents' heads. They were always closed-off to us both in the past and present, and I wanted to change that. After experiencing the Reid family, I thought we Davises could try for the same—or at least attempt a decent replica.

"On Jane?" Josh sounded surprised. "You know we love Jane. What kind of approval do you need?"

"I bought a ring today and am going to ask her to marry me on her birthday. I wanted you all to know and to be happy for us."

"Oh Max!" Mom declared. "You're getting married." Mom sounded like she was making a statement, but it also sounded like a question.

"Are you and Dad okay with that? I love Jane and believe we can be happy together."

"Of course we're happy for you and Jane. Your father and I think she's perfect for you. We liked Emily, but you and she were too alike. Jane has that extra sparkle that suits you perfectly."

"I think so too, Mom." I was relieved she and Dad approved.

It took a while but Dad finally spoke. "I know your mother and I pushed you three to succeed when you were younger. We probably weren't the most sympathetic of parents and to be honest with you, if we had to do it all over again, I don't know that we'd do it any differently. This was and still is who your mother and I are. We're sorry if we disappointed you throughout the years, but your mother and I are proud of all three of you. You've grown into fine young men who will become responsible citizens. We know now that our job is done."

Mom and Dad came over and gave us each a hug after Dad's grand speech. I had to chuckle. This was probably the most sentimental Dad's ever been with us and yet it was still not the most heart-warming of speeches. There were no warm-fuzzies, no tears, no I love yous. But in Dad's own way, he gave us his style of love, tears, and girly-sentiment. I guess this was a start. Once Jane joined the Davis clan, she'd loosen up my family and if she couldn't finish the job, our babies would do the trick. I'd wait and see how stern and robotic my parents could stay once they held their first grandchild. We Davises would learn what we could from the Reids, and I saw a beautiful future ahead for all of us.

Next, I was off to the Reid house to get Bobby, Sandy, Gram, and Roland's permission.

"Hello, Max. It was such a nice surprise when you called to have lunch with us." Sandy greeted me warmly.

"Hey, Son. What brings you by mid-week, mid-day?" Bobby had a glint in his eye because he knew exactly why I was here.

"Before we get into any conversation, come sit outside. I have lunch ready."

We sat and talked about school at first, but quickly dispensed with the formalities.

"I came here today hoping to ask your permission to marry your daughter."

"Yes!" Both Bobby and Sandy answered simultaneously. "Take her. We love her but she's too old to be living at home, and she's too difficult for your average man to handle her. You are the perfect balance of laid-back, but firm." Sandy spoke with an approving nod.

Bobby added, "She loves you, the family loves you, and even Jake was wondering the other day when you two would get married."

"You're okay with me and Emily having dated back in college? It's not too weird for you?"

"Nope. Look at Estelle and Roland—yours is not the only interesting story if we start unlocking closed doors on the Reid sagas." Sandy mentioned with a wink.

"Plus, thanks to you, we have Emily as a daughter and the twins as grandchildren. Ellie and James wouldn't be in our lives, otherwise."

"When will you propose?" Bobby wondered.

"I thought on her birthday?"

"Do you think she suspects a proposal?" Sandy asked.

"I doubt it. We've talked in general terms about the future. This proposal should shock her."

"I'm so excited." Sandy put her arms around me and gave me a side-hug. "You are perfect for our daughter."

"Your parents approve of Jane?" My future father-in-law sounded a bit concerned. "When we met them at the softball game, they seemed to like her, but liking someone and welcoming them into the family is a different story."

"My parents and brothers love Jane." I reassured them. "Our parents weren't ever openly loving or affectionate with us. They were always more of an authoritative figure than a friend, but something about Jane made them want to become closer to all of us. She's brought our family together in a way I can't explain. My parents and brothers absolutely approve and champion Jane."

"Well, we're glad to hear that. Welcome to the family, Max." Bobby and Sandy took turns giving me a hug.

"Well it's about time someone took that old maid off the shelf!" Gram answered with a smile when I asked for her and Roland's permission to marry Jane.

"You know she's my favorite Reid," Roland warned. "Don't do anything to hurt her or you'll answer to me."

"Roland, I can assure you that she's *my* favorite Reid as well and though I'm positive we will continue to fight, we will also grow closer as a couple. I love her and will do my best to be a good husband to her."

"All we can ask for is that you two try your best." Gram came over and hugged me. "I'm glad you're adding to our already perfect family."

After the approvals were given, I thought about leaving but something didn't feel right. Looking across the street, I knew I needed to let Jake and Emily know since those two were integral in not only getting us together, but also in keeping us together.

"Finally!" Emily ran over and hugged me.

"I don't care the situation, Emi. You are not to hug any man like you just did." Jake pulled her off, of course. "Congrats!" He then greeted me with a warm smile and shook my hand. "You and Jane are perfect for one another. She will complicate the hell out of your life, but you will love every moment of it."

"What made you decide to ask her now? What was the impetus?" Emily asked.

"I finally feel like I have stability in my life. Med school is almost over, Jane is at a good place in her life with the firm, and I love her more than I could imagine loving someone. When you and I broke up, I thought it'd be impossible to find that easy-going love we had. You were and still are the epitome of a perfect woman."

"That she is!" Jake declared and pulled his wife even closer into him.

"With Jane somehow, both our imperfections make perfection. I know it sounds silly, but I love every last thing about her."

"That's so romantic, Max. You don't know how happy I am for you." Emily attempted to pull away from Jake, but he held strong. "Of course, I'm thrilled for Jane, but you..." she began tearing. "You know you'll always have your own special corner in my heart. You were there for me after I lost the rest of my family. You were a friend when I felt lonely. I would have been lost had you not loved me and guided me. And for that, I will always love you in my own special way."

"Em." Shockingly, Jake actually let his wife come to me and he allowed me to give her a hug. "We were two lost souls who guided one another. Four wonderful years led us to meet our ideal mates. It's all come full circle." I hugged her and kissed the top of her head one last time, then let her go, lest I go into the Reid family with the future patriarch upset with me.

"Okay, now...more good news!" Emily declared. "Jake and I want you and Jane to be the godparents of our new baby. We were going to tell the family immediately, but why don't we hold off on that news until the proposal is done."

With Emily's announcement, everything did seem to come full circle. "Well, then now I have my answer."

"What was the question?" Emily wondered.

"While searching for a ring for Jane, I remembered that a certain unclaimed engagement ring was still sitting at the bottom of my closet. I wondered what to do with it and now, I think I finally have a solution."

"What's the solution, Davis? You better not be thinking of giving it to my wife as any sort of a gift."

I laughed. "I would love to give it to my new godchild when he or she is born, if that's all right with my almost fiancée and her husband?" I kidded.

"Our life really has come full circle, hasn't it?" Emily asked in awe. "I think that would be a beautiful gesture to keep that ring in the family. Thank you."

"Do I get a say?" Jake asked his wife.

Emily looked like she was going to say no, but she allowed it.

"Davis, you are very welcomed into the Reid family!"

Now that the hard part was done and I got everyone's approval, on to the easy part of making my girlfriend my partner in crime, partner in love, and partner in life.

What the Hell is Wrong with These Two?

"Nick would you take the twins outside and maybe walk around the hospital with them? They've been here the entire time and I think they would like some fresh air." I was not happy with Donovan and Jane. I needed to have a talk with them.

Both Nick and Doug knew that something was not right, and they didn't question my request. They picked up the twins and left the room as quickly as possible.

"What the hell is the matter with the both of you?" I asked really angry, really hurt for Laney.

That question caught everyone in the room by surprise. Of course, my protective husband got angry for me and glared at the guilty parties.

"I don't know what you two did, but I don't think I've ever heard my wife use a four letter word. What's got you so upset, Love?"

"These two were caught by Laney making out in a hospital room."

"How moronic can you be? You both told me it was over."

"What do you mean over? You knew about these two cheaters?" I was not only angry and hurt for Laney, but also for Max who had no idea what his girlfriend was doing behind his back.

"Emi. Calm yourself. Our baby is bordering on crying because his mom is upset."

I picked him up from his makeshift crib and rocked him the best I could.

"Well he feels no differently than his mother." I, too, felt like crying right now. "Jane, how can you do this to Max?" I asked dumbfounded and flabbergasted. "After all these months, after working out all the kinks in your relationship, you're going to throw it all away for a brief fling?"

She look like she wanted to fight back, but she knew better. She really had nothing to say in her defense.

"And Donovan what about you? You're a thirty-two-year-old man who's been around the block many times. Did you really feel the need to break up a happy relationship? Not only did you break up a happy relationship, you broke Max's heart and you broke Laney's heart."

"Emily," Donovan said in a repentant manner, "I know that I'm guilty of a lot of things, but I don't know what Laney's heart has to do with all this."

"Are you that dense or are you pretending to be stupid?" I couldn't believe I was saying all these things. I felt really bad on the one hand, and kind of nervous on the other hand, but I was really pissed off right now. "After trifling with her feelings for months, no make that years, you really had no idea that you would break her heart if she saw you with Jane?"

"And you," I was also angry with my husband who kept the truth from me. "Why didn't you tell me what was going on?"

"Well it all kind of happened when you were nearing your term and I didn't want to upset you, and I didn't want to put you into premature labor, Emily. I did this all for you."

"Explain to me now what is going on. What happened and why did Max leave so suddenly?"

"Who wants to start?" My husband looked at both guilty parties.

Jane gave her confession first and explained to me what happened the day of her birthday then Donovan gave me his confession and told me how sorry he was for breaking up Max and Jane.

"Okay then what the hell was that today? If it's over, if you two decided that it was over why were you making out again in the hospital room?"

"That was his brilliant idea," Jane said sarcastically.

"Jane, your attitude and sarcasm do not suit today." I heard Donovan and Jake laughing in the background so I turned to them and gave them an evil glare. They both stopped immediately.

I heard Donovan whisper, "Man I didn't realize your wife could get so upset. She's kind of scary when she's mad."

"I didn't know she can get this mad either! I better watch myself. Though I've got nothing to worry about. I never make her mad." My husband chuckled.

"Okay Mr. Godfather to my children, or soon-to-be ex-Godfather of my children, explain to me about this kiss today."

"I'm sorry, Emily" he apologized over and over again. I was not appeased. "I just wanted to make sure one last time that she and I did not suit. The first time we kissed—the only time we kissed—it was kind of disgusting. It was like I was kissing Becky and she was kissing Jake so we both decided at that point that it was incestuous for us to date."

We could hear Jake practically singing in the background, "You're preaching to the choir. This is what I have been telling you since day one."

"So if kissing Jane is like kissing your sister, why'd you do it again?"

"We didn't. But stupidly, when I saw Jane again today, I needed to satiate my curiosity one last time. I needed to be 100% sure that she and I had no attraction for one another."

"You both disgust me." I was still too angry for words, but I couldn't help chastising them. "And you know what? You both deserve one another. You're both the epitome of selfish. You could care less who you hurt in the meanwhile as long as your curiosity is satisfied. If everybody lived by your standards, we'd all be having affairs."

I could see that Jane was angry with me for chastising her. I didn't care. They had both hurt two people whom I loved dearly.

"Why don't you both leave before my wife gets really upset." Jake started laughing again and shooed them out. I didn't even say goodbye.

It was at this point that I started crying. My heart hurt so much for Max and Laney. Max had been so hurt all his life by his parents, by me, and now by Jane. I thought that he finally found happiness with her. What would I do, what could I do to make things better for him? And Laney must've felt so betrayed by her own cousin. And it was all for naught. These two weren't even in love with each other. They were just testing the waters.

"Don't cry my love. It will all work itself out. I promise."

"How do you know?" I asked in between sniffles. "What are we going to do for them Jake? I want Max and Laney to be as happy as you and I are. What can we do to help them?"

"Jane already has her head on straight, and she is going to go grovel to Max out in Mexico as soon as she can. I believe she's planning on leaving this week. Donovan...well I don't know what to say about my best friend. I do believe he and Laney are meant to be, but there's only so much we can do when he doesn't believe in the same thing. One day soon he will open his eyes. Trust me, I see the attraction, but he is fighting it. I believe that he will come to his senses."

With those encouraging words he came and laid down in bed with me and brought our newborn in between us. This love, warmth and comfort is what I hoped for with Max and Jane and Laney and Donovan—but it didn't appear to be in the cards for any of them.

I'd call Laney as soon as my little one went back to sleep, but for now, it was time to be a mother, again.

Donovan's Plight, Flight

"You gonna go after her?" My best friend had been miserable since he made a mess of things with Jane, and Laney left believing that he and Jane were together. Funny thing, the same reason that forced Laney back to England was the reason Donovan woke up to smell the coffee.

"Are you the one who sent me this?" He picked up what looked like a small notebook of sort. "It must've been you. I don't know who else would've had access to this."

"What the hell are you talking about? Are you going after her? Have you come to the realization that my cousin is your soul mate? The key to your happiness? Your happily ever after?"

"You've been reading Ellie way too many fairytales. I don't know of any such thing." He was still denying it.

"After witnessing my marriage, your parents, my parents, your sisters...you still don't believe in happily ever afters?"

"You sound like a chick, now. Emily has done some number on you, my man. When did you become such a believer in fairytales?"

"Since I met my wife." I decided to go in for the kill. "You can't understand the wonders and beauty of being with the one woman who makes your world go around. There's not a day that doesn't go by when I wake up to her and smile. When you find the woman, your Emily, she'll make you smile and thank God that you're alive to feel such love. Our little Laney is it for you. Why do you keep fighting it?"

I'd no idea why he was fighting it so much. I knew he was attracted to her and he continually wondered what could've been, with her.

"Dude, I've made a mess of things with every woman I thought was the woman for me. I've left Kate bitter, Jane angry—though I'm hopeful she and Max will work everything out, and Laney hurt because she believes she caught me kissing her cousin of all people. Both Laney and Emily were right. I am selfish. I want what I want at all costs, and have no care for others' feelings. What if I'm wrong about Laney? What if it's just lust?"

"I think you know it's not just lust. I've always known that Laney's had a special place in your heart since we were younger. She was the one you used to always protect, always cared for, always made sure she was comfortable. Even when you were infatuated with Kate, you still took the time to show Laney how special she was to you. Was this all in my mind?"

"All this time, I thought I did that because she was a younger sister who needed caring, not as a future partner."

"All right. Let's be honest with one another. What's got you in the dumps these days, then? You haven't been dating, you've been an asshole on many occasions, and you've been sniffling around my wife way more than I like." I didn't care for any man to be near my wife, demanding her attention if it wasn't me or the children.

"Emily doesn't seem to mind. In fact she said she liked having me over. And let's not forget Ellie, who gives me a bigger smile than she gives even her father, when I show up."

"Don't push it, Friend!" Jake warned.. "Or I'm gonna push you into that pool of ours that Ellie is so fond of jumping into with her godfather."

"Well, look who's here, again!" Nick and Doug waltzed into the backyard as though they owned the place. Each adult was carrying a child with Emily not far behind, carrying the infant.

Ellie gave me her famous smile, but refused to jump into my arms. She was happy to be with Nick this time.

"Traitor," I grumbled when she turned away from me. "What's Nick promised you to turn you away from me?"

"Look at their attire. They're going swimming as soon as dinner's done. She's done with you unless you can produce something more precious than the pool."

"Ellie, you wanna go take a walk with Uncle Donovan?" I tried to coax her away from Nick.

"NO!" She declared and shook her head fiercely.

"You wanna go swimming with Uncle Nick?" My brother was rubbing in his win.

She nodded her head fiercely, again and hugged Nick the way she usually hugs Donovan when he comes over and plays with her. Even a one year old was playing games with his mind and wreaking havoc on his emotions.

"Women! I can't seem to win any over, no matter the age. I concede and bow down to you," Donovan called out to Nick and showed his respect to the man who won, fair and square.

"Women issues?" Now Doug was taunting him.

"Smugness doesn't become you, Doug." Donovan answered in a pissy way, while the rest of the group laughed.

Doug did have a smug look. "I talked to Laney just now," he announced.

"You did?" Donovan said a little too loudly and enthusiastically.

Doug cracked up again. "Shit, Donovan! You're like a lovesick puppy. You're just as bad as her boyfriend."

"What the hell? What boyfriend? Laney doesn't do boyfriends. She just dates."

"Where've you been?" Doug was doing a great job of making my buddy jealous. "She's been seeing this guy pretty seriously since she got back to England last month. You know he's asked her to marry him?"

"Fucking hell? Are you kidding me? Is this the same idiot who called her his duchess? What the hell was that all about, giving up a dukedom? Who the hell has a dukedom?"

"He apparently will." My wife was now getting into this intervention. "He will inherit a large dukedom when his time comes. You may have to Your Grace our little Laney and her husband, after they get married, of course." Emily had a sly smile going. God, I loved my wife. I walked over to her and kissed her lips just because she was so damn cute.

"Are you kidding me?" Donovan was a bit outraged now.

"Nope. Laney told me that she spent a week at his grandfather's larger than imaginable country home."

"She talks to you, too?" Donovan addressed Nick. "Why won't she return any of my calls if she's talking to the rest of you?"

"Maybe she doesn't want to talk to you." Doug laughed at Donovan's torment.

"She and Michael called me right before we got here. They're going to Rome together to tour the city."

"What. The. Fuck! I'm so screwed." Donovan had his head in his hand. "You guys are all lying to me, huh? She and this Michael guy are not as serious as you say they are."

Now it was time for my intervention. "You heard Michael's speech about Laney being his sun and moon and whatever the hell he uttered. Poetic bastard, wasn't he?"

"*'She's the shine to my sun and the light to my moon. I'd give up my entire dukedom to spend a lifetime with her,*' was what I believe he crooned when he visited her in the hospital. That was the most romantic thing I've ever heard a man declare to a woman." My wife added. "That Michael could write romance novels with the way he was waxing poetic about our Laney." Emily smiled over to Donovan. "They both looked so happy in love."

"It doesn't get more serious than when you ask someone to marry you, Buddy."

"You are all making me delirious," Donovan was done. "I'm going home. Go ahead and be happy. I don't want any part of it." He got up and kissed all three kids. "Goodbye children." The twins waved bye to him in response.

"Did we do it? Will he go after her?" Emily asked.

"Hell yes! I'd bet one of my kids that he's on the next plane to London as soon as he gets his affairs in order."

"This is gonna be good! I wish I was a fly on the wall when he starts courting Laney."

"Perhaps we will be that fly on the wall and see his anguish. This could be high drama and Emmy-worthy entertainment." And I couldn't wait for the show to begin.

(Donovan) July 29, 2013

I give up!

After rereading the damn diary and convincing myself that Delaney wouldn't refuse my affection, I made a life altering decision. After weeks of torture, and thinking about her constantly, I knew she was the girl for me. Part of me was scared like hell. I'd gone through life thinking I was in love with Kate, only to figure out that the love part died when I went off to law school. Then there were the countless women I'd dated and left. Of course, my last failure was Jane. What the fuck was I thinking believing that we were meant to be? And how the hell could I have been sexually attracted to Jane? Damn! It grossed me out to think that I had any attraction towards someone I considered a little sister.

There was always the school of thought that Laney could turn out to be the same case as Jane. Shit! I knew absolutely nothing about true love—the kind that Jake preaches every chance he gets. But, I was going to try. It killed me to know that every day I wasn't with Delaney, she was with another man and forgetting the connection we had. I didn't know if I was an idiot, but since she refused to return any of the messages I'd left for her, I had to hope that she still had feelings for me. It was either that, or she hated my guts. I chose to believe in the former.

"Roland, you have a moment?"

Roland looked up from his paperwork and didn't say a word. I was feeling like a school boy at the principal's office.

"I'd like to transfer to the London office, as soon as possible."

Roland now looked at me funny, but still stayed mute.

"Would that be possible?"

"Depends on why you want to go to London." Finally, a word or two. "For what reason do you need to go all the way out there? Is it to renew your relationship with Kate?" There was a firm disapproval in his voice.

"No, Sir. It's to try and win over the affections of your granddaughter."

"Which granddaughter?" Damn! This wasn't going to be easy.

I lowered my head in a deeply apologetic way. "I'm sorry sir for being an asshole towards both your granddaughters. I shouldn't have trifled with Jane's feelings and caused a rift between her and Max. And I deeply regret that it's taken me this long to understand what Delaney meant to me. I'd like to try. I'll need to grovel, court, whatever the hell she wants, to earn the family's approval and Delaney's love."

"You mean that, Son? You're not going to hurt my granddaughter, are you?"

"No, Sir! I believe I'm in love with your granddaughter. I can't stop thinking about her. I hear her laugh in the middle of my day, I see her smile when I try and sleep at nights, I talk to her when I'm lonely. Is this an early onset of dementia, or is this love?"

Roland chuckled. "That's how I felt when Estelle left me for Jerry. I thought I'd go mad if I didn't see her one more time, hold her in my arms one last time, love her again for the last time."

"That's it, Roland. I need that chance with Delaney. And it won't be for one last time. I plan to win her over for a lifetime."

"You've got your work cut out for you. Hasn't Jake told you about Michael Bennington? He's pursuing her with all his might. I've never seen such ardor in a young man. My old buddy, Harry Bennington, his grandfather, is pissing in his knickers right now because Michael's in love with an American girl. But secretly, I know Harry is in love with our Laney as well. He's constantly having her over at his country home because 'Laney loves it here,' the poor fool keeps telling me. What do you have going for you that's going to give you one up on Michael?"

"I have her love, Sir. That's what I have." Was I kidding myself? Did I honestly believe that I had her love, still, after all this time had gone by?

"I hope you're right, my boy."

"Well it's about damn time!" My future father-in-law proclaimed when I went over to his house to ask his permission to court Delaney. "What the hell took you so long? Didn't you see how my little girl mooned over you since she was a...little girl? You're the damn reason she left here and now it looks like she may stay there forever if she marries this future Duke of England."

"Dad," Doug interrupted. "He's not the future Duke of England. He's just a duke of some area in England."

"Whatever the hell he is, I won't have my daughter living so far away from me. You go declare your intentions and bring her home," the Chief commanded.

"So, you don't care which man brings her home, as long as he's successful?" Doug laughed. "Maybe Josh will bring her home. I happen to know he still has the hots for Laney."

"You ready to treat my baby like the princess that she is? She's too good for the likes of you, Donovan. She's as pure as they come—a rarity in this day and age. She's never given her heart to anyone except you and all you've done is squashed her dreams."

Was anyone going to make this easy for me? "Yes, Chief. I will love her, take care of her, and treat her like my princess for the rest of our lives. Now do I have your permission?"

"You do, Son. Welcome to the family." My future family gave me a group hug.

Next was my grovel / apology to Gram, and after listening to her berate me for almost an hour, I escaped to Jake and Emily's.

"Damn! I've never had such a difficult day as I did today. I got an earful from the entire family."

"Why?" Emily asked.

"Because I've decided to move to London and court my future wife, princess, love of my life—feel free to choose the correct title as you see fit."

Emily threw herself at me to Jake's chagrin. Jake of course came over and peeled his wife away.

"Love, it doesn't make me happy to see you touching any man, not even my best friend."

She then came back over and kissed me on the cheek. "If my husband weren't here, I'd kiss you on both cheeks and the lips, you make me so happy."

"Let's not get carried away." My buddy was really unhappy now.

"You all right with me going out there?" I addressed Emily. "Please tell me, give me hope, Emily. If anyone knows Delaney's heart, it's you. Do I have a fighting chance?"

"I think you have better than a fighting chance. Go. Find her. Court her. Show her how much you will love her the rest of your lives!"

"Yes Ma'am!"

With that last bit of encouragement, I picked up and left the comforts of home to go after my princess.

Birthday Surprises

"You, to my left," Jake pointed at me, "and you, to my right," he pointed at Donovan and to our respective seats. After dropping off Jane at home, Jake took us to a swanky speakeasy bar.

"It's all good now, Jake. I'm not going to punch your best friend in the nose again."

"When the hell did that happen?"

"Last Friday when Donovan was making the rounds getting everybody's approval, going through his ten-steps to a better human being process."

Donovan busted up to the truth of my statement.

"After I punched him, I felt much better. But I think it was this morning that made me accept him as a friend and possible future family."

"What happened this morning? I didn't see any words being exchanged while I was giving my speech. You two weren't talking in the back were you?"

"When I saw your buddy standing in the back at a conference that he knew nothing about, at 8 o'clock in the morning when he had his own meeting to attend, I figured he couldn't be too bad of a guy. I'm sure everything you said went right over his head, but he was there to support you. That was all right in my book."

Donovan gave off a stupid grin, and even as a guy, I could see why women would fawn over him. He was a damn good looking man. Not that I'd admit that to anybody else but myself.

"When are you leaving?" I asked Donovan.

"Tomorrow after work. Do you by chance know what time she is leaving for this summer home?"

"I do, in fact. Michael told me that he was going to be on a hunting trip and he would be back late at night. Actually I got it wrong, they are leaving early Thursday morning. I don't think he knows that it's Laney's birthday on Wednesday. Or else I can't imagine him being away from her on her birthday if he knew."

"What are you going to do to stop her from going?" Jake spoke, doubtful that his best friend would be able to keep Laney away from leaving for this trip.

"Are you actually doubting me, Best Friend? You don't trust that I will win your cousin's heart in the end?"

Jake laughed as he took a sip of his bourbon. "Yeah I'm doubting you. You were stupid enough to let her go. You deserve every heartache that comes your way."

"Amen!" I spoke and drank my scotch to that statement.

"Speaking of leaving," Donovan handed me an envelope. "It's only fitting that I give this to you on your birthday as well."

I opened up the envelope and found two first-class tickets to any destination of our choice. "Are these the infamous tickets that separated me from my girlfriend for the last two months? The tickets that sealed your asshole status, the tickets that brought heartache to everybody involved, and the tickets that probably pushed Laney away as well?"

Jake was enjoying himself at the expense of his best friend. And his best friend was grinning, though I didn't know why the hell he was grinning when he was the perpetrator to all that I had accused him of.

"Yep. These are those infamous tickets. There are two tickets in there as you can see, one for Jane for her birthday and one for you for your birthday. Happy birthday and enjoy yourself at my expense."

"Considering what you put us through, I should ask you to provide lodging as well."

Both men laughed at me.

"If that's what it will take to clear me of my guilty conscience, I will get you the poshest lodging available wherever you decide to go."

"You're in luck," I said slapping his back. "Lodging won't be necessary since I think I'm going to take Jane over to London so she can see the London office. We will stay with Laney and Jake's family for a while during our time there. Thank you for the tickets." I put out my hand and as we shook, I decided to finally let go of all anger towards Donovan.

"If we are doing birthday presents, I have one here as well. I don't know what's in there, Davis, but my wife told me to give it to you as your birthday present."

Opening up a thin box that was beautifully wrapped, I saw that Em had created a photo album for me for my birthday. It went in chronological order for just about every year of my life starting from the day I was born to the picture of me and Jane and JR at the christening. And on the first page, there was a beautifully written letter from Emily telling me how much I meant in her and her family's life. It obviously was nothing inappropriate, but the love behind this gift was overwhelming.

"Your gift is starting to piss me off, Davis. Aside from the fact that it is way too sentimental for my liking, my wife must've spent hours getting this gift together for you. These are hours that she does not have, hours where she should be sleeping instead."

I ignored Jake and sent Em a text.

Thank you for the gift. I don't think I've received a better one in all my life.

"What did you write to my wife?" Jake was trying to look over my shoulder. "And what is she doing answering you back at this hour? She should be sleeping." I saw Jake pull out his phone.

"Love, why are you up at this hour?" Jake's voice went all honey on us. "You are? Babies are all down?"

"Oh brother, he sounds like more of a chick than his wife when he's on the phone with her."

I agreed with Donovan's comment.

"My wife wants me to tell you, 'you're welcome,' and to have a good time with Jane."

I grinned thinking about how different my life was right now with Jane, than when it was with Emily.

"What's that smile for?" Jake wondered.

"You really want to know?"

"Yeah, because I might have to kick your ass if it's anything inappropriate towards my wife."

I grinned even more. "I was thinking how peaceful and lovely my life would be right now if I had married Em."

Simultaneously, I stepped away from Jake while Donovan stepped in and grabbed him. All three of us busted up laughing.

"But," I said loudly, "I wouldn't change what I have right now for anything or anybody, even Em. Jane is all I need and she's all I can handle."

That appeased Jake. "Your life will not be easy—ever. My sister has never been quiet about anything."

"I know." I grinned like a fool in love.

We parted much later than expected and I came home to find Jane, donned in her negligee, sans underwear, but out like a light. Carefully, I opened up her legs and returned the favor she bestowed upon me this morning. This woman was the best birthday present any man could wish for, in all his living days.

(Max) August 26, 2013

Last (ing) Love

"Is this the last of her stuff?" Nick complained. "Damn! Why do women have so much baggage?"

I laughed. "Amen to that. They have way too much baggage in every sense of the word, but don't tell your sister I said that."

"You sure you want to commit yourself to my sister? She can be a bit of a psycho at times. You're going to live with that the rest of your life."

I laughed even harder. "But she'll be *my* psycho. And I love her every which way."

"Shit, you are gone if you're saying you love even the psycho side of her. Good luck, man. She's not easy to live with."

"I have my ways of controlling your sister."

This time Nick laughed hard. "Yeah. That's what you think. She ain't no Emily."

"She's Jane and that's who I fell in love with. Thanks for your help, Nick."

"You're welcome. See you later."

I looked around her new lodging and smiled when I laid out all her shoes in the small shoe closet that had her name written all over it. I'd live with her temperament, her shoe habit, her jealous nature and I'd love every minute of it. She was my life, my breath, my consummate love and we'd create a marriage like none other.

I fell in love with this girl during the course of a four-hour sushi dinner and over the course of our courtship, didn't take charge of our relationship and guide it in the right path. I harbored grudges, kept the pain to myself, and thought that being self*less* manifested the ultimate love for Jane. That was also how I almost lost this precious girl.

Our nine months of courtship wasn't easy. It started with an all-out argument on our first date, to copious misunderstandings concerning Joyce and Hannah, to the total disaster with Donovan. That one was not easy to bounce back from, but here we are, engaged to be married. I wait laughing, in anticipation of Donovan's comeuppance. I need not seek any retribution as Laney will be my avenger and kick his ass to the curb—many times over—before accepting him. In all ways, Laney stood out as the strongest of the Reid women. A soft-spoken tigress, lioness, a liligress,—a girl who accomplished much without any fanfare. She would show Donovan how much work it required to truly love and be loved. Yeah, I can't wait to watch it all from the sideline!

But in the meanwhile, my soon to be wife and I would have many more arguments before and after the wedding, but I'd be sure to resolve those arguments before the sun goes down. If I learned anything in the past nine months, I learned I needed to act swiftly and correctly and to always show my lady that I love her unconditionally.

Jane Sydney Reid, soon to be Davis,—I love her...I cherish her...and I'll hold on tight because I can't live without this precious gem.

Now that you've read about Max & Jane's happy ending, it's a must that you know what happened with Donovan and Laney. The following are early excerpts of Laney's journal. *Unlikely Attraction – Delaney's Story* is divided into three parts. First is the Mo(u)rning phase where we see Delaney mourning her "relationship" with Donovan. Next is (New) Day where we see Delaney in a new environment, surrounding herself with new friends and a new possible love. But in the end, her (K)Night will come to sweep her off her feet. There's something extra special about this book. I hope you'll get a chance to read it.

Unlikely Attraction
Delaney's Story

d. w. cee

Prologue

"What are you doing with this?" I couldn't believe I was holding my diary again, months after it'd been lost. "And where did you find it?"

"Well..."

"*DONOVAN TAYLOR! WHY DO YOU HAVE MY DIARY?*"

"This is going to sound bizarre, but it was mailed to my house. I got it in the mail with a typed note that said, '*FYI.*'"

"Please tell me you are joking. How did my diary get mailed to *your* house of all places and who would do that? And why you?"

"I'm a bit unsure as to why me, but it was, and now here it is."

"Well, I suppose I should thank you. I've been looking for this for months. I tried to remember where I last used it by remembering the last entry, but none of it would come to me."

"Oh, you wrote about being sad about leaving your home in LA, in your last entry."

"*YOU READ MY DIARY?*" I went a bit ballistic at this point. "*HOW COULD YOU READ MY DIARY?*"

"Well...I only opened it up, first to see what it was. Then I flipped through the pages to find the owner's name. Then...I read the first few pages to see if I could get a sense of who wrote the journal. And then..."

"Yes? And then...?"

"I got a little sucked into the journal entries."

I started convulsing.

"You're a really good writer, I must say."

"Is that *all* you have to say?"

"I enjoyed your writing?"

"Oh my gosh, oh my gosh, oh my gosh..." I walked in circles while hyperventilating.

This diary-stealing, diary-reading rat, stopped me dead in my circle, put his hand around the back of my neck and kissed me hard! I'd been kissed before, but never this completely.

"Mr. Taylor! Donovan Taylor! What are you doing?"

"You, Miss Delaney, are adorable!"

And then he grabbed me again and kissed me senseless. I gave up my fight...for now.

Mo(u)rning

It all started with a diary that my friend Alice Hancock gave me at my 9th birthday party. It was pink and sparkly and came with a lock and key. Of course, I quickly attached the key to my bracelet and starting August 7, 1999, I wrote in my diary daily. There was not a day that went by when I didn't record what happened to me. Looking back, most of the entries were boring, of course, but this is what got me writing and interested in a possible future career as a scriptwriter. And who would have known, that a wee bitty diary would lead me to the wedding of my dreams. But...I'm getting ahead of myself. The following are just highlights of what led to this beautiful Christmas Day.

AGE 9—Summer Vacation

"Laney, where are you? We're all loaded and ready to leave. Please don't lag behind. Your cousins and brother are waiting for you in the RV," Mom yelled while I searched for my diary. I had to take it on my trip since I was going to write about all the details of Yellowstone National Park.

"I'm looking for my diary," I yelled back. Of course, I didn't really yell at my mother, but I was getting a bit worried.

"If it's that pink book with a lock, I think I saw Doug with it in the RV."

"What?" I ran down the steps and hurried into the RV. Doug was holding my diary on a table and Nick had a hammer in his hand, raised up to the roof of the RV. He was about to swing down on my treasured book.

"NO!" I yelled as loudly as my nine-year old body would let me.

My scream freaked out both boys and the hammer ended up hitting Nick on his thigh on its way down, and Doug on the chin on its way up. Lucky for me, the diary was safe! The boys weren't too badly injured, either.

"What'd you do that for?" Doug and Nick yelled back at me. They looked so funny hopping around the RV trying not to cry from the pain.

After laughing as much as I wanted to at them, I argued back, "Serves you right for being nosy. I hope you both suffer the entire trip." With that, I ran out of our RV and into Jake and Jane's RV.

Jake is the coolest, smartest and best-looking boy cousin a girl could ask for. All my friends have a crush on him. He is going to be a senior in high school and he always dates the prettiest cheerleaders. I'm going into 4th grade, Doug is going into 6th grade, Nick is going into 7th grade, and my cousin Jane is going into 8th grade. We all go to the same school and Jake is the only one who says hi to me if he sees me on the playground. Of course, he isn't playing handball or tetherball like me and my friends. When he sometimes walks across the field and sees me, he'll rub the top of my head and call me *Squirt*. All my friends get so jealous because he only talks to me.

Jane is sometimes mean and ignores me. She is only nice when she wants something from me. But, since she is in the junior high campus, I don't see too much of her. My brother for sure ignores me. Nick generally says hi, but he is also on the other campus so I don't see much of him either.

"Why are you in our RV?" Jane was not nice today. Maybe she is on her period. I don't know exactly what a period is but that's what I hear the boys giggling about whenever she is in a foul mood.

"Nick and Doug tried to break open my diary, so I came here to get away from them."

"You and your silly diary. Why do you always write in that thing?"

"'Cuz I like it. Why do you always talk on the phone whenever I come over to your house?"

"'Cuz I like it," she said in the same way I did. I think she was making fun of me.

"Are you on your period?" I asked.

Jane screamed louder than I did when I saw my diary about to be hammered open. Maybe a period is something you don't want destroyed. Who knows?!?

AGE 10—He's THE ONE!

I saw my future husband today—the man I'm going to marry. He is soooooo handsome! He's even more handsome than Jake. He's the brother of Jake's girlfriend, Kelley (I love Kelley!), and Doug tells me that he's also Jake's best friend. When I asked Doug why I hadn't seen him before, he says it's because I'm stupid and I never notice anyone since I'm always either reading or daydreaming. Well, yes...I read a lot and daydream a lot, but NO! I'm not stupid! Why, I just got better grades on my 5th grade report card than Doug did when he was in 5th grade. You see! I'm NOT stupid! Anyways, my future husband's name is Donovan Taylor, and he's sooooooo dreamy. How can anyone be sooooo handsome? Today, Auntie Sandy was girlsitting me (not babysitting, but girlsitting) and Jake, Kelley and Donovan came home from school to pick up snorkeling gear before going to some place called Cabol? They kept saying Cabol this, Cabol that, and I didn't want to sound stupid so I just sat and stared at Donovan.

"Who's this pretty little girl?" my future husband asked.

"I'm Delaney Reid, but everyone calls me Lane or Laney."

"Hello Delaney Reid. Can I call you Delaney? I don't want to be like everyone else and call you by the same name. I'd like to be someone special to you." He winked at me.

"Stop flirting with my ten-year-old cousin. She's seeing stars right now between your smooth talking and 'dizzying good looks.' All women must be blind if they think you're 'devastatingly handsome.'"

"Oh, but he is..." Oh my gosh, oh my gosh, oh my gosh! Did I just say that? Aaaahhh! I wanted to scream and die of embarrassment right in my auntie's kitchen.

"You see...Delaney agrees, so it must be a fact that I'm 'devastatingly handsome!' I'll see you around, Delaney Reid." Donovan touched me. He really, really touched me. He patted the top of my head and told me he'd see me again. This was the best day evahhh!

AGE 10 (After Cabol)—I hate NEON!

The front door opened and I heard Donovan say hello to my father. *Whaaaa?* What was he doing in my house? Oh! My! Gosh! I wanted to die! My night retainers were on—you know the kind with the metal-wrap around the head? I was in my Cinderella "nightgown" and my hair was a mess in pigtails. And I had my neon green underwear that showed through my WHITE nightgown! Why, oh why, does Mom always have to buy me such bright and colorful underwear? And why, oh why, do I always forget that I'm not supposed to wear bright underwear with something white? I'm going to burn all my underwear next time Mom buys any more of them for me!

"How was your Christmas, Little Girl?"

"Why are you here?" I asked in a snippier way than I wanted to ask. Mom was always scolding me these days about sounding "snippy."

"Jake needs to talk to your dad and I'm tagging along."

"Are you going to be a doctor like my dad?"

"No way! I don't have any interest in being a doctor. I suck at science. What about you, Little Girl? You going to be a doctor like your dad?"

"Maybe. I'm good in science and I'm smart, too. I heard my mommy and daddy say I was way smarter than my brother. I don't think they wanted me to hear that, but I heard it."

"I'm sure you are, Cutie-pie. You're definitely cuter than your brother." He patted my cheek with his hand. I was NOT going to wash my face tonight. I'd even lie to Mom when she asked me later if I'd brushed my teeth and washed my face. "You must have lots of boys chasing after you, or maybe you have a boyfriend?"

"What? NO! I don't have a boyfriend..." I shot up from my belly-on-the-floor position and kinda ran around in circles. "I DO NOT HAVE A BOYFRIEND!" I yelled.

Donovan laughed and laughed at me.

"What in heaven's name are you doing?" Daddy asked as he walked in the family room with Jake and Doug.

"Nothing, Daddy." I stopped running, embarrassed I'd acted like a dummy, again.

"Well, whatever you were doing, you might want to know we can all see your neon green underwear!" my brother announced *REALLY* loudly.

"AAAAAHHHHH!!!" I screamed and ran up to my room as I heard all the guys laughing at me.

AGE 10—Valentine's Day!

I made Valentine's Day cards for everyone in my class. When I say I made cards, I mean, I REALLY drew, colored, and wrote personal messages to everyone—even the kids who bugged me! Of course, I made an extra big one for Donovan. I didn't know whether or not he'd stop by our house, but I hoped he would because Mom threw the coolest, craziest parties. She's the BEST party planner, evaaaaahhhh! She decided to throw a Valentine's Day party this year and the theme was PINK, my favorite color. Mom is the absolute best in every way. When I woke up this morning, the entire house was pink and filled with hearts and balloons. My room had streamers all over and on my desk sat a big box, bigger than my head—and trust me, my entire family tells me that I have a big head.

"What's this, Mom?"

"A present." *Did my momma think I was stupid?* Of course it was a present. "Don't give me that snippy look, young lady." *How on earth did she know what I was thinking?* "I know 'cuz I'm your momma." *Aaaahhh! She's psycho.* Or is it psychic? Whatever.

"Who's this from?"

"Open it," Daddy suggested.

I did open it, and it was the most fantabulous dress in PINK! "Thank you, thank you, thank you! It's so pretty. Do you think Dono..." I turned PINK myself and ran into the bathroom with the dress. I think my parents were laughing at me, but I ignored them.

School was soooooo boring and it lasted soooooo long. As soon as it was done, I ran home with Doug and helped Mom wherever she'd let me help. The party started at 6:00pm with a wonderful dinner that Mom did NOT cook. Mom is a great party planner, but not the best cook. Lucky for all of us, she catered the meal. Now, I'm not trying to be mean. She just doesn't cook. However, she does a lot of other cool things, so it's all good.

I quickly ate my dinner with my cousins at the children's table. Jane was pouting because she had to sit with us even though she said she was almost 15 years old. Jane looked gorgeous in her soft pink dress (it helped that Auntie Sandy let her put on blush and lipstick tonight—something my own mom would not let me do). I felt like an ugly duckling! Even worse, my dress was big and poofy; something a little three-year-old would wear. What ten-year-old wears a big, poofy, pale pink dress? Jane was in a long, slinky, pink dress. With her black hair, blue eyes, and the pale pink dress, she looked like a high schooler. With my blonde hair and the big poofy pink dress, I looked like cotton candy with a curly yellow bow on top. Ugh! I was going to have to stay away from my really pretty cousin.

"Hi Donovan!" Jane stood up and greeted him with a great big hug.

"Hello, Beautiful." He answered her with a kiss to her forehead. "Happy Valentine's Day."

"Same to you. Did you just get here?"

"Yeah. Your brother, Kelley, and I just popped in to say hello before heading over to the frat house."

Donovan chatted away with my cousin, and I don't know why, but my heart hurt so much to see him with Jane. And I felt so inadequate next to her. Quietly getting up from my seat, I went up to my room, found the card I'd made for Donovan and threw it in the trashcan. I also tried to take off this stupid dress but of course the complicated buttons in the back made it impossible for me to take it off. This was probably the stupidest thing I've ever done, and I knew Mom was going to yell at me till next Valentine's Day, but I got out the hugest pair of scissors I could find and searched for a way to get this dress off me. *Should I start cutting from the top, or the bottom?* I couldn't make up my mind. *What the hell, I mean heck.* Mom would be furious with my snippiness now...but she wasn't here to see it or hear it...ha! ha! ha!

"What the hell?"

I jumped back at the real *"what the hell"* and the scissor landed right between my big toe and the one right next to it. Would that be called the fore-toe? Second toe? The one right after the big toe? Who! The! Hell! cares what the toe is called when my foot hurts so badly? OW! OW! OW! I hopped around my room but held back the tears because Jake and Donovan had come in my room.

"I'll go get the first aid kit. You stay here with Laney."

"Jake! Please don't tell Mom! I'll be in big trouble!"

He laughed at me (again!). "All right. I'll clean and bandage you up myself," he answered and walked away.

"Why the hell did you have a pair of scissors the size of Jaw's mouth on your dress?"

"I couldn't unbutton the dress so the only way out was to cut it off."

I think Donovan thought I was coo coo for cocoa puffs—and by the way, isn't that a great saying? Daddy says that about some of his patients, though I don't think he means for me to hear it.

"Do you normally cut off all your dresses if you can't wait for your mom to help you take them off?" He was trying really hard not to laugh at me. WHY oh WHY do these people always laugh at me? WHY can't he just give me a hug and kiss on my head like he did to Jane? Instead, this boy, man, college student—whatever!—was always laughing at me. *Aaaarrrggghhh!*

"No." There was so much blood coming out and it hurt so badly, that's about all I could say.

"Laney." Uncle Bobby was here. Thank GOD! "Let's see what's happening."

Uncle Bobby is a doctor like Dad, but in a different part of the body. He must be much smarter than Daddy because Daddy only knows about the heart, but Uncle Bobby practices something called general medicine, which means he takes care of the whole body. I'd never tell Daddy I thought Uncle Bobby was smarter, but I think I'm right.

"It's bleeding so much." I croaked so I wouldn't cry.

"Ooh, this looks pretty deep. I'm going to have to suture the wound. Jake, give me my kit." My cousin did just that. "This might sting a bit. I'm going to have to clean it first."

As soon as Uncle Bobby put the cotton pad with antiseptic on me, I yelped, "SHIT," then added very quickly when I saw the look on all of their faces, "-take mushroom!" Uncle Bobby's body started con-vulsing, and he couldn't stop laughing at me. Then, Jake and Donovan joined in. I was probably redder than the red balloons in my room.

"You want me to hold your hand when your uncle starts with the stitches?" Donovan offered, and I was no dummy. The offer was taken even before the question was finished.

Getting stitches is not for the weakling. It hurt! But, I didn't cry in front of Donovan and this crazy weird feeling in my stomach that came on after Donovan started holding my hand, helped take my mind off the needle tying my two toes together.

"What do you keep muttering?" Donovan asked.

"Huh? I'm not saying anything."

"Yes you are. You keep saying all these words that don't have any meaning when stated together."

"Oh." *Shii*take mushroom! I didn't realize I was saying any words aloud.

"Say them louder, Laney."

"Do I have to, Uncle Bobby? I'd prefer to keep them to myself. It's just my private collection of words."

"I'd like to hear them," he said with a nice smile.

"Oh, OK. Here goes...*shii*take mushroom, Hoover *Damn, hell*-o, *ass*inine, ha*bitch*ual and there are a couple more but I think I'll stop before I get into any more trouble." My head went down. I waited for Uncle Bobby to have a "word" with me.

"Where did these words come from, Laney?"

"I make them up. And I promise I only use them in my head whenever the situation is extreme, like it is now. I don't use these words on anyone else. It's just my private collection of words, Uncle Bobby."

"So, it's like a substitute word for the actual bad word itself?" Jake was snickering at me. And so was Donovan.

It wasn't cool of them to make fun of me. I got mad! "Um, *HELL*-o, I think that's called a euphemism...," answered the girl who was in a lot of pain, and with a lot of snarkiness. After getting cut with a pair of scissors, I never wanted to use the word snip(py), ever again! Donovan and Jake were practically on the floor, shaking with laughter. Uncle Bobby was too. "Have I put you all in *stitches*? Can we finish up *my stitches* once yours are contained?"

"Where on earth did you get such a large vocabulary, Delaney? Who teaches you all this stuff?"

"Nobody teaches me. I read, unlike some people in this household." I pretended to cough and say Doug's name at the same time.

"I don't think we need to go anywhere for entertainment tonight. I could hang out with your cousin all night and be perfectly happy."

Really? Meeeee toooooo!

"I think you're all set, young lady. It will be up to you to explain to your parents what happened here."

"Thank you, Uncle Bobby. When you're too old to take care of yourself, I'll help you." Maybe that wasn't the best thing to say?!?

"Why thank you, Laney. Not even my own kids have offered help in my dotage. I'll keep it in mind."

"Bye." I called out to my uncle and expected the other two guys to leave. "Good-bye?" I said to the both of them.

"Before I leave, I want to know why there's a handmade Valentine's Day card in your trashcan."

Oh! My! Gosh! Donovan was almost at my trashcan picking out his card.

"NO!" I screamed. And that helped. He stopped long enough for me to grab the card out from under him.

"Is that for your boyfriend?" Donovan teased. "He must have the same initials as mine as I see a huge D in the front and a T in the back."

Mortification with a capital M—thy name is Delaney! I could be a bit melodramatic at times, but at this very moment, I should be nothing less. Donovan almost guessed my secret.

"Stop harassing a ten-year-old and let's get going. Kelley's going to be waiting."

"I can't leave till Delaney tells me who she made the card for and why it's in the trashcan."

"I made it for a boy. But I got mad at the boy for paying attention to another girl. So I trashed it." I looked him dead in the eye and dared him to challenge me. But inside, I was sooooo nervous he may challenge me. "Satisfied?"

He smiled his one-million megawatt smile and said, "Happy Valentine's Day, Little Girl. See you again, soon."

This was the best Valentine's Day evahhh!

AGE 10—Easter

Easter is always on Uncle Billy's boat in San Diego. His boat isn't that big, but somehow we all make it work. Today, with the weather being so nice, I was told we were sailing somewhere deep into the ocean. I love water! And when I make this statement, I mean what I say. I LOVE WATER! I can surf, much better than my brother, of course. I swim well enough to be on a swim team, and I love to jump off the high, high diving boards. I haven't learned to water ski yet, but I figure that's coming up soon—like maybe this summer in Hawaii.

"When did you get that dress, and with what money?" Mom was commenting on my Easter outfit. After that cotton candy dress fiasco, I asked Mom to get me a non-poofy dress. Her answer to my plea—a Lilly Pulitzer dress that would be great...if I were FIVE years old. I'm TEN now and can NOT wear a dress that makes me look like a baby. Plus, Jake is coming to Easter brunch with Kelley, and where they are, Donovan isn't far behind.

"I bought it." My proud announcement didn't sit well with Mom. If Valentine's Day taught me anything, I learned I didn't want to look like a baby, I didn't want any more pastels (sorry, RL and Lilly Pulitzer), and I didn't want to look like everyone else. I wanted to POP, and my orange dress POPPED! "Isn't it pretty?"

"It's beautiful, Baby." Daddy finally came out to the car, ready to leave. "Did your mother buy it for you?"

"No, I didn't. She must have taken my credit card and made another online purchase. Young lady," uh-oh...here came the scolding. "You are not to use my card..."

"Let her be, Babs. It's Easter, she looks gorgeous—in fact, that dress is much sweeter than the one you picked out for her. Maybe you should let her buy her own clothes from now on. Then we won't have this issue."

"Thank you, Daddy." I kissed him on the cheek and jumped in the car before Mom could continue her lecture.

Our ride to San Diego was boring, and as expected, Uncle Billy took the boat out to sea. Right before we left, Jake, Kelley and Donovan hopped aboard, and I knew today was going to be fantastic! But the water was choppier than usual, so I stood, holding the railing, hoping to ease my rioting stomach.

"Hey there, Little Girl. Whatcha doing here by yourself?"

"I'm feeling a little queasy so I thought I'd come here and calm my stomach."

"Laney," Doug yelled. "You want to jump in the ocean with us?"

Between feeling like I was going to throw-up and not wanting to take off my POP-orange dress, I didn't want to go in, but everyone was doing it and I didn't want to look like a chicken. I thought I should follow along.

"You going to jump in with all of us?" I hoped Donovan would join us, but I doubted it since he was wearing the most handsome suit, *evahhh!*

"You're not scared to jump in? You need me to hold your hand, again?" Donovan was teasing me and I liked it. I probably had on my dorky smile but all was good because Donovan was with me and not Jane.

"I'm happy to hold *your* hand, Donovan, if *you're* too scared to jump in," I teased back. Before he could get a word in, I grabbed his hand and pulled us both into the water.

"I can't believe you did that," he said while rubbing the water out of his face. "I'm fully clothed," he complained and started splashing water on my face, then swam over to dunk me in the ocean. We were both fully clothed. My bright orange dress floated in the water with me, but since I had a bathing suit underneath, it was a-OK.

"Race you back to the boat," I hollered getting away from Donovan. He swam after me, grabbed my right foot and pulled me under. He swam ahead, laughing away until I caught his jacket that trailed behind him. Hanging on, I let him pull me as he struggled back toward the boat. When he slowed, I took my chance and jumped on his back. He swam with me on his back over to the boat, up the ladder, and onto the deck. I couldn't let go because I didn't want to let go. That was so much fun!

"All right, Little Girl, let's get you dried up." Leaning back gently, he made sure my feet were on the deck and he placed the large towel around my body. I knew for sure, right then and there, that I loved Donovan Taylor!